SANTA BARBARA PRESS

STREET FIGHTS

A NOVEL BASED ON A TRUE STORY

JOE MARTORI

SANTA BARBARA PRESS

This is a novel. With the exception of certain well known figures from the worlds of crime, politics, law, business, labor, sports and journalism, whose actual names are used, the characters in this book are fictitious. Any resemblance to persons, living or dead, is purely coincidental and exists solely in the reader's mind. The names, incidents, dialogue, and opinions expressed are products of the author's imagination and are not to be construed as real.

First Edition

Published by Santa Barbara Press and Paragon Publishing Company
4554 North Central Avenue
Phoenix, Arizona 85012

815 Dela Vina Street
Santa Barbara, California 93101

ISBN 0-915643-24-3

Manufactured in the United States of America.

DEDICATIONS

To Barry and Bob Goldwater, Harry Rosenzweig, Tony Nicoli, Dan Cracchiolo, and the late Judge Paul LaPrade for hangin' in there.

To Lee Iacocca, John Sirica, John Scali, Mario Cuomo, Dennis DeConcini, Tommy Lasorda, Jack Valenti, Leo Buscaglia, Ronald Schiavone, Arthur Decio, Joe Garagiola, Jeno Paulucci, Joseph Califano, Peter Rodino, Ralph D'Annunzio, Antonin Scalia, Frank Carlucci, Rocco Siciliano, and Peter Domenici, too many of whom, I'm sorry to say, would be classified by a great number of Americans with the likes of Al Capone, Charles Luciano, Vito Genovese, Carlo Gambino, Joseph Bonanno, Carmine Galente, Paul Castellano and Tony Salerno.

To Frank Sinatra, whose plight is that of the public figure—in spades!

To Brown & Bain, P.A., a law firm that not only understands the meaning of free expression but espouses and encourages it.

To The *Uomini di Rispètto* (Men of Respect): Vince Accurso, Mark Apicella, Al Bonacci, Tony Bottagaro, Robert Burns, Sally Costanzo, Ed James, Herb Lieb, Pete Lo Bue, Paul Lo Duca, Ed Martori, Jr., Sonny Martori, Paul Muscenti, Joe Oddo, Rick Palmeri, Tony Pitetti, Johnny Ruocco, Dwayne Tatalovich, Bruce Vinci, Skip Wallach, Jerry White, Marvin White and Steve White, many of whom were there to help me through some pretty rough times.

To My cousin Art Martori; Frank and Jerry, my brothers; and my wife, Terres, for your respective strengths and stamina.

To Marvin Gaye, whose music all Americans should listen to *and hear*. What else is new, my friend, besides what I've read?

To Julia, *per la cosa nostra*.

Last, and most important, to Joseph, Christina and Arianne, my children. May you, your generation and the generations of kids to come never shed another tear because of your heritage.

ACKNOWLEDGMENTS

Many thanks to the women who helped with the technical stuff and inspired me with their encouragement: Donna Isaacs, Bev Markheim, Susan McCrillis, Kathy Miller, Diane Russell, Peggy Tramel and Donna Whitmore.

Special thanks to Julia d'Orlando Martori for contributing so much to the creative side.

To Toby Stein, my *Yiddish paisan* and editor: let me simply declare to the world that without you, this project would have remained a dream.

STREET FIGHTS

PROLOGUE

DAN BARNES

PHOENIX 1976

IT WAS HOT. Only early June, but the desert summer had set in. The reporter patted his damp forehead with his damp handkerchief and glanced down at the sheet of paper in his typewriter. Where the hell was he? Much as he dreaded moving out of his chair and leaving this air conditioning—temperamental though it was—he was excited about the meeting. If he didn't finish today's copy, he'd be late.

He pecked at the old standard for a few minutes, frowning from boredom. Then he shoved his chair back from his desk, threw back his head and stretched. He polished his thick glasses with the end of his tie. The newsroom blurred, but it didn't matter; there was nothing to see except two secretaries at the other end of the room. With the legislative session completed five weeks ago, the governor had finished signing all the bills, and if it weren't for the upcoming special elections, he wouldn't have been around, either.

The sound of the phone made him turn. Sure enough, the light was flashing on his desk. "Hey, Dan, where the hell is your story? I've got to get a paper out. You've got exactly ten minutes!" The receiver on the other end slammed down. Oh, to get out of this rat hole. It wasn't just this newsroom and his menopausal editor; it was the paper, the town, his whole goddamned life.

He yanked the paper from the typewriter, stormed across the room to the editor's office, threw the story on his desk and walked out.

Even after fifteen years here, Dan was never ready for that first encounter with the heat when he left an air-conditioned building. The sensation was like opening the door of an oven to check on a TV dinner. He looked around the blacktopped parking lot for his car. The waves of heat radiating up from the ground made the little red Toyota look like shimmering Jello. By the time he walked over to his car, his feet were burning. Turning on the ignition, he felt the heat from the seat penetrate his shirt and assault his back. He didn't dare turn on his Jap version of an air conditioner right off. He'd have to let the engine idle for five minutes. He leaned back, closed his eyes and concentrated. There it came, the cool breeze of a New Jersey summer. The smell of honeysuckle that kept him company as he climbed the hill to Short Hills High. He felt the breeze brush through his hair like a friendly hand. New Jersey in summer was even better than the Wisconsin summers of his childhood—it was sure better than here. Any place would be better than this parched inferno where all his thirsts remained unquenched—unless by some miracle this sleazy bastard he was on his way to meet was really on to something. Dan glanced at his watch: 11:15. As he shifted into first gear and the car lurched forward, he wondered when his life had gone off course.

Today was the third anniversary of his second marriage, and all the celebration he could afford, at forty-seven, was a pair of movie tickets and a cheap dinner. He switched on the air conditioner. The first blast of torrid air was like a hand grabbing him by the throat. What sadistic fate had decreed that on $20,000 a year he was supposed to support two families?

At the corner of Van Buren Street, Dan stopped for a light. On his right was a long, narrow park that stretched several blocks ahead of him. Lining the park were skinny, towering palm trees, topped off by small handfuls of fronds. They always reminded him of feather dusters, stuck in the ground by some faggot Paul Bunyan. The grass was littered with garbage, but the human refuse was worse.

On Third Avenue, Dan made a left and ordered himself to stop this defeatist attitude. Doors were about to open. Why shouldn't this loudmouth Simpson be for real? He knew him. They hung out in the same bars. He saw Simpson drinking with all the creeps in town. This time he'd hit the jackpot, he told himself. He could see the next day's headline: ATTORNEY GENERAL OWNED BY THE MOB.

Suddenly, the headline blurred, and then his thoughts. The road kept swerving, throwing him off balance, slowing him down—as though his whole life had led up to this ride that just possibly could straighten everything out. The heat and excitement were making him shake too much. Dan pulled over to the curb, flung back his head and took several deep breaths. Soon, he was less conscious of his heartbeat. His head cleared. His surroundings came into focus.

As he plunged back into traffic, he thought that maybe he was better off not seeing it all so sharply. What a slum! Derelicts stretched out under trees in the vacant lots he was passing. Tiny, ramshackle houses, their windows covered with aluminum foil, feebly fighting off the sun. Clothes scorching dry on sagging lines. Abandoned cars that looked like oversized, rusted pretzels dotted the street.

Easing to the left lane, Dan noticed for the first time the shabby, faded pink mission across the street. What a contrast to the pristine church of his childhood. Dan remembered Sunday mornings vividly. He and his brother would wander down to breakfast just as his father was returning from the bureau where he had gone to check on the night's news. The meal of fresh fruit, eggs and pancakes was a prelude to the one awaiting them later. Already the pies for dinner were baking in the oven. Breakfast over, everyone prepared for church.

The white frame building was gabled and had the expected bell tower. The church looked like something out of "The Midnight Ride of Paul Revere," but this was Wisconsin, not Massachusetts. No matter. A fine Calvinist church looked the same wherever it was. Inside were highly polished pews, white walls and an unadorned mahogany pulpit—quintessential simplicity.

The smell of new-mown hay accompanied the congregation into the church. Girls, wearing dresses with sashes tied in soft bows in the back, and boys, always in trousers and jackets with newly polished shoes, were on their best behavior. Dan consistently derived more comfort from the women of the congregation than from the preacher. The solidity and predictability of these women in their cotton dresses and straw hats, all smelling like Sweetheart soap, gave him a sense of security. Besides, he didn't need a minister to tell him about God. He had a relationship with Him all his own. Now Dan remembered it had been a very long time since he'd really spoken to God, and suddenly he wanted to re-establish that contact.

I'll never be my old man, I know that. But God, please let something happen to me today. I've been in the wrong place at the wrong time too many times. Today, let things break my way. I keep seeing that Wop at the country club telling me how he buys drinks for twenty or thirty people a day. Why should a greasy immigrant succeed while I—a real, honest American—am still in the small time?

Yellow lights flashed in his rear-view mirror. An emergency truck of some sort was coming up behind him. How could he swing to the right when he had to turn left? Sweat drenched his neck and back while the confusion of the preceding moments reverberated between his temples. The piercing lights were closing in, but where was the shriek of the siren? Could it be a tow truck? Something was written on the front. As the vehicle loomed closer, the lettering sharpened. Finally, utterly clear, the words filled the mirror: JESUS SAVES.

As the truck closed in on him, Dan stared in terror. His tongue flicked over his dry, salty lips while he turned to see who was driving. With his destination in sight and no relief from his tail, shards of light reflected off the windshield, blinding him. A deafening explosion catapulted Dan through the driver's door of his mangled Toyota.

''My God,'' he agonized, as he lay in a red puddle on the blistering pavement. ''I'm not ready to die. Not now. The Mafia. Embassy. God, why did you let them get me? Please let me live.''

Shout at the Devil!

BOOK
I

JOE

BROOKLYN 1956

CHAPTER 1

OFFICIALLY it was still summer. In a few days the calendar would attest to what everyone already knew: autumn had arrived. The giant oaks and maples that cover Avenue T like a canopy bore as many red, yellow and orange leaves as green. In the gardens in front of the large brick houses chrysanthemums were sprouting new buds while the roses were clearly dying out. A fifteen-year-old boy, his light brown hair growing out a crew cut, books under his arm, turned right off the Avenue and started up a driveway that ran alongside his house, 351 Avenue T, in the Gravesend neighborhood of Brooklyn. Five-nine, with broad shoulders atop a long torso and short legs, he walked up the alley with his distinctive, rolling gait. Around back of the house he opened the screen door and went in.

He heard the sound of voices coming from the living room, and went in to find his parents and Mr. Ashworth, his father's English teacher, engaged in a heated debate.

"But if I no gotta da time to study, what I should taka deesa lessons for? Atta da start, you tola me dis no problem."

"Please, Mrs. Corelli, explain to him that we have a contract," Mr. Ashworth implored.

Joe listened to his mother explain to his father in Italian what Mr. Ashworth had concluded was nothing more than a language problem. Surely once his wife told Mr. Corelli that he had an obligation to continue the lessons or pay for them anyway, the whole matter would be settled. As his mother finished speaking, Joe's father sat quietly, nodding comprehension. Mr. Ashworth looked from one to the other waiting for someone to say something. Finally the old man got up and shuffled across the room to where Mr. Ashworth was sitting and said, "Ledda me see deesa contract."

The English teacher opened his briefcase and pulled out a single sheet of paper.

"Isa dat ita?"

"Yes, Mr. Corelli. Would you care to inspect it?" Mr. Ashworth asked, as he offered him the contract.

"No, no. I beleeva you," he muttered as he reached into his back pocket and took out his watermelon knife. As he felt the blade of the knife against the right side of his neck, Mr. Ashworth burst into a sweat. From the corner of his eye, he looked at Joe's mother in a silent plea for help, but the only part of her that moved was her chest going up and down double time.

"Now you tear it uppa inna smalla, smalla pieces."

"Eh, ah, excuse me, sir?"

"I saida tear it uppa, uddawisa Ima gonna tearra uppa you facea inna smalla, smalla pieces."

"Just as you say, Mr. Corelli. Certainly."

Joe watched as the trembling man tore the contract into shreds and handed the pieces to his father. The knife back in his pocket, Giuseppe Corelli offered Mr. Ashworth his hand. "It's beena ma pleasu'."

Mr. Ashworth slammed his briefcase shut, grabbed up his hat, and scurried out the door.

"Nice goin', Pop," Joe laughed, announcing his presence.

His father looked at him and winked. His mother began to shout.

"What kind of behavior is that? We'll be lucky if the police aren't at the door. If he tells anyone what just happened, what will people think of us?"

In the middle of her tirade, Giuseppe pulled on his sweater and sauntered out the front door.

She turned to her son for sympathy. "My Lord! What's come over your father lately?"

"Come on, Mom, the only thing you were worried about was that Pop'd cut that jerk's throat and get blood on your pink chair." He walked over to his mother and kissed her on the cheek.

Maria Teresa Corelli was a stubby, stoop-shouldered woman who could have posed for a Daumier peasant. She sighed and went into the kitchen to get his supper. Thursday was macaroni night. The only surprise was the form it took. Tonight was spaghetti with squash. While his mother filled his plate, Joe flipped through the sports section of the *Brooklyn Eagle*.

She put his plate in front of him, and wiped her clean hands on her apron. "So, Joseph darling, how was school today?"

"School's okay," he said. "The spaghetti's not bad, either."

"School's important," she said.

"Absolutely," Joe said. "But spaghetti's important, too, no?"

His mother nodded. Stopped. "You're teasing me."

Joe shook his head. "Ma, really, this is delicious. Nobody makes better."

She smiled deeply, her fear of what the neighbors might think about her husband's handling of the skinny schoolteacher forgotten.

As his mother watched him eat, Joe thought about the way they did certain things in their house. Dinner was served at noon when his father came home from work. His mother would eat with his father and listen to him recount the night's events. After eating, his father would sleep for a few hours before getting up and going back to work at six. Mr. Ashworth might know English, but he was pretty stupid to show up to talk to Joe's father during his sleeping time. There was no way his mother would have awakened his father, but he must have heard Mr. Ashworth and decided to come down and settle things.

Joe laughed. He'd once come up on a sleeping German shepherd too fast and gotten bitten good.

That funny connection wasn't deep. Joe thought his father was exactly what a man should be. Smart. Honest. Hard-working. Tough.

In a neighborhood where some people seemed to hang around for a living, the way his father worked made as strong an impression on Joe as Giuseppe Corelli's toughness. Somewhere deep in Joe's psyche, it was already written: he, too, would be honest, hard-working and tough. He was already smart. It was a fact about him, like his height; his height was average, his brain was above average. At this point in his life, Joe would probably have traded some IQ points for two or three inches in height, but he was smart enough to know it was just as well it couldn't be done. He was also smart enough so that while he admired his father, he knew he would have more choices about what to do with his own life.

Not that his father minded *his* life. Giuseppe Corelli was in the wholesale produce business. When he left in the evening, he drove into Manhattan to the Washington Market, where railroad cars filled with fresh fruit and vegetables from all over the world were emptied and the contents sold to wholesalers from the entire metropolitan area. Success in Giuseppe Corelli's business hinged on knowing produce and your customers, for while an occasional customer might call and place a special order, buying for resale to retailers was very tricky. The goal was to buy enough of the right items to fill all the orders without having highly perishable leftovers. To succeed, it was vital to know the ethnic groups you were supplying and which fruits and vegetables were traditional in a given season. Thus, one would be in a position to anticipate demand and to know, in light of the price that varied from day to day, how much you could sell and to whom.

After all these years, Giuseppe had the operation down to a science. Among the other wholesalers, he was known as the peach doctor. The minute a bushel of peaches was opened, he could tell from the color if closer inspection was warranted. Peaches communicated with him in some mysterious but infallible way so that if Giuseppe said he wouldn't buy them, no one else bought them.

Around midnight, trucks would begin arriving, and the wholesalers would turn over to their drivers responsibility for getting the orders loaded and delivered to their warehouses, while they, at an hour when most people were already asleep, would go to a local diner for lunch. By four o'clock in the morning the night's purchases were sorted and stacked and ready to be sold to neighborhood storekeepers.

When most people were on their way to work, the wholesalers had concluded their day's business. The next few hours were spent tallying up the receipts, preparing the bank deposit and cleaning up the warehouse. Day's work over, they'd head home for dinner and an afternoon of sleep. Six days a week, fifty-two weeks a year, the cycle was repeated. For a man content to spend his whole life working to better his family's circumstances, it was an ideal business.

Giuseppe Corelli was such a man. A sturdy, compact man with powerful, square hands, he started each day by packing his loaded Italian pistol in a shoulder holster resting to the left of his heart before descending the spiral staircase leading from his bedroom to the dinette. Before he left the house, he'd have two or more of the many cups of espresso he would drink before the long night was over.

One day looked much like the next; this year was indistinguishable from the last. Only family events marked the passage of time. A baby starting school, a son beginning to shave, a daughter getting married. These rites of passage, all moments of pride, made the hard work worthwhile.

But every man wants his shot at immortality. Giuseppe Corelli's one chance lay with his namesake.

Giuseppe's chance was Joe, Jr.'s cross.

CHAPTER

2

JOE LOVED Fridays. Football practice was never too strenuous the day before a game. His coach was superstitious about Friday injuries. Normally Joe came home from school by going down East 5th Street to Avenue T, but on Friday he detoured at Avenue U to see if anything special was going on. From Monday to Thursday he was Joseph Corelli, honor student, football player, sports writer for the *Lincoln Log* and member of the student council; but from Friday to Sunday he was Joey, Avenue U street kid. The funny thing was, he had no preference. He liked being both Joes equally.

On either side of Avenue U, clusters of teenagers were gathered on the sidewalks. On the north side of the street the meeting place was under a green-and-white Breyer's ice cream sign that identified Happy's Candy Store. Directly opposite, over a large picture window, white letters spelling Tommy's Sweet Shoppe stood out from the shiny, black background. Whether they hung out at Tommy's or Happy's, the kids looked the same. The boys were wearing tee shirts with short sleeves rolled up to hold the mandatory pack of cigarettes. Their pegged pants and featherweight shoes were the neighborhood trademarks. They wore their hair long, slicked back on the sides and formed into elaborate pompadours on top. A cigarette jutted from the corner of a mouth or dangled between the fingers of a studied hand. Shoulders thrust back, hips forward, crotch the center of gravity, they preened and posed as much for each other as for the few girls who dared to hang out with them.

The girls also had a prescribed look. Whether their hair was in pony tails or loose, long or short, a required wave hung over one eye. At least the visible eye was heavily made up, and their mouths were constantly in motion, loudly cracking gum between deep drags off some boy's cigarette. They were wearing their father's or brother's shirts, with the sleeves rolled up to the elbow, over a pair of dungarees rolled halfway up their calves, or circular skirts that hung to about the same spot. White ankle socks and black flats grounded them a little.

As Joe approached the corner of East 4th Street, he noticed a powder-blue Cadillac heading in his direction. By the time he crossed the street, the car had caught up with him and the driver was clearly trying to get his attention. Joe stopped on the corner in front of the Club Solitaire and waited for the car to pull up alongside.

"I wanna talk t' ya. I'm Raymond D'Allesandro. My friends call me Raymo."

"Oh, hello, Mr. D'Allesandro."

"I hear you're wunna the best sports pickas aroun'."

Joe hesitated, wondering how to answer. "Well, I like sports," he said.

"Do ya think ya could pick da games good? Ya know, da winnas an' da loosas."

"Well, ah, I like sports. But, I don' know. Ya want me t' pick em, I'll pick em."

"If you pick me winnas I'm gonna give ya five dollas for every game ya pick me a winna."

Joe hesitated. From what he knew about the D'Allesandro family, he thought it might be smart not to get too involved with any of them. On the other hand, the man wasn't asking Joe to work for him; he was only asking him to say which teams he thought would win—something Joe figured out every day anyway, to place a small bet himself, or just for fun. What harm could it do?

''All right,'' he said. ''Sounds good.''

''Okay. Get in. We'll get somethin' t' eat an' you can tell me who ya like t'morra.''

''All right, but could we stop by my house first so I can get rid of my books?''

He climbed into the car and directed Raymo to his house. The interior of the car was immaculate. Special containers attached to the top of the dashboard held mints, breath spray and cigarettes.

Raymo was close to forty, and what was left of his sandy-colored hair was starting to turn grey. He was about Joe's height and build, with the muscular remains of his days as Golden Gloves champ still evident. Everyone in the neighborhood knew the D'Allesandro family, because there were so many of them. Raymo worked as a shop steward for a New Jersey shipping company, but it was his loan sharking operation that kept him in Cadillac money. His twin younger brothers, Sally and Nunzi, made book, and while Joe had not met Raymo before, he knew the twins well.

The car pulled up in front of Joe's house. As he opened the kitchen door, the odor of simmering parsley water hit him.

''*Madonna*. How can you stand to make that stuff?''

''What can I say, darling? Your father thinks it's good for him. If it keeps him happy, what's the harm? So, how was school today?''

''Fine. Listen, I might not eat home tonight. I'm gonna go out and see who's around. Maybe I'll get some pizza with the boys. Okay?''

''Make sure you stay away from the bums.''

His hand didn't move, but in his mind Joe crossed himself. ''Yeah, all right, Ma. See you later.''

He walked down the hall to the ''little'' room, dropped his books, made a quick stop in the john and headed out the front door to avoid the possibility that his mother might have decided to get more specifics about his plans for the evening.

Outside, Raymo was stretching his legs. From the look of him, you'd never guess he was one of the neighborhood's torpedoes. Just like a college man, he wore loafers, slacks and a button-down shirt with a pullover sweater. Back in the car, Raymo made a U-turn and headed for Coney Island Avenue.

Bernie's Diner looked like an aluminum trailer without wheels. It sat just off the corner of Avenue U and Coney Island Avenue on a lot big enough to have its own parking, an unusual luxury. Bernie was behind the counter when they walked in. Raymo waved to him and Bernie hurriedly put down the glass he was drying to escort them to a table.

"How's it going, Raymo?" he said as he gave the spotless table another cleaning.

"Can't complain, Bernie. How's business?"

"Good. Good. I just got some fresh bagels from next door. Can I interest you?"

"An' some coffee. This is my friend, Joe. See what he wants."

"I know Joey. He comes in here with his friends sometimes. What's yer pleasure, kid?"

"A jelly donut and milk."

"You got it. Be right back."

"I'm wondering, Mr. D'Allesandro, who told you about my interest in sports? Was it your brother Sally?"

"Yeah. An' Ace an' Nunzi. Ya gotta reputation. People think you're pretty smart. Word around is you're goin' t' college."

"That's right. I'm goin' to Notre Dame like my brother Jerry. That's how I got interested in college football. I'd listen to the Notre Dame games on the radio, and feel like I was with him. Kept me from missing him so much. I haven't missed a game in nine years."

The waitress was coming toward them with their order. She looked like a bottle of mucilage. Her orange hair was piled on top of her head like a beehive, and her face and uniform were the same shade of yellow. Joe wondered whether if he squeezed her neck, glue would ooze out of her mouth.

Joe waited for Raymo to spread cream cheese on his bagel before picking up his donut. When he finally bit into it, his teeth met with plenty of resistance. He took it out of his mouth and pressed it between his fingers.

"What's the story, kid? Somethin' wrong with the donut?"

"Yeah. This isn't a donut, it's a hockey puck."

Raymo looked over at the counter where Bernie was cutting a piece of pie and yelled, "Hey, Bernjamin!"

Joe chuckled as Bernie tripped all over himself getting to the table. He didn't get service like this when he was here with the boys.

Raymo looked up at him and said, "Bernie. Ya let me down. My friend here says this donut's past its prime."

"I'm so sorry. Dis waitress is new and I gotta watch her like a hawk. No brains."

He seized the donut and scurried off, while Raymo pulled a card out of his pocket and handed it to the boy.

"Here's the teams that're playin' t'morra. Now, you're sure you unnastan' all dese point spreads?"

"Yeah."

"Okay. Whattaya like?"

Joe took the card from Raymo. As he was looking it over, Bernie returned with a fresh donut and apologized again.

"Don't worry about it," Joe said benevolently. "Have ya got a pencil I can borrow?"

"Sure. Here. Keep it. I got plenny." He pulled a pencil out of his apron pocket and handed it to the boy.

Joe circled his picks and handed the card back to Raymo.

"Are you fuckin' crazy? You can't pick sixteen games."

"You asked me to pick. These are the games I picked."

"But there's too many games."

"Why?"

''Pick a few a them.''

''I can't. These are the games I like. If I pick a few now I might pick the wrong ones!''

''*Madonna*. All right. All right. We'll do it your way.''

The next morning, Lincoln beat New Utrecht 23-14. As Joe turned his bike onto Avenue T he could see his father in the front yard raking leaves.

''Hi, Pop.''

''Pepino, where you go so early dissa mornin'? Itsa Saturday. Why you no sleep?''

''I had t' get some work done in the library. The storm brought down a lot of leaves last night. The streets are very slippery.''

''I putta my salesa slips and books onna you desk. Maybe you betta do 'em before you go outa again.''

''Come on, Pop, that's my Sunday job. Have I ever been late gettin' 'em done?''

''No. You a good boy, Pepino. Whenever you ready's okeh.''

He wondered if his father'd think he was such a good boy if he found out Joe was lying to him.

CHAPTER 3

HE HATED not being able to share his love of football with his parents, but they were vehemently opposed to the game. They believed it was too dangerous. If he defied them openly, they'd worry, and the constant bickering would take away all the fun. He decided that what they didn't know wouldn't hurt them.

Joe rode his bike around to the back and went into the kitchen. His mother was unpacking a carton of olive oil.

"Is that from Uncle Sal?" he asked.

She nodded. "Mrs. Murdocco's second cousin just came from Reggio. She called this morning, and your father went to pick up the packages. Uncle Sal sent this, some *Caffè Bianco* and some *Calabresella*. I keep telling Dad, when you write your brother tell him not to send this terrible perfume. It's dreadful, just dreadful. Does he listen? Of course not."

As his mother spoke, she punched a hole in the top of the oil can and began to empty it into a glass bottle. She shot a quick glance in his direction and asked, "Can I get you some lunch? Your papa and I have already eaten."

"Yeah, I could use a sandwich. I'll wash up and be right back."

When he came back into the kitchen, his mother was removing the top of the can. Just as he thought. Inside the drained oil can was a *sopressata*, a Calabrese salami. Italian meat products were contraband, but no Italian-American had ever heard of anyone getting sick from eating a *sopressata*.

After lunch Joe decided to go over to Shef's poolroom. It was a good place to hang out and convenient to Jean's Candy Store, where he could check on the football scores.

In Gravesend, like anywhere else in the city, there was generally at least one candy store to a block, but none of them sold enough candy to satisfy even one serious sweet tooth. In front of all of them there was a green wooden newspaper stand on which the city's eight dailies were stacked, each pile held down by a heavy metal bar advertising either a magazine or a brand of cigarettes. On Avenue U, the *Brooklyn Eagle, Il Progresso* and the *Morning Telegraph* outsold all the other papers.

Inside, a counter displayed tobacco products, candy and chewing gum next to a soda fountain with five or six stools. Some candy stores were also luncheonettes, the ethnic make-up of the neighborhood reflected in the menu; on Avenue U there was a brisk trade in sausage-and-pepper sandwiches, while ham turned the iridescent green of a horsefly.

Locals always knew one candy store from another. For a discussion on the current state of affairs in college or professional sports, you'd go to one shop. For the outcome of the fifth at Aqueduct, to another. If you needed money, you would purchase your candy at still another store. But if grass was what you were after, you'd go to a candy store outside the neighborhood: on Avenue U "junk" was nowhere to be found. Junk brings cops, and cops are bad for business.

The sky had clouded over, and the wind was whipping slimy leaves around. He headed down East 2nd Street, snapping his jacket closed and shoving his hands into his pockets.

"Hey, Joey, wait up."

He turned, not to see who it was because he'd been hearing Vinnie Lo Bianco behind him since he was two years old, but just to give his friend a chance to catch up. Vinnie was Joe's height, but slighter. His black hair always had enough Brylcreem in it to withstand hurricane winds, and his small, pencil-thin moustache gave him the appearance of an Italian Charlie Chaplin. His fingernails were bitten down to the quick, and his small, black eyes darted around like a ferret's. Vinnie had good reason to be nervous. Local shylocks and bookies were always after him trying to collect old debts. Vinnie didn't gamble when he felt like it; he gambled like he brushed his teeth, just because it was a new day. His parents weren't much better. His father had made a fortune in the olive oil business, successfully marketing his products to most of the supermarkets in Brooklyn. The Lo Biancos had two children: Vinnie, their spoiled baby; and Concetta, their older, undisciplined, retarded daughter. They passed on to Vinnie not only their preoccupation with gambling, but also the funds with which to indulge the habit. Lately, though, their generosity had been decreasing, while Vinnie's addiction was growing.

''Where ya goin', Joey?''

''Over t' Shef's.''

''Oh yeah. Maybe I'll come witcha. Shoot a few. Relax,'' he said as he lit a cigarette.

''Yesterday after school, I ran into Raymo D'Allesandro.''

''Yeah. You been bettin', Joey?''

''No. He wanted me to pick some games for him. Said he'd give me five bucks for every winner. Haven't heard any scores, have ya, Vinnie?''

''Nah. I didn't make any bets today. I'm busted. Ace is threatenin' to break both my arms.''

''Well, whattaya doin' goin' t' Shef's for?''

''Jesus Chris', Joey, I gotta get glasses! Who the fuck is dat on the corner?''

Joe's eyes, even with glasses, weren't good enough to tell for certain, but it looked like it might be Sammy the Bug. No sooner had he said that than Vinnie dove head first into the bushes.

''D' ya think he saw me?''

"No. But if I stand here and talk to these hedges much longer he'll know you're in 'em. See ya aroun'."

Shef's was on East 1st Street, two doors down from Laurel Chemists, which was right next door to Tommy LaRosa's barber shop and diagonally across from A. Torregrossa & Sons Funeral Parlor. In this neighborhood that did not have a single bank, bookstore, movie theater or gift shop, funeral parlors were second in number only to candy stores. Occasionally, Sabbatino & Sons, right down the street, and Cusimanno & Russo on West 6th Street and Avenue T, caused Joe when he was little to speculate on the health of the race. But by now Joe knew that the success of these three enterprises had little to do with local actuarial statistics, for through their embalming rooms passed the heaviest members of three of New York's five "families." Dead or alive, Joe thought, shivering at his grim joke.

Shef's was better to think about. Shef got his name because he was known in the neighborhood from the days when he drove a horse-drawn milk wagon for Sheffield Dairy. Now, in his vast spare time, he shot pool. Shef was the undisputed king of the neighborhood pool sharks and had held his own with such notables as Willie Mosconi and Willie Hoppe. His life's ambition to open his own pool hall finally materialized in the basement of a store that went out of business. Patrons entered the dimly lit caverns of Shef's by going down a dark, narrow staircase that led off the street. At the bottom of the stairs loomed a green steel door on the other side of which sat Shef, perched at his counter.

Shef was a little guy, maybe 120 pounds with a pool cue in his hand. His baseball cap pulled snugly over his forehead, combined with his thick glasses, rendered his eyes invisible. Shef charged by the hour. When a guy came in he'd mark down the time and send him to a table—if one was free. On weekends a wait was inevitable. Behind the counter, Shef had a refrigerator where he kept Cokes, Yoo Hoos and Manhattan Specials, coffee drinks that were probably the best seller on Avenue U. He also stocked a few candy bars. Customers who wanted anything else to eat or drink went across the street to Jean's.

"Hey, Joey, how's it goin'?"

"Okay, Shef. Looks like a packed house. Any'a the boys around?"

"Yeah. The Riccios got a table in the back. I hear you guys beat New Utrecht t'day. Didja see any action?"

"Yeah, some, but not enough. We really had some laughs. All week long during practice, me an' Bruno Marino kept telling Patsy De Primo that New Utrecht had a tackle that was layin' for 'im. 'Number 73 an' his name's Rigor Mortis, and he's tellin' everybody you're a pansy an' first play he's gonna put your lights out.' Well, by the time kickoff comes around, Patsy's so psyched up we can hardly control him. On the second play from scrimmage he yells t' me, 'Hey, Joey, which one's Mortis?' So I point to 73 an' next play he cold cocks the guy. He comes into the huddle an' says, 'Didja see the shot I gave that fuckin' Mortis?' The plan worked. Number 73 didn't come back into the game until late in the second half."

Shef laughed. Everyone knew the De Primos as the neighborhood Neanderthals.

Joe looked around and, catching sight of the Riccio brothers way in the back of the poolroom, made his way toward them. He kind of wished Louie weren't there. Much as he really liked Johnny "Boy" Riccio, he always suspected that Louie was a charter member of the zippered-pocket club.

"Hey, Joey," Johnny called out. "Whatta game! We kicked their fuckin' asses!"

"Beats losin'. So where is everybody?"

"I don't know. I haven't seen anyone today. We're goin' t' the victory dance tonight, right?"

"Hell, yeah! I was gonna ask Lo Bianco t' come but ya can't talk t' that guy anymore. He's got so many shys after 'im ya can't walk a block without 'im divin' behind garbage cans or duckin' up some alley."

"Ah, fuck 'im."

"You guys heard any football scores?"

"Nope."

"Listen, while you finish this game I'm gonna run up to Jean's. Want anything?"

Joe walked across the street to Jean's candy store on the corner. How convenient if Shef would sell food. But the unspoken rule on the Avenue required everyone to stay on his own turf and not cut in on his neighbor's livelihood.

Joe loved the smells along Avenue U, especially the wonderful fragrance emanating from Rome Bakery. Filling the glass showcase, and in baskets behind the counter, were loaves of bread of every size and shape. Small loaves for hero sandwiches, large, cross-hatched Neapolitan loaves and the braided bread of the Sicilian; round and flat, white or whole wheat, dough to make pizza and *frezella* were all sold here. This was a bread store only. Pastry was another art, the province of LoBasso's, next door.

A few blocks away, across West Street, clouds of aromatic smoke drifted out of Albie's back door. Albie owned the neighborhood *latticini* store, which had the best smoked mozzarella in the world, probably. Other forms of mozzarella would be soaking in a tray of water. Still others, resembling the back of an old lady's bunned head, had been salted. Fresh ricotta, packed into tall, metal tins that looked like milk-shake glasses, sat on racks so the excess water would drain out. Strictly speaking, *latticini* stores specialized in dairy products, but outside Albie's were baskets of dried cod, or *baccala*.

Mingled with the odor of smoky cheese was the smell of fish from the shop immediately next door. On the sidewalk alongside Albie's *baccala* were large, metal tubs filled with ice and clams and baskets of snails, called *babalooch* by the locals. Inside, customers walked on a sawdust-covered floor while they inspected the day's catch. Whole blues, swordfish, fresh tuna, flounder, sole and mackerel were cleaned, filleted or cut into steaks only when they were bought and the fishmonger was told how to prepare them.

From across the street wafted the smell of rice balls frying at the neighborhood-renowned *focacceria*, Joe's of Avenue U. A strictly Sicilian restaurant, its specialties included such delicacies as *vasteda*, lamb innards mixed with ricotta; *sufritto*, beef heart and lungs cut into small pieces and cooked in a very spicy tomato sauce; and *sanguinaccio*, a pudding made of pork blood. Joe knew that the poverty of Italy accounted for using every last piece of a slaughtered animal. When he ate here, he did his best to enjoy the food without identifying its ingredients.

Joe preferred Jean's. Jean was behind the counter making sandwiches. She reminded Joe of Gina Lollobrigida. In her late thirties, she had two beautiful daughters about Joe's age. What made this lady unique was that she was divorced, a true phenomenon in the neighborhood.

''Hi, Jean. Ace around?''

''Yeah, Joey. He's in the back with half the neighborhood.''

Joe held up his hand in a parting gesture and headed for the back room. Through the haze of smoke, Joe saw Mauro ''Ace'' Fiore holding court at his corner table. With him were Frankie ''Cheech'' Fusco, a local bookie, and Bobby Balducci. The smoke-filled room was crammed with tables of card players listening to several radios blaring football games from all over the country. The crowd consisted of the older guys in the neighborhood, most in their thirties and forties, with a few just a couple of years out of high school and not yet married. They worked as bricklayers, stevedores, longshoremen, truck drivers, printers, bartenders, or, as was the case with three of those present, numbers runners for local bookies. One of the radios announced that Wake Forest had just scored another touchdown on Clemson, putting them ahead by four points. Cheers erupted all over the room. You'd think this was an alumni gathering. The truth was that these guys didn't know Wake Forest from

Sherwood Forest, but they did know about covering a point spread.

Joe walked up to Ace and thrust out his hand. Ace was a business agent for a construction union when his duties as the neighborhood loan shark didn't interfere. Ace had a fifty-six-inch chest and huge arms. Tattoos adorned both his forearms. "Death Before Dishonor" was emblazoned above a six-inch panther on his left arm and a four-inch faded heart with "Mary" in the center was on his right. He always had a Garcia y Vega in his teeth, a diamond ace or star sapphire on his right pinky and a diamond key chain in the shape of an ace hanging out of his left pants pocket. He was always tan, with manicured fingernails. He wore his fedora brim-up and belted his pants halfway up his massive chest.

"Joey, ma boy. Have a seat."

The kid nodded to the other two men and sat down.

"Have ya got scores on any of the college games yet?"

"Yeah, who da ya want?"

Cheech Fusco passed the kid a sheet with all the day's games listed on one side and columns for each quarter on the other. Joe looked down the list for teams he had given Raymo. So far, eleven of them were winning. He couldn't believe it.

Ace watched as a big smile spread over Joe's face. "From your puss, I'd say you were doin' okay."

Joe looked up to see Bobby Balducci studying him with expressionless eyes. Bobby always wore a suit on his slight frame, didn't talk much, smiled hardly ever, and never lost his temper. Despite his unimpressive size and disposition, word on the street for as long as Joe could remember was, "Ya don't fuck with Bobby Balducci." Although no one—alive—had ever seen him with any kind of weapon, his reputation as a button man was well known.

"Yeah, Ace. I picked sixteen games today, and most of them are ahead."

Cheech Fusco, who specialized in sports, looked at him in surprise. ‘‘Who ya bettin’ wit’, Joey?’’

‘‘Nobody. But I did make a private bet with a friend, and he told me no one could pick so many winners. Looks like I might come close. To tell ya the truth, I thought he was right.’’

He handed the list back to Ace. ‘‘Thanks.’’

‘‘Sure, kid. Any time.’’

As soon as he got home that night, Joe turned on the radio to find a station that was broadcasting the day’s football results. If he wasn’t dreaming, he had picked thirteen winners. He had earned himself a net fifty bucks!

CHAPTER

4

SUNDAYS, his mother dragged him off to the ten-thirty Mass at Sts. Simon and Jude. Everyone in the neighborhood knew that Maria Teresa Corelli raised "good" boys. Girls weren't mentioned, only because that went without saying. Unless young Joe was at her side, the old ladies would whisper among themselves that Tessie was losing her grip. Joe hated to sit still for what seemed like forever while some priest with his back to him flailed his arms and mumbled unintelligibly in Latin. But sit he did, because his mother had inculcated in him a fear of God's wrath—and hers. So he was paying tribute to one more "Don" to keep Him off his back. He didn't know it, but he was also acquiring the self-discipline critical to survival on the streets.

■ ■ ■

WALKING BACK from communion, Joe slipped out the back door of the church and headed down McDonald Avenue toward the Gravesend Social Club. A group of kids from across West 6th Street were shooting craps in front of Hy's candy store. Every candy store in the neighborhood had a Sunday morning crap game outside as though it were an unwritten law. He crossed Avenue V and walked up to the social club. By the cars parked along the street, he knew who would be there. It always amazed him how many Mafia guys would gather in one spot, their flashy, unique cars parked one behind the other. He was certain the light-blue Fleetwood belonged to Dominic ''Lilo'' Ferrara, and the copper Eldorado was Sally D's. Just like running a full-page ad in the paper. If there weren't peace among the families, and if the cops weren't so well taken care of, the boys would never risk being so obvious.

Italian social clubs, whether they were in Gravesend, Little Italy, or Harlem, looked the same. Ostensibly deserted stores, no sign out front, the clubs invariably had a green shade over the window to keep passersby from peering in. A distinguishing feature of this one was a small ''GYC'' logo centered on the front door. Nunzi D'Allesandro had given it to Lilo Ferrara. Since Gravesend Youth Center was just up the street, Nunzi thought the association might lessen the heat at the social club. Inside, bare bulbs hanging from the ceiling provided a harsh light by which the men played cards. On Sunday mornings, at the back of the room, a large table was set up next to the bar with a *marganetta*, espresso cups and freshly baked Italian pastries. Ace, Sally D'Allesandro, and Lilo ''worked'' this club, on behalf of Don Carlo. It was a rare Sunday that Carlo Gambino wasn't perched at one of the back tables looking like a giant sea gull devouring at least three cups of coffee, a rum *baba* and a *pasticiotta*. Ace had offered young Joe the opportunity to serve coffee there on Sunday mornings, and while he didn't pay him, a fellow who was having a lucky run of cards would be inclined to tip very generously. Sunday-morning patrons of the social club were mostly Bankers and Brokers enthusiasts. They'd wander in before and after church; before and after—and during—the time their wives and mothers were at church, because few of the men had seen the inside of a church, except for weddings and funerals, since grade-school days.

Joe had been working for about an hour when Raymo D'Allesandro walked in.

''Joey! Hey, how's my man?''

''Hi, Mr. D'Allesandro.''

''What's with dis Mr. D'Allesandro? Call me Raymo. In dis joint, if ya call me Mr. D'Allesandro, t'ree guys are gonna answer you.''

''Okay, Raymo. Whatever you say.''

''What I say, kid, is you're a fuckin' genius. You know how much money you made me yesterday?''

''I know we had a good day . . .''

''Well, I bet a hunerd bucks a game. That's how much fait' I had in ya, kid. An' ya didn' let me down.''

He reached into his pocket, pulled out a roll of bills, counted out sixty-five dollars, and handed it to Joe.

''Thanks a lot, Raymo. But all you should be giving me is fifty bucks. We won thirteen games and lost three. The net was ten winners.''

''Dat's a fair point but on a weekend like dis, ya deserve a bonus. The udda bonus I got planned for ya is ta take you wid me next week to Rosalie's and have her woik both of us over. And don't t'ank me, Joey. I should be t'anking you. At this rate I'm gonna retire.''

CHAPTER

5

SNOW BEFORE Christmas was very unusual. It was the first day of school after the Thanksgiving holiday, and for the last few hours enough had fallen to cover the sidewalks. At three-thirty in the afternoon, the students working in the *Lincoln Log* office had to turn on the lights.

Joe looked out the window at the blowing snow and decided to leave. His college-boards prep class was at four, and the street looked slippery.

As Joe negotiated the wet stairs, he heard a horn honking. Double parked in the service road along Ocean Parkway was Raymo's car. As Joe approached the window, Raymo yelled to him to get in. The boy debated whether or not to obey. He'd been avoiding the older man because he was too embarrassed to face him. He was also just a little scared. Ever since that glorious day at the beginning of the football season when Raymo announced that he would retire on Joe's football genius, the boy had nearly busted him. Joe couldn't pick the right *time*. He must have lost Raymo fifty grand—it was in-fucking-credible. But somehow Raymo kept showing up. He'd bet a hundred dollars or more on each game and then lose four out of four, six out of seven, or nine out of twelve. But he didn't seem to give a damn about the money. The less he cared, the harder Joe tried. He was analyzing his ass off, but he couldn't pick a winner.

"Ya got ya class today?"

"Yeah."

"Get in. This is no weather to be walkin' aroun'."

This wasn't the first time he'd found Raymo outside school waiting to take him to his class. Raymo seemed as concerned as Joe that he do well and get into a good school. Maybe he figured Joe had better go to college because he sure as hell would never make a living betting on football.

"God, Raymo, I'm sick! Ya gotta stop bettin' with me. I'm so fuckin' cold, I'm gonna put ya in the poor house."

"F'get it, kid. It's only money. Ya try, dat's the main t'ing. Besides, excep' fer the bowls, the season's over, anyway."

"Thank God. This is makin' me old before my time."

"Relax. Ya worry too much. Jus' so ya know, I really neva have given much of a shit about money. I neva been married, I live in my ole lady's house. It's a kinda simple life. I got more dough on da street, woikin' for me like a fuckin' slot machine, den I could ever need or lose on gamblin'. Deese last couple a months have been about da best in my life. It's really nice havin' somebody t' look forward t' seein'. Win, lose or draw, kid, I wanna be witcha to watch ya grow up an' succeed in a bigger way den anybody in dis broken-down, fuckin' neighborhood's eva done. Ya know, even dough I put money out on da street, I ain't sucha bad guy. I can't leave my mom all alone, and dat's why I ain't neva got hitched. But I really wisht I would've had a kid. In fact, once I signed up for wunna dose big bruddas programs, but I guess dey musta checked out my rap sheet cause I neva gotta call from nobody. An' dat's even afta I checked da box dat said I'd be willin' to take a colored kid as my little brudda. I don't know why I'm talkin' to you like dis, kid, but just so ya know it, Joey, I figure you'll be my little brudda."

Whatever Raymo did for a living, he was sure being more than decent to Joe. "Just so *you* know it, Raymo, I think those big brother *chooches* made a real big mistake."

Joe put his head back and closed his eyes. Another damn headache. Ever since that scumbag Mitberg had thrown him on his head, he'd get these headaches and sometimes blurred vision.

"Hey, Joey, look smart. Ya gotta go study."

"Ya got any aspirin?"

"In the glove compartment. Ya got anudda headache? What's goin' on wid you? Don't sweat deese exams. You still got a year before dey count."

"Nah, it's not that. A few weeks ago I was goin' by the Boody schoolyard an' about twenty guys were pitchin' dimes. Anyway, I hear Paulie De Luca callin' me t' join 'em. Well, I wasn't too busy that day, so I went in. After awhile, Lefty Mitberg, the Boody coach, comes out while it's my turn t' pitch. He comes up behind me and gives me a shot on the backa the head, and I go flyin' with my forehead on the ground. Jesus Christ! I saw fuckin' stars. Since then I haven't felt so hot."

"Is dat da same guy they t'rew outa Lafayette?"

"Yeah."

"Did he know who ya wuh?"

"I don't think so. He just called me a Wop son of a bitch."

"An' he teaches at dat school?"

"Yeah, he's always been a real prick."

"Lemme go talk t' im."

"Raymo, f'get it."

Raymo stopped the Cadillac in front of Mrs. Abramowitz's house. Mrs. Abramowitz was a former Lincoln teacher who operated her SAT preparatory course out of her house. She had a great track record. But some argued that the kids who cared enough to go to her would do well no matter what. No matter. Joe was covering all his bases.

There wasn't any other way to hit a home run.

CHAPTER 6

LATER THAT week, Joe ran into Mikey Gilberti leaving the school building. Mikey came up only to Joe's shoulder, but he played first-string fullback on Lincoln's football team. He was built like a fireplug. Guys twice his size gave him respect.

"Leavin' early today, huh, Joey?"

"Yeah. Thought I'd go t' Jean's for an egg cream before I go home."

"I'll go witcha."

Paulie De Luca was leaning on the jukebox, filling it with nickels. *Wake Up, Little Susie* by the Everly Brothers was playing on the large Wurlitzer. Behind the jukebox, Junior Aversa was lounging at one of the tables, while Vinnie Lo Bianco crouched in the phone booth on the back wall.

"Hey, Paulie, what'd ya play?" Joe asked, as Mikey walked to the back and joined Junior.

"Let's see, uh, *You Send Me* an' *Little Darlin'*."

"Move over." Joe reached into his pocket, pulled out three nickels and played *Donna, Come Go With Me* and *Blanche*.

"Hey, Jean, can I get an egg cream?" he called.

"Just as soon as I finish this malted."

Joe walked to the back and joined his friends at the booth.

''We got the inside track on some tickets for the Alan Fried Christmas Show at the Paramount, Joey. Ya wan' in?'' Junior asked.

''How much are the tickets?''

''I ain't sure yet, but we have t' go fer a fin, at da least.''

''Okay, count me in. I'll see if I can sell a few Christmas trees for my ole man an' earn some money.''

Vinnie hung up the phone, wiped the perspiration from his forehead and sat down.

''What the fuck's the matta witcha, Lo Bianco?'' Paulie asked.

''My ole man's cousin in Miami called this mornin' wit' a tip on the toid at Hialeah today. I just put my last fifty on it. I gotta get a hit or Raymo's gonna cut my heart out.''

''Hey, Joey,'' Paulie interrupted, ''what the fuck did you say ta Raymo?''

''About what?''

''About that cocksucker Mitberg?''

''Why da ya think I said anything to 'im?''

''Well, I seen Richie Borzano, an' he tole me dat yesterday he was shootin' some baskets in Boody schoolyard when Raymo D'Allesandro comes up to 'im. He ast 'im where he could find some guy named Mitberg, so Richie takes 'im down t' th' locka room. Well Raymo goes inta Mitberg's office an says, 'You Mitberg?' an' Mitberg says, 'Uh-huh, what's it to ya?' All uva sudden Raymo pulls out a toity-eight an' suddenly Mitberg's sittin' so far back in 'is chair he's practically fallin' ova. Raymo shoves th' rod in 'is ear an' says, 'I bin hearin' t'ings aboucha, ya Jew prick. T'ings dat get me very upset.' So den he goes ahead an' tells 'im th' storya da day Mitberg gave ya that *scyof* on the head. Mitberg's sittin' there crappin' all ova 'imself.''

None of the boys cared why Raymo had laid it on Mitberg; that he did was enough. They'd all been on the receiving end of Mitberg's savagery at one time or another. Raymo had avenged them all.

"After Raymo leaves, Lefty says t' Richie, 'Siddown, kid! I'm gonna call the cops an' you're gonna tell 'em what just happened here. We're gonna put that maniac away.' So Richie says, 'Whattaya talkin' about, Mr. Mitberg? Tell 'em 'bout what?"

"The stupid fuck!" Mikey exclaimed. "What th' hell would make 'im think Richie'd squeal?"

"Ah, whattaya expect from a slimy prick?" Paulie responded.

"Ya know, I didn't ask Raymo t' do anything. The other day, the weather was lousy, he sees me walkin' and offers t' give me a ride. He sees I've got a headache again an' asks me how come I been gettin' so many headaches. So I tell 'im. How should I know he's gonna work the guy ova? Not that I mind."

Vinnie's eyes were popping. "Ya know, Joey, I figured by now Raymo'd have blown your head off wit all da bum tips you bin givin' 'im."

"Well, I never thought he'd blow me away, but I can't make 'im out, either. Who knows, maybe he just likes me as a person."

Joe shrugged, finished his egg cream and got up. "I'll see you guys."

As he walked around the corner on East 2nd Street, he ran into Johnny Riccio.

"Hey, where ya headed, Joey?"

"Home. I've got homework. Besides I wanna catch my pop before he goes to the market. You wanna sell trees with me again this year?"

"Yeah."

"Okay. Well, let me get home so I can put in our order."

"Good. Ya wanna go to a dance at Our Lady a Grace Saturday night?"

"Yeah."

"Okay. Let's meet at Jean's at eight an' we'll go ova together."

By Saturday evening, the grey, winter landscape had been transformed into a fairyland of cotton and crystal. In the muted glow of the street lights, drab houses wore long, sparkling earrings. When Joe left the house, snow was still falling. The powdery snow fell over a thin layer of ice. The streets were quiet. As he walked, the crunching of Joe's feet sounded loud in the stillness. The usually harsh sounds of Avenue U seemed muffled by the snow.

Until Joe arrived at Jean's, he wasn't sure who was going to the dance. Inside the front door, Johnny, Vinnie, Mikey and Petey De Primo were shooting the breeze with Crazy Nancy. Nancy was Raymo D'Allesandro's sister. She also lived in her mother's house, in an apartment on the top floor, with her husband and son. Nancy was a degenerate horse better. Every night at eight o'clock when the delivery of the *Daily News* and the *Morning Telegraph* drew all the dead-serious gamblers, she was among them. Her salt-and-pepper hair was strewn all over her head, and under her open coat she wore a dirty housedress. Her whole life was horses; her only interest in winning was staying alive—winning brought the money to stay in action.

"I was beginning to think you weren't coming," Johnny said as Joe walked in the door.

"Are you all waitin' for me?"

"Yup. This is all of us. Let's go," Mikey urged. Nancy gave him the creeps, and he was anxious to get out of there.

Inside the front door of Our Lady of Grace Church, the boys could hear *La Bamba* blasting on the record player in the basement. The floor of the large room was finished as a basketball court. The nets and scoreboard hung over the crowd of teenagers milling around. For the boys, the least of the attractions at these dances was the opposite sex. For the most part, they had very little interest in girls, and if it weren't for the few couples going steady, a newcomer to the scene would never know that these gatherings were dances. The sparsely populated dance floor served as a gulf between the preening girls on one side and the boys on the other, all but oblivious to them.

The truth was that the boys didn't need confraternity dances to meet girls. The few girls who hung out at the candy stores were always available for a gang-bang in the back of a car, in a schoolyard or in the basement of Mario's Pork Store. What else was there to do with them?

It was different for most of the girls. If they were ever caught hanging out, their fathers would grab them by the hair, drag them home and beat them black and blue. But they could go to a confraternity dance and keep their reputation intact. After all, the dances were sponsored by the church. The church, for its part, could point to the dances and CYO basketball games as evidence that it was keeping the adolescents occupied and off the streets—a perfect gesture in a world where form was everything and substance unimagined.

As the boys filed into the gym they caught sight of a group from Avenue X: Sonny Balbi, Angelo "Brown," Nicky Corella, and Frankie Mangellino standing near the record player, along with Big John Macri and some of the boys from West 10th Street. Avenue X was a street of serious violence. No harmless numbers running or crap shooting for them; they carried guns and used them. The group from Avenue U had little in common with them, but knew the rules. Peace reigned between the two Avenues, and Joe and his friends meant to keep it that way.

"Hey, whatta you guys doin' here?" Sonny called out as the boys approached.

"We were invited," Johnny Riccio responded.

"Yeah," Nicky chimed in, "I t'ought we could use a few more guys here. Looks funny at a dance when ya got too many broads."

"Hey, watch yer language. My sista's ova dere."

"Frankie, come on. I didn't mean no disrespect. It's just an expression."

"I'm gonna get some punch," Vinnie Lo Bianco announced. "Anybody else want some?"

No one seemed to hear him, so he turned and headed across the no-man's-land to where the punch bowl and the girls were. Awareness of an approaching male traveled around the group like electricity as the girls nudged each other, felt their hairdos and smoothed out their skirts.

Goddam girls, he thought, as their attention became riveted on his progress across the floor. Why the fuck do they always have to hang around the fuckin' punch bowl? A guy can't even get a drink without stickin' out like a fuckin' sore thumb.

"Hi, Vinnie," Anita Lipari called out.

"Hi, Anita. Andy witcha?"

Andy was Anita's younger brother. Even though he was a couple of years younger than the other boys, they liked him, and he hung out with them sometimes.

"He walked me over but he didn't stay. He'll be back later to pick me up."

In addition to having the hots for Anita, Vinnie liked her. He was debating whether or not to ask her to dance when a commotion broke out behind him. He turned to see that a bunch of guys from across Coney Island Avenue had barged in.

Sonny Balbi moved out first to challenge them, with the rest of the Avenue X gang close behind. Suddenly one of the Coney Islanders pulled out a .22, aimed it at Sonny's belly and threatened to spill his guts all over the gymnasium floor.

"You can take that fuckin' piece an' shove it up your fuckin' ass!" Sonny yelled.

The girls took care to get out of the line of fire. Cockfights were nothing new; the code of the street protected the females as long as they were smart enough to stay out of the way.

Joe and his friends exchanged glances. They didn't have to see the other guns to know that the one aimed at Sonny was not the only one in the room. The gang from Avenue X had better believe that the Avenue U boys were ready to die with them or they were dead meat anyway. As Joe and the boys from Avenue U moved up, Big John Macri and his guys joined them, in an unmistakable gesture of support for Sonny and his friends. Just at that moment, Father Cafelli came into view. Instantly, the boys scattered. It was enough to make Joe believe in all those Italian miracles.

Until the time Father Cafelli *didn't* show up in time.

CHAPTER 7

AS FAR back as anyone could remember, the Natales had been bakers. When the young immigrants, Biaggio and Pasqualina Natale came to Brooklyn, they opened a bakery on Carroll Street. They and their ten children labored in that store night and day to earn enough money to stay alive. By the early thirties they had married off some of their children; however, the bakery now had to support their sons' families. Bakery bread was a luxury during the Depression, a reality that threatened the family's survival. Fortunately, their oldest daughter, Maria Teresa, had married Giuseppe Corelli, whose produce business was virtually unaffected by the disastrous economy. Giuseppe bought the mortgage on the store and in so doing saved the Natale's pride. In time, they moved the bakery to Avenue U between Lake Street and Van Sicklen, right across the avenue from Lady Moody Square, named for the English baronet's widow who became one of the first female political leaders in the colonies, attracting nonconformists of every ilk. Joe, whose father had told him all about Lady Moody, sometimes wondered what she'd think of the nonconformists who inhabited her neighborhood now.

When young Joe and Johnny Riccio set up their Christmas tree business, they did it on the sidewalk in front of Natale's bakery. The boys would meet Giuseppe's truck driver, who'd deliver a small load of trees to the aspiring entrepreneurs. The week-old snow was starting to melt. Shoveled snow that had been piled like a retaining wall along the curb was turning into putrid slush.

The boys were waiting in front of the bakery for the delivery truck, rubbing their upper arms and bouncing from foot to foot to keep warm. It was a typically chaotic Friday before Christmas. Avenue U was thick with trucks making extra deliveries. Anxious proprietors screamed orders to porters and delivery boys while harried patrons came to blows with each other over the last *cannoli* or few pounds of broccoli *rapini*. The same people who during the year would call a shopkeeper a thief, cast aspersions on the circumstances surrounding his birth or assign him to Dante's lowest circle over a nickel increase in price were ready to kill for the privilege of paying twice its worth for a Christmas item.

"I'm freezin' my fuckin' balls off here," Joe complained.

"Me too. Let's make fast worka dese trees an' blow dis iceberg."

"Right, but first we need trees. I wish that stupid Polack'd hurry up," Joe said as he stood on tiptoe trying to catch a glimpse of his father's truck. "Listen, you keep your eye out for Tom. I'm gonna go see if my Uncle Vito's got a garbage can we can build a fire in."

In a few minutes Joe returned with an old, rusted oil drum, newspapers and some coal. The boys filled the drum with crumpled-up papers until they covered the hole in the side that used to be the spigot. On top of that they put the coal. Before long they were warming their hands over a healthy blaze.

"It's too bad your uncle doesn't have a rack to put ova the can, Joey. We could go across the street to Sally D's fruit store and buy some *castagnas*. We could sell roasted chestnuts along wit' da trees."

"You dream. I bet you there isn't a chestnut left on this street. The old ladies have been hoarding them for weeks. The other day I was collecting for my old man over at John Ricciardi's, and some old hag was in there calling him a *sfacim*, *fidende*, accusing him of hiding chestnuts in the back for his special customers. I thought, 'Lemme get outa here before this guy decks 'er.'''

Their laughter was interrupted by the sound of yelling and a honking horn. Tom had arrived.

The three of them made short work of unloading the trees. After Tom had left, the boys began lining them up along the bakery wall.

''Hey! What the fucka you kids doin' here?''

The boys turned to find Louie the Torch watching them.

''We're sellin' trees. What's it look like?'' Joe answered.

''Looks like you're gonna burn down the whole fuckin' neighborhood,'' Louie said indignantly. ''Ain't nobody taught you guys a healthy respect fer fiah? Look how the wind is blowin'. See where ya flames is leapin'? Pretty soon yer air hole's gonna turn into a fuckin' torch an' you got twen'y trees all set t' go.''

The boys could see that he had a point. Even if they didn't, they would have moved the trees. Louie was the king of the local arsonists, and no one would dream of arguing with him about fire safety. Joe and Johnny had both heard Bruno Marino, Louie's star apprentice, extol his virtuosity with fire.

The young salesmen did quite well, considering they weren't really set up until afternoon.

But, by Saturday, which was Christmas Eve, they still had better than half their trees left. Their fire wasn't doing them much good because the air was more wet than cold. It was one of those winter days when it was impossible to tell whether or not it was raining. If you stood outside long enough, water would collect on your hair and clothes. If the wind blew, you could feel a spray, but you would feel foolish carrying an umbrella.

Joe and Johnny were huddled under the awning outside the bakery when Mr. Goffredo came by.

''Hey, Joey. Heard you was sellin' trees again dis year. Ya got a bargain fer me?''

"Sure, Mr. Goffredo, all our trees are bargains," he answered.

"Lemme see dat one in da back," Mr. Goffredo demanded as he pointed to a twelve-foot tree leaning against the bakery window. "How much?"

"Five bucks," Johnny said.

"Five bucks? Five bucks! *Madonna*, what crook a ya workin' f' here?"

"Look, Mr. Goffredo," Joe said in as reasonable a tone as he could muster, "you came to us because we sell our trees for half what everyone else wants. Five bucks is our price. If you know where you can do better, we ain't gonna feel hurt."

"I know where I can do betta, but I ain't got no gills an' if I stay out here much longa, I'm gonna drown in dis air. Gimme the fuckin' tree an' lemme get outa here."

He handed Joe a five-dollar bill, took the tree from Johnny and left.

"Everybody can do better somewhere else. Everybody accuses us a rapin' 'em. An' when they get all done with the song 'n dance, they buy the fuckin' tree. Y'd think that part of what they're buyin' is the time t' do their routine," Joe observed.

"Pepino, *vene ca!*"

Joe's grandmother was motioning to him to come to the bakery door. In one hand she held a plate with a few slices of pizza and in the other two paper cups.

"Whatcha got, Nona?" he asked as he took the cups from her.

"You boys mus' be hungry. *Mangia.*"

Joe took a sip from one of the cups.

"Hey, Nona, this is wine."

"*Chooch!* You t'ink I don' know? It keeps you warm so you no getta sick. Go, go back t' woika," she ordered as she closed the door on him.

By four o'clock they had sold out. Johnny was counting the proceeds while Joe doused the fire.

''You guys sold out already?'' Paulie Mangano asked. ''I was gonna get a tree from ya.'' Paulie was Sammy the Bug's father. Sammy was a bookie, and his father took numbers.

''Try Taverna, he may still have some,'' Joe suggested. ''Before ya go, gimme 819 an' box it,'' he said as he pulled six dollars out of his pocket.

''Okay. How about you, Johnny Boy?''

''Well, my birthday was this month, maybe it'll be lucky for me. Give me 126.'' He took a dollar from the money he'd been counting and handed it to Paulie.

''Come on, Riccio, spring for the six bucks and box it,'' Joe urged.

''Whattaya mean, box it?''

''You serious? You pullin' my joint?''

''So I neva played a numba. What's so hard t' believe?'' He looked back and forth from Joe to Paulie, getting pissed.

''Okay, okay. Settle down. One twenty-six can be mixed up into six combinations: 216, 612, 621 an' like that. When you box a number you're bettin' on all the possible combinations. So if your birthday's this month an' we just made some money, go for it. Maybe it's your lucky day.''

Johnny scowled throughout Joe's explanation. He felt like a jackass. He looked at Paulie, then at the money in his hand and pulled out a five.

''Box it!'' Turning to Joe he said, ''Okay, Corelli, we got fifty-four bucks here minus the six I just boxed. You take six an' we split the remainder. Okay?''

''Okay.'' Joe picked up the oil drum and walked into the bakery.

When he returned Johnny said, ''Ya know, we forgot to deduct what we owe your old man fer the trees.''

Joe smiled. ''I guess he'll want what he took last year.''

''Yeah. What was that? I don't remember.''

''Nuthin.''

Johnny stood frowning quietly for a few moments. "Ya mean he didn't charge us?"

"Yeah."

"Wouldn't it be a lot easier for 'im t' just hand ya twenty bucks?"

"Not him. Ya gotta understand how he thinks. If he handed me twenty bucks he wouldn't have t' order the trees, have his men load up the truck, and send Tom ova here t' deliver 'em. But then I wouldn't stand out here for two days and freeze my *cullyonis* off or slug it out with these *chooches* to earn a buck. Therefore, he misses an opportunity to teach me what my life is gonna be like if I don't do well in school."

"But you *do* well in school. You already got the message. Why keep sending it?"

"Johnny Boy, did you eva see my pop mail a letter?"

"Mail a letter? Whatta we talkin' about here?"

"When my pop mails a letter he opens the box, pushes the envelope back as far as it will go and then closes the door. Next, he opens the door again to be sure it's down. He does that about three times before he walks away. After a few steps, he goes back, opens it one last time and peeks in. Ya got it?"

"Yeah. You're lucky your old man talks t' ya so much. My pop doesn't say anything unless there's a problem."

"Talks t' me? Are you kiddin'? My old man hasn't said eight words t' me in all my life. But in one *scyof* on the head or one nod of approval, he says more than most people do when they make a speech. He teaches by example. Like the mailbox numba. Whenever he's not working, he's either reading or writing.

"Enougha this! We earned the bread f' the rock 'n roll show and the Holiday Festival at the Garden with money left ova—so let's get the hell outa this pea soup. We only got a week until it's back t' prison."

CHAPTER

8

JOE SAT at his desk in the ''little'' room. He could hear his mother's favorite Italian radio program coming from the kitchen. He was going through his scrapbook of souvenirs from his political campaigns in junior high. In seventh grade he'd run for G.O. Vice-President. His supporters wore yellow paper bow ties with a green ribbon stapled to the middle. On the tie, in green crayon, was written ''7th yr Veep'' and under it ''CORELLI.'' His slogan that year was ''Get More For Your G.O. Dough, Vote For Corelli And Watch Him Go.'' Since he had skipped eighth grade, his next campaign was in ninth. That year he'd handed out ink blotters, white with brown lettering: ''Let's Go, Joe!'' was printed in each corner. Both campaigns had been successful, and he was toying with the idea of recycling one of them in his bid for the presidency of Lincoln this term.

''Joseph, supper's ready,'' his mother called.

As he walked into the dinette he heard on the Italian station, *''Mangia Troppo, Beve Troppo, Brioschi Pronto Ti Aiutera.''* The radio clicked off and moments later his mother came in with his dinner.

''How was everything at school today, darling?'' she asked as she put a steaming bowl of chicken and sausage in front of him.

"Okay. I made a decision today. I'm going to run for student-body president."

She sat down across the table from him. "Does that mean president of the whole school? Five thousand kids?"

"Yeah. I was just looking over some things from my junior high campaigns to see if I could use one of my old gimmicks, but I'd better not. I'm gonna need the support of my friends from junior high, and they might remember 'em and think I'm unimaginative."

"Do you think it's wise to do this?"

"Why not? I've always won before."

"But Lincoln is so big and everyone is Jewish. They always elect Jewish presidents. I'm afraid you'll be hurt."

"Look, Ma, I know what you're sayin'. But don't worry. Lemme tell ya how I have it figured. My opponents will probably be Harvey Haddad and Norman Schwartz. Who's gonna vote for Haddad? All the Jews? No. Only Syrian Jews will vote for him. The other Jews'd rather vote for an Italian than a Syrian, even if he is Jewish. You know how it is. Then there's Schwartz. Now, if he were one of the Jews from the honors classes, I'd have a problem. But he's not. I figure my classmates in honors, especially the ones I went to Boody and 215 with, Jewish or not, will vote for me. Then there's all the kids from Avenue U an' Avenue X, who'll vote for the first time because they have an Italian to vote for."

"I hope you're right, darling. But please don't count on it too much. You know how hard you take things when they don't work out for you," she warned, shaking her head.

As the conversation ended, Joe thought how proud he was that his mother spoke English so well, in spite of her sixth-grade education.

■ ■ ■

FEBRUARY WAS the dead of winter, so it wasn't at all unusual after three days of rain for the temperature to drop suddenly, turning the world into an oversized ice-skating rink. That's exactly what Joe found when he left for school the following morning. Next door the Gurians were salting their stoop.

"Good morning, Mr. Gurian. Has Philip left yet?" Joe asked.

"He left early today, Joseph. The weather, you know."

The Gurians were cousins of Israel's Prime Minister David Ben-Gurion, despite the difference in spelling. Joe had always thought it was curious that East 2nd Street was the borderline between the Italian and Syrian Jewish neighborhoods. The demarcation began with the Gurians, who were Jews but not Syrians. Joe's friend Mervin Dayan, who lived down the street from the Gurians, claimed his Uncle Moshe was some big shot in the Israeli army. He found himself wondering how German Jews and Polish Jews and Syrian Jews, who in Brooklyn wouldn't live in the same neighborhood or worship in the same temple, managed to get along in Israel. He didn't have too much time to speculate because halfway to East 3rd Street he heard Carlo "Whitey" Gentile calling him.

"Wait up, Joey. I'll walk witcha." Carlo got his nickname from his coloring. With his platinum-blonde hair and pale-blue eyes, he looked more Norwegian than Italian. "What's happenin'?"

"Not much. Where ya goin'?"

"Thought I might go t' school t'day. There ain't nuthin else goin' on."

"Well, get yourself t' school on election day 'cause I'm runnin' f' student-body president. They neva elected an Italian before an' I plan t' be the first. But I need all the boys with me t' do it."

"Yeah? They neva elected an Italian? Whatta dey elect, only *mazza creestos?*"

"Yeah."

"Hey, Joey, it takes money t' run a campaign, right?"

"Sure."

"I gotta great idea. How about I be yer fund raiser?"

''No! No, thank you. It doesn't take that much money. Besides, I wanna be president of Lincoln, not Sing Sing.''

''Hey, Joey, whattaya talkin' about? Yer hurtin' my feelin's.''

''Look, Whitey, remember last summer I told you I was broke and couldn't go to the track with you an' the boys?''

''Yeah, I remember. I tried t' help ya out then, too.''

''Right.'' They'd gone up to Bear Mountain on a confraternity picnic, and Whitey had his burglary tools stuck inside his socks. They weren't there two minutes when he was breaking into camp sites stealing people's cheap utensils and coffee pots. ''You were gonna finance my day at the track with fenced coffee pots. I still don't know how you thought you could get enough of them on the bus without being noticed to raise enough money to pay for admission, no less bet on the races. Please, don't help me. Just vote.''

''Relax. Your trouble is ya worry too much. Wait a minute, will ya?''

Whitey vanished. As Joe stood there waiting for him he heard the sound of something ripping or breaking, he wasn't sure which. He thought he saw something move inside the screened-in porch at the home of the Matalans, one of the wealthier Syrian families in the neighborhood. By the time Joe was able to absorb what was going on, Whitey was back with a large television in his hands.

''Here,'' he said, as he handed the set to Joe. ''My campaign contribution.''

Joe gaped at the TV. It seemed as though he had been standing there for hours before his hands and feet would respond, and he could drop the set and run, slipping on the ice over and over again all the way to school.

That evening, Joe was sitting at his desk doing his homework when he heard tapping at the window. Between the condensation from his breath that was fogging over the glass and the darkness outside, he couldn't tell who was out there, but the tapping became so insistent that he finally opened the window.

"Christ! What the fuck took ya so long? I'm freezin' t' death out here."

"Whattaya doin' here, Whitey?"

"I brought ya yer cut. Mario ga' me twenny bucks fer the set. I coulda gotten more but ya broke some tubes when ya t'rew it inta d' bushes."

"Look, Gentile, let's get somethin' straight once and for all. I don't wanna cut. Keep yer money, an' stay the fuck away from me." Joe slammed the window so hard that his mother came running in.

"Joseph, what's going on in here?"

As he turned to face her, he couldn't hide his rage.

"What was that noise? And why are you so upset?"

"I, uh, slammed the drawer too hard and my fingers were in the way. It's nothing. I'm okay."

"I think you work too hard, darling. Come have some hot milk and go to bed. You'll be better off."

"Really, Mom, I'm okay. I'm almost done, anyway."

She didn't argue. As she left, he sank onto the couch. Whitey was going to give him a heart attack yet. By the time he had gotten to school the next morning, between sprinting and panicking, he thought his heart would break right out of his chest. Maybe running for president wasn't such a hot idea after all. If this was the kind of help he was going to get from the neighborhood maniacs, he might win the election but not be healthy enough to take office.

CHAPTER 9

BY FRIDAY NIGHT Joe was ready to break loose. All week he had been coiled like a spring waiting for the police to arrive at his door. He couldn't believe that no one had seen or even heard about the burglary at the Matalans. But as the week rolled to a close, he decided that if he were in trouble, he'd know it by now.

It was quiet for a Friday night on Avenue U. The cold had driven people indoors. Even the usual crowd of horse lovers that gathered nightly at Jean's was smaller than usual. Finding no one at the candy store, Joe walked across the street to Pippy's Bar.

Pippy's real name was Giuseppe Verdone. To his friends and customers, he was "Joe Pippy." He owned the bar on the corner of East lst Street and Avenue U. Most of his patrons were older guys in the neighborhood who'd drop in to have a drink and to find out what was going on. Word on the street was that if you heard it at Pippy's, you could "bank it." As Joe entered, he saw Billy "Jap" at the pinball machine. Billy, who got his nickname from his slanty eyes, stopped playing long enough to look Joe over and satisfy himself that he was a harmless local. Joe considered him someone to avoid because his name was often linked with the episodes of violence talked about in the neighborhood. Joe had digested the difference between strength and violence, and while he had the stomach for the latter, he had little taste for it.

The bar had about a dozen stools. The one to the far left, under the flashing ''Rheingold'' sign in the window, belonged to Albie from the *latticini* store. Joe had never been in Pippy's without seeing Albie on that stool, drinking quietly, not talking to anyone. At the other end of the bar Gino Barese, Vinnie ''Sicilian,'' Philly Trambelli, Tommy Lo Cicero and Jimmy Puccini were listening to Pippy tell about his trip to Las Vegas. Getting to Las Vegas was the ultimate neighborhood fantasy. Just about every night for the last six months, Pippy had been entrancing his patrons with his stories about the games he'd played and the broads he'd screwed. Jimmy Puccini lapped up Pippy's stories as much as anyone, although he probably didn't understand some of them. With an IQ of no more than 70, he wasn't capable of doing much except some simple errands for his sister Jean. He was about twenty years older than Joe, and his balding head tended to bob. He loved Joe, and the feeling was mutual. If Jimmy's eyes didn't shine with intelligence, they had their own kind of light, Joe thought. From goodness. Sometimes, looking at Jimmy, Joe would wonder if being slow made it easier to be good on Avenue U—or was it only that being smart didn't necessarily mean you were smart clear through?

Joe sat down next to Jimmy and ordered a scotch and soda. It didn't occur to him that he might be asked for an ID any more than it occurred to Pippy to ask. Not that they didn't know about the eighteen-year-old drinking age—it just wasn't relevant. The neighborhood had its own rules about drinking that took precedence over those of the outside world. No one was afraid that large crowds would gather in the bars because Italians rarely went to them. There were no races to see who could chug-a-lug a pitcher of beer the fastest, because even if there were two people crazy enough to try it, no one would be interested in the outcome. Drunken brawls were unheard of; the local bosses wouldn't tolerate any behavior that attracted cops. These people prided themselves on having quiet, ''safe'' neighborhoods. Discreet, private savagery—yes; conspicuous crime—no! Since all the players understood the rules, there was no risk in serving minors.

Before long, Rudy ''the Hawk'' joined the group at the bar. He ordered a drink while reaching into the bell jar that Pippy kept filled with pickled eggs and peppers. Rudy was a well known longshoreman, highly respected by everyone. He came home from World War II in terrible shape. The story was that he had gone AWOL, and when he returned to the base his sergeant had him confined to the ''Black Box.'' He spent months locked in that box in the hot sun. About a year later, when the war was over, he started making trips to Newark over the weekends. Rudy knew the sergeant was from Newark, and he began systematically checking every family in the city with his sergeant's common last name until he found him. Then Rudy's hunt really began. It took him just over two years to catch the sergeant in the right circumstances to waste him. To the Newark police, it was still an unsolved homicide. On Avenue U, it was a simple matter of vengeance, the matter-of-fact source of Rudy's nickname.

Joe put his hand on Jimmy's shoulder. ''Ya know, I'm in the mood for a movie. T' tell ya the truth, James, I don't even remember the last one I saw. Maybe you could pick us a good one, an' we'll go t'morra? Whattaya say, buddy?''

''Gee, Joey, I been t'inkin' I'd like t' see *Rumble on the Docks*.''

''Okay, yer on. But you gotta find out the times and where it's playin'. Deal?''

''There ya are, Joey!'' His conversation with Jimmy was interrupted by Paulie De Luca and Mikey Gilberti, who had just come in the front door.

''This place is like a morgue,'' Mikey commented, as he made his way to the jukebox in the back.

''What's goin' on? I looked all ova fer the guys. The street's deserted,'' Joe said.

"Didn't ya hear? Shef's had a real big game goin' on t'day. Heavyweights from all ova. Ponzie's ova there representin' the neighborhood. He's doin' okay. They ain't gonna go back to Queens, da Bronx or wherever da fuck dere from an' say dere's bananas in Brooklyn."

Ponzie, a local pool shark, got his nickname because, when he wasn't hustling pool, he made his living promoting pyramids and other assorted schemes. Ponzie was only one of the virtuosos with a cue who gathered at Shef's. While these impromptu tournaments were very exciting events for the guys in the neighborhood, they cost Shef money, because while everyone watched they didn't play.

You oo've got the magic touch. It makes me glow so much. As the jukebox came to life, Mikey joined the others at the bar.

"So how's the race goin' for Lincoln's first Italian president?" he inquired.

"Okay. I'm convinced I'll win if there's a heavy turnout. I hope you guys are out there pitchin' for me. I'm gonna really need your help t' pull this off."

"Don't worry, Joey. We're campaignin' fer ya. In fact, my Uncle Bill's gonna make you some great signs. I'll bring 'em t' school on Monday. Ya know your slogan, 'Don't Take A Chance'? Well, he's got a hand flippin' a coin ona dynamite background so it looks kinda 3-D. It's gonna be a smash," Paulie said.

Bill De Luca owned the local sign shop, so it was very easy for the boys to believe that the posters would be great.

"I'll bet they're gonna be a knockout." Joe couldn't wait to see them. "That's awfully generous of him, Paulie. Tell him I'm grateful."

"It's his pleasure. He said he wants t' see an Italian win an election, even if it is jus' high school. Ya gotta start somewhere, right, Joey?"

"Yeah, Fiorello La Guardia, move ova," yelled Gino, who'd been listening to the boys' conversation.

■ ■ ■

THE NINE candidates for the three G.O. offices sat on the stage in Lincoln's auditorium. They were required to give their campaign speeches to the entire student body at assembly. Three regularly scheduled assemblies were necessary to accommodate the large number of students. As the candidates watched the last group file in, all were glad that this day was almost over.

Lincoln's auditorium was the size of a large theater, right up to a full-size balcony. As the final assembly got underway, Joe could see Whitey, Nicky Corella and Fredo ''Wing'' Pistilli in the front row of the balcony. The sight of the three of them together made Joe's hair stand on end. From the time the candidates' posters had started going up, Haddad's and Schwartz's had begun disappearing. Then word got out that the boys were conducting their own independent poll of the electorate. Voters foolish enough to prefer one of Joe's opponents were threatened with a broken head and neck unless they quickly saw the error of their ways. As Joe learned of each new episode, he'd beg and plead with the boys to cut it out, certain they were hurting and not helping. He'd lecture them on the dos and don'ts of the democratic process, but no amount of civics tutoring worked.

■ ■ ■

ONE DAY the previous week as Dr. Goldman, the dean of boys, rounded a corner, he had seen Fredo tearing up one of Harvey Haddad's posters. Fredo was not unknown to Dr. Goldman; indeed, he had achieved a certain notoriety in the school the previous year when he had poured a can of red paint all over Abraham Lincoln's statue on red-letter day.

''Halt!'' shouted Goldman when he caught sight of the boy.

Fredo, five-eight, pudgy and sandy-haired, turned to confront the short, dark man with a pencil-thin moustache, fondly known to the student body as Hitler. Goldman could not wait until Fredo turned sixteen to throw him the hell out of school, and witnessing the boy's latest act of destructiveness caused him to come unglued. He began to scream and yell about the rights of others. The boy watched him impassively. When Goldman finished, Fredo unzipped his fly and pissed carefully all over the dean's shoes. Goldman went bat shit. "In my twenty-five years at Lincoln, they've defaced my office, defaced my car, they've cursed my mother, they've cursed my father and they've cursed me! But no one has ever urinated on me before."

Fredo tipped an imaginary hat and walked off.

■ ■ ■

THERE WAS no doubt in Joe's mind that the boys would once again give him reason to question the wisdom of having gotten involved in this election. He hoped they'd play their hand quickly and put him out of his misery. The tension was giving him a stomachache. He didn't have long to wait. No sooner had Harvey Haddad stood to speak than they jumped up, slammed their seats and stamped their feet in mock restlessness. The teachers on duty quickly silenced them and Harvey began again. This time they hissed and booed. Once again, the teachers rushed to control them. On Harvey's third try, the boys pulled out all the stops. Before anyone realized what was happening, a volley of tomatoes, probably stolen from one of the many gardens in the neighborhood, was hurled at the speaker. The boys jumped over seats and students as they made their escape with a pack of enraged teachers close behind.

It came as no surprise to Joe that at the end of the assembly Dr. Goldman took him aside. Rumor had it that Goldman hated Italians. Although, in light of recent events, Joe wondered if he could blame him, he was nonetheless wary. Not only did Goldman blame him for everything that had happened, claiming it was campaign strategy, but he accused him of having broken the election rules by paying for professionally made posters. Despite Joe's assurances that he had done everything in his power to stop his "friends" and that the posters were a contribution from a student's uncle, Goldman threatened to have him disqualified from the election.

"If that's what you feel you have to do, Dr. Goldman, then I will take my case to Dr. Weiss." Joe knew the new principal of Lincoln really liked him and would at least give him a fair hearing.

In the end, he not only stayed in the race, he won by a landslide.

CORELLI	1816
HADDAD	781
SCHWARTZ	768

His mother cooked a victory dinner of mussels with hot sauce, linguini and clams, stuffed mushrooms and eggplant parmigiana. Slipping a ten-dollar bill into his hand, she whispered, "Don't tell your father I gave you this little present. It'll make him mad."

Giuseppe was so proud he couldn't decide whether to laugh or cry. He grinned from ear to ear; his face was flushed and tears filled his eyes. He pulled a twenty-dollar bill from his wallet and stuffed it into his son's pocket while he held his index finger over his lips and gave the boy a conspiratorial wink.

Joe would keep both their secrets. His own secret was a growing confidence in his ability to beat the odds. Everything was breaking Joe's way. He was hot. He knew he could parlay this windfall into a big hit. But how?

CHAPTER

10

HIS QUEST took him to Jean's on the brightest, sunniest Saturday morning that the Northeast had seen in almost a month.

At first glance, it looked as though everyone from East 2nd Street was scattered around in the back booths. *Earth Angel,* playing on the jukebox, was barely audible over the noise.

''There's Joey. Let's ask him,'' suggested Junior Aversa.

''Ask me what?''

''We need some basketball games fer t'night. Lo Bianco says Syracuse. Ace an' Sally D're both in the back. Dey like da Knicks against da Celtics. Whadda you think, Joey?''

''I don't know very much about basketball, fellas. I go on the bookies' line and my gut,'' he answered. ''I'm lookin' for a good bet myself. I'll be right back,'' Joe promised as he headed for the back room.

The tables were filled today. A quick look around and Joe could see that Cosimo Roselli was placing a wager with Cheech Fusco. Joey never quite understood the deal Fusco had with Sally D concerning which of them would take a given wager. His hunch was that when the action was big, it was Sally D's exclusive province.

Roselli was the neighborhood hijacker. He was as nice a kid as there was on the street. As a child he'd had rheumatic fever and was out of school more than he was in. He was left back so many times that by the time he got to seventh grade he was fifteen years old and almost six feet tall. In the eyes of the other kids he was the school dummy. Worse, that's what he was in his own eyes. Predictably, at sixteen he dropped out and turned to the street for something to do. The boys put him to work in the hijacking business. A couple of months before, he had been picked up after a high-speed chase. He was caught red-handed on his way to Mario's Pork Store with a load of men's clothing he and Louie the Turk from Avenue X had hijacked at a truck stop on the New Jersey Turnpike. The cops had worked Cosimo over pretty good in an attempt to determine which of the higher-ups had masterminded this bust, but, true to the neighborhood code of *omertà,* Cosimo took his lumps without breathing a word. Had he cooperated with the law—a choice that never really occurred to him—he would, as a first-time loser, have had a shot at a suspended sentence. Instead, he now nervously awaited a jail sentence after pleading guilty to two felony counts.

On the street side, Mario's Pork Store was a meat market. He kept sheep heads hanging in the window for his Neapolitan customers. Inside, in his showcase, he had sausages, tripe, veal cutlets and anything else that the neighborhood demanded. In the back there was an elevator, not much larger than a dumbwaiter, that transported his customers to his fencing operation in the basement. When Cosimo would arrive with a heist, he'd back the truck up to Mario's elevator and unload the cargo. By the next morning word would be all over the street that Mario's Pork Store was running a special. Joe's parents stayed away; Joe stayed away, too. But he was always friendly to Cosimo, whom he genuinely liked.

Now, Joe walked up to the back table to pay his respects to Ace and Sally D.

''Hi there, kid. Have a seat,'' Sally offered as Joe extended his hand.

''Hi, Ace. Sally. I haven't seen you in a long time,'' he said to Sally.

"Well, Joey, I've had a few restless natives on my hands. Business. But I been hearin' about ya, anyway. My brother Raymo thinks a lotta ya, kid."

"He's been a real friend to me, Sally. I like him a whole lot."

Sally could tell the kid wasn't telling him what he thought he wanted to hear. "Lemme tell ya about Raymo, kid. He shoulda had kids. If he had, he'da liked you t' be it. He really loves ya, kid."

The boy was astonished. Not that the information itself was so surprising; the candor was. First Raymo and now Sally. Italians are not up-front about their feelings, especially the men. Maybe what made it possible for Sally was the use of the third person.

"Ya need somethin', kid? Or is this a social call?" Ace asked, breaking the awkward silence.

"Got any tips for me? I fell on thirty unexpected bucks an' I'm feelin' hot. The boys out front are talkin' basketball. Word's out Sally's toutin' the Knicks."

"Listen, kid, I don't know nuthin," Sally said. "The Knicks ain't a bad bet."

"But they ain't good enough to shoot thirty on," Ace added.

Satisfied that there wasn't a fix going down, Joe returned to his friends. It seemed that only college games got wired.

He wanted to call his bookie, but Ralphie Cardillo was on the phone, so he went and sat down next to Vinnie.

"I'm gonna bet the Knicks," he said.

"Yeah. Ace an' Sally tole ya?" Vinnie asked.

"No. It's my idea."

"Okay, fuck d' Nats, I'll do the same. We'll watch the game at my house tonight. Bet the Knicks four times fer me."

Joe got up and started to pace. "What the fuck is Ralphie doin' on that phone? He's been talkin' since I got here."

"He's talkin' t' Isabelle, whattaya think? Ya know his mudda. If he called from home an' she caught 'im, she'd whack his *cullyonis* off," Vinnie said.

Impatience was rising from Joe's gut and choking him. From time to time feelings like these would overtake him. They'd start as anxiety and grow into rage. They frightened him because he wasn't in control. Joe would stand outside himself and watch while his behavior became more and more incomprehensible, and no matter how loudly he screamed at himself to settle down, he couldn't be heard. These episodes left him drained and listless. His mother told him he got it from his father. According to her, Joe had needed a blood transfusion when he was born. His father had his blood type, but was drunk when he donated it to him. The message was clear. Whatever was wrong with him was his father's fault, not hers.

In this one way, Joe didn't want to be like his father. On more than one occasion, he had watched in terror as his father reduced the house to rubble. When his rage was spent, his dad would crawl into bed, where he'd stay for days, claiming he was about to die. Joe would sit at the foot of the stairs, crying and waiting. Every time it happened, he really believed his father would die, and the more he cried the angrier his mother would become. "Don't pay any attention to him," she'd yell. "He's crazy." Was she right? Was he crazy? Were they both crazy? Like father, like son? He didn't want to think about it. He turned suddenly and stalked out of Jean's.

The cold air smacked him in the face. Somewhere inside him the brakes went on, and he remembered that he wanted a phone.

He found one at Tommy's Sweet Shoppe. He took out a dime and dialed Olfield 6-8000, a number in Hackensack, New Jersey, that rang in a bookie parlor on Avenue X, right up the street. As soon as he heard the receiver picked up on the other end, he identified himself.

"This is Joe fer six."

"Yes, Joe."

"What's the line on today's games?"

"The Knicks a' five an' a half over the Celtics. The Lakers a t'ree over the Nats. . . ."

''Gimme the Knicks eight times.''

That night at Vinnie's house, the boys watched the Knicks lose outright by sixteen points. Their bet never even had a shot.

The next day, when he arrived at the social club to serve Sunday coffee, the bookie's runner announced that he owed $440 on yesterday's bet.

''You gotta be nuts! I neva bet $400 on anything in my life.''

The runner gave him a knowing look, sighed, shrugged his shoulders and left.

That evening Joe was sitting in the ''little'' room doing his father's books when the doorbell rang. His father had gone to work, and his mother was at Mrs. Princiotta's for their weekly poker game, so he answered the door.

''Jesus Christ, Joey, have you heard? We're in deep shit with Angelo Cacciardi,'' Vinnie said as he pushed his way past Joe.

''I heard this mornin' he thinks I owe 'im 440 bucks. But that's ridiculous. I'm not worried about it. They'll realize they've made a mistake.''

''Yeah? Then how come we're ordered to a sitdown t'morra night?''

''Sitdown? I haven't heard about any sitdown.''

''T'morra night, eight o'clock at Club XIX on Avenue X.''

CHAPTER

11

THE NEXT morning, the *Lincoln Log* election edition headlined his triumph: JOSEPH CORELLI CAPTURES LINCOLN G.O. PRESIDENCY.

■ ■ ■

THAT EVENING the boys trudged along in silence to Club XIX, Angelo Cacciardi's bar on East lst Street and Avenue X. Vinnie was totally absorbed in trying to resolve the dilemma of how to smoke and bite his nails simultaneously. Joe, for the first time in his life, noticed that every other house had a shrine in the front yard: Our Lady of Fatima in a grotto of rock and broken bricks; the Infant of Prague in a limp, water-stained cape; St. Anthony and some faded pink flamingos. Joe concentrated on each one to keep his imagination in control.

In the back of the bar, seated at the last table, were Angelo Cacciardi, two bodyguards and Raymo.

The boys sat down, and without the usual formalities, Angelo went on the attack.

''You fuckin' scumbags! Whattaya tryin' t' pull?''

''Mr. Cacciardi, we're not tryin' t' pull anything,'' Joe said.

But Cacciardi was not so easily convinced. He called them every name they'd ever heard—plus a few. After a while Joe stopped listening. At every pause he repeated his story exactly.

"I said eight times and not eighty times. I've never bet more than ten times in my life; check your records." He kept wondering why Raymo was there. Finally Angelo slowed down, his language became less graphic, and he even seemed ready to listen. "You scumbags better talk fast," he ordered.

Since Joe had nothing new to add, they all fell silent, looking at each other. Just as Joe was beginning to feel like he was breaking out in hives from the tension, Raymo spoke up.

"I know both these kids. Joey's good people. Normally I'd say ferget Lo Bianco, but if Joey says he made the bet fer both a dem, I'd believe it."

Once again silence descended. Angelo looked at Raymo for what seemed to be forever. Slowly his gaze shifted to the boys.

"Get outa here!" he ordered.

The boys got up. Joe pulled thirty dollars out of his pocket and put it on the table. "Take the vig outa this."

Vinnie watched his friend, looked at Angelo and reached into his jacket pocket.

"I got only five. I'll get ya nine t'morra."

The gorilla on Angelo's right started to get out of his chair.

"Ah, wait a minute," Vinnie squealed. "I jus' remembid. I t'ink I got some more money in my pants."

It was late when Joe got home. Except for the kitchen light, the house was dark. Upstairs, he looked into his mother's room to say goodnight.

She was kneeling by the side of the bed, rosary beads in hand, her missal open in front of her. The only light in the room came from the votive candles that she routinely lit every night before praying. The centerpiece of her statue collection on top of the dresser was the Virgin Mary, an arch with a bas-relief figure crushing the head of a snake. The virgin was flanked by the Sacred Heart on one side and St. Joseph, every Italian's patron saint, on the other. Perpendicular to the dresser, on top of a chest of drawers, was a collection of saints with special meaning for her. There was St. Gerard, who had appeared to her in a dream when she was pregnant with Joe's older brother, Jerry. The saint informed her that she would have a boy, who must be named after him. If they were to have a second son, Giuseppe expected him to be named Joseph, an issue she had raised with the saint at the time. When Maria Teresa told Giuseppe about the dream, he went wild. Still, she remained implacably loyal to the orders from on high. The apparition prevailed, and the name Gerald entered the family for the first time. St. Jude was next, because he had answered her prayers when the process of bringing Joe into the world had nearly cost her her life—a fact she pointed out to both him and his father with regularity. Last, but not least, was San Gennaro, the ranking Neapolitan saint.

"Good night, Mama," Joe said softly.

She looked up at him impassively and nodded while the beads continued slipping through her fingers. Then she returned her full attention to her saints.

Say one for St. Raymo, he thought gratefully, closing the door without a sound.

CHAPTER 12

SCHOOL HAD been out two weeks for everyone but the staff of the *Lincoln Log*. Getting out the last edition of the paper was always frantic. It was summer and cabin fever had reached epidemic proportions. The tender green of spring had matured into the vibrant colors of summer. It was harder than usual to concentrate on galley proofing when the outdoors was so seductive.

Sprung at last, Joe all but ran back to Avenue U with the final issue of the *Log* under his arm. He hurried up the street searching for his friends, finding them at Shef's. Vinnie, Mikey and Johnny Riccio were standing with Shef and some of the older guys, talking about something that, from the look on their faces, Joe guessed was serious.

"Hi, Joey," Johnny said distractedly.

"Hi. What's goin' on?"

"Didja hear about Bruno Marino?"

"No. What about him?"

"His body turned up in Bath Beach with five bullet holes in it," Johnny responded.

"Why? What'd he do?" It wasn't unusual for bodies to turn up almost anywhere in Gravesend, but Joe never quite got used to it. In this case, the body was a kid he'd known all through school. Somehow, it came too close to home.

Everyone knew Marino as one of the neighborhood animals, not only because of his huge size, but also because of his disposition. A budding arsonist, he had been sent to Boston on his first job by a local gangster named Babe Capria. Unfortunately, Bruno bungled the assignment. Three nights before, he had been in a Coney Island bar with his girlfriend when Babe came in. Babe joined them and before long began upbraiding Bruno for blowing the Boston job. With his pride at stake, Bruno felt compelled to beat the living daylights out of Babe, thereby signing his own death warrant. Word of the beating had spread throughout the neighborhood. Everyone except Joe, who had been holed up in Lincoln's newspaper office, had been waiting for the other shoe to fall.

He didn't want to hear any more. He was finally out of school, and he wanted to have fun, not listen to a dirge. ''Anybody up for a little pool? I don't know about the rest of you, but I came here to shoot a few racks,'' he announced as he walked to a free table, setting the *Lincoln Log* on a nearby chair and racking up the balls.

The boys followed him.

''Hey, Riccio, listen to this,'' Mikey called. Mikey picked up the paper that Joe had left on the chair and decided to ride his friend.

''Says here, 'The following is a list of those students who maintained an average of 95% or over during the previous semester, in the order of their performance:

GLORIA EDIS
MARILYN SILVERMAN
SHELDON JACOBOWITZ
CAROLE KAPLOWITZ
JOSEPH CORELLI
EMANUEL NADELMAN
STEPHEN GOLDMAN
EUGENE ROSENBERG
ELIZABETH HOLTZMANN.'

How did they let you on this list, Corelli? Looks like you need a Bar Mitzvah to qualify.''

''You're a real comedian, Gilberti,'' Joe answered.

''Johnny Boy, when I get my copy in the mail, I'm gonna bring it to your old man,'' Mikey said. ''I wan' him to see he was right to send ya to Lafayette. There ain't no company like dis ova dere.''

''Lay off, Gilberti. Are you shootin' or what?'' Johnny said with irritation. He had hoped to go to Lincoln. Lafayette wasn't in the same league academically, and he, like Joe, wanted to go to a good college. But his father, for reasons that were unclear to him, couldn't stand Jews, and the academic track at Lincoln was almost all Jewish. So he went to Lincoln's ball games and dances with his friends and only went to Lafayette long enough to go to class and then got the hell out.

''You're up, Gilberti,'' Vinnie called. As Mikey got up to shoot, Vinnie pulled Joe aside.

''Listen, Joey, I got us a great deal. Ya know how Shef's been talkin' about paintin' dis place?''

''Yeah.''

''Well, I got us da job,'' he said proudly, as though Joe'd been waiting all his life for this news.

''Whattaya mean? We don't know anything about painting.''

''What's t' know? Ya buy paint an' a brush an' ya put it on the wall. Simple.''

''Look, Vinnie, even if I was interested, starting t'morra I've gotta be up every day at four in the mornin' to go to the market an' load watermelons for my pop.''

''That's okay. We'll do it when ya get home.''

''I don't get home till noon, and even if I had the energy then, this place is already jammed.''

''That's the beauty a dis, Joey. That's how come Shef hired me. I know the place an' the guys. He don't hafta close down. We can work aroun' his customers. Ya think a stranger'd do dat?''

''I don't know about this, Lo Bianco. How much are we gettin' paid?''

''Seventy-five bucks. Where else could we get that kinda money? An' I gotta have it, Joey. My name is mud aroun' here. Things are so bad I gotta go outa the neighborhood to make a bet anymore. Ya gotta help me!''

Eventually Joe capitulated. Not because he thought Vinnie's plan was any good—he didn't—but because he hated to let a friend down. Besides, some extra money would come in handy. It was going to be a long summer.

Later, thinking about caving in to Vinnie's dumb idea, it came to Joe for the first time that he could afford to give in to Vinnie. Sometimes, he decided, giving in proves how strong you are.

BOOK
II

JOE

BROOKLYN 1957–1958

CHAPTER 1

A MONTH into his senior year at Lincoln, Joe was primed and ready for one of the most important years of his life. He had already sent for applications to Notre Dame, Georgetown, Harvard, Yale and Columbia. He played the anxiety game so as not to appear self-confident, but in his heart he knew he'd be accepted everywhere. Indeed, that was his greatest fear. His brother Frank was relentless in pushing for Harvard, and while he knew that Frank's position won all the points for logic, his endocrinal attachment was to Notre Dame. This dilemma, however, did not so much as dampen his excitement over the prospect of getting off Avenue U and out of Brooklyn.

A few weeks earlier he represented Lincoln for a week at a seminar on human relations at the National Conference of Christians and Jews Camp in Hyde Park. He had no sooner gotten back when Raymo decided to take him on an educational trip of his own. On a glorious Saturday afternoon, they drove to Hoboken and attended a Teamsters meeting, run by Tony Provenzano. Raymo was treated with great deference by the union leaders, and he saw to it that they understood Joe was "good people." Smart, too. The kid was gonna be a lawyer, maybe a labor lawyer. Who knew? He made sure Joe understood that although it might look like the Teamsters were Hoffa's exclusive property, appearances could be deceiving.

■ ■ ■

IT WAS Saturday night, and all he cared about was getting to Jean's to meet Vinnie Lo Bianco, Johnny Riccio, Mikey Gilberti, Junior Aversa and Johnny's brother Louie. They were going to the confraternity dance at St. Rocco's on West 11th Street, well off their turf. But they didn't care; they were on a senior-year high, ten feet tall and ready to play. Even with girls.

Shortly after they arrived, Mikey asked one of the girls to dance. In no time flat, he felt a tap on his shoulder. He turned to find himself nose to nose with ''Jack the Ripper'' Novella. Jack was Mikey's height, but thirty pounds lighter and had a face that looked like it belonged on a wanted poster.

''Hey, you cuttin' in?''

''Nah. I wan' ya should get the fuck outa here.''

Mikey was surprised. If Jack had been cutting in he would have let him. Gilberti was quiet, even shy, and despite his strength, he didn't like to fight.

''Look, Jackie, I ain't botherin' nobody. Why don't ya let me alone?''

''Ya heard me, wise guy. I don' like youse guys comin' here an' dancin' wit' th' wrong girls. Dis is ow backyard, an' we wan' ya outa here.''

Mikey ignored him, finished the dance, and walked over to his friends.

''What did Jack the Rippa want witcha?'' Vinnie asked.

''He said I was dancin' wit' the wrong girl.''

''Yeah? So what'd you say?''

''Nuthin. What's to say? The guy's comin' in on t'ree engines. Wants me t' go out an' fight 'im.''

All of a sudden an open bottle of Coke hit Gilberti on the side of the head, soaking his hair, face and shirt. He went berserk! As he lunged for Novella, Joe and Johnny each grabbed an arm and tried to stop him. He pulled away from them as though they were a pair of anemic girls and tore up the stairs and out onto the street after Jack.

Outside, the Avenue U crowd watched in horror as Mikey caught Jack, picked him up under the shoulders, and slammed him against a telephone pole, knocking him senseless. By now, about ten of the West 10th Street Gang joined in the fray. Their leader, ''Big John'' Macri, who was a full head taller, grabbed Mikey from behind, took a swing at him—and missed, giving Mikey the opportunity to corner John and pulverize him.

Meanwhile, Jack had recovered sufficiently to get back on his feet, pull a knife and lunge for Joe. Joe took a quick step out of the way and ran out into the street. Novella followed him with the knife. Joe decided that the best strategy was to stay as close to the church as possible, so instead of running away, he began circling a parked Chevy Impala. A couple of turns around the car and Johnny Riccio started chasing Novella. For some time the three of them went around and around, no one gaining on anyone else. A newcomer to the scene would have been unable to tell who was chasing whom as they proceeded Sambo-and-the-tigers style.

Joe was running out of steam when, from the corner of his eye, he noticed that Johnny, on one of his turns around the car, had picked up a garbage can from the sidewalk. Counting on the unexpected having a paralyzing effect on Jack, Joe stopped short, turned, threw up his arms and yelled, ''Time out!''

It worked. Novella stopped dead in his tracks in a state of absolute confusion. Before he could gather his wits, Johnny caught up with him and clobbered him over the head with the can. With Jack out cold on the ground, Johnny leaped on his back and continued beating Novella with the garbage can.

Meanwhile, no one from the Avenue U group or the West 10th Street Gang had made a move to intercede in the Gilberti-Macri fight. Joe rushed over to Mikey and screamed at him to stop. By then, John Macri was bloodied. Mikey got off him and stood gasping and shaking his head from side to side while trying to regain control of himself. Johnny Riccio, meanwhile, had dropped the can and joined Junior, Vinnie and Johnny's brother Louie on the sidewalk.

The six boys regrouped and surveyed the damage. Macri and Novella were out cold on the street. The West 10th Street boys stood still, making no move toward Joe and his friends or to help their buddies. The Avenue U boys looked at each other and, without making any sudden moves, turned and walked away.

CHAPTER

2

JOE SAT on the stage reviewing his notes. This was the first assembly period on Monday afternoon, and he was very excited. Every year, Lincoln gave an award to someone who had made an outstanding contribution in the field of education, philosophy or social work. This year the students had voted to give the award to Helen Keller, who, with her teacher, Annie Sullivan, was at this very moment seated on his left. As student-body president, Joe had full charge of the program.

As usual, he would start out with a reading from the Old Testament, followed by the flag ceremony. Next, his address:

> Today is Helen Keller day, a day on which we honor with the Lincoln Award a famous lady, who is known throughout the world as an example of courage and determination. Stefan Freifeld will recite a short poem called 'Invictus,' which means unconquered. It was written when William Ernest Henley, the poet, refused to give in to the difficulties surrounding him.

After the poem, he would introduce Mr. Plaut, who would talk about the Lincoln Award, followed by Joyce Levine singing "You'll Never Walk Alone." Immediately after the music, his vice-president, Susan Stein, would tell the audience why Miss Keller was chosen as this year's recipient of the Lincoln Award and then Dr. Abraham Weiss would present her with the award.

The program went off like clockwork. Accepting the award from Dr. Weiss, Miss Keller took her teacher's hands in her own and began to deliver her speech. Joe sat mesmerized by the magic of the woman's hands. He knew what it felt like to have his head racing ahead of his mouth; how much more frustrating it must be to have to use your hands. Just as he was thinking that the only ideas he had ever seen communicated with fingers couldn't be repeated in mixed company, a disturbance in the audience drew his attention.

Everything happened so quickly that the scene took on a surrealistic quality. A few members of the Avenue X Gang had barged into the auditorium and, armed with eggs and tomatoes, were attempting to rush the stage to pelt Miss Keller. Faculty members were trying to tackle them from behind, while the little Jewish hothouse plants seated down front stood holding hands trying to block their way.

The chaos in the aisle flowed in slow motion as Joe sat there wondering why these aborigines had to be Italian. His mother's words, "What will they think of us?" flashed through his mind. From the time he had begun his campaign for president, Joe had found himself suffering periodic bouts of humiliation caused by some of the other Italian kids. As school president, he was ashamed for the school when these savages broke loose, but as an Italian, he felt it even more deeply. He had to summon up all his intellectual ability to convince himself that these cretins did not reflect on him, that he would be seen as a separate person. Still, it was a monkey on his back and on the back of every Italian who wanted to make something of his life and wanted to do it honorably.

He looked over at the two women who were proceeding as though nothing unusual was going on. Of course. Helen Keller could not see or hear anything. Unless Miss Sullivan stopped her and explained, she'd have no way of knowing, and why would her teacher tell her how the Visigoths were receiving her?

Joe turned and looked back at the aisle where the invaders had been contained and were being dragged from the auditorium. Why was this woman, a genius, imprisoned in a dark and silent world, while these imbeciles were blessed with all their senses? Why should those without vision see? Why should people incapable of understanding hear? What kind of God gave them all the tools to create havoc while this woman struggled? Sometimes it was easier to believe in the small-minded, capricious gods of his ancestors than in the Christian God of wisdom and love.

On his way home from school that afternoon, Joe had just crossed Avenue T on his bike at East 2nd Street when he saw Louie Riccio walking toward him.

"Hey, Joey! I was just at ya house lookin' for ya."

"Oh, yeah? What's up?"

"Joey, we're in deep shit! Today at school everyone was talkin' about the fight Sataday night. Dere's one big rumble goin' down. Big John Macri's got word out all over Lafayette dat the West 10th Street Gang should arm demselves fer war Wednesday night. They're gonna kill us!"

"Christ, Louie! They must have a hundred guys in that gang. Look, I gotta get home an' do my homework. You busy now?"

"Nah. Even if I was, I couldn't concentrate. I got diarrhea already."

"All right. Look, calm down. See how many a the guys you can find an' let's meet afta dinna at Jean's. We're gonna have to figure out what to do about this."

"Good. Good idea, Joey. See ya lata."

When Joe got home his mother was eager to hear about Helen Keller, but all he could think about was how to avoid winding up dead on the street, and he certainly couldn't talk to her about that. If she knew about his life on Avenue U, her hair would fall out. As he made his way to the "little" room, he mumbled something about courage.

At seven-fifteen, Joe walked into Jean's. In the back, filling a couple of booths, were the Riccio brothers, Vinnie, Mikey, Paulie, Junior Aversa, Billy Donadio and Butchie Di Costanzo. They waited a while to see if anyone else would show up, shooting the breeze about everything but the problem at hand. Butchie had just come from Pippy's, where Armando Mattarese, the neighborhood's last word on matters scientific, because he worked at Raytheon, was holding the crowd of regulars spellbound with his latest revelation: that the atom bomb was the size of a golf ball.

By seven-thirty no one else had come, so the boys decided to get down to business. Louie began by suggesting they call the cops.

"Are you fuckin' crazy?" Joe said. All we need is a buncha cops down here on Avenue U, an' we'll get it worse from the big guys than from Macri's guys. So why don't we just play it by ear? This is a bona fide street fight, a war! Lemme try to work out our strategy."

"We're witcha, Joey. Whatta we gonna do?" Mikey asked.

"For starters, we need help. Macri's gotta have a hundred guys in his gang. We don't have a gang. I'm surprised all you guys showed up. I say we go to the Avenue X boys an' ask 'em to help us."

"Who's we?" Vinnie asked.

"Me," Joe said. "I'll go straight from school tomorrow. We meet here again tomorrow night."

CHAPTER 3

THE NEXT afternoon, after school, Joe rode over to Avenue X and ran into Sonny Balbi, Nicky Corella, Rico Porta and Patsy De Primo.

"Hey, Joey! Whatcha doin' ova hea?" Sonny called.

"Lookin' fer you guys. We gotta talk."

"Yeah? Okay. Let's go ina candy store an' siddown."

The boys sat down and Joe told them the whole story. He bet on the ongoing rivalry between the two gangs to have the Avenue X guys view him and his friends as natural allies.

"Look, Joey, I t'ink I could get twenny, maybe toity guys to come down," Sonny offered.

Before he could respond, Porta leaped out of his seat.

"I tell ya what! I got dis Civil War cannon. We'll put da cannon in da Protestant churchyard downa dead-end street from Shef's. Den we'll draw 'em down da street. Den ar guys split inta the alleys an' I'll start firin' the fuckin' cannon on dose cocksuckers."

Joe turned pale. God Almighty, he thought, this guy's gonna start blowin' guys away with cannon balls. "Rico, please, no way!" he said.

"No, no! Dis is the greatest. I been wantin' t' use dis cannon fer a lon' time. They're all a buncha scumbags. We'll get 'em."

''Look, Porta, we'll kill people that way. We can't do that. These guys, I don' know whether they're gonna come down wit' bats or what, but I don' think there's gonna be any killing.''

Much to Joe's relief, none of the other boys liked Rico's idea, either.

''Look, Sonny, if you guys're seen up on Avenue U, maybe we'll blow it,'' Joe said. ''Macri's smart enough to have somebody scoutin' the area, an' if they see you, they'll know we're ready for 'em, an' come some other time. So, hang out in the park on Avenue V an' play cards, like ya usually do, with one guy in the candy store across the street. We'll get the number on the pay phone over there, an' station Vinnie Lo Bianco at Hy's on McDonald Avenue. Soon as Macri's gang crosses McDonald Avenue, Vinnie'll call ya. In case they come from two directions, I'll put Louie Riccio at Mr. Bongiorno's printing shop at West 5th Street an' Avenue T. I'm sure Mr. Bongiorno'd let Louie use the phone.'' (He better make sure, Joe thought.) ''Fer sure, I'll call his son Anthony in advance to get clearance. If Louie sees anybody come down Avenue T, he'll call Vinnie at Hy's an' Vinnie can tip you off. How's that sound?''

The boys looked at each other, nodded, and agreed to help.

Any guy could use his fists; not so many could use their mouths to win an argument, Joe thought. This business of making people see things his way, it felt real good. That must be the way lawyers felt when they won a case. Real good. And powerful.

■ ■ ■

THAT NIGHT at Jean's, the boys met again. Joe filled them in on the plan he'd worked out with the Avenue X Gang. A bunch of the Avenue U boys would gather at Shef's and wait to be joined by the Avenue X guys after Vinnie tipped them off by phone from Hy's. Others would be stationed at Tommy's Sweet Shoppe and Happy's waiting for the arrival of the Avenue X guys on Avenue U. While nothing short of the National Guard would make them feel truly secure, they were no longer talking cops.

By the next night, the boys were wired. Street fights were not their style. Word spread all over the Avenue, so that a lot of the neighborhood kids came out and stationed themselves at Pippy's and Jean's where they could see what was going on without getting in the way.

Meanwhile, the principals had positioned themselves according to plan. Mikey Gilberti, whom Joe wanted out of the initial line of fire, took a dozen or so guys up the street to Tommy's Sweet Shoppe to wait until Macri's bunch descended on Shef's. Vinnie was in the back of Hy's watching. Joe was at Shef's waiting for Vinnie to call. Louie was at Ralph Bongiorno's to monitor any sneak tactics.

■ ■ ■

AS VINNIE sat by the phone peering out, he noticed Tommy "Black" Cutrone come in the front door of Hy's. He owed Tommy so much money that he'd rather face the entire Macri gang single-handedly than have Tommy spot him. He quickly slammed shut the door of the phone booth and crouched down on the floor. He could hear Hy and Black talking.

"Hy, how ya doin' today."

"Okay, Tommy. Can't complain."

"Business good?"

"Nah. Lousy. My wife's already tormentin' me about buyin' temple seats for the holidays. Her sister's got $200 seats, an' she's gotta have 'em, too. I tell her, 'Sadie, I'm not a big-shot doctor like Jake. I sell a few newspapers, some cigarettes. Ya can't get blood from a stone.'"

Vinnie was going nuts. Why the hell didn't the stupid bastard just give Tommy the protection money so he'd get out of there? Suddenly, the noise from outside signaled an approaching crowd. Christ, he thought hysterically, they're comin'.

Hy, looking out the window, turned to Tommy. "Say now, Tommy, get this. That's an awful big buncha kids. What d' ya suppose they're up to?"

''Nuthin that'd interest us. I could use a cigarette.''

''Sure. Here, take the pack.''

''T'anks. So, ya got your premium payment?''

''Ya know, I had a real slow month, Tommy.''

''Hy, Hy. What kina talk's dis? Slow business beats no business. Right?''

''Right, Tommy. Right. I'll get it.''

Vinnie's heart was racing, and he had broken out in a cold sweat. He could hear Hy counting out the money for Tommy.

''Whatta life, huh, Hy?''

''Whattaya mean?''

''Here. In da paypa. Ike's off on anodda golf trip. Mus' be rough. Us poor slobs here slavin' away jus' t' keep body an' soul t'gedda.''

''Yeah, Tommy. Yer right.''

''Well, see ya nex' mont'. Happy holidays.''

Vinnie heard the door close. He waited a few seconds to be sure Tommy wasn't coming back. Then he slowly pulled himself up and peered out the window. The Macri gang was gone. The plan was shot to hell. They'd lost the element of surprise. Too late to call anyone except the police.

While Hy and Tommy were discussing current events, Joe, Paulie, Johnny Riccio and Billy Donadio were shooting pool at the back table in Shef's—three feet from the phone.

Paulie's palms were so sweaty that every time he doused them with talc, it turned into paste. Joe was pacing, lighting one cigarette with the hot ash of the last.

''What's takin' 'em so long to make their move?'' Johnny asked the cue ball.

''If anything's gonna happen, it's gotta happen soon. It's afta dark,'' Billy said calmly.

Just then the phone rang. The boys stood frozen, all except Joe, who jumped to grab it.

''Hello.''

"Joey! Joey, I blew it. Macri mus' be dere already."

"Here! What the fucka ya talkin' about?"

"Don' worry, I called the cops."

"You what?" Joe shrieked into the phone. "You mothafucka! You degenerate bastard! *Putana miseria. . . .*"

Joe felt a sharp pain in his right kidney. He wheeled around to find himself staring at the large gold horn hanging from John Macri's neck. Suddenly the pain moved to his gut. Looking down, he saw what appeared to be a .45 shoved under his rib cage.

"Upstairs, you prick!" Big John hissed through clenched teeth.

Joe's mind went blank. His heart, wildly racing just seconds ago, stopped cold. His mouth went dry; his hands were ice. He knew he was dead. He let the phone fall and started walking toward his execution.

Out on the street the two boys marched in silence to the corner. Macri shoved him to the left, and they continued walking until they came to Tommy La Rosa's barber shop.

"Get in dere!" he ordered, gesturing to the alcove over Tommy's front door.

Inside the hallway, John put the barrel of the gun against the left side of Joe's head.

From far away a strange voice began to speak.

"Ya wanna blow me away, Macri? All we did was come t' ya confraternity dance. We didn't pick on anybody. We may have been dancin' wid girls who hang out at your church, but dat's no different den when you guys came ova t' Ar Ladya Grace and danced wid the girls who hung out at ar confraternity. Johnny, it wasn't your fault. You didn't start the fight. But you were on your turf an' Jack Novella started the fight, that little wimp. An' ya know what? There was only five or six of us. There was fifteen or twenny a you. The mistake that Jack Novella made is that he picked on Mikey Gilberti. Now Mikey Gilberti, as you found out, could kill any fiva ya. I unnastan' exactly where you was comin' from. Ya hada do what was right. Yer in charga your turf. So you were gonna help Jack fight Mikey, but cha didn't realize that Mikey could take on fiva ya. Now Mikey's not a hood. He doesn't do anyt'ing wrong. But he plays football, so he's very strong. So you got y'self in a kina trap, not because ya wanted t' hurt us or we wanted t' hurt you, but I unnastan' where you was comin' from. You hada do what was right unda da circumstances, an' ya got ya fuckin' brains beat in by Mikey Gilberti. The resta us, me, Johnny Boy Riccio, Vinnie Lo Bianco, Junior Aversa, we jus' came t' have fun, jus' like you come t' ar place t' have fun, an' we all hada fight. We all hada fight. Now you're all pissed off cause fiva us took carea fifteena you. An' now ya wanna kill me f' dat. But yer wrong. Ya mada mistake, an' if I were you I'd admit I was wrong unda the circumstances. I wouldn't wanna kill ya. I mean, I'd be a little pissed at ya, because I lost face wit' my own guys but maybe, maybe we could work it out some way. Maybe I could make ya a trade. Maybe I could tell ya dat, ya know, you guys, if ya feud wit' anybody, ya feud wit' the guys from Avenue X, not us, 'cause we don't fight wit' nobody. We play ball. Nunna us do anyt'ing wrong. We hang aroun' Shef's pool room, but we're basically a buncha at'letes. I tell ya, ya f'get about dis an' if ya eva get inta a battle or a rumble wit' da guys from Avenue X, we'll stay out of it. Dose guys are crazier den you. Yer an even match f' one anudda an' dat's d' only promise I could make. An' the udda t'ing I could say is dat you an' Ernie Brocco are supposed t' be the guys dat run da West 10th Street bunch. Now Ernie Brocco is my father's godson. My father confirmed Ernie Brocco, because his father is a customer of my father's in the produce business an' he asked him t' confirm Ernie. You know, some kina honor. Now, how's it gonna look if you blow my head off?''

''You guys started it. You messed wit' ar girls.''

''Who? You name the girls we mistreated. You name anybody we were disrespectful to or anybody we said anyt'ing wrong to.

If we t'ought we weren't welcome, we wouldn'a come dere, but we figured you guys always came t' ar dances an' we treated ya like gentlemen 'cause we t'ought we'd be treated the same way. Ya big mistake was ya picked on Mikey Gilberti, the wrong guy t' pick on. Hey, Johnny, remember the time y' were down at Ar Ladya Grace an' we were all dancin' aroun' an' havin' a good time an' you, me, an' Sonny, an' Nicky, an' Frankie were bullshittin' dere an' alluva sudden dose guys from the udda sidea Coney Islan' Avenue show up an' the guy sticks a fuckin' piece out at Sonny Balbi an' says he's gonna blow his fuckin' head off? An' you're standin' dere an' I'm standin' dere an' Balbi tells him t' shove that fuckin' piece up his ass? We were blood brothers den. We were ready t' die t'getha. Now y're gonna kill me?''

The voice stopped talking. Joe kept watching the rhythmical movements of the horn around Big John's neck as it rode the peaks and troughs of the gunman's breath. Joe thought about all the *corni* he had ever seen, large and small, gold, coral and ivory, hanging around necks, pinned on babies, attached to wrist watches, on men and women, old and young. Maybe he should get one. In a world like this you needed all the help you could get. The thing was, he should have gotten one yesterday.

CHAPTER

4

"YA GOTTA deal."

The voice wasn't inside his head. Joe risked a glance. Macri had lowered his gun. He slipped it into his belt, pinched Joe's cheek, and walked away.

Joe's first awareness was of his legs. They hurt. He looked down at them and realized that he had begun crouching. His feet were numb. He didn't know how long he'd been there in the corner, in the dark. As the fog lifted, he heard sirens in the distance. He pressed his palms against the wall and, one hand at a time, inched his stiff body upright. He looked around. He was in the doorway outside the barber shop. Now he began to feel pins and needles in his feet. He'd never imagined pins and needles could feel so good.

He listened to his voice. He said it again. Listened again. "I'm alive!" It seemed to be true. His mouth had won another case. A capital case this time. He wondered if a lawyer ever got soaked through with sweat while he was pleading a case. Pleading was sure the right word, he'd learned that tonight. And when it was appropriate, to feel scared shitless. And, even then, refuse to fold up and die for someone.

The sirens got louder. Suddenly he was surrounded by their relentless whine.

Jesus Christ. Cops all over the street. I've gotta get outa here.

He peered around the corner of the alcove. The red-and-yellow flashing lights of a police car had just passed ''Peanuts'' Barrentino's bar and were coming straight for him. He ducked back into the blackness. His head was pounding. He could not afford to get picked up. He looked out again. The car had stopped up the street at Tommy's Sweet Shoppe. Two policemen jumped out and ran inside. The neighborhood was always crawling with cops, so even though he only saw the one police car, he knew that more would come tearing around a corner any time now. Directly across the street, behind Pippy's, was an empty lot overgrown with weeds. If he could just get there, he could make his way home through back alleys. He couldn't stand around thinking about it forever or he'd miss his chance. He bent over as low as he could get and still keep his balance, almost as if he were in his football stance. He looked out again, checked both directions, and made a beeline across Avenue U, diving head first into the weeds. At that moment a police car came screaming down East lst Street, rounded the corner of Avenue U on two wheels and tore right past him. Joe hugged the ground. When the patrol car had passed, he raised his head a little and glanced around. The lot was strewn with zip guns, baseball bats, tire irons and lug wrenches. Those guys had come ready to do some heavy damage. He crawled through the lot around Pippy's and came out onto East lst Street. He crouched behind the hedges of the house next to the bar. Suddenly the dog inside started barking. Joe panicked. He had to get out of there before the owners came out and found him. As he bolted into the middle of the street, a car screeched to a halt, missing him by a hair. It was a beat-up old Mercury. Behind the wheel sat Ali Baba, Joey Gallo's driver-bodyguard. Next to him was Joseph ''Little Strunz'' Patti, a Gallo enforcer. The back door swung open and a hulking figure flew out, grabbed him by the shirt and tossed him onto the back seat of the car, where he landed beside Joey Gallo.

"What the fuck is goin' on?" Ace demanded, pushing in after Joe.

Joe closed his eyes and blurted out the whole story.

"I don't believe dat I'm hearin' dis. Yer supposed to be a smart kid. Ya let yer plan hinge on Lo Bianco? I got a parakeet dat's more reliable. I don't blame him, I blame you. You should know betta."

"Ace, God, I'm sorry. I told them all not t' call the police. I figured I needed t' keep Vinnie away from the action so he wouldn't fuck it up. He folds unda pressure. I thought this was a nice, easy job for 'im."

"Why didn't ya tell 'im to stay home an' play wit' 'is joint? Why didn't ya come to me? Macri works fer Mimi Scortese. I coulda tipped 'im off. Macri woulda foun' religion an' nunna this woulda happened."

"I didn't thinka that, Ace. Christ, I'm sorry."

"Lemme tell ya, kid, ya don' know how sorry ya should be. Not only did ya kill all the action on the street f' weeks, but ya busted up a sitdown."

He gestured toward Gallo sitting in grim silence on the other side of Joe.

"My *paisan* here came all the way ova from President Street to meet with Don Carlo and settle a little family problem. We meet ova here, because we gotta protected neighborhood. Now what am I gonna tell Signor Gambino? He's ridin' down the street, and suddenly there's heat everywhere. He's not a patient man. He doesn't like to waste his time."

Joe thought he would puke. These men were killers. Ace was his friend, but business was business, and Joe had fucked up royally. What could he say? They drove in silence. He had no idea where they were taking him. Finally the car stopped.

"Look, kid," Ace said quietly, "ya made a mistake. Everybody makes mistakes. That's how ya learn. So ya made yer mistake an' y'll learn. But I'm tellin' ya, dis is your graduation day, *capeesh*?"

Joe nodded. From the corner of his eye, he saw Gallo reach over and open the door. As he started to climb out, he felt a hand on his arm. He turned and looked at Gallo who, up till then, had not so much as moved a muscle.

''Dat was one helluva party ya t'rew out dere, Joey. Dere was guys from all ova Brooklyn. But cha know what? I didn't see nobody from President Street. Whatsa matta, we offended ya?''

Joe dropped his eyes. What was he supposed to say?

Then, as though he'd read Joe's mind, Gallo said, ''Don' worry, kid, ya ain't gotta ansa. Dat was one a dem rhetorical questions.''

Joe looked back at Gallo and for the first time registered a pair of magnetic eyes watching his every move. ''Rhetorical''—had he heard right? A silent exchange took place between them. He had heard right, and Gallo knew he had scored a bull's-eye.

''So the nex' time ya t'row a party, make sure I'm on the guest list,'' Gallo said quietly. With a barely perceptible gesture, he motioned Joe out of the car.

Joe stood on the sidewalk and watched the taillights vanish in the night before he dared look around to see where he was. He had just been taken for a ride by four men, each of whom believed that murder was a reasonable solution to most any problem. Breaking a law of the street was that kind of problem. And that's what Joe had done. Yet when they were through making sure he understood that he wouldn't be allowed to screw up again, they dropped him off, safe and sound.

Right in front of his house.

CHAPTER

5

LIFE AS he had known it was over. Next week, he'd be on a train for South Bend. As he climbed the stairs in back of the post office, he could hear the noise coming from Mother Cabrini Hall. Joe's friends had started his going-away party without him. "Going away" on Avenue U was usually reserved for exotic places such as Dannemora and Leavenworth. Only when Jerry, Joe's brother, had left ten years before did Notre Dame join this elite group of destinations. He opened the door at the head of the stairs and walked in.

Mother Cabrini Hall was the place for all occasions. During World War II, the neighborhood Fascists used it for meetings and rallies. Joe had vivid memories of their parades. Dressed in their brown shirts, Italian flags flying, they'd march out of the post office, cross Van Sicklen Street and go all the way to Ocean Parkway, singing "Giovenezza" at the top of their lungs. He often wondered who suffered greater prejudice: the innocent Japanese who were interned for fear of their potential mixed loyalties, or the Italians whose blatant sympathy for Italy wasn't taken seriously? Now, on the threshold of his going-away party—on the threshold of a whole new life—Joe vowed that he'd be an Italian who was taken seriously.

Most of the wedding receptions he had ever been to had taken place in this hall. The room was ideal for a "football wedding" with large, bare walls and bare floors. The bride provided her own tables and chairs so that nothing belonging to the hall could be destroyed. There was plenty of room for a band, dancing, boxes of sandwiches, a reception area for the family's oldest to hold court, with room left over for general milling around. Sandwiches, tossed from table to table, that unwrapped in mid-air or were overshot, landed on the floor and were quickly ground into an oil slick. Squealing children slid through the slime while the groom's second cousin, who would surely replace Richard Tucker if he could only get a break, sang—not one, but three—arias from *Pagliacci*.

Today's scene wasn't so different. The noise level was the same, decor identical, food predictable. The major difference was the guests. With the exception of a few of the better known ladies of the street, they were all male. Italian women belonged in the house, like the espresso machine or macaroni pot. Taking them out for anything other than a family occasion was unheard of.

All the guys from the Avenue were there, including the boys from Avenue X. Word about a party spread like the clap, so there was no telling who'd show up at one. Still, Joe was surprised at all the heavyweights who had come. Ace, Sally D and Raymo. Joe Bonfiglio, an enforcer for the Gallo mob, who lived around the corner from Joe, was more likely present to keep his eyes open than to play.

Tommy Black was sitting at a table with Carlo Gambino and Lilo Ferrone, who clearly stood out from the crowd. Lilo looked like a beach ball with arms and bushy white eyebrows, where ninety percent of his hair resided. He always wore flamboyantly checkered suits with a white carnation in the lapel. If you looked at him too long, your vision would begin to blur.

Standing by the bar was Joe's brother-in-law Rocky and Rocky's uncle, Johnny "Neck Road" Bono. Johnny was a Don in the Profaci family, second only to Joe Profaci himself. Rocky wanted to be a "made man" in the worst way, but his uncle wouldn't hear of it. Joe remembered the night he had had dinner at the Bono house, listening to Johnny tell Rocky how he'd spent all his life walking a tightrope between the law and the "family" to make more money than he'd ever dare show, let alone spend. It hadn't been worth it to him, and he wouldn't help his nephew make the same mistake.

They were the first people Joe greeted.

"Rocky. Mr. Bono, what a nice surprise," he said as he shook hands.

Rocky had a pleasant face with a bulbous nose and was the most nervous person Joe had ever met. He couldn't say three words without interjecting a preposterous giggle, and he always had a cigarette in his shaking hand. Joe's father had never been able fully to accept this Sicilian as his son-in-law. But Joe really liked him. He was a guy from the street.

"Ya didn't expect me to miss my own brother-in-law's goin' away party, did ya?"

"I guess not, but I'm very honored that Johnny took the time t' come."

"Well, Joe, I came to say I'm gonna miss seein' ya around the social club on Sundays. Can ya suggest a replacement? Not any ole *cedrulo*, now. I mean someone with your finesse with a coffee cup," Johnny teased.

Joe laughed. "Count me out. You guys are on your own."

"That's really why everyone is here, Joey," Johnny said as he looked around at his fellow chieftains. "We'll all be sorry to see ya leave. But speakin' just for myself, get your ass off these streets, kid, and don't bring it back."

"Believe me, Johnny, I won't!"

At that moment Ace joined them.

"Can I break this up for a minute? I need a few words with my pal here."

"Sure," said Rocky. "But go easy on 'im, Ace. Don't go corruptin' 'im or I'll never hear the end of it from his sister."

As Ace walked off with Joe, he took the boy's hand in his paw and put a small brown bag in it.

"What's this?"

"Open it an' see, but don't be too obvious. I don' wanna embarrass anybody."

He shook the contents of the bag into his hand. It was a solid gold keychain with a large gold medallion on the end. On one side was carved a shamrock engraved "Notre Dame" and on the other, Joe's initials. He looked up at Ace with tears in his eyes.

"This is so you remember there's a lotta guys rootin' for you here. Do good an' always do the right thing," he said as he slapped him on the back.

"Ya know, Ace, I invited Gallo. When ya see 'im, tell 'im this time *he* offended me."

CHAPTER 6

JOE AND Vinnie were standing in front of the candy store arguing over how many more games it would take to clinch the National League pennant.

It was the worst possible time of day to get a car down the Avenue. At six o'clock the sidewalks were jammed with people hurrying home from work. Shoppers were shoving their way into the crowded stores to pick up a last-minute item for dinner. Trucks were double-parked while the drivers scurried to make their deliveries. Cars monopolizing the bus stops forced the buses to stop in intersections or right in the middle of the street to disgorge their passengers. The clutter of bodies and machinery reduced the Avenue to one lane of traffic going in two directions simultaneously.

New Yorkers, at best impatient, are transformed at this hour into rabid combatants. Drivers honk at double-parked cars, then double-park. Pedestrians run out from behind trucks, and swear at the car that almost hit them. Add the Italian temperament to the scene, and you've got one hell of a spectacle.

In the midst of this chaos, Joe spotted a new silver Eldorado that had been cruising lazily down Avenue U. It became ensnarled in traffic in front of Mario's Pork Store. A fat, balding man leaped from the car and ran diagonally, breasts bouncing, across the street to Happy's.

''Hey, kid!''

Joe found himself face to face with his neighbor, Joe ''Bonehead'' Bonfiglio.

''Mr. G wants a few words witcha.''

He looked where Bonfiglio was pointing, then turned to speak to Vinnie who, not surprisingly, had vanished.

''Sure,'' he said, shrugging, and started to weave his way through the maze.

Bonfiglio led him to the passenger side of the car and opened the back door.

''Get in,'' he ordered.

Joe peered into the back seat. Hunched up in the corner behind his driver sat the diminutive form of Joey Gallo, gazing at him from under the brim of a blue-gray fedora.

''Hey, *chooch*. Where's your manners? Ask the kid polite.''

''Hey, kid! Wouldja do me the honor of gettin' in the back of the fuckin' car?'' he said, as he bowed from the waist. Joe laughed as he climbed in next to Gallo.

''This is some fancy set of wheels you've got here, Joey,'' he commented as he looked around the lush interior.

''Hot off the assembly line.''

''Oh, yeah? How hot?''

Gallo reached over and pinched his cheek. ''The kid's a comedian. Whattaya wastin' yer time goin' to college for? I'll get you booked at the Copa.''

His driver interrupted the laughter to let Mr. G know that the traffic had started moving.

''How about a ride?'' Gallo asked.

''Don't mind if I do.''

Gallo leaned in the direction of the open door and yelled, ''Hey, Bonehead! Get in.''

The fat man jumped in the front seat and the car rolled down the street.

''The kid likes your car, Bonehead.''

The passenger in the front seat turned and smiled. He was ugly enough when he was serious, but when he smiled his features twisted into a grotesque caricature. It took no imagination to believe he was the ruthless executioner everyone in the neighborhood whispered about.

"Bonfiglio's wired with some Cadillac dealer. Dis here's a '58. Ya can't even buy 'em till next month."

Gallo reached inside his jacket pocket and pulled out a pack of Camels. "When the ashtrays get filled, we trade it in."

He took a cigarette from the pack and stuck it in the corner of his mouth. "You smoke, college boy?" he asked, holding out the pack to Joe.

"Yeah, thanks."

Joe's eyes had been riveted on the older man's face since this little game of cat and mouse had begun. Gallo's eyes were mesmerizing. Joe could no more look away than if Gallo's eyes were a double-barreled gun.

From the front seat, Bonfiglio offered the kid a light. Without diverting his eyes, Joe inhaled deeply. He became aware that the car had turned right and they were speeding down Ocean Parkway toward Coney Island.

"Ya know, Mr. Gallo, ya missed a hell of a party."

"Gee, kid, I'm honored. Wid all dose people, ya knew I didn't show."

Leaning forward in his seat, he smacked Ali Baba, the driver, on the back of the head. "Ya hear dat, Ali? The kid missed me. Ace is right, this is a helluva guy."

He fell back and turned to Joe. "Don't take it personal, kid. Sometimes in life business comes before pleasure. My brother Larry decided to go into da union business, and ya know how dese blue-collar workers are, dey're slow learners. No college boys. Anyway, Professor Joey here had t' give 'em a little education. But cha know, I t'ink it's better dis way. If I'da come to da party, dere woulda been a coupla hundred people and we woulda danced and got a little drunk and I woulda slapped ya on da back and said, 'Good luck, Joe,' and dat woulda been it. 'Dis way I t'ink, I should see dat kid before he goes. Word on the street is he's some smart guy, in school and out. So, here we are havin' dis chat and gettin' to know each other even betta."

The limousine emerged from an underpass facing Lincoln High School and swung a hard left onto the ramp that led to the Belt Parkway overhead.

"So, I hear yer headin' west. Takin' the advice of dat reporter, 'Go West, Young Man?'"

"Horace Greeley. I don't know if he was a reporter, but that's what he said."

"He didn't say it. He wrote it in a newspaper. Ya ain't startin' to believe what ya read in the paper, are ya, kid? 'Cause if ya are, dat ain't no way to get an education. Reporters are a packa fuckin' liars. They live by da commandment 'Dow Shalt Sell Paypas At All Cost.'"

"The press has nothing to do with it. Remember, my brother Jerry went to Notre Dame," Joe said, holding back a smile.

"Yeah, I remember how proud he was to get in! Where is it, again?"

"South Bend, Indiana."

"Is dat anywhere near Philadelphia?"

Joe didn't laugh. He was used to it by now. He'd never met a New Yorker who knew any more about what lay west of the Hudson than he could see by driving up the West Side Highway. What's more, Joe had never met one who cared.

"No, it's farther west than that. South Bend is on Lake Michigan, near Chicago."

"Michigan. Ain't dat where Detroit is?"

"Yeah. But Chicago's closer."

"Listen, we got some people in Detroit. We done a lotta favors for Don Pepe dere. You remember dis name—Joe Zerilli. You need anyt'ing, you tell 'im I said he should help ya out. He's a real heavyweight out dere. He'll fix ya right up. I'm gonna get

Peanuts or Benny Fats to get ya da names of our contact guys and dere telephone numbers, too.''

The highway had sloped down to street level and now ran right next to the water along Sheepshead Bay. Here and there along the water's edge were emergency turnoffs, meant for disabled automobiles, that were put to more use after dark by urgent adolescents. Joey ordered Ali to pull off at the next one he came to. Then he directed the boy's attention to the freighter that was steaming toward the Narrows.

''Ya know where dat boat's goin'?''

''To any one of a dozen harbors in the area, I guess.''

''It's goin' to New York. New York's the greatest country in da world. What da fuck are ya leavin' for? What's in Indiana? Een-dee-aana,'' he drawled dramatically. ''Dat's da Italian word for Indians. Dey got Indians dere? Maybe I should buy ya a bow an' arrow for a goin' away present.''

''I'm not the only comedian in this car.'' Joe, beginning to feel freer to be himself, laughed. ''If my folks were here, my pop'd kid my mother that you must be Naboledon because only Naboledons can open their mouths that wide.''

''Yeah? So how come he'd say dat t'ya mama? She gotta big mouth?''

''No. She's Naboledon.''

''Ay, *paisan*, yer papa's right. See, I knew I liked ya.

''Here.'' Gallo reached inside his pocket, pulled out a thick wad of money, and handed Joe a hundred-dollar bill. ''I didn't make yer party, but I din' ferget you should get a graduation present.''

Joe shook his head. ''No thanks, Joey,'' he said. ''I'm all set, really.''

''Whatsa matta, kid? You afraid t' take money from a gangster?''

His tone was light, but Joe could see he was really offended. ''Hey, Joey,'' he said. ''Whatsa matter with you? I'm here, we're having a fine time, right? So what's money? It's just not necessary."

Gallo looked *halfway* convinced. "Look," Joe told him. "I'll make ya a deal. If I ever need money for any reason, you'll be the first one I call."

"You remember dat," Gallo said.

The car came to a stop and Ali turned off the motor.

"Hey, Bonehead. Go take a walk. Get yer blood circulatin'. You could use da exercise. Ali, you go wit' 'im in case he gets lost. And make sure da rods stay here. I don't need no Sullivan Law violations to fuck up my visit wit my *paisan* here."

The two men pulled their guns out of their shoulder holsters and shoved them under the front seat with such force that they were in sight—and reach—of the passengers in the back seat. The availability of the weapons and the departure of the two men made Joe increasingly curious as to just what this caper was all about. He put his arms out to his side, palms up, and said, "Is this where I get it?"

"Hey, kid. I told ya. You're my *paisan*."

"Well, if we're here for the submarine races we're too early. Besides, you're not my type."

"Enougha the jokes. Ya know the Sicilians, like your neighbor Mr. Bonfiglio, they don't take us Neapolitans seriously. They think all we can do is sing "O Sole Mio" and pick a few pockets. We need some tough, smart guys like me and you to teach them some respect. Sally D has an awful lot of respect for you, kid. He could fix you up real good. I could set you up even better. This is where ya belong. Why do ya wanna go west and fuck around with a buncha Irish pricks for? Those *sfaceems* stab one another in the back on a regular basis.

"Stick with the Italians, kid. Don't ever forget we come from the land that gave this country its name—America. It was our ancestors that created the maps that enabled all these fuckin' highbrows to arrive here before us.

"How many times would men have had to invent the wheel over 'n' over if Pliny hadn't recorded the knowledge of the time? Would we even know when the Pilgrims landed on Plymouth Rock if Julius Caesar hadn't come up with our calendar? Who knows if American children would be studying literature if Virgil and Livy hadn't created the art? Shit, we gave language to more than 500 million people."

Hearing so much knowledge roll off Gallo's tongue amazed Joe. He'd heard, of course, that the man was brilliant and crazy, but the emphasis had always been on crazy. Seeing he had the boy's undivided attention, Gallo went on. "Italian tailors designed and sewed the elegant clothes that the upper classes wore to hear Italian tenors sing Verdi. It was Italian marble cutters who laid the floors and built the columns for the museums filled with Roman sculpture and the paintings of da Vinci, Tintoretto and Modigliani. Italian bricklayers built the homes of the robber barons, whose architects were trained in techniques developed by the Romans and refined in the styles of Bramante, Brunelleschi and Bernini.

"The sons of Italian carpenters, stonemasons, barbers and bakers only wanted to pass on generations of family tradition. You think they were motivated to improve their lot? How can ya improve on the pride of a fine craftsman?

"Stick with the Italians, kid!"

The improvement in Gallo's English after his two bodyguards disappeared took Joe by surprise. Then he realized that he, too, spoke differently, depending on whom he was with. When he talked with Mr. Weiss, he talked *like* the principal; when Big John Macri had him cornered, he talked the way Macri talked—if he'd sounded like Mr. Weiss, he wouldn't have lived to graduate. He didn't switch on purpose, exactly; it was more like a reflex. A defense mechanism, you might say. Joe smiled inwardly at the idea that he and Joey Gallo might share the same defense mechanism. As he was thinking, Joe unconsciously started to run his finger over his left pocket, where he had put the gold key chain that Ace had given him as a going-away present. He remembered all the times Ace, Sally D, Raymo and Johnny Neck Road had made sure he wasn't in the wrong place at the wrong time, and when he was, how quickly they fixed it. *They* wouldn't fix him up the way Joey meant. They were proud of him for getting off the streets. In some way, he felt, they lived vicariously through him. They were all Sicilians. Here was this guy calling himself his *paisan* and encouraging him to fuck up his life.

He spoke carefully. "Ya know how it is, Joey. My mama goes to Novenas at Sts. Simon and Jude every Friday night. She brags to the other women about her son the concert pianist and her son the doctor, and now she wants to add her son the dentist. But I told her, 'Ma, I'm not spending my life digging bubble gum outa braces. I'm gonna be a lawyer.' Even though she'd have more use for a dentist, she'll take a lawyer. She can still brag. What would she say if I went to work for you guys?"

"Hey, look, kid, don't tell me about Neapolitan mamas. I wrote the book. You gotta brother who's a doctor. That already puts your mother one up on everybody in the neighborhood. You drive up in a car like this, buy her a fur coat and more jewelry than she can wear at one time and she won't ask or give a fuck what you're doin'. Just don't get caught. Wrong is gettin' caught. And you won't get caught, kid. You're too smart."

"Ya know, Joey, that's only half the story. The other half is my pop, a real Don Giuseppe! Let me tell ya about him. Once when I was a little kid I walked into his bedroom while he was getting dressed, and I saw these scars all over his ass. So I said, 'Papa, what happened to your *culo*?' Well, he tells me that when he was a young man in Italy, during World War I, he was in the army and he was machine-gunned. Then he got tetanus and was doubled over in the hospital for months. King Victor Emmanuel came to see him while he was touring, because my old man was such an unusual medical case. He should have died. But my father's too pigheaded to die. He's a Calabrese. So they gave him a bunch of medals, and he was a hero. Just this last year I found out that he got tetanus from rubbing against a rusty wire right after he was shot. Why in the fuck did he want to die for a government that didn't even know he was alive in the first place? He didn't, so he came to America.'' Joe stopped. He'd really been running on.

''No,'' Gallo said. ''Don't stop. Tell me more about your old man.''

Joe shrugged. ''Pop went into the wholesale produce business with his cousins. A dog's life. Seven in the evening until noon the next day, just about every day of the year. Here he carried a gun. Here he fought. The same man who refused to fight people he didn't know, who wouldn't risk his life for politics, left the house every night with a pearl-handled baretta. Because now it was his independence, his integrity and his family that were at stake. Ciro Terranova wanted a cut on the artichokes. Before submitting to a shakedown, my pop would have blown Ciro's head off or died trying. You can't push a Calabrese. Right and wrong is in here,'' Joe tapped his temple with his forefinger, ''and in here.'' He put his hand on his chest. ''Living with yourself comes first. Forget the cops! I've seen my dad drive nails into wooden crates with his bare hands. I don't even want to think about what he'd do to me if I did anything that was wrong in his book.''

Gallo had been listening carefully, making no move to interrupt. Now it was clear that the boy had finished, and he nodded at him appreciatively.

''Ya come from a good family, kid. That's important! Family's all we Italians got. It gives us strength. It gives us courage. It gives us security.

''The biggest threat to our families has always been the fuckin' educational system in this country. The vast majority of Italian immigrants wanted nothing more than a new setting in which to continue their old traditions. But this Anglo society had other ideas. Supposedly, the purpose of the public school system was to ensure an educated citizenry for the survival of democracy.

But the sudden influx of southern and eastern Europeans gave the system a new goal—Americanize the foreigners! Our response was resistance. Italian children brought into their homes ideas that threatened centuries of honored tradition—loyalty to the father and the family before the state. So we invented a way out: passive aggression. We avoided Americanization. We strengthened our bonds to our families and scared the shit out of these Anglo-Saxons.''

Joey bared his teeth in laughter. ''What happened, college boy, was that we Italians entered the American world just long enough to earn a living. But not long enough for the non-Italians to learn anything about us.

''We were the first real immigrants. Still, all the fuck ya eva hear is gangsters, Mafia, Black Hand! Amen!

''Be thankful you got a good family. Ya know, I don't know too many Calabrese. Everybody says dere crazy. Hot-headed. My ole man always told me to watch out for 'em, because they talk with their teeth clenched. Even the Sicilians are afraid of dem. So, I hear ya. Ace tole me you're gonna be a lawyer. That's good. Right now everybody goes to Adelman. All we got is Jew lawyers. And that's okay. They're our blood brothers, but it'd be better if we got some Italians. We gotta do something about that Sentencin' Sam Berkowitz. He's not like mosta the Jews. Fuck! All an Italian's gotta do is belch and that lousy cocksucker gives 'em thirty years. Without Italian lawyers, we ain't gonna get any Italian judges. Raymo tells me he took you to see Tony Pro. That's good. He's comin' up in the world. Those fuckin' Teamsters are really a wild bunch. Now that I'm in the union business myself, I see there's a few of us who could use a good Italian lawyer.''

Mr. G paused and looked out over the water. The sun was setting, leaving in its wake a trail of colored ribbons across the bay. In the distance, the lights on top of the Marine Park bridge started to rotate, dotting the sky with flashes of red and green. ''I hear you went to Lincoln with all those Jew geniuses.''

"Yeah, I wanted to go to Brooklyn Prep, but my pop said no. He said if I wanted to get anywhere in this world I'd have to compete with Jews and it was important to understand the competition."

Suddenly, Joe understood what this meeting was all about. He latched onto Joey Gallo's eyes, and this time he didn't look away.

CHAPTER

7

IT WAS a test. A time-honored Italian device for assessing the people around you. Gallo, pushing thirty to Joe's seventeen, thought of Joe as a promising young talent that had blossomed on his turf, and of himself as a talent scout. He liked what he'd seen and heard and wanted to stake a claim. He wanted to be taken seriously, that was why he had dropped the 'dese,' 'dems' and 'dose,' not because Ali and Joe Bonfiglio had left the car.

"Ya gotta smart papa, kid," Joey said. "Maybe that's why you're so smart. Another smart man graduated from Lincoln, a Jew. Arthur Miller. Ever hear of him?"

"Sure. We had the same English teacher, Mrs. Goldstein. And don't think at least once a week we didn't hear that she taught him everything he knows."

"Oh, yeah? What'd she teach him—English? Did she teach 'im about Italians and lawyers, too?"

"I don't get ya."

"Didn't Mrs. Goldstein have you read her prize student's prize play, *A View from the Bridge*?"

"I've heard of it. It was on Broadway recently, but I never read it. Should I?"

"You bet your sweet ass you should read it. If you're gonna be an Italian lawyer in Brooklyn you gotta meet Alfieri. How else are ya gonna know what ya gettin' into?"

"Look, Joey, if you've got a point to make, make it."

"I got no point to make, but Alfieri does. As an apprentice lawyer, you should know what Alfieri said. So let me tell ya." Gallo pulled out a crumpled piece of paper from his pants pocket and began to read.

> You wouldn't have known it, but something amusing has just happened. You see how uneasily they nod to me? That's because I am a lawyer. In this neighborhood to meet a lawyer or a priest on the street is unlucky—we're only thought of in connection with disasters, and they'd rather not get too close. I often think that behind that suspicious little nod of theirs lie three thousand years of distrust. A lawyer means the law, and in Sicily, from where their fathers came, the law has not been a friendly idea since the Greeks were beaten.

Without realizing it, Gallo had looked up from the paper and was reciting from memory.

> I am inclined to notice the ruins in things, perhaps because I was born in Italy. . . . I only came here when I was twenty-five. In those days, Al Capone, the greatest Carthaginian of all, was learning his trade on these pavements, and Frankie Yale himself was cut precisely in half by a machine gun on the corner of Union Street, two blocks away. Oh, there were many here who were justly shot by unjust men. Justice is very important here.
>
> But this is Red Hook, not Sicily. This is the slum that faces the bay on the seaward side of the Brooklyn Bridge. This is the gullet of New York swallowing the tonnage of the world. And now we are quite civilized, quite American. Now we settle for half, and I like it better. I no longer keep a pistol in my filing cabinet.
>
> And my practice is entirely unromantic.
>
> My wife has warned me, so have my friends; they tell me the people in this neighborhood lack elegance, glamor. After all, who have I dealt with in my life? Longshoremen and their wives, and fathers and grandfathers, compensation cases, evictions, family squab-

> bles—the petty troubles of the poor—and yet . . . every few years there is still a case, and as the parties tell me what the trouble is, the flat air in my office suddenly washes in with the green scent of the sea, the dust in this air is blown away and the thought comes that in some Caesar's year, in Calabria perhaps or on the cliff at Syracuse, another lawyer quite differently dressed, heard the same complaint and sat there as powerless as I, and watched it run its bloody course.

The last hour had taken on a dreamlike quality that seemed to be sliding ever more rapidly from reality to fantasy.

As he listened to Joey recite, the boy had closed his eyes. But when he opened them he was still there, sitting next to this thug—this fascinating, electrifying thug who had recited a lengthy passage from a play Joe had never even read, and although he couldn't know for sure, every instinct told him that Gallo's recitation was verbatim.

"What does that passage mean to you, Joey? Why did you take the trouble to memorize it?" he asked.

"Memorize it? Nah. I read it a couple of times before. I guess I got one of those photogenic memories."

"You mean photographic," Joe said politely. "Photogenic means to take a good picture."

"Yeah, that too."

"Let's get back to the quote. What are you trying to do, warn me against mediocrity?"

"That's only part of it. Alfieri's a symbol. If I wanna lawyer I can get one the same way I get an eggplant or a pound a sausages." Mr. G leaned forward slightly, thrusting his right hand in front of him and rubbing his fingers back and forth along his thumb.

"So what does that mean, Joey? Lawyers sell a service. Whattaya think *you* do?" Joe kept his tone polite, but said what had to be said to keep things in perspective. "Gambino's got some guy making a fuckin' pain in the ass of himself. He calls you up and says, 'Hey Gallo, I got this fly buzzin' aroun' my head.'

So he pays you to swat 'im. But someday the cops'll catch you with the swatter in your hand and you'll be goddamned glad to be able to buy a lawyer to get ya out of the flypaper. That doesn't mean you're for sale, does it? That's commerce, Mr. G.''

As the sky began to darken, Ali Baba and Joe Bonfiglio reappeared. They stayed within sight but out of earshot.

''This sea air is givin' me an appetite,'' Joey said, changing the subject. ''How about some mussels in red sauce? I know a great place not far from here.''

''I'm ready.''

Joey stuck his hand out the window and gestured to the waiting men.

''Jesus Christ! I think somebody stashed a body out there. It stinks!'' Bonfiglio said as he climbed into the car.

''Shmuck! How long ya gotta live in Brooklyn t' know swamp gas when ya smell it?'' Joey responded.

''Ali, we're goin' t' Gargiulo's.''

The car pulled out onto the Belt Parkway. It was pushing eight o'clock, and the rush-hour traffic had just about vanished. Joey turned back to his companion. ''You're a smart kid. You gotta be sure when ya get t' that fancy school that you don't let those Irishmen make ya stupid. I bin goin' back an forth t' Washington lately t' talk to this Senator McClellan. The prick's got a real hard-on for Italians. Anyway, he's got this fancy lawyer named Bobby Kennedy. So I'm sittin' in the waitin' room and Kennedy's in his office and all of a sudden some guy comes along an 'e heads right in. Well, I give the high sign t' one a my boys an' 'e gives this guy the once ova. Ya know what I mean? Well, this guy, he don't know what's goin' on so he gets outa there fast. So I figure if I'm gonna keep comin' down here t' see dis Kennedy we better get a few things straight. So I told 'im, 'Listen here, Mr. Kennedy, sir, with all due respect, what the fuck're ya doin' widout no bodyguards? You go around stickin' yer nose in udda people's business like this and, sure as shit, somebody's gonna get pissed off. Maybe try t' blow ya head off. I'd hate t' see it happen. Yer not a bad guy. But fuck, man, if somebody's gonna get ya, and I'm anywhere around, you know who's gonna get blamed, don'tcha?' I offer to have a couple a da boys watch 'im until he can get some cover. But he ain't gonna pay no attention. He thinks I'm a psycho. That's because these Irish fucks don't know nuthin about street fights. They jus' get drunk and swing at each udda. You ever bin in a street fight, kid?''

''Well, Joey, I've been in plenty of fights, both on and off the streets.''

''Kid, I ain't talkin' about no brawls. I'm talkin' about keepin' yer eyes open. Understandin' what's goin' down around ya. About keepin' yer eye on the enemy when 'e don't know yer lookin'. Like the Indians. They never let anybody take 'em by surprise. They did the surprisin'. If the ground is hard and dry and there ain't no footprints, that don't mean nobody's there. Maybe there's a squashed flower on the ground that ain't had time to turn brown. Ya know what I mean? Trouble don't come unexpected if ya know how to read the markings on the trail. You gotta have the stomach to split a guy's head open before he can do it to you. If ya stick a gun in someone's mouth or tattoo 'im with a lug wrench on the back of the head, you better not be squeamish about a little blood squirtin' on ya.''

''Joey, ya sound like Polonius. You know who that is?''

''Yeah, I know who that is. I read *Hamlet*. Whattaya think, I'm a fuckin' illiterate? Before ya start gettin' too smug, college boy, lemme tell ya, life's a street fight. Everything ya learned on Avenue U you'll need out in corn country. It won't be so easy t' tell the good guys from the bad guys when they're all well-scrubbed and milk-fed, with diplomas from Emily Post. You'd be smart to stick with the Italians an' stay away from those midwestern Irish bastards. Don't forget, they only let ya come there so they can feel superior.

''One last thing, Professor. You're goin' to a Cat'lic school. The Church ain't been known for steppin' up to bat to protect the innocent. *I'm* a gangster, right? Some guy steps outa line, I gotta waste 'im. That's my business. Tell me what the Pope's business is—and who's the *gangster*! I ain't sat back an' sang 'Joy to the World' while six million people got gassed who didn' do nuthin wrong to nobody."

"I've heard all that crap about the Pope and his pact with Hitler, but I got my doubts."

"I got *my* doubts, kid, an' ya wanna know why? You really want me t' believe the Pope actually worried about what Hitler would do t' the Cat'lics? Half the fuckin' Germans are Cat'lic. How many people can ya turn inta soap? Nobody's that dirty. That's the easy answer. Right unda da Pope's nose, Italians hid Jews. They smuggled 'em outa the country while the Nazis had their backs turned. The ones who got caught got it between the eyes. The Pope, moral leader of the world, safe and sound in his palace with 'is own army, didn't have half the courage of the peasants, who knew betta than 'His Holiness' what's right an' what's wrong. What could it have cost him on Easter Sunday morning, 1939, with millions of his sheep crowdin' inta St. Peter's Square, insteada the white satin robes an' the gold and jewels and his whole fuckin' festive numba, if he comes out on the balcony in one a dem black Jew suits, with the big black hat and the long coat and a Star of David arm band? Well, Professor, how many Jews do ya think woulda died? Six million? Gimme a fuckin' break!

"Ali, *andiamo*!"

The limousine pulled off the highway and turned down Neptune Avenue. The main street of Coney Island was a throbbing mass of people of every size, color, shape and description, all there because the summer was coming to an end.

Joey drew the boy's attention to a car full of shrieking youngsters who had just flown by on the Cyclone. "Ya been noticin' colored people comin' t' this park?"

"No. I guess I haven't been paying attention."

"There was a time they wouldn'a come here. Not just 'cause they didn't have the dough, but they was afraid to travel through the Italian neighborhoods. Italians broke a lotta black heads just because they was black. Dat was bullshit, but I'm sorry to say it happened. Shit, we ain't been anythin' more than d' colored people in dis fuckin' country since ow parents left Ellis Island. All we been is European *moolinyanas*. But the Irish looked down on the Italians, so the Italians would look down on the blacks. But ya see, everybody starts t' loosen up. The Irish let you go to their school. Italians let the coloreds come to the park. That's good. But don't get too relaxed. One of these *titsoons* bumps up against some Italian kid a little too hard an' he's dead meat. Things ain't changed that much yet. There's a little trouble in an Irish school an' the shit's gonna come down on some Italian head. Be smarter than Mr. Kennedy, kid. Don't let your guard down.''

''I won't, Joey,'' Joe said.

Not even with you.

BOOK
III

JOE AND DAN

PHOENIX 1971

CHAPTER

1

IT WAS past midnight when Joe got home. He unlocked the door that led from the carport to the kitchen. Just inside the door, at the table in the dining area, sat Angela with a look on her face that would stop a clock.

"So, what dragon were you out slaying tonight?"

He went into the kitchen to get a glass of water. What the fuck was she doing up? For some time, he had made a point of coming home long after he expected her to be asleep precisely to avoid these confrontations.

"Which one of your ever-growing list of stray dogs needed your aid and comfort this evening? Whose needs were so critical that you couldn't even take the time to call and say you wouldn't be home for dinner?"

He sank down in the chair across the table from her. Joe was too tired for this, and tired of it.

"How is it that as the list of important people in your life grows longer, Joseph and I keep getting bumped to the bottom? Even the goddamned janitor takes precedence over us."

Joe knew from long experience that she neither expected nor particularly wanted him to answer. Most women would scream, cry, throw things. Not Angela. As she vented her anger, her voice got quieter. Maddeningly rational when she was calm, rage made her more so. If you hurt her feelings, she'd rather cut your heart out than let you suspect that you might have hit a soft spot. She robbed him of the male need to protect the female. It drove him wild. He hated her for it.

"If this situation is going to continue, I suggest you make up a list of explanations for me to give your son when he asks me where you are and why you don't come home. I've run out of shabby excuses. It's your turn, Dad—unless, of course, you're planning to cut this shit out!"

"I can't stop," he answered quietly. "He who stops is lost."

She stared at him with undisguised disgust. "You're quoting Mussolini." Slowly she leaned forward in her chair until she was practically on top of the table. "You know what they did to Mussolini. If you're looking for a role model, why don't you choose one who came to a happier end?"

She got out of the chair with such force that it flew into the wall. Turning, she raced from the room. As she vanished into the bedroom, Joe stared after her, clenching his teeth, biting down hard on the anger.

He wanted to coldcock her. But hitting women wasn't his thing. Actually, hitting anything, even an animal, wasn't his style. Even as a kid, when some bully had chosen him to add one more notch to his belt, Joe always tried his wits before his fists. Yet somehow this woman provoked him to the point of wanting to push her face in. Sometimes he would wake up, his heart racing, and he would have to turn on the light and make sure he hadn't broken her nose. The nightmare of having smashed her small, straight, beautiful nose, smearing it all over her face, was a recurring one—a flagrant contrast to his dreams about Ashley.

When he was upset, worried, angry or in the throes of a full-fledged temper tantrum, Angela would sit quietly and listen to him for hours on end. She never interrupted, never begged off; she didn't move a muscle. Sometimes he wondered if she'd died while he was talking. Most of the time, when she finally did respond, he wished she hadn't. She would look at him with her brittle, black eyes, and when she was sure she had his attention, she would, without flinching, proceed to tell him the very last thing in the world he wanted to hear. While that was just the sort of event that triggered his nightmare, it was also the single biggest reason he stayed married to her.

■ ■ ■

HE COULDN'T remember when he had stopped loving her. He wasn't even sure he ever started. His taste in women—how often she took the trouble to remind him she knew—ran to blonde, flashy, compliant. Angela was none of those things. The trouble was, she'd been the perfect wife for an Italian boy from Brooklyn on his way up. For starters, she was Italian. He was too tied to his roots to marry someone who wasn't. But unlike most of the Italian girls he had known, she was bright, well educated and had a frosty aloofness that he'd never seen before in any Italian.

They had met through Brendan Flaherty's friend Mary Buitoni, of macaroni fame, one summer afternoon in Mary's apartment at 69th Street and Park Avenue. It was difficult to know, when Mary was around, if other people were naturally quiet or simply unwilling to fight for the floor. While the others let Mary, with her iconoclastic wit, keep them in stitches, Joe watched Angela. She had short, black, curly hair, and small, sharp features that reminded Joe of an Italian sculpture. These days, he might have thought "shrew" a better description. Anyway, she intrigued him, and he wound up driving her home.

They were both seniors in college. He liked to talk to her. She knew how to listen. She understood his ambitions.

She had insight. They formed a powerful intellectual bond, and on top of everything else, his father adored her. Calabrese, she could do no wrong.

He remembered the first time he brought her home to Sunday dinner. Everyone was there: Frank; Jerry and Cyd and their two children; even Kay and her kids were in town. After dinner, as his mother was clearing the table, Angela took out a cigarette.

As she lit it, Kay turned pale; his brothers froze; his mother dropped a plate and Joe nearly had a coronary. Women did not smoke in front of his father. To this day, at forty-six, his sister hid in the bathroom to have a cigarette. Why hadn't Joe thought to warn Angela? And then, the unimaginable. His father got up to get her an ashtray.

When they got married, his mother had apoplexy. What kind of wife could a woman who had gone to college be? What could she possibly know about cooking and cleaning? Well, his mother was half right. Angela couldn't clean, and learning how was definitely not on her agenda. But she could cook. So well, in fact, that it upset his mother *more*. He'd never understand women.

■ ■ ■

JOE SAT forward in his chair, rested his elbows on the table, and rubbed his eyes with his palms. He needed air. He walked out the kitchen door and around to the back of the house where he could look down on the Valley below. The truth was, it had been a long, hard road from Avenue U to the foothills of Camelback mountain, and Angela had traveled most of that road with him.

In a sense, she had helped him cut his last ties with the old neighborhood, because he could not go there with her. Every time he tried to get together with his old friends, she reacted as if they had lice. She didn't know how to talk to them and didn't want to learn. She said they were cretins and couldn't imagine what he could have in common with them. He'd hated her snobbery, but, at the same time, it had made him feel good about himself. She never thought of him as one of them. He had begun to see himself through her eyes, and lost some of his self-consciousness. She made him believe that he could handle himself on the Manhattan side of the bridge.

In those days, she would do anything for him, from spending her evenings in Notre Dame's library doing research for his law-review articles to checking his papers for any mistakes in English. She even typed them, a task she enjoyed almost as much as house cleaning. This same woman, who was speechless when confronted with Raymo or Vinnie Lo Bianco, could sit down to dinner with the dean of the law school and charm the fillings out of his teeth. While nothing Joe asked was ever too much, Angela was extremely demanding about what she expected from him—and aggressive about it to boot.

He had expected that, because she was Italian, she would appreciate the culture, understand the traditional roles of men and women and their respective duties and privileges. He was right. She did. The mistake he made was to assume that she bought it for herself. She did not. If she was very clear about what she expected from him and the marriage, it was nothing like what he had observed, or was prepared to give.

This fundamental difference was responsible for the chaos in their marriage, for despite Angela's forbidding exterior, she had an explosive personality. One night they went out for Mexican food with three other couples, including his cousin Tony and his wife, Jean. The eight of them polished off a dozen pitchers of margaritas and, on the way home, they had to stop the car for Joe to vomit. Tony, who was driving, flatly refused to let Joe back in the car. When the couple finally did get home, Joe took out his fury on the bathroom. When Angela tried to stop him from smashing everything in sight, he shoved her out of the way. The next thing he knew, she had grabbed a solid wood towel rack, torn it out of the wall, lifted it over her head, and brought it down on his, leaving a path in the ceiling and splinters on the floor.

All his life, his violent temper had gotten him what he wanted. This woman's refusal to be intimidated by him, her insistence on telling him he was wrong when he was, despite the reaction her disagreement might produce, supplied the ballast in his life.

In the final analysis, when everyone around him told him he was right, she was the only one he could believe.

How ironic that now when he was fighting to protect everything they had set out to build, she should be so determined not to understand.

Ashley always understood, even when she'd had only two lunches and her intuition to go on.

CHAPTER

2

"GOT A minute?"

Tom Brady turned off his Dictaphone. "Sure. What's on your mind?"

Joe strolled into his partner's office and sat down on the colonial couch under the window.

"I spent last evening with Uncle Joe. Then he called at seven-thirty this morning. He's all excited about this." Joe stretched across the desk to hand Tom an article from the Sunday paper.

THE VALLEY HERALD
Phoenix, Arizona, Sunday October 18, 1971

Starting Next Sunday
THE HIDDEN CANCER

Call it what you will . . . the Mafia, La Cosa Nostra, the Syndicate . . . it exists. And it's at work here, in the Valley of the Sun.

Organized crime . . . that is "The Hidden Cancer."

Starting next Sunday, The Valley Herald will release an astonishing story.

Until now, most Valley citizens have believed the Mafia was concentrated in Tucson. The Herald series will reveal that dozens of crime leaders have landed in Phoenix from Chicago, Detroit, Las Vegas and points east.

Seasoned investigative reporter Dan Barnes spent months on this project. Risking grave consequences, he interviewed many individuals identified by law enforcement authorities as members of the crime community. Barnes will expose the cancer within our state in a series which will name persons, places, dates.

Don't miss "The Hidden Cancer." It starts next Sunday in The Valley Herald.

Excitement wasn't good for Uncle Joe, and that meant this article wasn't. Joe watched Tom reading it, wondering if his partner, knowing that Uncle Joe wasn't even really Joe's uncle, could understand how much the old man meant to him. Uncle Joe was a cousin, but because of the tremendous age difference, sixty to thirty, Joe called him uncle out of respect.

■ ■ ■

JOSEPH T. CORELLI had come West as a young man looking for an opportunity. Back East, he'd been in the produce business with his father and his cousin Giuseppe, Joe's dad. But he had tired of it. Restless, young and full of energy, in Arizona he'd struck out on his own and gambled his money on crops. He'd buy a piece of a carrot deal; when it came in, he'd throw everything he had into a lettuce crop, only to parlay it again in melons. Success followed success, leading to an empire of land, ranches and other businesses that supported him and his five younger brothers in lavish style. With no sons of his own, he had warmly welcomed his young cousin—an attorney, no less—into his life.

"Does this mean something to him?" Tom was asking, handing the paper back to Joe. "I know you guys are meeting with Barnes this week. But why's your uncle getting so exercised over this?"

"I don't know. He wasn't making any sense. I'm going to meet him at the club for lunch to find out. I just thought I'd find out if you'd seen the piece and had any reaction."

"I never did get to see the paper yesterday, but I think we've been too close to the nerve center of this state not to know if there were major organized crime here. Heck, the state's run out of the club."

"And any day I'd happen to miss having lunch there, you'd be bound to," Joe said. "I agree. If there were Mafia in the political structure, we'd at least have heard a few hints from Bob Goldwater or Uncle Joe."

"Well, it can't hurt to hear him out and calm him down."

Tom was very cerebral. Despite a competitive attitude and a harsh temper, he rarely lost his objectivity. His ability to see things rationally often had a settling effect on Joe's more volatile nature.

The two had met early on in law school. At the end of each semester, Notre Dame would post the class rankings. Joe finished first, first semester, with Tom second. "Well, Brady, looks like it's you and me," he declared when he had tracked Tom down. He was right. That was precisely how they went through their entire three years. Joe sometimes got the feeling that Tom had never forgiven him for that. Yet, here they were, four years out of school and partners in their own law firm.

"Well, Tom, I'll hear him out but I don't know about the calm-him-down part. If you ask me, the paper's got a little Valachi fever. Ever since that guy started singing and the reports were published, instead of Communists, the paranoids see Mafia behind every bush."

The young men laughed and Joe headed over to the Phoenix Country Club.

Joe stood in the doorway of the Men's Grill searching for his uncle, who, as usual, was going from table to table, talking to everybody. The older man virtually ran his business from there. Now, catching sight of Joe, he rushed up to greet him.

Uncle Joe looked terrible. His face was beyond red. The old man's health history read like a medical encyclopedia, and from the way he looked today, Joe wouldn't be surprised if he had a stroke before nightfall.

"I've got a table over here." Uncle Joe led the young man to a corner in the back.

"Christ, you look terrible. Are you taking care of yourself?"

"Yeah, yeah. I'm fine. I'll be even better when we get our injunction against the paper."

"Injunction? For what?"

"Did ya look at the article I told ya about?"

"Sure, it's here in my briefcase. But that still doesn't explain why you want an injunction."

"They're gonna print lies about me! I want them stopped!" Uncle Joe couldn't sit still.

"Please calm down. We're gonna meet Dan Barnes tomorrow afternoon. Why assume that they're going to say anything about you? You're not in the rackets. You're not from Chicago, Detroit, or Las Vegas, and you have no connection with any of these places he mentions. Why are you getting yourself so worked up?"

"How about 'points east'? I'm from New York, remember?"

"New York is New York, not points east. You're making too much of this."

"Okay. Ya wanna know something ya don't know? Lemme tell ya," Uncle Joe said, the tension in his voice increasing. "Years ago, when the Paradise Valley Country Club first started admitting Italians, I used to golf there every now and then. Horace Perkins, as in the *Valley Herald* Perkins, golfed there too. He had the habit of walking off the green without putting the flag back in the cup. Finally, after I'd had all I could stand of it, I asked him to please put the flag back in the cup so people behind him could tell where the hole was. I wasn't being picky. It was irritating, right? Am I right?"

"Hey, what do I know? I've golfed exactly once. Ya know, we didn't have too many golf courses on Avenue U. Boccie was our game." Joe laughed. He waited for his uncle to laugh. No such luck.

"You done kiddin' around? Can I finish my story?"

"Yeah. Go ahead," Joe sighed, resigning himself to the old man's intensity.

"Well, Perkins starts yellin' at me. 'You greasy Wops, you're nuthin but trouble. I told them not to let you people in this club. You're as bad as Jews. Thank God we don't have any of *those* yet. Let me tell you, the day the bleeding hearts let them in, Horace Perkins goes.'

"Now I'm very calm, and I stay calm, and I look him straight in the eye and I say, 'Mr. Perkins, now you listen real close to me. The next time you play ahead a me and you don't put the flag back in the cup, I'm gonna take the flag and ram it up your ass so hard that it's gonna come out of your mouth. I hope I've made myself clear.' That's it. I walk away. But I know this guy's had it in for me ever since then, and I just know this is his big chance. I can feel it. That's why we gotta get an injunction to stop them from printing."

"Please, let's wait until we talk to this guy tomorrow."

"I don't wanna wait. What the fuck am I payin' you for, to tell me to wait? I don't need a lawyer fer that. I can get anybody to tell me to wait. I want you to do what I'm tellin' ya. Stop them from printing!"

"You can also get anybody to tell you what you want to hear. A whole lotta guys do that to you every day. I'm telling you that what you want is a prior restraint order, and no court in this country is going to give you one. It's unconstitutional."

"What the fuck do you know about the Constitution? You're a tax lawyer. You make business deals. You're just a kid. I'm wastin' my time with a fuckin' kid. I'm gonna get another lawyer."

"Okay. You want another lawyer? I'll get you two lawyers. Do you remember when we were negotiating with Cesar Chavez and all those people from the United Farm Workers Union over unionizing the labor at the Marblehead Ranch? Remember Rex Lee, Bozell's attorney? Well, he's one of the foremost constitutional scholars in the country. We'll get him. Then we'll get Herb Steinberg. He beat Perkins and his paper in a big libel suit. An' ya know what? Steinberg doesn't have any love for Perkins, either. Perkins screamed at Steinberg from the witness stand, calling him a 'fuckin' kike.' Would you like either or both of those guys?''

''Ya see, I told ya that Perkins 's a bigot.''

''I don't know what he is. You tell me you want another lawyer, I'm suggesting some. But they won't tell you anything different. You can't get a judicial order to stop the press from publishing in this country, even when a fair trial is at stake. The courts act as though the right of the press to be free goes above and beyond the rights of the individual. Trust me, I know what I'm talking about. The most we can do is wait for them to publish and see if they libel you. Then we can sue for libel. That's it.''

The promise of a future law suit quieted Uncle Joe a little.

''Look, go home,'' Joe urged. ''Rest. I'll see you here tomorrow at three, and we'll find out just what this guy Barnes has on his mind.''

CHAPTER

3

UNCLE JOE never ceased to amaze him. Here he was, as up, optimistic and jovial as he'd been down, depressed and bullying the day before. The two of them sat with Dan Barnes, a crew-cut, corn-fed hick, and his assistant, an innocuous fellow named Preston Baker. For two hours, Barnes questioned the old man about his past. He was looking for dirt. He wanted to find a jail record, sleazy associates, questionable business transactions, connections with known mobsters—anything. It sounded as though Barnes were reading from the index to *The Valachi Papers*. While Uncle Joe looked bewildered, Joe mentally checked off the names he recognized and people he knew. The questions themselves were slanderous. Joe kept interjecting some of his uncle's achievements.

"Tell me, Mr. Barnes," he said when his uncle went to the men's room, "in all the research you've been doing, did you discover that my uncle was the Boys' Clubs of Phoenix Man of the Year?"

Barnes stared at Joe blankly.

Which turned Joe's tone confrontational. "Bob Hope gave him the award, and said my uncle was a better stand-up comic than *he* was," Joe continued. "I've always thought it was that part of his personality and his willingness to dig into his own pockets that made him so successful in raising large sums for various charities.'' Joe paused, waiting for Barnes to respond.

The reporter's vacant expression turned to irritation. ''I'm here to do an exposé, not write a testimonial,'' he said and got up to leave.

Watching their backs, Joe downed a glass of water as though it were a shot of scotch.

''Where are they?'' Uncle Joe asked, returning to the table.

''They're gone. I guess they either got what they wanted or gave up.''

''Well, I'm in the clear. They're not gonna write anything about me.''

''What makes ya think so?'' He just couldn't hold it in.

''Because, couldn't ya tell? All those people they asked about, I neva hearda any of them.''

''But they came here for a reason. Asking you all those names—Zerilli, Licavoli, Bonanno—they were looking for something.''

''Yeah! But you told them all the top-flight people I hang out with. Ya told them about my awards and charities. They were barking up the wrong tree and they knew it.''

''Just think for a minute. They could make you look bad by simply saying, 'Joe Corelli denied alleged friendships with Peter Licavoli, Carlo Gambino and Joseph Bonanno.'''

And how could they make *him* look? Joe thought. One Joe Corelli was as easy to besmirch as another. Joey Gallo popped into his head. Guilt by association. Hell, guilt by just having been born on Avenue U.

CHAPTER

4

THE VALLEY HERALD
Phoenix, Arizona, Sunday October 25, 1971

Today's Chuckle

If you can't say anything good about a person—let's hear it.

THE HIDDEN CANCER
A Mafia Haven
By Dan Barnes

An abundance of organized crime lucre has filtered into the Valley and has been uncovered in a no-stone-unturned probe by The Valley Herald.

The Herald has located more than 100 Valley residents or frequent visitors who are members of organized crime or who have strong ties with them.

It is now clear that the Mafia lives.

Joseph Valachi, from prison, told the story in meticulous detail to the Justice Department in June 1963. Then, Mario Puzo fictionalized the existence of several Mafia chieftains. The Puzo book, ''The Godfather,'' performed a valuable service.

There are plenty of rocks in Arizona for the Mafia snakes to hide under, and they've done so.

Our sources have indicated convincingly that 100 of the state's leading citizens get their major source of income from crime.

How can we stand for this?

> A major weak spot is the Arizona Racing Commission. Last year, Congressman Paxon charged that a 50 per cent owner of Arizona's dog tracks, Embassy Corp. of Buffalo, N.Y., repeatedly had done business with organized crime leaders.
>
> And he named them: . . . Moe Dalitz, . . . Raymond Patriarcha, Dominic Corrado, Giacomo W. Tocco, and Anthony Zerilli.
>
> Every honest citizen of Phoenix must be outraged!

Joe closed the paper and went to call Don Perrino. Don viewed himself as a potential target. Barnes had wanted to interview Don last summer, but he limited the reporter to a few questions on the phone. He and Joe had discussed their options during the course of the week—and concluded they had none. All they could do was sit and wait. Now Joe was curious to see what Don, also an attorney, thought about today's article.

"How are ya doin', Donny?"

"You saw the article, too?"

"Yeah. Whattaya think?"

"What scared me more than anything was the Daily Chuckle. Do you think some clown at the paper slipped that one past Barnes? As for the article, it didn't say a damn thing."

"I agree. He claims to have done four months of research, but if ya ask me, he probably read a few books, *The Valachi Papers, The Godfather* and Bobby Kennedy's *The Enemy Within*, and took it from there."

"That was kinda my feeling. Could you believe him saying that Mario Puzo performed a valuable service with *The Godfather*? Real valuable—enough to have set back Italian-Americans a couple of generations. What do you think Barnes is gonna fill the other nine articles with when this one was such a zero?"

"I don't know, Donald m' boy, but let's hope it's not us. I have a real bad feeling about those Italian names he strung together when he talked about Paxon and the Racing Commission."

''How's your uncle doing?''

''I haven't spoken to him today, but I'm sure I will. He's become pretty paranoid this week. I'm worried about him.''

''Well, I'll see you tonight at the Goldwater bash. And Joe?''

''Yeah.''

''You better spread your juice around to cover us all.''

CHAPTER

5

TUXEDOED MEN with jeweled women on their arms streamed into the main ballroom of Del Webb's Towne House. Joe scanned the festive room for table seven. Goldcor, a corporation that took its name from the two families that had founded it—Goldwater and Corelli—had naturally bought a table for this dinner honoring the junior Senator from Arizona, Baron Morris Goldwater.

Bob Goldwater and Uncle Joe were there already, seated closest to the dais. This wasn't one of those obligatory affairs; people were genuinely pleased to be present. Out of real respect—out of love—they came to honor Arizona's favorite "favorite son."

Alan Jamison, the president of The Valley National Bank, and Parker Northridge, a young attorney with Snell & Wilmer, had beaten Joe to the Goldcor table, and were seriously discussing bringing a heart institute to Phoenix. Stanley B. Jokinski, the brilliant young heart surgeon who had operated on Uncle Joe in Houston, was ready to strike out on his own. The timing seemed perfect.

"Hey, Bob, tell Alan and Parker the story about the black medical technician you met in Uncle Joe's hospital room," Joe urged.

Bob and Joe, Sr., exchanged glances and started to laugh.

"Okay. Well, maybe you know I went to Houston with Joe. Anyway, I did. Right after the '64 election. So I go on up to his room the afternoon before his surgery, and he's laughing and carrying on about Arizona with this colored guy. You know Joe. Give him ten minutes and you're old friends. Well, this fella is a technician who's come t' get some blood, and as I walk in he holds out his hand and says, 'Johnson's the name.' So I take his hand and say, 'Goldwater's the name.' Old Joe here nearly bursts his aneurism laughing. Poor Johnson, he didn't know whether to believe me or not.''

When the laughter died down, Jamison said, ''I played golf with Horace Perkins today. He'll be another supporter. By the way, he's all bent out of shape because he didn't get an invitation to this dinner.''

Alan's last comment was clearly directed at Bob, but, except for a barely perceptible shrug, he did not respond.

''Why the hell would he expect to be invited?'' Uncle Joe shouted. ''Doesn't he realize that Harry Rosenzweig would have made up the guest list? Surely Rosenzweig wouldn't invite the town's leading bigot! Not to mention that Perkins has used his paper to keep Harry under a microscope ever since Harry's become the state Republican Chairman. Perkins's done everything but crawl up his asshole. Harry's predecessor didn't get that kind of treatment. Why Harry? 'Cause his name's Rosenzweig?''

''Look, Joe, I know. Horace is my friend, but I'm not blind to his shortcomings. Still, the night's for Barry, not Harry. He should have been more objective.''

''Well now, Alan, I'll tell you,'' Bob responded, scratching his head. ''We Goldwaters are no strangers to prejudice. I remember once trying to enter a PGA tournament, and the president at that time, Joe Novak, told me I couldn't play 'cause I'm Jewish. So I said that was okay, I'd only play nine holes because I'm only half Jewish.''

Everyone laughed, but Bob had made his point.

"Say, Alan, since you and Perkins are so tight, maybe you know why he thinks I'm such a menace to the community?" Uncle Joe asked.

Joe buried his face in his hands.

"Menace? If he thinks you're a menace, Joe, he hasn't filled me in on it. Why do you say that?" Alan asked in surprise.

"Well, his head stooge, Barnes, came to interview me for that series that started yesterday, 'The Hidden Cancer.' Haven't you been reading it?"

"Yeah, I have. In fact, I was asking Perk last week what Barnes could have learned in a four-month investigation that I, who was born here, who knows the intimate details of every major business transaction that takes place in the state, would not have gotten wind of. I can't wait to find out where the mob's been hiding."

"Did Perkins offer any clues?" Northridge asked.

"No. He said I'll have to wait and read it like everybody else."

■ ■ ■

THE PROGRAM for the evening was typical. The bishop of the Episcopal Diocese of Arizona gave the invocation, followed by the Pledge of Allegiance. A medley of Barry's favorite Indian songs was performed by the Glee Club from the Phoenix Indian School. Bob, who had taken his place on the dais, stepped up to serve as the Master of Ceremonies.

Joe wondered how many present knew that Bob's relationship to Barry had little to do with his selection as MC. His dry sense of humor, coupled with his mastery of the art of understatement, made him a well known and highly sought-after toastmaster. Tonight's assignment was to introduce the ninety-two-year-old Carl Hayden, the first Representative to Washington from the brand-new State of Arizona.

Following Hayden's introductory address, the crowd got what it came for. As Mr. Conservative came to the podium, the assemblage rose to its feet and applauded and cheered as though this were the 1964 Republican Convention. Many, having never forgiven their party for hanging up an "Out to Lunch" sign that year, had tears in their eyes for this man who had been crucified by his opponent and the media—the all-time low point in presidential politics.

"I feel like I just got an Academy Award," the Senator said, smiling. "But before you all panic, I'm not going to bore you with a long list of thank yous. In fairness, however, a man doesn't get where I am tonight without a lot of help and sacrifice from his family and friends.

"You know, when I decided to run for the Senate in 1952, Senator Hayden wasn't kidding when he said we Republicans met in an ice-cream parlor—we probably could have fit in the phone booth. Everybody in the state was a registered Democrat. The only real vote was in the Democratic primary. We were a southern state in that respect. 'Course, without Ike that year, a lot of us wouldn't have made it.

"Now that I'm done with preliminaries, let me tell you who I blame for getting me into this rat race." Barry turned to Harry Rosenzweig, seated to his right, and slapped his friend on the back to ensure that everyone knew exactly whom he was talking about. "My old buddy, Rosie.

"After World War II, Arizona started growing in earnest. The City of Phoenix was as wide open a western town as you'd find anywhere. Well, a group of public-spirited citizens tried to bring some morals and decorum to the city, but the government at the time was so damned corrupt, they couldn't get anywhere. So they decided to throw out the old system and put in a group of reformers. They called themselves the Citizens for Charter Government, and they came to see me about running for the City Council. Well, trying to elect Republicans was one thing, but running myself was another. I turned them down. Next thing I know, Harry invites me to dinner, gets me tanked on a bottle of Old Crow and before I know it, I'm running for City Council.

Turns out they wanted me 'cause I'm Jewish. These fellas figured that if they got businessmen and union members and Catholics, Mormons and Jews, then everybody'd be represented. When one of the businessmen dropped out because reform didn't seem real good for business, they wound up with two Jews, me and Harry.

''The first thing we did after the election was ruin everybody's fun, ours included, by making gambling and prostitution illegal. Naturally, we didn't eliminate it, just drove it underground. That taught me the most important lesson of my political career. Laws are meant to protect us from each other, not ourselves. When we try to legislate morality, interpose our standards on those who don't share them and use the law as a club for enforcement, then we make a mockery of the system. We clutter the books with laws that won't be obeyed and can't be enforced. Friends, that's the heart of conservative philosophy and was the beginning of my own evolution as a conscious conservative.

''Now, Harry, after two terms, had enough. He had all the running for office he was ready for. But we both got the bug for politics from this experience. I discovered I loved the challenge of holding public office. Harry liked working for the party and its candidates. So we became a team. For twenty-five years now I've been going to Harry for advice and while I may not always have taken it, Harry, in my heart, I knew you were right!''

Joe, laughing as hard as anyone, noticed out of the corner of his eye that Uncle Joe wasn't laughing. He probably hadn't even heard Barry's joke. His face was scrunched up, his eyes turned inward. Damn Barnes's maligning heart! He wasn't going to spoil all this. Too many people had worked too hard to let that bastard get the last laugh.

CHAPTER 6

THE NEXT afternoon, Joe parked his car in the lot behind Corcoran's, a popular steak house and one of Uncle Joe's favorite restaurants. The main entrance led through the kitchen, where the heat was so oppressive that it was a relief to emerge into the smoky dining room.

''Mr. Corelli,'' the maitre d' greeted him as he walked up to the station. ''Looking for your uncle?''

''Yes, Mike. Is he here?''

''I'll show you to his table.''

Not surprised to find his uncle's table abandoned, Joe sat down, ordered a drink and waited for the older man to return. Undoubtedly socializing at another table, Uncle Joe would eventually wend his way back, stopping numerous times en route.

Finally he heard the familiar, rasping voice behind him. ''Been here long?''

''Uh-uh.''

''So what did ya think of today's article?''

''I didn't like it. If I were Guido Battaglia, I'd be sick.''

''Did I hear you men mention Guido Battaglia?'' asked Jack Corcoran, approaching their table.

''Yeah. Joey here thinks Guido got a bum rap. I don't see that Barnes had anything on him. Not even a fuckin' parking ticket,'' Uncle Joe answered.

"Well, I agree with the kid. If this is his so-called 'exposé', a lot of innocent people are going to get hurt. If it's a crime to do legitimate work for someone with a record, or write a letter to a parole board, we're all in trouble."

"Jack's right," Joe said to his uncle. "That's why I'm getting more and more worried about this. If a gangster came in here once a week because he liked Jack's steaks, based on this kind of thinking Corcoran's would be called a gangland hangout."

"I never even thought of that," Jack responded. "Thank God I'm not Italian!"

As Jack walked away from the table, Joe said to his uncle, "You know, Barnes reached a record high for the series today—he hit 20 Italians and 2 Jews!"

Uncle Joe put his arm around Joe and whispered in a somber tone, "Let me tell you something, Clarence Darrow. If he hits us, he's gonna someday, somehow, learn what a real fuckin' hit is all about."

CHAPTER 7

THE VALLEY HERALD
Phoenix, Arizona, Friday October 30, 1971

Phoenix Weather
Cloudy, breezy and a little cooler today. High in the mid-80s. Yesterday's high 89, low 62. Humidity: high 51, low 18. Details, page 15.

THE HIDDEN CANCER
Detroit Gangsters Invade Arizona
By Dan Barnes

The Detroit Mob has an effective grip on Arizona.

Ask Mother Goose's president Mel Adelbaum.

Or lawyer Donald Perrino.

Or a number of other Valley residents.

Law enforcement authorities say the top Mafia leader in Detroit now is Joseph Zerilli, FBI No. 795171C, although others believe the Detroit Mafia is ruled from afar, by multimillionaire Pete Licavoli of the Grace Ranch, Tucson, and to a lesser extent by retired elder Joseph Massei of Florida. Other capos are William ''Black Bill'' Francone, and John Obraggi, according to authorities.

[Continued on Page 16]

Joe had a knot in his stomach as he turned to page 16. Mel Adelbaum had been Uncle Joe's partner in the Mother Goose's chain; maybe that was where Barnes got the name Corelli. Besides, his friend and colleague Don Perrino had finally come up, and he wanted to see in what context. Looming before him, in bold print, the headline read DETROIT GANGSTERS INVADE ARIZONA; MANY ARIZONANS INVOLVED. Directly under the headline were three pictures, with names below: JOSEPH CORELLI, MELVYN ADELBAUM and DONALD PERRINO.

> Adelbaum said he accidentally ran into Licavoli and his son Mike in Tucson about a year ago when Adelbaum went there to discuss buying pre-packaged potatoes from distributor James Jenkins. He said he met Jenkins, a former upstate New York produce dealer who suffered financial reverses in the Willcox area, through Adelbaum's former partner Joe Corelli. Corelli, on the other hand, said he met Jenkins through Adelbaum.
>
> A visit by this reporter to Detroit two years ago to check police reports and news clippings resulted in exposure of Joseph Zerilli's interest in this area at that time. In 1955, he and several California and Detroit produce men incorporated Marblehead Ranches Inc. and bought 3,000 acres in the north Glendale area for $2.7 million.
>
> Zerilli comes to Arizona infrequently. The last time was two or three years ago when Zerilli and Don Perrino lunched at the Phoenix Country Club and Corelli "came over to say hello." Corelli said he knows Perrino but doesn't know Zerilli, and said he couldn't remember meeting Zerilli or having lunch with him.
>
> Marblehead became one of the state's largest growing centers of lemons, oranges, grapes, nectarines, peaches and cotton. In 1959, Marblehead Ranches was sold for $5 million cash after a flood.
>
> One buyer of Marblehead was Del E. Webb, one-time carpenter, owner of two Las Vegas casino-hotels, and developer-builder of Sun City.
>
> In 1966, the ranch was sold again for $3 million, to Robert W. Goldwater, the senator's brother, and Corelli. They hold it today in Goldcor Investment Corp., formed March 27 of this year by Goldwater, Corelli and his family and Frank Vincente of Glendale.

Goldwater said Zerilli has no interest in the ranch now, and he doesn't know Zerilli.

Perrino has told The Herald he went to school in Detroit with Anthony Zerilli and knew his father Joseph then. "I've seen him (Joe) two times in the 30 years I've been in Arizona," Perrino said. "The only time I've known the guy has been in a purely social situation. We've got no interests with him, never have had, and don't intend to have."

The Perrinos own much land and have other enterprises in southern Arizona under the names of Perrino Joint Venture and Cochise Enterprises Inc. Cochise Enterprises is run from the office of Tucson accountant Stefano J. Tramburello.

Tramburello has for years been the accountant for Licavoli and Joe Bonanno. Federal authorities say Tramburello often takes the Fifth Amendment before investigative bodies.

Law enforcement authorities said they can only guess at the range of the Detroit mob's interest in Phoenix and environs. A Licavoli associate has been active in construction in this area. Another runs a restaurant firm incorporated by Phoenix lawyers.

Scottsdale sources also have reported that former Teamster President James Hoffa of Detroit, who has been alleged to have syndicate ties, owns land in Paradise Valley and Scottsdale through numbered (anonymous) trusts.

Another Detroit foray was made into Arizona 15 years ago, according to the late Corporation Commissioner Milt Husky. He said two emissaries from Hazel Park, the Detroit area racetrack run by Anthony Zerilli and Giacomo Tocco, tried to buy the Apache Junction dog track but didn't complete the deal. Today a half-owner of the Apache Junction track is Embassy Corp. of Buffalo, N.Y., which also has had a stock interest in Hazel Park.

Joe dropped the paper and seized the phone to call Don. His secretary said he wasn't taking any calls. Grabbing his jacket and briefcase, Joe rushed downtown to his office.

He found Uncle Joe pacing frantically. "There you are! You always get in so late! What are ya, a fuckin' banker?"

"Calm down and come into my office."

Uncle Joe followed him, hollering at his back: "I wanna sue! Today! Right now! Let's get started."

"Sit down and stop yelling. You've got to listen to me. I don't like this any more than you do, but we've got to stay rational."

"Have you spoken to Donald?"

"No. He's not taking any calls. I'll keep trying."

"I don't give a fuck what he does! I wanna sue!"

"The series isn't over. We've got to wait until it's over to do anything. An important factor in libel is damages. It's too soon to tell what they might be. And we don't know if they've said all they're going to say about you."

"Whattaya talking about? They called me a Detroit mobster! I never been in Detroit in my life! How am I gonna do business in this town with people thinkin' I'm a fuckin' criminal?"

"Calm down. The article barely mentions you. It's that stupid picture that's so horrendous. Anyone who reads the article will know they haven't said a goddamn thing about you except that you once said hello to Joseph Zerilli. That's not a crime."

"I never told them I said hello to Zerilli! That jackoff Barnes told *me* I was seen at the club sitting with Don Perrino and Zerilli having a drink. Remember, I said, 'That could be, Donald's my friend and I buy probably twenty or thirty drinks a day for my friends. But I don't remember nobody called Zerilli.'"

Without missing a beat, Uncle Joe continued. "Do you know how many Corellis live in this town? How many of the kids are gonna hear in school today that they come from a family of gangsters? Do you think over breakfast anyone read past the picture? No! But as some hard-on is eating his Wheaties and lookin' over the paper he remarks, 'Gee, Cathy, ya know that Corelli kid you go to school with? Family's in the Mafia.' How'd you like your son to come home and ask you if you're a killer? Well, I got two daughters and grandkids. My brother Vince's got a son, Artie and Frankie got five kids each, Rocky, seven, and Tony, three. Do you know how my brothers and their families are gonna react to this pack of fuckin' lies? And you want me to stay calm? On my father's grave, I'm gonna bury these mothafuckas!''

''Joe, I know how you feel. Remember, it's my name too. You aren't the only one who's worked hard to get where you are. So have I. But we can't jump the gun. We've got to wait till the series is over.''

''Listen, kid, in New York, we went to work every day with guns because we were being hassled by Ciro Terranova. We weren't giving him a cut on the artichokes. No one could protect us but ourselves. Adding insult to injury, my father testified before the Dewey Commission on organized crime. Do you have any idea what could have happened to us for that? For months we slept with one eye open. I can't take this kind of shit calmly, when we risked our fuckin' lives keeping clear of the Mafia. What the fuck does this WASP mothafucka know about mobsters, anyway?''

His face purple, hyperventilating, Uncle Joe collapsed into a chair. Joe handed him a glass of water and waited for him to settle down a bit. Then he said, ''You're right. My father tells the same story with as much passion as you. He's still got the gun he used to carry every day. On Avenue U you grow up having a sense of being Italian that's cut into your psyche, your character, your personality—you name it. We were taught that every minute you had to be on the lookout for danger. On the Avenue, that's how the guys live. Insecurity, suspicion and fear govern their lives. Look at our history! Invasions made us suspicious of strangers. And the Church teaches us to fear God, death and, inevitably, life itself.

''You may not know this, but I didn't always go to Notre Dame. I started law school at Harvard. In the fall of '63. That's when the Valachi hearings were monopolizing the press. Even the *New York Times*. Day in and day out I followed the coverage. Let me tell you, an Italian at Harvard Law School was a phenomenon as common as a tap-dancing cockroach. Those hearings made me furious. One day they carried an article in the *Times* about my neighborhood, calling Tommy's Sweet Shoppe on Avenue U a 'school for crime.' I hung out there sometimes. It wasn't anything like that. Day in and day out, Valachi."

Joe got up from his desk and, after a minute's search, removed a newspaper clipping from his filing cabinet. "Here, read this."

As his eyes ran down the old clipping, Uncle Joe nodded his head in sympathy.

"Well, when I saw those pictures and that headline this morning I felt just as angry. I wanted to rip Barnes apart."

"Forget Barnes, kid. Barnes is just an overpaid flunky. It's Perkins. Perkins's responsible.

"I wanna sue him!" he shrieked as he flew out of his chair. "If you won't do it, I'm gonna get Mark Jennings."

"Mark Jennings can't help you. He represents the paper."

"You think Mark Jennings's gonna represent the paper against me? I've known him for almost thirty years."

"He's not going to represent the newspaper against you, but he won't represent you against the paper, either."

Uncle Joe bolted from the office, stormed down the hall and slammed the front door.

Seconds later, Tom Brady appeared in Joe's doorway. "Got a minute?"

"Sure. Come on in."

"Your uncle just made quite an exit. I gather he isn't taking today's article too well."

"Why the hell should he? If he were in better health, I wouldn't expend so much of my energy trying to calm him down."

"To tell you the truth, I'm concerned about this myself. A lot of people will recognize the name under that picture and think it's you."

"That's true. And even if they know it's not me, he is my cousin."

"This could be very harmful to the firm's image. We're too new in this community to withstand an attack on our reputation."

"What's your point, Tom? Is there something I can do?"

"I guess not, but we'll have to monitor general reaction to the article for negative repercussions."

Joe looked at Tom, but didn't say a word. He knew all about negative repercussions. On Avenue U, negative repercussions ranged from having your face pushed in to having your heart carved out of your chest. In allegedly more civilized places he'd been, they settled for breaking your spirit.

BOOK
IV

JOE

NOTRE DAME 1958

CHAPTER 1

> Who shall put his finger on the work of Justice and say ''It is there?'' Justice is like the Kingdom of God. It is not without us as a fact. It is within us as a great yearning.
>
> George Eliot

JOE WALKED walked out of the College of Business thinking how much easier his accounting final had been than he'd expected. He stood on the steps in front of the building and snapped his Notre Dame jacket closed. It was eighteen degrees. As he looked up at the grey January sky, he almost smiled. If there was one thing no one would ever come to South Bend for, it was the weather.

He started back to Farley Hall. Late in the day, exams over, the campus was quieter than usual. He was glad. He didn't want to run into anyone. All he wanted to do was get back to his room, pack and get out of there. What a far cry this was from the way he'd set out a few months before!

■ ■ ■

HE HAD never taken a trip alone. It was exciting. Once the *Twentieth Century Limited* cleared the labyrinth of underground tunnels and was out in the sunshine, Joe went into the bar to get a

Coke and a feel for where he was. The train shook and twisted along the track, and he had difficulty maintaining his balance. As he stood there trying to look sophisticated, he heard a voice say, "Your first train trip too, huh?"

He turned around to find a fellow approximately his age and about three inches shorter. He offered Joe his hand and said, "Hi. Lou Scibello."

"Joe Corelli. And it's not my first train trip—it's my second."

"Where ya headed?"

"South Bend, Indiana. I'm gonna be a freshman at Notre Dame."

"Me, too! Wherea ya from?"

"Brooklyn. You?"

"Queens. How'd ya decide to go to Notre Dame?"

"My brother went there. That's how I took my first train trip. When I was eleven, I came out here with my mother for his graduation. Why are you goin' to N.D.?"

"Well, it was the only school I got into that my mother liked. I wanted to go to Syracuse. My advisor wanted me to go to Columbia. In typical Italian fashion, Mama won out."

Joe laughed. "What high school did ya go to?"

"Stuyvesant. Ya know, the home of the fat Jews and short Italians. Where'd you go?"

"Lincoln. Home of the fat Jews and killer Italians."

"Man, you ain't kiddin'. I played football at Stuyvesant. In my junior year we scrimmaged Lincoln. There was a guy on your team that was the biggest white man I've ever seen."

"Patsy De Primo! I played football, too. We must have played against each other. But ya know, our other tackle, named Carmen Parisi, was about as huge as Patsy—a little shorter, but ten pounds heavier."

The boys were getting tired of trying to stay on their feet. In the men's room, they found a couch. Sunrise found them still there, laughing and trading stories.

■ ■ ■

IT DIDN'T take Joe and Lou long to discover that the name "Fighting Irish" was not entirely accurate. Not only were there more Italians on campus than either one had anticipated, but the most highly touted athletes in their class were Italian. Nick Buoniconti, Angelo Dabiero and Tony Barone in football; Armand Reo in basketball; Mike Giacinto and Joe Balistrieri in track. The captain of the football team was Chuck Puntillo and the All-American was Nick Pietrosante.

The first organization the boys joined was the Italian Club. Their faculty advisor was a priest, nicknamed "88 O'Toole" by the students, because everyone who took his class got an 88. If an 88 didn't suit you, he'd bowl you for your grade. At the first meeting, president Charlie Lo Piccolo, son of an alleged Midwest Mafia Don, led the group in the singing of the club song, *"Va Fanculo Tutti Quandi,"* with the Irish priest smiling benignly. When the group got to new business, Vince Langella suggested the club invest in black jackets for its members. Pete Contadino, whose father was one of the major guys in Milwaukee, jumped up and yelled, "Siddown, you moron. We can't even afford buttons!" Within the club was a very select society, known as the Seven Italian Dwarfs. Lou qualified, along with Rich Catenacci, John Baldo, Dino Marino, Vinnie Noce, Bob Naro, and Bob Policastro. Joe, at five-nine, was much too tall.

Joey Gallo had been right in a way. Joe was, for the most part, more comfortable with these Italians than he was with his roommate, Brendan Flaherty, and the other non-Italians with whom he came into daily contact. Flaherty was an Irishman from New Jersey who fancied himself a sophisticate. He took one look at Joe's sharkskin suits and featherweight shoes and gagged. He appointed himself Joe's Henry Higgins and immediately set about the business of civilizing the uncouth Brooklynite. Not only was he determined to eradicate Joe's accent, but he introduced him to cordovan shoes, rep ties and herringbone jackets. The finishing touch that he had in mind for himself was to change his name from Brendan to Brendon—less Irish, you know. While Joe never really understood or related to him, he seized the opportunity to learn from him.

■ ■ ■

PASSING the La Fortune Student Center, he stopped under the blue-and-gold sign marking "The Huddle." He was freezing and considered going in for some hot chocolate. Joe had had one of his more educational experiences of the semester in this snack bar, one he wouldn't have wanted to get out on Avenue U.

■ ■ ■

BEHIND the tables where students sat to have burgers or milk shakes were several pool tables. Joe would often go in to relax and shoot a game or two. About a month into the school year, he had wandered in looking for a game, when he met a kid named Jim Bushnell, who was from Joliet, Illinois. They had been shooting the breeze for a while, when Jim asked Joe if he'd like to play.

"Sure," he said.

"How about we play for ten bucks?"

"Okay. What'll ya spot me?" Joe quipped, thinking he would take a shot at snookering this hick.

"I'll spot ya twenty-five on a hundred an' you break."

Joe couldn't believe his ears. This hillbilly from Illinois was gonna spot him twenty-five balls. This would be like taking candy from a baby.

Each of the first four shots was played "safe," until Joe had finally unintentionally opened up the rack sufficiently for Jim to shoot. Joe could see from the way Jim made his first three shots that he might be in serious trouble. This guy was positioning the table beautifully, leaving open shots three ahead. In no time flat he had run the rack, with the last ball and the cue ball situated in such a way that his next shot would open up the rack for his next run. With his opponent marveling at his finesse, Jim ran sixty-five balls before Joe got the chance to shoot. His mind blown away, Joe made three shots and then missed, leaving Jim the opening to run out and finish the game before Joe ever got another chance.

"Ya know, the most I ever ran in my life was twenty-four balls. In my neighborhood they'd never let me live down gettin' sucked in like this."

"Don't worry about it. There probably aren't any future NCAA pool champs in your neighborhood."

They became good friends after that. Joe'd go into town with Jim from time to time and watch him hustle the locals. It was fun as long as he wasn't the hustlee.

■ ■ ■

HE DECIDED to do without the hot chocolate. Instead of continuing to Farley Hall, Joe turned abruptly and headed toward the heart of campus, slowing down at the statues of Father Walsh and Father Sorin. The dense greenery that had protected them from the sun when he arrived in September was long since gone. On their shoulders, as on the skeletons of the dormant trees, were reminders of the last snowfall. Behind the statues was the Golden Dome, lackluster in the darkening sky. He stopped in front of Sacred Heart Church and tried the doors. They were locked. Instead, he made his way to St. Joseph's Lake. The snow from the last storm had all but vanished, but the ground was still frozen. Brown bristles were all that remained of the summer grass. The bleak surroundings matched his mood. Joe sat down by the water's edge and looked out over the lake. Here and there lights went on in the buildings in the distance, their reflections bouncing off the ice. He reached into his pocket and pulled out a wad of bills. He counted it again. Three twenties, two tens, two fives and ten singles. More than enough.

Getting the money had certainly been an experience. If he'd called home for it, he would have had to tell his parents why he needed it. So he called Joey Gallo.

"Hey, watsa matta, kid?"

"Ya told me before I left if I needed money t' tell ya. Well, I'm tellin' ya. I gotta get home. I'm broke. Could ya wire me twenty-five bucks for bus fare? I'll pay ya back soon as I get t' Brooklyn."

"Wya? Whattaya mean wya?"

"Western Union. Ya go t' their office. They send the money by telegram."

"I neva hearda dis. I'll get it t' ya wit' somebody ya could trus' and ya don't gotta pay me back nuthin. I'll leave a message t'morra f' ya t' call Mr. G."

"Okay, Joey. Thanks a lot." Gallo had never even asked why he was coming home.

The next day Joe got word from Brooklyn to meet a bookie from Elkhart named Pasquale at the main entrance to the Notre Dame Stadium at sundown.

"I'm sending you a hundred dollars. Take a plane. Forget the fuckin' bus," Gallo had ordered when he called to set up the contact.

From Gallo's diction, Joe could tell he was alone. "Thanks, Joey, but I want to take the longest, slowest way home. I'm in trouble, an' I need time to figure out how to break it to my folks."

"Okay, kid. Whatever ya say. You need anything else?"

"No. Joey? Thanks a lot."

■ ■ ■

JOE WAS numb from the cold. He got up, rubbed his behind to restore his circulation and walked over to the Grotto. Inside the rock arch was a statue of the Lady of Fatima. The prie-dieux were empty. A few votive candles were flickering in their cups.

Everyone came here to think. Somehow Joe found the lake more soothing. At that moment he felt a hand on his shoulder.

"Worried about exams, son?"

Joe looked up at the imposing figure of the university president, Theodore Hesburgh. "No, Father."

"Good. Students usually do better than they expect."

"Well, I'm only a freshman, so I wouldn't know."

They began to walk alongside each other. "That's what I thought. If it's not exams, what is troubling you?"

Omertà, Joe reminded himself quickly. No matter how genial Father Hesburgh seemed, he was still one of the authorities.

"Nothing in particular, Father. I think I'm just tired."

"Son, this is a bad time of year. It's so cold and gloomy, it's easy to get depressed. But just wait till spring. It's glorious! Makes these winter months worthwhile."

Joe smiled and nodded. They came to a fork, and Hesburgh turned left while the boy continued on to his dorm.

His room was cold enough to hang meat, a clear sign that Brendan had been in. He slammed the window shut and stood by the radiator to get warm. One nice thing about going home was he wouldn't have to sleep in ear muffs and a hat. His bloodless Irish roommate was a fresh-air freak who had to have the windows open at all times. Some mornings he'd have to shake the snow off his blanket. Joe pulled out his suitcases, tuned the radio to the campus station and opened his closet.

"Oh Donna, Oh Donna"—the song was ending. "For all you listeners out there, it's six o'clock Notre Dame time, and this is your favorite sports announcer, Don Criqui."

Joe smiled as he listened to Don's unique voice come into the room. Don was from Buffalo. Joe'd met him through Brendan, and the two of them had really hit it off. A cub sportscaster at the university station, WNDU, Don always managed to weave Joe's name into his broadcasts. He was either in fifth place in an NCAA tennis tournament, or passed the time trials in a bicycle race or something equally obscure.

"And now for the results of the feature race at Hialeah . . . and Son of Dancer, with Joe Corelli in the saddle, finished third."

Joe sat down hard on the edge of his bed, put his head in his hands and sobbed uncontrollably.

CHAPTER

2

ONE LOOK and he knew. Someone had rifled his desk. Whoever did it had been very careful. A less meticulous person would never have known, but Joe was compulsively neat. On top of the desk was a leather pencil box. Pencils were always point up. Inside the center drawer on the pencil ledge was a ruler to the left, erasers to the right. Lined up next to the ledge was a box of paper clips, a box of rubber bands, a staple gun and a box of staples. Next, on the left, was a box of typing paper; to the right, carbon paper. In the file drawer, every piece of paper had a file, and every file was arranged according to a system Joe had devised. So, one file out of place, one pencil upside down, and it was like setting off an alarm. The only question was, who?

It couldn't have been Brendan. Not only because he hadn't yet returned from Christmas vacation, but because in the semester Joe had lived with him, he'd never gone near Joe's desk, not even to leave a message. Why would he start now? So far as Joe knew, no one else had a key and the door had not been tampered with.

He hadn't even finished unpacking his suitcase when he had his answer.

"Come in," he responded to the knock on his door.

Father Maguire, the Rector of Farley Hall, walked in. When Joe saw him, he got a sinking feeling in the pit of his stomach. Father Maguire had a key to the room!

''I have some bad news for you.''

''What's that, Father?''

''During your absence we entered your room and we looked in your desk. We found pages from the *Catholic Commentary on Holy Scriptures* that you ripped out of the book in the library. There's been serious pilferage from the library. You'll have to go before the Prefect of Discipline and the Discipline Committee to determine whether or not you'll be expelled from school.''

''Father, how come somebody could go into my room?''

''Well, the university has the right to enter the rooms at all times.''

''Right,'' Joe said, trying to suppress his anger.

The boy and the priest stood staring at each other. Father Maguire had a reputation for being a mean son of a bitch. Yet he had always been very nice to Joe. Once he'd caught him throwing water balloons at someone in the halls, and chose to ignore it. Joe always assumed that his top grades had something to do with the priest's myopia.

''Let me just warn you,'' the priest continued. ''Father Cardinelli wants your head.''

Joe was incredulous. ''He what?''

''He is the leader of this investigation, but Father Finley will be calling you.''

Father Maguire closed the door behind him, leaving Joe standing there dazed.

■ ■ ■

HE DIDN'T have long to wait. First thing next morning, Joe received word from the Assistant Rector that Father Finley, the Prefect of Discipline, wanted to see him. This man made Father Maguire seem like a pussycat, and Joe set out for the Administration Building nauseated and light-headed from anxiety.

In Father Finley's office he sat on the edge of the chair across the desk from the Prefect of Discipline. P. Leonard Finley, C.S.C., had grey hair and the red face that seemed as much the mark of a Catholic priest as the Roman collar. As Joe wondered if they were connected, his inquisitor came to the point.

"Joe, we know you took the pages out of the *Catholic Commentary on Holy Scriptures*."

"How da ya know that?"

"Because you couldn't have written your term paper without them, and we found them in your desk. Another student had an excellent paper almost identical to yours and we confronted him with it."

"Who's the other student?"

"I can't disclose that to you."

The boy glared at the priest.

"Joe, you have to appear at a hearing of the Discipline Committee at the end of the week to determine if you'll be expelled."

"All right," the boy answered, becoming impatient. "Is there anything else?"

"Yes. You're going to be accused of stealing a number of other books as well."

He listened while Father Collins read off a list of about twenty books Joe had never even heard of.

"Father, you can accuse me of whatever you want to accuse me of, but that is so much bullshit!"

"Those books are missing."

"That history book you mentioned sure is. I know. I've been over to the library trying to get it and they never have it. But I never even heard of the rest of the books you just named. In my family, Father, books have always been sacred. My father doesn't speak much English, but he reads and reads and reads. Mostly in Italian. We didn't have enough money to buy books so I'd go to the public library once a week. Until this crazy mistake, I never defaced a book. And I *never* stole a book! Shit, I was never even late in returning a book to the library!"

"Well, Father Cardinelli seems to think you're the person who took them. And just so you are fully informed, he was recently appointed to head a subcommittee concerned with pilferage from the library and the book store."

"What does Father Cardinelli know about anything? I'm in his class. I'm his top student. I probably have the highest grade of almost three hundred kids. What the hell does he know?"

"Well, he feels very strongly about this. He says you've disgraced Italians."

"Listen, Father, you know what Father Maguire found in my desk. Now, what do you think I did with all these other books? Did I sell them? Did I ship them back to Brooklyn? The guys in my neighborhood don't even know how to read. Did I burn 'em? I didn't take any of those books. I did take the three pages from the *Catholic Commentary on Holy Scriptures*. Let me tell *you* something now. I was assigned the Book of Job. I went to the library one night and found that there are two copies of the *Catholic Commentary on Holy Scriptures* and three hundred guys who needed it. There was an hour wait for the book. I waited an hour. When I got the book, guess what? There was no Book of Job. It was ripped out. I didn't have another hour that night to wait for the other copy. The next night I went back again. I waited again, and guess what? I got the same book I'd had the night before. No Book of Job. On the third night, I finally get the copy with the Book of Job in it. They tell me I have fifteen minutes to look at the book. Have you ever seen this *Catholic Commentary* book? It's about two feet long and eighteen inches wide. Ya need six magnifying glasses to read what it says, and the Book of Job is ten pages. Nobody in the world, not even Evelyn Wood, could read this thing in fifteen minutes. It's *impossible*, Father. So I removed the last three pages neatly, brought them to my room where I could read them, wrote my paper, and put the pages in my desk drawer so I could bring them back to the library and tape them back in the book. You know the guy, and I know the guy, whose paper tipped you off to me. So let's stop the kiddin' around and let me mention Anthony Barone, one of your up-and-coming star football players. Biggie's a good friend of mine, and even if he weren't, I wouldn't rat on him. You know it's Tony Barone as well as I know it's Tony Barone.''

''Yes, I know,'' Father Finley admitted reluctantly.

''He comes to me and says, 'Joey, I got this Book of Job in Cardinelli's class. Whatta you got?' I got the Book of Job, too, so he's in luck. 'Could I borra your paper and maybe get some ideas?' 'Biggie, here's the paper, but do me a favor, do not copy it word for word. Cardinelli will know you didn't write it, because I got a 96 average in his class an' you got about a 68 average.' 'I swear t' ya, Joey, all I wanna do is look at it, just t' get some ideas.' Now you can bust me, Father, but I guarantee you, if he didn't copy it verbatim, it was damn close. I don't know that for a fact, because I never saw what he turned in. But Cardinelli nailed Barone, an' he led ya t' me. That's the story. I took the pages. As fer the other books, you'll have to find the guilty parties on your own.'' Joe ended his account of what had happened substantially calmer than when he started it, confident he had made his point.

Too soon.

''Joe, come at eight in the morning on Friday,'' Father Finley said firmly, standing to signal the end of the interview.

Joe dragged himself to the dorm. Barone's room was just inside the side door of Farley Hall. The door was open, but Joe kept on walking.

''Hey, Joe. Come here.''

Billy Ford, Tony Barone and his roommate, Rocky Sturges, were sitting around looking like they were at a wake.

''Did you talk to Father Cardinelli?'' Joe asked Barone.

''Yeah. He called me in. Said my paper was really well done and thought I might have stolen it from you.''

''Well, what did ya write in the paper?''

"I didn't copy it, Joey. I swear. Sturges helped me. Right, Rocky?"

Rocky, a walk-on, was one of the brighter ballplayers around. He nodded.

"Did he ask you how you got your research?"

"Yeah. I said I got it from you."

"Ya know, Joe," Billy interrupted. "I'm in the same section of Cardinelli's class as Tony. Let me tell you, he's got one fuckin' hard-on f' Biggie. If Cardinelli weren't a dago, I'd say he's got it in for Tony because he's Italian. Maybe it's football players he hates. I think he took a shot in the dark. Decided t' rattle Tony's cage t' see what would fall out."

"Well, guys, it was me, an' I'm still fallin'."

At that moment, someone hurled a snowball through the open window, hitting Barone on the side of the head. He went bat shit. Leaping up, he sprinted out of the room, Ford and Joe in his wake.

"You cocksuckers! Stop! Wait'll I get my han's on you—I'll teach ya to t'row snowballs at me."

The three culprits turned, and Joe recognized Nick Buoniconti, Bob Bill and Norb Roy, all freshman football players.

"Look, Tony, you'd better simmer down," said Joe. "There's three a them an' two an' a half of us. I've already taken my lumps t'day."

Biggie stopped immediately. As he looked down at his friend, a snowball grazed Joe's ear. Their eyes locked in silent understanding. A snowball fight. Just what the doctor ordered.

■ ■ ■

SITTING ACROSS the room at a conference table were Father Joseph Maguire, Rector of Farley Hall; Father Richard "Black Mac" McCauley, Rector of Cavanaugh Hall and a member of the Library Committee; Father Francis X. Cardinelli, Rector of Walsh Hall; Father Joseph Muldoon, Assistant Rector of Walsh Hall; and Father Finley, Prefect of Discipline. Father Finley declared this formal meeting of the Discipline Committee in session. Before he could say another word, Father Cardinelli started yelling at Joe.

"You are an utter disgrace! You're an Eye-talian! How could you do such a thing? In a religion course! You should be thrown out forever and go to work in the streets where you came from."

CHAPTER

3

THERE WERE hoodlums in every line of work.

Joe bit his tongue. He looked at each of the black-robed figures sitting before him. Alone, he was supposed to defend himself on vague charges before a tribunal of priests who had the power to alter his life irrevocably. It was obvious he was in for a long morning.

"Francis, now calm down. He has to get a fair hearing, and he has to have the opportunity to tell all the facts," Father Finley admonished his colleague.

Then, in a scrupulously neutral tone he said, "Joe, please tell this Committee the story you told me a few days ago in my office."

Joe repeated his story. When he had finished, Father Cardinelli leaned across the table, pointed his finger, and said venomously, "You're lying."

"Father, it's not a lie. It's the truth. There's no reason for me to lie. I wanted to put the pages back. If I hadn't, why would I have saved them? Surely you aren't going to accuse me of being stupid! If I'd torn them up and thrown them out, you wouldn't have them as evidence. You wouldn't have known who took the pages."

Joe read the faces of the Committee. Father Finley and possibly Father Maguire believed him.

"You took the books of Ecclesiastes, Ruth, Isaiah and Leviticus!"

"Father Cardinelli, let me tell you something. This project of yours was the most boring thing I ever did in my life. I would have no more interest in reading any of those other pages than I would in jumping off this building. I told you what I took, and I didn't take anything else."

"You must have. Who else would have taken them?"

"Come on! There are about 300 guys taking this course."

"Do you know who the thieves are?"

"Not all of them."

"Well, tell us whom you know."

Joe shook his head. "You aren't going to hear it from me. You know as well as I do that I didn't take all these books unless you think I'm sellin' 'em. There're a lot of guys stealin' books and pages."

The interrogation went on for about three hours with the same questions being asked over and over again and Cardinelli hurling insults at Joe at regular intervals. Finally Father Finley called a halt. "Enough, Francis. That is enough.

"There's nothing further we have to ask you, Joe. Go back to your room, continue on with your classes and take your final exams. I'll call you very shortly and let you know the decision of this Committee."

The boy rose slowly to his feet. In a way, this had been like the sitdown he and Vinnie had gone to on Avenue X, but there were glaring differences. The bookie had been willing to take him on one-on-one. Angelo Cacciardi had had a beef with Joe, and that's who had heard Joe out. Angelo invited a character witness, someone who knew Joe well but who was also a respected member of the brotherhood. He didn't try to decide if a kid he didn't really know was telling the truth. They also came to a quick determination of the facts. They didn't tell him to go home and study for his finals while they decided whether or not to blow him away.

It turned out, Joe didn't have long to wait. Two hours hadn't gone by when he received a call that Father Finley wanted to see him.

"Joe, I want you to know I believe you. However, you lost by a vote of three to two. You are to be expelled for a semester. At the end of the semester, you are invited to come back. I want very much for you to return. Come to summer school. You can make up the time very easily, but for now, you are to leave at the completion of this semester's exams. Take your exams and get your grades. You'll have a completed first semester. Furthermore, there is no other penalty. Father Cardinelli is to grade you objectively. You are to take his final exam and whatever you get is your grade."

Joe sat quietly, hearing Father Finley out. When it was clear that the priest had nothing more to say, Joe got to his feet and turned to leave.

"Joe, isn't there anything you'd like to say?"

"Is there any kind of appeals process?"

"No."

"Then what could there possibly be for me to say? I told my story. Three out of five people didn't believe me. You tell me you believe me, and you're the Prefect of Discipline—but I'm out anyway. I grew up believing that the truth is irresistible. So I guess I learned an important lesson—truth is not the best defense. It's no defense at all."

"Please sit down. I can't let you leave here with that attitude."

Joe glared at the priest, neither sitting nor making any attempt to leave.

"I'm the Prefect of Discipline. You imply that if I believe you, that should be enough. Instead, the university, in an attempt to be fair, has decided that a group decision in matters of such a serious nature protects the student. Surely you can see the danger of one man, for whatever reason, making an arbitrary decision?"

"Sure, in theory, group investigations should produce justice. But this group? First off, there's no one to look over their shoulder and call foul. Where are the rules that control their behavior? Who was there to talk for me? You ask a seventeen-year-old freshman to appear alone at a hearing conducted by five adults—all priests, no less. One of them with such a hang-up about being Italian he expects his Italian students to be super-human to compensate for his own inadequacies. The second member of the group is his assistant, and the third member, Father McCauley, is a member of the Library Committee. Three out of the five had an axe to grind. Each of them had a message to send to the university community. Father McCauley's was what happens to you if you steal books, a problem that must be costing this school a small piece of change; Father Cardinelli's, some kind of reverse discrimination; and his underling's, the need to go on living with his boss. This wasn't a trial before a jury of my peers! These guys set out knowing what they wanted to find, and when they didn't find it they took a grain of truth and twisted, stretched and distorted it, to make it come out the way they needed it t' come out. Hey, I was wrong to tear out the pages, but under the circumstances, can you honestly say that the punishment fits the crime?"

Instead of responding, Father Finley repeated his request for Joe to return for summer school.

"Look, Father, I work in the summer for my dad, hauling fruit, loading trucks an' just plain giving him a hand. He counts on me, so he'll have to decide that. In fact, I don't know how he'll feel about my coming back at all. He knows I'm not a thief. When I explain what happened, he'll believe me—not whatever the letter of suspension says—and he'll be furious with Notre Dame. My father's not too crazy about the Church in the first place. I don't have to tell you there are perfectly fine colleges in New York. I could get a good education and live at home where I'm safe from arbitrary searches."

Father Finley bristled. ''Look Joe, I understand that you're angry and hurt, but let's get one thing straight. In your housing contract, in large print, the university reserves the right to enter students' rooms at any time. In light of the circumstances, I believe we had reasonable cause. What's more, you have to admit that no one ever pressed you on the issue of plagiarism.''

''Okay, Father, I apologize for the wrongful search crack, but you'll forgive me if I'm not impressed with your generosity as to plagiarism. The first week I got here, the Dean of Students assigned me the task of 'tutoring' Mr. Barone. It was clear to both of us that I was to help get him through school. Has anyone here ever done a comparison of the papers of 'bonus babies' and those of their tutors? I'm being treated unfairly, but it's okay, because I'll recover. And I will think about what you said. But maybe you an' the powers that be around here should think about the greater unfairness being done to the Tony Barones of this world.''

Joe left Father Finley's office feeling a lot better. He knew his punishment, and he'd deal with it. What's more, he'd gotten quite a lot off his chest, so he had a clear head to get him through finals.

Joe set to studying. He was determined to get the highest grades possible. In Cardinelli's class he was already light years ahead of everyone, but he'd work harder for that exam than any of the others.

■ ■ ■

WITHIN TWENTY-FOUR hours of an exam, grades had to be posted—in this case, both the exam grade and the semester grade. Except for one four, Joe's grades were fives and sixes; fives and sixes were A's. In Nieuwland Science Hall, outside Father Cardinelli's classroom, the boy looked for his grade. Final exam: 97. Final grade: 3.

Thief! Cardinelli was a thief and a cheat. At least on Avenue U, thieves stuck to the house rules.

Well, this was one thief who wasn't going to rip him off without a fight.

It was a straight shot from Nieuwland to Walsh Hall, Cardinelli's dorm. An enraged Joe stalked across the grass that lay between the two buildings. At his knock, Father Cardinelli opened the door. The priest, both shorter and slighter than Joe, barked at him: "What do you want?"

"I wanna talk to you."

"What do you want?" the priest repeated.

Joe pushed in the door. "Take off that collar!"

"What?"

"Take off that fuckin' collar, you bastard. I got an A on the final, and you gave me a C!"

"You're a disgrace. You stole all those books. You lied."

"Listen, you son of a bitch. Father Finley tole me an' he tole you that the only punishment I was to have was to be expelled for a semester. I have been expelled. You know that."

"Yes, but you are a disgrace to the Eye-talian people!"

"Take off that collar, you cocksucker. I'm gonna kill ya, you son of a bitch."

"You're a disgrace! *You* are a disgrace to our heritage and all my Italian ancestors! I'll have you know my grandparents came to this country from Italy. You've caused me such embarrassment!"

"Are you gonna take off that fuckin' collar or am I gonna kill ya with the collar on, you muthafucka?"

The priest had been backing away and now he was up against the window. Joe grabbed Father Cardinelli by the neck.

"I'm gonna kill ya, you muthafucka. Ya ruined my fuckin' life cause ya such a fuckin' hypocrite!"

The priest's face contorted as it dawned on him that the boy was going to strangle him.

"You're a fuckin' degenerate hypocrite! You're a scumbag and a motherless, fuckin' prick, you son of a bitch. You call yourself a priest? I tole you the fuckin' truth the other day. You didn't want to believe it because of whatever fuckin' hang-up ya got, you rat bastid. It ain't my problem—it's your fuckin' problem! There's a lotta other guys here who'd like t' kill ya, but I'm gonna do it first.'' Suddenly, the look of utter terror in Father Cardinelli's eyes compelled Joe to relax his grip on the priest's neck. He dropped his hands to his sides.

''Get out of here,'' the priest whispered hoarsely.

''Fuck you an' your mother—an' everybody else!''

Joe whipped out of the room, headed straight for Father Finley's office.

Bursting in, he said, ''Father, I want you to know that I just almost killed Father Cardinelli.''

''You what?''

The boy told him what had happened.

''Joe, go home immediately. Just go home. I'll take care of this. Don't worry, let me deal with Francis Cardinelli,'' the priest said somberly.

But his eyes said he might enjoy this round more than the last one.

CHAPTER 4

EARLY FRIDAY morning the Trailways bus rolled into the Port Authority Terminal. Joe was exhausted, physically and emotionally. He had so much money left over that he decided not to wrestle with his belongings on the subway, and took a cab to Brooklyn. His father would still be at the market, but his mother would be home. It was Friday, and that was the day she waxed the floors.

When Tessie Corelli opened the front door, scrub brush in hand, foam-rubber pads strapped to her knees, it took a minute for her to absorb the fact that Joe was not an apparition.

"Joseph. What happened? What are you doing home? How did you get here? Take off your shoes so you don't get the floor dirty," she said in a rush of confusion and concern.

Telling her was hard, but he had to get it over with.

She looked as though someone had died. "What a disgrace! What will we tell the family? What will people think of us? What are you going to do? I guess you'll just have to go to work for your father in the market now. Your whole life is ruined," she moaned.

Slowly she got up and shuffled across the room.

Just this once he'd have liked her to understand. At least give him a little support, some encouragement.

''Here, this is a telegram from Father Cardinelli,'' she droned, holding the envelope out to him.

''Father Cardinelli? What's it say?''

She shrugged. ''You read it. I didn't even understand it.''

He grabbed the telegram from her hand. ''I made a mistake. Your grade is five, not three. Sincerely, Francis X. Cardinelli, C.S.C.''

■ ■ ■

THE SOUND of someone shoveling snow woke him. He had slept all day Friday and through the night. Several inches had fallen, and from his window he could see his father clearing the front steps. As he opened the window to cool off his stifling room, a woman passing by stopped to chat with Giuseppe.

Joe went down for breakfast. He was starved. He couldn't remember the last time he'd eaten. Halfway through his meal he could hear his father at the back door, stomping the snow off his boots. He opened the door, letting in a blast of frigid air.

''Joseph is awake. He's in the dinette eating breakfast,'' he heard his mother say. Joe could feel himself tense. ''I'll bring you some coffee.''

As his father seated himself across the table, Joe looked up.

''So, Pepino. You home.''

''Yeah, Pop.''

''You mama tola me wada happen.''

''I'm sorry, Pop.''

His father reached into his pocket, pulled out a piece of paper and handed it to him. Notre Dame had already sent a bill for all the missing books.

Joe was surprised at his own calm, but what more was there that could upset him? It was over. ''Don't pay them, Pop. I didn't take the books,'' he said quietly.

His father nodded. ''Whatta youa gonna do?''

''I don't know, Pop. Father Finley wants me to come back for summer school. I told him you need me.''

Father and son maintained silence while the boy finished his breakfast. Finally the older man spoke.

"You remember wena you was a littla boy, you aska me how I gotta alla dose marks on my *culo*?"

"Yeah, Pop. You said you were machine-gunned in th' Italian Army."

"Dida you eva tinka abouda how you getta shota in d' backa?"

Joe had not thought about it. Now, he looked at his father and waited for him to say it.

"I wasa runnin' away. You hear me, Pepino? I wasa runnin' away. You no run away. I no needa you disa summer. Go backa to disa school and show dese son-a-ma-bitches dey no breaka d' Calabraise."

As much as he hated Cardinelli, he loved his father twice again. Joe swiped at the salty moistness at the side of his mouth and nodded. Over and over he nodded until the tears stopped.

CHAPTER

5

"JOEY. YOU'RE BACK," Jean called as she looked up to see who'd come in.

"Hi, Jean. What's goin' on?"

"Ya know, a few days ago Ace tole me that if I see ya, t' tell ya he's lookin' for ya. I guess he knew you was back. Is everything okay?"

"Yeah, Jean. How's Jimmy?"

"Ya know Jimmy. Nuthin eva changes f' him."

Joe looked around the candy store. That didn't change, either. "Have ya seen Ace t'day?"

"Sure. He's here."

"See ya later, Jean."

The boy walked to the back. Inside were the same card players, the same smoke, the same noisy radios. In some mysterious way, time on Avenue U was frozen. At the back table, in the corner, Ace was sitting at his usual place. With him were Sally D and Joey Gallo, engrossed in a serious discussion. Something was going down. As he was trying to decide whether or not to interrupt them, Ace caught sight of him and signaled him to come over.

"Sidown, kid," Sally said after Joe shook everyone's hand.

"So Joey, whattaya doin' here?" Ace asked.

The three men listened to the boy's story, making no attempt to interject questions or comments. When Joe had finished, the men exchanged glances and Sally nodded his approval.

''Joey, ya took the rap like a man. You didn't rat.'' He slapped Joe on the back, beaming with pride.

''Don't worry about those fuckin' priests. Whadeva ya want, it's yours. Come here, woik in da candy store. I'll pay ya whadeva ya want. Six months, ya go back. Don' worry. The good t'ing is ya didn' tell on anybody. Fuck dose guys. Ya learnt good,'' Ace said.

Joe couldn't believe it. He was a hero!

''Ya gotta be a glutton f' punishment, goin' back dere wid dose degenerate scumbags,'' Gallo said. ''Stay here wid me, kid. I'm gettin' big. I could use a smart guy like you. I tole ya dis before.''

From the look Sally and Ace exchanged, Joe knew that they didn't see things in quite the same way.

''Thanks, Joey. And thanks for the loan, too,'' he said as he reached into his pocket and pulled out a hundred-dollar bill. ''It meant a lot to me to be able to wait till I got home to tell my folks what happened.''

''Keep it, kid. T'ink of it as a down payment.''

''I can't do that, Joey. First of all, when I got home, my pop asked me where I got the money for the bus. I tole him I borrowed it from a friend. He gave me this to return. Said I should neva owe anybody anything. And besides, I'm gonna go to college somewhere.''

''You remember I tole ya I could get ya inta the University a St. Louis?'' Sally asked.

''Yeah.''

''Lemme do it now. They'll treat ya right dere. Dese ain't da same kinda fuckin' priests dey got at Notre Dame. Dese are da best—da Jesuits. Plus, St. Louis ain't no one-horse town. We gotta lotta our people dere in case ya eva need 'em.''

"I wanna tell ya guys somethin' about Notre Dame. The day of my last exam I hada pack. I was leavin' the next day. But I needed a little air, a walk, t' say good-bye. An' as I'm strollin' aroun', Father Hesburgh, the president of the whole university, comes up t' me an' asks me if I got a problem. In all the time I was there, a week didn't go by that I didn't see 'im talkin t' students. Now, that'd be like Don Carlo walkin' up the Avenue every week an' shakin' han's with all d' kids at the candy stores. Then we got this Italian club. Ya know what our theme song is? *'Va Fanculo Tutti Quandi.'* "

The men got hysterical.

"Dey letcha sing dat in a Cat'lic school?" Sally asked.

"Yeah. An' ya know what? One day I say t' my buddy, Danny Russo, 'These Irish shmucks, I wonder what they'd say if they knew what the song meant?' Up comes the club sponsor, Father O'Toole. He puts his arm aroun' my shoulder an says, 'Joe, I remember your brother Jerry. We had a few Italians here in his day, too. Angelo Palumbo, Don Penza, Patsy Bisceglia, Jack Alessandrini, Frank Varrichione. You think because I don't spoil your fun, I was born yesterday?' In fact, Joey, ya know what? There was a guy in the club from California named Joe Gallo. He was from a place called Modesto. His family's big in wine."

"Wine? Someone named Gallo stompin' on grapes fer a livin'?" Joey Gallo laughed. "Wimps like dat couldn't be related t' me. Plus, I ain't got no relations west a' Joisey City."

Joe looked at him. Gallo had a way of reacting to people who were legit as though they were some sort of jerk or coward. Joe didn't like that. Something about this man made him nervous. Joe couldn't figure him out, and he hardly ever agreed with what he said.

"Ya know, kid," Sally said, "one t'ing dat troubles me in dis story. Dis guy Barone. I t'ink maybe we should fix 'im so he neva plays football again. I'll get his legs busted up so bad he won't even walk again—f'get football. Dis Italian stooly, *sfacime*."

Joe put his hand on his forehead and pushed his hair back. ''No, Sally. God no! These Italians from the Midwest, they ain't like us. They're different. I met this guy, Dickie Orlan. He's a pig from someplace in West Virginia. Wears overalls, chews tobacco, spits. A *preemordina* hillbilly. Ya know, d' guy's Italian. Name's really Orlando. Barone's kinda like that. Until Notre Dame found him, his life's ambition was to own a bar in Benton Harbor, Michigan. He doesn' know he did anything wrong. He doesn' understand. Believe me. Football's his only real hope in life. He's a nice guy. See? These people aren't Eetalians. They aren't even Italians. They're Eyetalians.''

''Especially the priest, I bet,'' Gallo growled.

''Especially the priest,'' Joe admitted

The men exchanged looks. If they didn't quite understand, they were plainly impressed with Joe's plea. Joey Gallo looked at his watch and stood up.

''Take carea y'self, kid.''

Sally watched Gallo leave. When he was out of sight, Sally leaned over and put his arm around Joe's shoulder.

''He's right. He is gettin' big. Too bad he ain't gettin' smart. Stay away from him, Joey. He could be a dead man. *Capeesh*?''

Joe understood, all right. His instincts were sharpening. He didn't plan to be seeing much of Joey Gallo.

Sally asked, ''Ya need some money?''

''Sure.''

''I want ya t' bet Tennessee against Kentucky t'night.''

''Sally, I think they're playin' at Kentucky. Nobody beats them at home.''

''Put all the money ya could beg, borra or steal on it, Joey. Take th' points an' bet on Tennessee. Don't tell anybody. Dis is a special present f' you.''

He shook hands with Joe and Ace and left.

Ace, who'd been sitting with his chin resting on his thumb, changed the subject.

''So, ya gonna do a little time. Okay. Monday you come here. Help Jean. Ya make some meatball san'wiches, wash a few glasses, an' when ya start feelin' sorry f' y'self, kid, ya tinka Cosimo Roselli. Eight to ten. Dannemora. He's a stand-up guy. When he gets out, he'll neva hafta worry about nuthin again. We'll take good carea him.''

''Dannemora? Christ! He's so sickly, ya mean *if* he gets out.''

Ace threw up his hand, turned his head and closed his eyes. Joe understood. Whatever God wants!

He also understood that, in Ace's mind, he and Cosimo were two of a kind. Just two stand-up neighborhood guys.

But he and Cosimo were not even close. And if it took him his whole life, he'd prove it to the neighborhood and to Notre Dame and to the whole fuckin' world.

CHAPTER 6

AT HOME he found his father reading *Il Progresso*.

"Pop! Ya gotta loan me fifty dollas. I wanna bet Tennessee-Kentucky."

"*Fidende*! I killa ya. Whattaya talkin' about? I wouldn't loana ya one penny. You a college boy. Is disa whatta I'm spendin' alla disa money for?"

"Look, Pop. This isn't gambling. The game's been fixed. I'll win the money to pay for some of the books."

"F'geta d' books. I pay f' d' books. Den deesa fuckin' priests leava you alone. But I get 'em. Donchu worry. Ya know dose ugly little nuns wita no teeth who come to ma store every day? Dey come for fruita. For d' poor people, dey say. Dey want cherries an' peaches *in January*."

He held out his right arm and smacked the inside of his elbow with his left hand.

"*Ma k*. From now on, I give dem *cipólle*. F'get about disa bettin'."

■ ■ ■

HIS BROTHERS arrived for Sunday dinner. His mother had summoned them to discuss the family crisis. Joe put down the paper and came down to say hello. Tennessee had won outright.

"What are you going to do till June?" Jerry asked.

"I'm gonna be a short-order cook at Jean's."

"Whattaya talkin' about? Go work for Dad at the market an' stay away from those misfits."

"I don't wanna do that. Then Dad's gotta explain to 'is customers what I'm doin' there. No. I'll work at Jean's."

"Joseph, why do you have to work anywhere?" Frank asked. "Go up to Columbia. Take some courses. You can always transfer them to Notre Dame. To tell you the truth, I don't know why the hell you'd even go back," he said with disgust. "I told you a long time ago, you should be at Harvard. I don't know why you turned them down, but you should re-apply."

"I'll look into Columbia. That's a good idea," he answered, neatly sidestepping the subject of Harvard.

■ ■ ■

TIME PASSED quickly. Jean's was the center of more activity than Joe had ever realized. Mafia chieftains were in and out all day long. Joe served coffee, took orders and watched the waltz of the Dons. The same men, three or four times a day, would greet each other, shake hands, ask after each other's wives and children—as though changes of monumental consequence could have taken place in the two hours since they last met.

Every day a fellow who worked next door at Lou's came in for lunch. He looked familiar, but Joe was unable to make a connection. One day he asked Jean.

"That's Tommy the Champ. He just got outa Sing Sing. Was boxing champ dere. Dat's how 'e got 'is name."

"What'd 'e go up for?"

"Burglary. Broke inta Dr. Biaggi's house. Stay away from him, Joey. He's *disgraziata!* Crime against an Italian —*Madonna!*"

STREET FIGHTS

■ ■ ■

ONE AFTERNOON at Jean's, Joe was watching a couple of the local *chimbrones* trying to decide who to vote for in the city's most popular annual beauty contest, "Miss Rheingold 1959."

"How come dese broads is always Irish or German?"

"How couldja say dat? Look, dere's an Italian girl. Rossi."

"Oh yeah. I gonna vote f' huh."

"Shmuck! She ain't gotta chance. Dere's a Jewish broad. Alla Jews'll vote f' huh, Italians'll vote f' da ones wit da biggest cannons, an' some Irish bitch'll win, as usual."

Suddenly, the boss from Marine Park, Jimmy Flynn, stormed into Jean's and headed for the back where about fifteen heavyweights were holding a meeting. With the door wide open, he started yelling at the lot of them at the top of his lungs.

"I want you fuckin' Wops t' stay outa Marine Park. Dat's my territory an' I don't want no Guineas dere. Ya unnastan'?" he screamed. He went on in that intransigent way for what seemed like ten minutes.

Finally, Flynn turned and started to walk out. One of the men got up, pulled out a .38 and shot him three times in the back. Frankie Scarpatto, who'd been on watch with Bobby Balducci, got up, grabbed Flynn by the hair and pulled him out into the middle of Avenue U.

Passing cars and buses narrowly avoided running over the bleeding body lying face down on the Avenue. No one dared stop to help. Flynn's own "wheel man" had taken off.

In five minutes the street was infested with cops. Cops everywhere. But nobody had seen anything. Crossing Avenue U was very dangerous. It was important to look both ways. How did he get three bullet holes in his back? He must have had an accident with his gun. Probably shot himself.

Somehow, Flynn survived.

■ ■ ■

TWO DAYS later, Ace came into Jean's like a wild man. He seized Joe by the shirt and pulled him out onto the sidewalk.

"I know what you did, you cocksucker! Get the fuck off the street! If I see your face, I'll kill ya! If I eva wanna see ya again, I'll letcha know. Unnastan'?"

Joe was in shock. "Ace! What th' . . . ?"

"Shut up, you bum! Get outa my sight! Ya hear?"

Joe ran home as fast as he could. His heart was racing. What the fuck was going on? He hadn't done anything. He knew enough to be afraid, and he stayed close to home.

■ ■ ■

ALMOST A week later, Raymo came to the house. It was the first time he had ever rung the front doorbell at 351 Avenue T.

"Ya gotta coupla hours, Joey? I'd like t' take ya t' see a friend a mine."

Joe was very wary. "Who?"

"His name's Frankie Amendola. Lives in Garden City, Long Islan'. His son Angelo got accepted t' Notre Dame an' Holy Cross. He can't decide where t' go. Frankie wants 'im at Notre Dame. I thought maybe you could talk to 'im."

Joe didn't answer. He stood there studying Raymo, not knowing what to think. He trusted Raymo. He'd always been his friend. But then so had Ace.

"By the way, Ace says t' come back t' work t'morra."

"What's goin' on, Raymo?"

"The FBI swept the street clean yestaday. We all knew da bust was goin' down an' hadda get ya da fuck outa dere. Ace got d' assignment. So whattaya say, will ya talk t' my friend?"

Joe managed to hide his relief. "Sure."

"I gotta make a stop first at West 12th Street," said Raymo. "Get in the car and we'll be on our way."

As Raymo proceeded west off Ocean Parkway, Joe looked at his watch and the odometer. *I'm finally gonna figure out just how big this world of mine really is.* Two lights, four minutes, eighteen seconds, and eight-tenths of a mile later, the baby-blue Cadillac crossed West 10th Street and Avenue U.

In another fifty minutes, Raymo's car stopped at the gate of an estate surrounded by an eight-foot wall. All Raymo had talked about during the entire drive was the "heat" in the neighborhood caused, mainly, by "dat fuckin' hayseed from Arkansas." Senator John McClellan's Senate Select Committee on Improper Activities in the Labor or Management Field was in high gear.

Two men not looking much like typical suburban security guards walked up to the car.

"Raymond D'Allesandro. Mr. Amendola's expectin' us."

The men nodded and opened the gate. When Raymo and Joe arrived at the house, they were admitted immediately and were led into a lavish living room, decorated to satisfy the taste of any "Early Italian" wife. Pastel satin covered the Louis XIV chairs, and plastic covered the satin. A surprisingly young man, dressed in a brocade smoking jacket, shook hands with Raymo and turned to Joe.

"Call me *Doncheech*. Angelo does."

Sitting on a hassock and looking very Ivy League was a boy about Joe's size, legs spread, his clasped hands dangling between his knees. He got up to greet them.

Angelo got them all drinks while a maid came in with a huge platter of Italian cold cuts and a basket of fresh bread.

"Eat!" Frankie Amendola ordered. "It's good. Dey deliva it special t' me from Little Italy."

The two men sat quietly as Joe answered all of Angelo's questions and added a few spontaneous observations. Suddenly he missed Notre Dame. Until these months of working at Jean's, he'd never truly realized the extent of the savagery in his neighborhood. During the drive with Raymo to Garden City he'd focused sharply on the size of his universe. He didn't want to live their way. Maybe he wouldn't go back to Notre Dame, but he couldn't stay home much longer, either.

Finally, it was time to leave.

"I'm awfully glad you came, Joey. Ya helped me decide. Where can I find ya when I get there?"

"Well, I don' know, Angelo. I'm not a hundred percent positive I'm goin' back. My father wants me to. My brother doesn't. I'm torn."

Raymo looked at Joe, making no move to go. They sat and read each other, while Angelo and his father watched the silent exchange.

Joe broke away first. He concentrated on the ice in his glass as he swirled it around, totting up the vig he'd just been assessed, imprinting yet another lesson on his soul. "Angelo, how 'bout if I call you when I get my dorm assignment?"

Raymo stood and walked to the door.

BOOK
V

THE MEN FROM THE BOYS

PHOENIX 1976–1977

CHAPTER

1

JOE DID know a lot about negative repercussions early on. But he was mistaken, back in his Notre Dame days, to think he knew all there was to know.

He hadn't known the half of it.

■ ■ ■

AT TWO-TWENTY a.m., on May 25, 1976, Joseph Tomaso Corelli died in St. Joseph's Hospital, Phoenix, Arizona. The official cause of death was a heart attack following a stroke complicated by diabetes.

■ ■ ■

JOE WAS standing off by himself. He'd come early, to make sure that Joyce and the girls were satisfied with the arrangements he'd made—and because he didn't know what else to do with himself.

He needn't have worried about how Tom O'Rourke would lay out Uncle Joe. O'Rourke's might not bury as many Italians as Sabbatino and Sons on Avenue U, but they knew how to do it with class. Joe particularly liked the way the floral arrangements were displayed, less like trophies and more like the loving tributes they were. His own red roses looked very nice. If one red rose is for love, he thought, what are six dozen red roses? *Redundant*. He didn't smile. He wished there *were* a way to show how much he had loved Uncle Joe, beyond making every single arrangement so Joyce wouldn't have to lift a finger to make a single call. He could have done all that out of duty or respect—and he felt those—but that pain in his mid-section wasn't from duty or respect. Uncle Joe's hotheadedness, his tantrums—nothing touched how loving he had been to Joe. If Joe thought of his cousin as an uncle, Uncle Joe treated him like a son. He hoped that when Uncle Joe had needed him most, he'd found him a good son.

Before the unanswerable question got to his tear ducts, Joe forced his attention to the people who had come to pay their respects to Joseph T. Corelli. Uncle Joe had been an important man in town for a long time, and Joe expected a crowd, but half of Maricopa County seemed to have come. The room, O'Rourke's biggest, was jammed. Sizing up the situation, people didn't stay very long; but others kept arriving, so that now, at nearly nine o'clock, the crowd had not begun to thin out. Angela had come almost as early as he, but was keeping away from Joe. Actually, everyone was leaving Joe alone. If he were they, he would, too. He knew what a look his face could get when things weighed on him.

Joe was grateful that Uncle Joe would be waked for only this one evening, not three, like back in Brooklyn. This was much more civilized. It had to be easier on Joyce and Uncle Joe's daughters. In Phoenix, Joe thought, Catholics were almost as sane about death as the Jews, who got a man into the ground before the sun set on the day after he died. Sane, and smart. Only after a man was buried could you even begin to distance yourself from the pain of knowing he hadn't just left the room for a minute. That, in Uncle Joe's case, he wasn't just off table-hopping. He was gone.

Angela, wearing a cream silk suit, passed by without turning her head in his direction. If he'd seen her before she left the house, he'd have told her to change. To wear black. But it looked as if, finally, the Italians had met Angela more than half-way—more than she'd ever been willing to meet them. Because none of the women here was wearing black, the Italians no more than any of the other Phoenicians. Even Joyce was wearing a navy-blue dress. Where, oh where, was it written that a widow had to wear black, not only right after her husband died, but forever after? Here, in what Joe still thought of as God's country, they'd torn that page out of the book. Sometimes, Joe thought, tearing a page out of a book has only salutary effects.

Joe watched them, the men in their lightweight woolens and the women in their pastel suits, as they came in, stopped for a minute at the coffin—Catholics kneeling, others merely bowing their heads—and then went over to Joyce to take her hand and say a few words to which she would nod graciously. After, they'd congregate in small clusters, talking quietly. You didn't hear any jokes or laughter; but neither was there any of the wailing that went on during the wakes of his childhood. *It doesn't mean that no one here is crying inside for you, Uncle Joe.*

Joe checked his watch. He still had time to call the country club to make sure everything was in place for the lunch tomorrow after the funeral. Having the lunch at the club, Uncle Joe's turf, was Joe's idea, and would be on his tab. Uncle Joe deserved one last good bash in his honor.

What difference did any of it make? Dead was dead. Joe swiveled his head so no one could watch *him*. Uncle Joe had been sick, sure; but he'd have fought all that off. What he couldn't fight off any longer were the cancerous lies and half-truths. They had eaten away and eaten away at him, until there wasn't enough of Uncle Joe left to live. Joe felt a shard of pain in his chest. Damn Barnes! Damn all the fuckin' snoops!

"Mr. Corelli? Mr. Joe Corelli?"

Joe raised his head. Too high. He looked down at the man in front of him, who seemed as thin as he was short. But his suit fit perfectly. Not off the rack, Joe registered. *The things you notice.*

"Yes, I'm Joe Corelli," he said. *Not the best Joe Corelli, but the only one available.*

''Excuse me for intruding on you in your hour of grief,'' the man said.

''That's all right,'' Joe said. ''Is there something I can do for you?''

The man shook his head. ''I thought I recognized you—I saw you a couple times, years ago. You looked so sad, I had to come over.''

Joe regarded this stranger coolly. Now he *was* intruding.

''No,'' the man said, reading his face. ''I didn't come over because I thought I could make you feel better. But, you see, I feel the same as you—forgive me, maybe not exactly, because I was no relation to Mr. Corelli. But in my heart, I feel such a sadness . . . I had to be for a moment with someone who knew what a man has died.''

There was a dignity about the old man. Why couldn't Joe place him? ''How did you know my uncle?'' he asked.

''Oh, from way back. Years ago, I was a bartender in one of Mr. Corelli's restaurants.''

Bartenders don't wear custom-made suits. He didn't say a word, but the man had his attention now.

''My wife, she gave birth to a little girl with terrible problems—her heart didn't work right. The doctors said her only chance was to have operations—they didn't say how many, but I understood *many*. The way my wife looked at me from her hospital bed—begging me to help—I thought I was going to die from shame. Mr. Corelli, he heard about what happened to us from the manager, and he came in person to talk to me. He asked me if I had any savings. I didn't earn much, but my wife and I were careful people. I had $2,235 saved. 'Good,' he says. 'Give me two thousand. I'll invest it for you in a good land deal.' I only stared at him. Invest it! The baby needed operations *now*. 'Don't worry,' Mr. Corelli said. 'I will call the hospital and tell the doctors to send the bill to me for whatever your little girl needs.' 'But I'll never be able to repay you,' I said. 'You're wrong,' he told me. 'In a year, eighteen months at most, you'll be able to repay me every cent.' And he was right. In one year, my $2,000 became $12,000!''

''And your little girl? Was she all right?''

''Yeah,'' the man smiled. ''My 'little girl' is a college professor now. In three months she'll be giving me my first grandchild. I think I know what his name will be.''

Joe was having a hard time swallowing. ''What if it's a girl?'' he managed.

The man shrugged. ''A girl is good, too. What's the matter with Josephine?''

''Nothing,'' Joe said. ''It's a very nice name.''

The custom-made suit still intrigued Joe. ''Tell me,'' he said. ''When my uncle sold the restaurants, what did you do then?''

''Oh, I left before.'' He was trying not to show his pride, but he'd just grown from five-three to five-five in ten seconds. ''Mr. Corelli was a saint, what he did for us. But he was a *smart* saint. And when my little girl was better, I thought a lot about what a smart man could do around Phoenix with a little money. I saved very hard, and when I had enough, I began to buy some land on my own. And I had a knack for what land to buy. Now, I am an apartment-house developer. As fast as I can put them up, people want to move in. Or I sell them to other investors. This is still a boomtown, you know.''

''Yeah,'' Joe said. ''I know. Thanks for coming over to me.''

''I tell you,'' the man whispered. ''Thanks to Mr. Corelli, the help he gave me, the start he gave me, I'm a very happy man today. Except *today,*'' he said. ''Today, inside, my heart is sighing.''

Suddenly, Joe thought he undertood. ''Listen,'' he said, ''helping you gave my uncle pleasure. I know that. Seeing your little girl get the care she needed—that's all he needed.''

The man put his index finger in front of his own mouth, but Joe got the message and shut up. ''Mr. Joe Corelli, I was able to thank your uncle. Many, many times I thanked him. When his daughters got married, I gave them beautiful gifts. He danced at *my* daughter's wedding. My heart hurts because I will miss him. The earth will miss him.''

This time, Joe knew enough to keep his mouth shut. So it was only to himself that he said, Wrong. The earth will have him.

Impulsively, Joe pulled the little man toward his chest, and held him for a moment, very tightly.

CHAPTER

2

ONCE AGAIN, Joe thought he had lived through the worst that could happen.

And, again, he was wrong.

■ ■ ■

''WELL, I can see I didn't have to worry about bringing this along today.''

The familiar voice brought Harry back to the present, as he looked up at his boyhood friend. ''Do you look older today, or do I just feel older?''

''Could be both.'' Bob Goldwater dropped the morning paper on an empty chair and settled himself across the table from his companion.

''My guess is plenty of folks in this town are going to get a whole lot older before this is over.'' Harry Rosenzweig folded the paper he had been staring at blankly and put it down next to the other one.

''You think the son of a bitch will make it?''

''Don't know. According to the paper, things aren't looking so hot.''

''Good afternoon, gentlemen, can I get you something from the bar today?''

''An extra-dry martini on the rocks. How 'bout you, Bob?''

''The same, please.''

A man from the other side of the dining room signaled the two of them to join him.

''Think I'll go say hello to Vic. Want to come?''

''No, you go. I'm not feeling up to socializing today.''

Harry watched Bob walk away. He couldn't remember the last time he had felt so melancholy. He just couldn't shake the feeling of dread. The dining room, glassed in on the north and east sides, offered a magnificent view of the meticulously manicured golf course. Lush lawns were framed by a variety of trees—fan palms, date palms, banana palms, olive and fig trees, oak, cottonwood and pine. Across the golf course and over the treetops loomed the mountain peaks that formed the northern end of the Valley. Harry was sure no place on earth could be more beautiful.

''Were you waiting for me, Harry, or hadn't you noticed our drinks are here?''

''Look out there, Bob. Would you believe we're in the middle of the desert? Can you believe that this is the same town we grew up in?''

Bob Goldwater studied his old friend. He and Harry were not as close as Barry and Harry. Although they were both nearing seventy, Harry was the older—closer to Barry's age—and today he looked as if he'd earned every one of the snow-white hairs that covered his head. Bob couldn't hide a worried frown as he said, ''I hate to see you let this thing get you down so bad, Harry. I called Barry this morning and read the article to him. You know what he said, don't you?''

''Yeah, I know. He said, 'Ah, what the hell!' But you know, after what happened to him in '64, nothing bothers him anymore. But it sure as hell galls me. It bothers me for him, and for you, and for me, and our kids, and our wives, and our friends, and everybody around us that this'll rub off on. I'll never get used to getting up in the morning and reading this.''

He picked up the paper and recited between gritted teeth:

> The conspiracy to assassinate Barnes began last week when he received a telephone call from a man who told Barnes about information relating to a land deal allegedly involving Sen. Barry Goldwater, R-Ariz., and Harry Rosenzweig, former GOP State Chairman and lifelong friend of Goldwater.

"Whether the guy lives or dies, unless they find out real fast and without a doubt just who put the bomb in his car, we're all gonna go through another 'Hidden Cancer.'"

"Now, Harry, you'd better settle down. You're getting all red in the face. Nobody ever took that newspaper series seriously."

"I know that, but it caused a lot of us a lot of personal misery until all the articles finally appeared. Even then, look how they affected so many of our kids. This guy lives or he dies, the paper's already laying the groundwork for his canonization. Bob, listen to this! A direct quote from the publisher:

> This terrible, unprovoked, criminal attempt on the life of a reporter, a fine citizen and a trustworthy, courageous newsman, cannot—in a civilized city—go unpunished.

"Of course this has to be punished! But was he a fine citizen? Was this guy courageous and trustworthy? Everyone knows that his days with the paper were numbered. But this horrible episode'll give the paper an excuse—as if Perkins's wife needed one—to drag every prominent figure in the community through the mud!"

"I'm not going to disagree with you, Harry, because you're 100 percent right. But we'll come through this just like we did before. The press'll do its guilt-by-association routine. It'll come to its usual unfounded conclusions. We'll be the subject of gossip for a while, and we'll have to sit still for a whole lot of crap. But in the end there's nothing to expose, nothing to prove, and it'll all go away."

"But what'll we go through in the meanwhile? I don't have the energy for this anymore. Shit, I feel like I'm in mourning."

"Mourning for what?"

"For Phoenix. For the world we grew up in. For the town where people didn't have keys to their front doors. For a world where men judged each other by their personal experience and not what someone else said—or imagined. For our childhood. Because I'd rather be eight and sitting with you and Barry in our cave, than be here."

"Gentlemen, are you ready to order?"

"How we doing on time?"

"Fine, Bob. It's only one-twenty. I think I could use a cup of coffee before we go. Can you imagine what it would have done to your dad if he had seen today's paper?"

"I guess it might have killed him. Your family was a bit more straightlaced than mine, but my dad wouldn't have been too happy, either. You don't think the Valley Bank gave me a seat on the Board when I finished college because I was such a knockout banker, do you? Nah, it was out of respect for my dad. As they said at the time, there might not have been a bank if it weren't for old Baron. Believe me, Harry, it's a good thing none of our folks lived to see these slanders."

"Harry, Bob. You guys look like you're here for the duration. Haven't forgotten the Goldcor board meeting, have you?"

"Hi there, Joe. Nah, we're coming. Bob and I were just talking about today's paper and all the insinuations that are being made about who's responsible for what happened to Barnes yesterday."

"You know, guys, I was with Uncle Joe the day before he died—only a couple of weeks ago—and he still couldn't forget 'The Hidden Cancer.' When he finished talkin' about it, he grabbed my arm and winked—like we'd finally come out of it clean. And then this comes down. I almost thank God he's gone."

The men looked suddenly uncomfortable.

"I was tellin' Bob how sick I got when I saw the article."

"Harry, that's because you're not Italian. When you grow up Italian you learn to expect the press to have knee-jerk reactions. After all, only the Mafia can plant a bomb in a car, right? You just watch. If they don't nail this fucker soon, everybody whose name ends in a vowel will be suspect!"

Harry looked up at the young man in astonishment. "You mean you get used to this?"

"I didn' say ya get used to it. You just learn to read the handwriting on the wall. If your *paisans* in Europe had developed that instinct, they wouldn't have turned up in Nazi living rooms disguised as lampshades. Take my word for it, gentlemen, the light at the end of this tunnel could very well be on a runaway train."

CHAPTER

3

JOE NEVER understood how so many of his friends could manage to read the morning paper from one end to the other before heading out to the office. When his alarm went off, he'd grab a cup of coffee, take it to the bathroom and drink it while he showered, shaved and dressed. Then he'd head for his car.

This morning was no different. Besides, yesterday's news had been so big that he couldn't imagine the paper coming up with anything as searing today.

But when he got to his office, one look at the front page set him straight. Starkly outlined, leaping off the page, was:

THE VALLEY HERALD
Phoenix, Arizona, Wednesday June 18, 1976

WE SHALL NOT FORGET

Dan Barnes is dead. But his spirit and devotion to ferreting out the truth will live on.

The Valley Herald cannot let the death of a man like Dan Barnes go unavenged. We make no attempt to hide our outrage. We shall stop at nothing to see that those responsible for this terrible crime are brought to justice.

Let all civilized members of our community join together to eliminate the cancer in our midst.

Dan Barnes cannot have died for nothing. We shall not forget!

—Arla Perkins

Alongside was a picture of a flagpole with the flag at half-mast and an article headlined "Governor Orders Flags at Half-Mast." The story ended with a quote from Barnes's minister: "That is the least we can do for this reporter. Perhaps the action will make people think of the situation around us."

With his death, Barnes's dirty dream of journalistic stardom had become a reality. Joe had seen enough. He threw the paper on his worktable and hit the intercom to his secretary. "Jan, will you bring me a cup of coffee?"

Jamming his hands in his pockets, he started to pace his office. Glassed in on both the north and east sides, it offered a panoramic view of the airport as well as the recently built Hyatt Regency Hotel. There were times when incoming planes seemed so close to the building that he thanked God for Phoenix's fog-free climate. Angela had given him a telescope as an office-warming present. He had thought to ask her if her intention was to enhance his view of the bathing beauties around the Hyatt pool, but for once he'd bitten his tongue.

Jan brought in the coffee, read his mood, and exited without a word. As he gulped the strong, hot liquid, Joe focused on the steady flow of arrivals and departures at the airport, and the rhythm began to steady his churning gut.

He was struck by how much the wild-west mentality still existed in Phoenix. The publisher of the only paper in town had used it to call for vengeance. Joe tried to imagine the publisher of the *New York Times* writing an article like that. The *Daily News,* maybe. The *Post,* probably. But in New York, if one newspaper took an extreme point of view, another paper, another publisher would be certain to take a divergent stance—precisely, in his opinion, the essence of the First Amendment.

As Joe contemplated just what it might mean for Arla Perkins to pursue her pound of flesh, his whole body suddenly shuddered. Damn that woman! She was not going to make him lose control.

Joe slammed down the cup so hard that the handle broke off in his hand. *Good start, Joe*. It was just as well he had a breakfast meeting with Herb Steinberg. With Herb, he could get this poison out of his system. By the time he got back, he'd be in better shape to do some work.

■ ■ ■

''I'LL SEND the waiter right over with some coffee for you, Mr. Corelli,'' the maitre d' said, holding out the menu.

''Thank you. Well, good morning, Herb,'' Joe said, managing a smile. ''You look like you're surviving the summer.''

Herb was smoking his inevitable stogie. He was never without the fattest cigars Joe had ever seen, either stuck in the corner of his mouth or grasped between his knockwurst-like fingers. Herb called himself ''A Great Man.'' Modesty prevented him from calling himself ''*The* Great Man.'' Promoting his image as the terror of the legal community, Herb hoped that the mere sound of his name would strike panic in the hearts of all who discovered him on the other side of a dispute. But ten minutes with an astute appraiser of human nature and the jig was up. Under his rough carapace, Herb was a gentle man. Still, when his passions were aroused, he could be genuinely fierce, and nothing aroused him more than a duel with Mr. Perkins's paper.

After the men had ordered, Herb came directly to the point. ''Have you ever heard of the IRG?'' he asked.

''Sure you don't mean the IRS?''

Herb didn't smile. ''Investigative Reporters Group.''

''Never heard of them. Should they interest me?''

''A few facts and then we'll move on to supposition. The initial meeting of the group was held in Charlottesville, Virginia, on February 22nd of this year. By April, they were incorporated as a non-profit corporation with more than 300 members from newspapers, radio and TV. Now, let's see if you can guess who one of their very first members was.''

''Barnes?''

''Bingo!'' Herb pulled the cigar out of his mouth.

"The first convention was scheduled for May 19th and 20th in Indianapolis, Indiana, home of the *Indianapolis Beacon,* the other Perkins paper. Polish up that crystal ball again, and see if you can tell me who couldn't afford the trip."

"Barnes."

"And what did the *Herald* say when he asked the paper to subsidize him?"

"No dice?"

"You're batting a thousand, kid. Just one more right answer and you win the jackpot. What would you imagine is being considered as the subject of the team's first investigation?"

Joe's hand began to tremble. He put down his cup, carefully. No spillage. *Good. Stay calm.* "The Barnes murder," he said dully.

Herb sat back in his chair, and worked his cigar while the waiter served their breakfast.

"Last week," Herb continued, "a member of the group, Bob Grogan, came to Phoenix to do a feasibility study. He spent most of his time with Peter Steele, the paper's city editor. For the record, Steele supports the idea with certain limitations. He refused to work with these out-of-town reporters on the Barnes death, only the broader issues of organized crime and corruption. He has to see this as an invasion of his turf."

"Then why cooperate? Anything like this ever been done before?"

"I doubt it. You're saying, if there's no precedent, why go along?"

"Exactly."

"Well, are you ready for this? Arla Perkins's granddaughter is one of the IRG founders. I can't say if someone pressured Steele directly, because I don't know. But it's clear that the paper made a decision to focus in on Barnes's condition during his last ten days—a public deathwatch orchestrated by the *Herald*. Every time Barnes had a limb amputated, regained consciousness, lapsed back into a coma—you name it—the paper was there.

God knows, I'm not trying to trivialize the tragedy, but you'd think nothing else was going on in the world.''

''No question the bombing has been good for the paper. The longer the story stays alive, the better for them.''

Herb turned his attention to his eggs. Joe pushed his own eggs around on the plate, took one bite of toast, and chewed over what Herb had told him. Ever since the bombing, the paper had been trying to make Barnes look like Woodward and Bernstein combined, instead of just another reporter covering the state legislature. It seemed to him that any cub could do what Barnes had been doing lately. Arla didn't even think he was worth a plane ticket to Indianapolis. Still, the more important they made Barnes look now, the bigger the story. What could be better than a bevy of reporters from all over the country, paid by someone else, to do what she'd have to pay her staff to do? In the end, if they did a good job, the *Herald* would get credit. If they didn't, the *Herald* could disassociate itself from the project. Hell, if he were in her shoes, he'd see this as manna from heaven!

Herb was looking at him. ''The picture's pretty clear,'' Joe said. ''You see me fitting into it somewhere, don't you, Herb? Those are worry lines marring your pristine forehead.''

''I have a hunch that Barnes's last words, 'Mafia, they finally got me,' coupled with the set-up message, 'Meet me at the Sunburst Hotel, I have information about Goldwater, et cetera,' plus all the attention Goldcor is getting these days in the paper about labor problems at the Marblehead Ranch would make the Goldwaters and Corellis prime subjects for this kind of investigation.''

''My hunch is your hunch is on the money. Thanks for the warning.''

"You haven't eaten anything," Herb said.

"Anyone ever tell you you're a Jewish mother?"

"You. A thousand times. Joe, you're going to need strength the next few weeks. Eat a little egg."

"Strength I have. What I need, Herb, is a little help and a lot of luck."

CHAPTER

4

Joe headed for the club, found the pro, and played the meanest racquetball he'd played in months.

When he got back to the office, the first thing he did was call Parker Northridge. Told he was in a meeting, Joe did some work, not failing to notice that he was able to concentrate on someone else's problem. He *was* in control.

Jan buzzed him to say that Parker was on the line.

''What's on your mind?'' Parker asked.

''Thanks for getting back to me so quickly. I had breakfast with Herb Steinberg this morning, and he told me a few things that I'd like to check out with you.'' As Frank Snell's protégé, Parker was in a position to know a lot about what was going on, but since Snell & Wilmer did work for the paper, would Parker talk?

''Sure. You know me, always happy to help.''

He'd know soon enough. ''Have you ever heard of a fellow named Bob Grogan? He's a reporter from out of town.''

''Not only have I heard *of* him, but *from* him.''

''According to Herb, he represents a bunch called the Investigative Reporters Group, which is considering sending a team of reporters to Phoenix to investigate the Barnes murder.''

''That's right. Grogan's from *Newsworld,* a paper in New York, and apparently he's won a pile of awards. However, it's not the murder they want to investigate. It's the 'climate' that interests them. Grogan struck a deal with Peter Steele. Barnes is the exclusive property of the *Herald,* but Steele turned over all their files on corruption, organized crime and the Barnes investigations to Grogan. Grogan fancies himself—and the team of what he estimates will be twenty to thirty reporters from all around the country—as an avenging angel. When you add that to Steele's mentality, we ought to have quite a donnybrook going on."

"What do you mean by Steele's mentality? I don't know anything about him except that Herb seemed to think he felt forced to cooperate."

"Well, journalists tend to be a jealous, competitive group, not known for a willingness to cooperate with each other. Steele looks at solving the Barnes murder with nothing less than missionary fervor. When he wants somebody, his reporters go out under orders to find something to 'nail the bastard.' I've never heard of a reporter coming back and saying, 'We've got the wrong guy.'"

"What about Grogan?"

"The group regards Grogan as the ultimate authority on investigative journalism. That's why they chose him to do the study and lead the pack. He wants the assignment. He thinks he's hit a gold mine here in Phoenix."

"How? What the hell do people in New York care about corruption in Phoenix?"

"Well, Joe, we do have some names with national appeal: the Goldwaters, Rosenzweig. The paper's convinced that they're the real power in the state, that they are behind the corruption, especially land fraud, and that they're protected by friends in high places, like Richard Kleindienst. Grogan believes that Barnes's 'Hidden Cancer' series is unplowed turf. I told him that Barnes had over-plowed, but he didn't buy it. Joe, I think all that ancient history is going to get recycled."

Joe's stomach started to imitate a cheap motorboat. All his hard work threatened again!

It was hard to talk without raising his voice. He made himself do it. "Well, what's your reaction to all this, Parker?"

"I think it's bad news. We're looking at people who don't know the state—its strengths or its weaknesses. They understand nothing of local issues, yet they think they have the right to air whatever they decide is our dirty linen. Who are they to judge us?"

"I'm afraid their credentials aren't going to be what people pay attention to," Joe said tightly. "I'd like us to keep in touch on this."

"By all means."

Joe could not concentrate on the work he'd been doing when Parker called. In fact, he couldn't concentrate, period. His gut was in an uproar, his head a shambles. He had to get out of there.

■ ■ ■

HEADED NORTH on the Black Canyon Freeway, his stomach began to unclench and his head started to function. Obviously, Grogan's being from New York was a lousy draw. Inevitably, Joe's name would come up. An experienced investigative reporter could easily uncover the fact that he'd come from a neighborhood Robert Kennedy had called the worst breeding ground for crime in the country. Kefauver, McClellan, Kennedy, the Valachi hearings and the Gallo-Profaci war had all produced a veritable directory: Who's Who on Avenue U. His friendship with Ace and Raymo, his family connection with Johnny Bono, Sundays at the Gravesend Social Club with Carlo Gambino, Joe Profaci and Tommy Cutrone, the letter Joey Gallo sent him after eight years in Green Haven, still trying to have his sentence overturned on the grounds that the publicity had denied him the right to a fair trial. Joey's sister Carmela had tracked down Joe's whereabouts. Joe had not forgotten that Joey had bailed him out when he was in trouble, without so much as a single question—and he had wanted to help Joey. But too much time had passed. Not even Louis Nizer could have sprung Joey from Green Haven. He hadn't been able to do a thing for Joey, but still they could say he represented criminals. They could say he came from a Mafia family, that he had been on the payroll. Why not? They'd done it to others on a lot less. Finally, he thought, after all these years, he and Joey Gallo had something in common: being beat up by the press.

Soaking wet from perspiration, he pulled off the highway at the next exit. Off to his right were a Shell station and a diner. Leaving his jacket and tie in the car, Joe opened up his collar, rolled up his sleeves, and went in for a cold drink.

He ordered himself not to exaggerate the problem or lose his perspective. But wait and see? No way. Not after the way "wait and see" had backfired on Uncle Joe.

CHAPTER

5

JOE FELT compelled to share his fears with his partners. Spencer was out of town, but Tom and Judd were both free for lunch on Friday.

Although they were temperamentally very different, all three had come from hard-working, middle-class families. Everything they had they had broken their backs for. That was why Joe believed both men would feel as threatened by the proposed IRG investigation as he did.

With time at a premium, Joe didn't wait to order before relating his conversations with Herb and Parker.

''I'm not sure that you should worry about this,'' Judd suggested mildly when Joe finished.

So what was new? Judd never worried about anything. He always expected things to work out, and somehow, at least for him, they did.

''What about you, Tom? I remember 'The Hidden Cancer' series made you pretty nervous. Are we ready to face that again?''

Tom cleared his throat. ''Well, I don't think nervous is an accurate characterization of my response. I felt that bad publicity could be harmful to the firm, and I wanted to be sure we monitored the community's reaction carefully, but I wouldn't say I was nervous.''

"Okay. I used the wrong word. But gimme a break! Would it be fair to say we shared a common concern?"

"Yes, that would be fair."

"All right. Do we share a common concern now?"

Tom shifted his weight in his chair. He was uncomfortable, and Joe knew it. His body language was the prelude to an equivocation. Joe had miscalculated; they didn't see this the way he did at all. Dammit, he should have known. Why didn't he ever learn his lesson? Tilting at windmills isn't a team sport.

"I'm always concerned about our reputation," Tom was saying. "I don't have to tell you that. But I think it is a bit premature to conclude that it's at risk. I think you'll acknowledge that Herb has a certain prejudice against the paper. Not that it isn't warranted, mind you, but his attitude does color his outlook. I realize that we also have Parker's input, but whenever I've approached him for information, I've had the feeling that I was pandering to his self-importance. I'm not implying that he was in any way dishonest, but there is a side of him that enjoys supplicants at his feet, so he's likely to exaggerate the significance of what he says. That's why I feel it's important not to overreact."

"Tom, Dan Barnes was only one man, but 'The Hidden Cancer' had all the righteous of Phoenix out hurling rocks through Goldcor's windows. You got a short memory? Do you remember Barnes justifying the bombing of Joe Bonanno's patio by reporters and FBI agents on the ground they were frustrated that Bonanno refused them an interview? Think what damage a whole horde of reporters could do."

"Now, Joe," Judd interjected. "Is there a horde? I can't imagine many papers investing in a wild goose chase. Most would rather let someone else do the work, and then, if the story's worthwhile, pick it up off the wire services."

"That's a good point," Tom agreed.

Joe sipped his wine and rotated the glass in his hands. How much of his private fears could he share with them? Tom grew up on the streets of Chicago; maybe he could understand the world Joe'd come from. But Judd'd never be able to relate. Judd grew up in Phoenix, went to Jesuit schools, married his high-school sweetheart, and had six all-American kids. His life was a script from a '50s movie. What would he know about hanging out with bookies, numbers runners, killers? Even Tom would have trouble relating to a world where a kid's ambition might be to become a world-class arsonist. Hell, even Angela, who had grown up in Brooklyn, didn't understand it. Maybe you really had to be from Avenue U.

"If the IRG decides to come, I'll exercise every option available to protect my privacy," Joe said calmly. "I'm not going to sit on my duff. This time around, I'm going to be prepared."

"What did you have in mind?" Judd asked. "I'll be happy to help you if I can."

"I agree with Judd. In fact, if you don't mind, I'd like to talk to Parker myself."

"Sure, Tom. But meanwhile I do have some ideas. For starters, I'd like the firm to stay loose for a while in terms of contingent-fee cases and pro bono work, because if the vultures descend, I'd like the firm's resources available."

"In what respect?" Tom asked.

Could he really be that puzzled, or was that face a warning sign? "In terms of legal and secretarial manpower." He kept his voice steady. "I wanna head these guys off. I may need some of the litigators. You know I don't know my way around the courts. That's what I mean," he added very quietly.

Judd and Tom exchanged glances. They recognized that quietness. In a moment, Joe would be shouting. The time for reasonable discussion had ended; the time to pacify him had arrived.

"Well, if a litigator is what you need, I'll try my best to be available," Judd assured him.

"The IRG meets next month. Is that right?" Tom inquired.

"Yep!"

"Okay. Well, we don't have long to wait. If you hear anything between now and then, be sure to let me know. Let us know." Tom gestured toward Judd, who nodded in agreement.

Joe nodded, too. But what he was seconding was a voice inside his head that said these guys were not about to go to the barricades with him.

Luckily, he'd eaten very little. He made it down the elevator and into his bathroom before he retched.

CHAPTER 6

IT WAS like when someone you cared a lot about was terminal. You slept less and dreamed more, but you still got up in the morning and went to work. Your daily existence wasn't all that different, really. Except that every time the phone rang, you wondered if this was it.

That was Joe's first thought when, a few weeks later, Parker Northridge called.

''Before I head over to Coronado for the rest of the month, I wanted to let you know that the IRG met. The board of directors approved the project and has allocated substantial monies to fund it.''

''What's substantial?''

''I don't know. Some contributions from private sources, but I haven't heard who or how much. I'll be in touch after Labor Day. Nothing will happen before then. No one in his right mind comes to Phoenix in August.''

''Thanks, Parker. Enjoy the cool air. Mail me back some, will ya?''

''Sure,'' he laughed.

Phoenix was like a ghost town in the summer when Joe had first moved here. By July fourth, the migration started. Phoenicians set out for Prescott and Flagstaff in the north or Payson in the White Mountains close to the New Mexico border, or, of course, California. But Phoenix was now so large, it seemed that all but a privileged few were in town all summer long.

Joe put his hands behind his head and rocked back and forth in his chair. After a while, he decided to check the morning paper.

As he scanned the reception area for the *Herald,* he chuckled, recalling how he and his partners had agonized over the decor. He lobbied for contemporary, Tom insisted on early American, and Spencer voted for classical stuffy. And so they went, back and forth, round and round, until someone suggested the "eclectic" look, which essentially meant that each of them could have a little of what he wanted. Tom got wing chairs. Joe got glass-topped tables with chrome legs. Spencer got heavy oak desks and brass spittoons, and they all got highly polished parquet floors with oriental rugs. The result was an unexpected smash hit.

"Say, there, Joe, did you see the referral that came in today from Cravath?" Spencer Winthrop's deep, well-oiled voice interrupted him.

"No. That's great. What's it about?"

"Come down to my office if you've got a minute. I'll show you the file."

He followed Spencer down the hall, shaking his head. Spencer sported the crushed Brooks Brothers look. His pants were held up by either old, cracked belts or bright red suspenders. Joe teased him about buying his ties in the gift shop at the Miami airport, but that was the extent of the jocularity that existed between them. Despite Spencer's efforts to appear boyishly disarming, there were too many times when he made Joe feel itchy.

The case was one involving massive securities fraud. Spencer had developed his expertise in securities law back when he was an associate with Casey & Stonemartin in New York. Cravath, Plimpton & Dodge, the source of the referral, had a Winthrop of its own, Spencer's father. In fact, Spencer came from a long line of attorneys. His grandfather, Spencer Winthrop I, had been the managing partner of Root, Ballantine & Harlan, just prior to the tenure of presidential candidate Thomas E. Dewey.

Not only was Spencer's legal lineage old and distinguished, he was also descended from New York's original Dutch settlers, a member of the "400." His wife, Melissa, was a von Buswirk, and on her mother's side, a Boston Brahmin. Imagine if the papers in those cities carried stories tying the closest thing in the American experience to "blue blood" to crime and violence in the Valley of the Sun!

"I must confess, I read through that several times and didn't find anything to smile about," Spencer said. "What did I miss?"

Joe hadn't realized that his sense of the ironic was showing, but Spencer was more right than he knew. The future for this sort of referral looked bleak.

The fact that the *Herald* had chosen to play down the IRG didn't mean that participating papers in other cities would follow suit. If this was a story elsewhere, he wanted to know about it.

He called Rocky Parlati. Joe had first met Rocky in New York during a business trip back East. The two of them had hit it off immediately. Rocky, tall, slim, dark and very good-looking, had grown up in south Philadelphia. A militant Italophile who had managed to work himself into a middle-management position with American Airlines, Rocky was meticulous to a fault about absolutely everything. Joe trusted him to search the local papers with a fine-tooth comb.

"Hey, Joe. Good to hear from you. Are you in town?"

"Kind of wish I were, but I'm calling because I need a favor, and if you think you can do it I'd be grateful."

"What is it? You know if I can, I will."

"I do, buddy. Here's the story."

Rocky listened quietly while his friend told him what was happening.

"Rocky, it would help me to anticipate what's going down if I knew how the investigation was being billed in these guys' home towns. The head honcho is a fellow named Bob Grogan from *Newsworld*. Do you think you could get your hands on that paper pretty readily?''

''Easy. I'll keep my eye out for the other papers, too. We shouldn't overlook magazines. Unfortunately, this is great feature material.''

''I owe you one.''

''No, you don't, Joe. This one's for me, too!''

■ ■ ■

AS THE summer wore on, Joe's attention became increasingly absorbed by what was turning out to be the biggest case of his career. Merging six large corporations with hundreds of subsidiaries and offshore holdings left him no time for his local clients. His life was being consumed by a project that was riddled with complex legal and financial issues and clients who weren't much help in understanding the maze. Telephone calls day and night. Unexpected weekend meetings. Countless intertwining business relationships for no apparent reason. Joe could not remember ever having a legal matter that made him feel so pressured or emotionally drained.

Any other time, he would have regretted taking this case. But no less-wild one would have accomplished what this one did: keep his mind off the impending IRG investigation for as much as fifteen minutes at a time.

CHAPTER

7

A FEW weeks later, Joe had a terse message from Rocky Parlati, asking him to call back as soon as possible.

"Your message sounded important. What's up?"

"I think it might be. Do you get the *New York Times*?"

"Only on Sunday."

"Well, today's paper carried a story with the headline '18 Reporters Begin Joint Inquiry Into Arizona Crime.' I'll send you the article. Are they there?"

"Not that I know of. You don't, by any chance, have the time to read it to me, do you?"

"Sure."

As Joe listened, he felt his body heating up. He yanked his tie loose and opened his shirt collar. Rocky finished reading.

A beat. "Joe?"

"I'm here." Amazing how normal his voice sounded. "Do me one more favor. I want to hear one paragraph again. Near the beginning. About the atmosphere here."

"'There is obviously an atmosphere in this state . . . ?"

"That's the one. The quote from Grogan."

Rocky read again:

> There is obviously an atmosphere in this state where some persons, or group of persons, felt the murder of a reporter was a reasonable and appropriate response to the work he was doing. . . .

"Presumptuous motherfucker!"

"Joe, don't let the bastard get to you this bad."

"I'm okay. Thanks for calling, Rocky."

Joe caught Herb on his way out the door.

"I've got just enough time for one quick question."

"I've only got one. Is the IRG in town?"

"Yup! Got in yesterday. They set up headquarters at the Adams. I've been planning to call you, but I'm working twenty hours a day instead of eighteen lately. Gotta go!"

As Joe replaced the phone, he stared at his white knuckles. He flexed his hand a few times to make the blood come back. There are days, he thought, when I wish I were the kind of guy who could waste a trouble-making scumbag like this.

CHAPTER 8

JOE HAD been sitting on the news that the IRG was in town. He was waiting to hear more. By Friday night he decided to go out and do a little investigating of his own. He headed over to Irv Wolfe's new place, The Polo Club.

Irv was seated on the bar stool closest to the door so he could eye everyone coming in. As soon as he saw Joe he got up to greet him.

"Hey, *paisan!* Where ya been? Haven't seen ya around lately," Irv exclaimed, smacking Joe on the back.

"How're ya doin', Irv? How's business?"

"Can't complain. Weeknights are still slow, but the weekends are crazy. Come sit down. I'll buy ya a drink. I'm feelin' generous t'night."

Irv, a soft-looking man with monochromatic coloring, loved Joe. Actually, he liked most Italians. His greatest disappointment in life was that he wasn't Italian.

"So what's the latest word around town, Irv? I've been too busy to socialize."

Irv shrugged. "Same old things."

"Any strangers in lately, asking questions?"

Irv laughed. "Whattaya talkin' about? What questions? About who? What?"

"Oh, I just thought ya mighta run into some of these reporters who've come to town because of the Barnes murder."

"I ain't heard nuthin about it."

"Benny Soleri hasn't said anything to you?"

"Benny? What would he know?"

"Well, I heard they set up their headquarters at the Adams. Benny mighta seen them in the dining room or in the bar."

"I ain't seen Benny for a month or so. Since I opened this place I ain't had a night off. Ya know how it is. Ya got a place like this, ya spend yer life in it. So, who are these reporters? Why're ya askin' about 'em?"

"Got a private table somewhere? I'll fill ya in."

"Sure. Follow me."

Joe told Irv just enough so sounding him out about Benny would fly.

"I first met Benny through my Uncle Joe, back when he was working at the Towne House. When Uncle Joe had a special occasion or was just in the mood for a good Italian dinner, he'd call Benny, tell him what he wanted, and Benny'd cook it for him. That's about all I know about him. But he used to work for you. Tell me, is he a stand-up guy? Good people? Can he be trusted with a job that takes a little finesse? Street smarts?"

"Oh, yeah! Benny's okay. Especially if he talks t' me first. He feels very strong about bein' Italian. He's worked hard for his family. He's got a son trying to get into the contractin' business. Who knows, with all the building Goldcor's doin' aroun' town, maybe you can help each other out. Ya know what I mean?"

"Sure. I read ya, Irv. So ya think ya can set up a meeting? At my place?"

Irv smiled benevolently. "No doubt about it. Benny'll do anything I ask him."

"Good. Let me know when. Not to change the subject, but who's that dynamite-looking broad at the corner table?"

■ ■ ■

AT EIGHT o'clock on Sunday morning, Irv and Benny arrived at Joe's house. Benny's job as maitre d' at the Adams Hotel's main dining room left him very little free time. Early morning, before his prep people came in, was best for him, because he also supervised the kitchen. The early hour, combined with Joe's reluctance to be seen in public with a man he hoped would be his spy, made Joe's house the ideal meeting place.

He met the men at the double oak doors and led them into the large, sunny living room. On the coffee table, they found coffee and fresh blueberry muffins. Joe seated himself in the club chair in front of the window, while Irv and Benny sat across from him on the couch.

"Have some breakfast. Angela made the muffins. They're not bad."

"They look good," Benny said. "How have ya been, Joe? Haven't seen ya in a while."

Benny had large features and square, powerful hands that made him look like an aging longshoreman instead of a gourmet chef.

"I know it sounds like an excuse, but I've been involved with a case that I sometimes think has me chasing my tail."

"All the more reason to come down to the Sandpainter and have a long, leisurely meal. Call me ahead, tell me what ya want and I'll cook it special, just like I useta for your uncle."

"Thanks. I'll do that. Right now, though, I need a different kind of favor. Did Irv fill you in at all?"

"He did, but he didn't tell me how you think I can help."

"All I need is you to keep your eyes and ears open. Who are these guys? What do you hear them talking about? What are their habits? Tastes? Who drinks too much and shoots his mouth off? The *New York Times* says there's a gal in the group—same thing for her. In short, I need some warning if they're snooping around something that will lead them to me or my people. I'm absolutely determined to keep our names out of the paper, and in order to do that, I have to see it coming. I can't stress enough the need to keep this among the three of us. If they think you can't be trusted, they'll either clam up or feed you dummy information. What do you say? Game?''

''Count me in. I'm raisin' kids in this town. They need a good reputation. I remember when that son of a bitch Barnes did 'The Hidden Cancer.' You'd think being an Italian bartender or restaurateur was proof of Mafia connections. That poor bastard Sally Fillippi, then Joey Corso. What the fuck did those guys do? Hell, I'm as guilty as they are of 'dealing' with criminals. How the fuck do I know what the people I serve dinner to do for a living? What's more, why should I care? They behave, pay the bill. I have to know something else?''

''Right on, Benny! I told Joe you were a clear thinker.''

''Look, Joe, thanks for breakfast. Tell your wife the muffins were delicious. Meanwhile, you can rely on me to find out whatever I can. I gotta get goin' before those *chooches* come in and fuck up my kitchen. Ya just can't get good help anymore.'' The two men shook hands.

''Listen, Benny,'' Irv explained, as they walked to the door. ''I'm gonna tell ya how we did things like this back in d' ole days in Chicago.''

Joe shook his head and laughed. Irv Wolfe, the world's most unlikely tough guy.

CHAPTER 9

BY THE end of September, Benny Soleri had provided some feedback. The IRG was making its intentions clear to a lot of people in the community. The reporters were extremely interested in anything or anyone connected with the Goldwaters. Breakfast, lunch and dinner, Goldwater, Goldcor, Marblehead Ranch and Embassy Corporation dominated the conversations. They were also looking at the big boys like The Valley National Bank and the Del Webb Corporation. Meanwhile, Joe had calls from Don Perrino, Herb Steinberg, Parker Northridge, Phil Evans, Larry Clouse and Judge Paul Lorano. All of them, or their clients, had heard from someone representing the IRG. The impression was unanimous: "The Hidden Cancer" was their springboard. They were questioning everyone about Joe's Uncle Joe, Vito Garbi, Mel Adelbaum, Don and everything and everyone that Barnes talked about. How thin the facts in those articles were didn't seem to deter them a bit.

With each succeeding piece of information, Joe's anxiety level mounted. He needed desperately to talk about all this with someone who could identify with his feelings. Ashley would listen, but she couldn't really help. Immediately Steve Ankewitz came to mind. Joe called over to the Big A Construction Company to see if Steve was free to go out and blow off some steam with him. He was.

He always was. Steve was a friend for all seasons. If Joe wanted to party, Steve was available; if Joe needed to cry, Steve would bring the tissues; if Joe had to release tension, Steve would team up for racquetball.

They had met through Steve's father, Jerry. Jerry had a construction company in Los Angeles that was looking for fertile, new territory on which to build. Phoenix was made to order. He and Uncle Joe found each other at a time when the aging farmer had fancied himself a builder. One apartment complex later, Goldcor decided it needed a construction partner.

Shortly after a deal had been struck but before the legal documents were signed, Goldcor got a vastly more advantageous offer for the land from another buyer. To the never-ending amazement of the elder Ankewitz, Uncle Joe, who had more than a little of the old Calabrese ethic left in him, stood on his handshake. The deal, and the friendship, were sealed.

■ ■ ■

''COME ON, Joe, have another drink. If ya pass out, you can spend the night on the couch,'' Steve was saying.

''Okay, but make it light.''

''Hey, listen, call Angela. Tell her you're staying here—then it'll be decided. You can relax and not worry about having to drive.''

''No call! I don't wanna talk to her. She's no fuckin' help. If they did a front-page headline calling 4230 East Lincoln 'Corelli's Whorehouse,' the only thing that'd bother her would be that they had published our address! They could say anything they fuckin' pleased, and she wouldn't bat an eye. You can bust me if I can figure her out. To hell with her!''

''Sorry I even mentioned it.'' Steve retreated to the bar.

Handing Joe his fresh drink, Steve sat down on the coffee table and spoke soothingly. ''I know ya feel rotten, Joe. I can't say I've ever experienced any prejudice because I'm Jewish, but my dad has and I guess I've absorbed his feelings. Because I do take it personally when I hear about cases of anti-Semitism. Ya know? It gets to me. Hey! Why don't Italians start their own anti-defamation league?''

Joe took a long pull on his drink and shrugged. ''Maybe because we're so diverse. We just aren't a cohesive group.''

''Hell, neither are Jews.''

''Yeah, but in times of crisis Jews band together. With Italians, everyone outside the family is a potential enemy.''

''Even another Italian?''

''Right. They don't trust each other any more than they'd trust you.''

''Somebody's got to be in your corner,'' Steve said fervently.

''Funny, that's what I thought. Like my partners—my old buddies.'' Joe shook his head as if he still couldn't take it in. ''They listen politely enough if I corner them, but they aren't really interested. They humor me and hope the whole thing will go away without it taking any of their time and attention. It's the old ostrich approach.''

The two friends talked most of the night. By the time Joe fell asleep, he had resolved to have another meeting with Judd, Tom and Spencer.

■ ■ ■

JOE CALLED a dinner meeting. Although he wasn't eating much these days, he wanted to keep things friendly if he could. Equivocating about his position didn't figure into that, though.

He got to the restaurant a little early, so his third drink arrived with the others' second. Raising his glass, he said, ''I want to propose a toast,'' and waited until the others lifted their glasses. They looked apprehensive.

''Now this toast has three parts, so please try to contain yourselves until I finish,'' he said. ''First, to us, to CBP&W, long may we wave.''

Joe noticed that Tom, at least, relaxed slightly. ''Second, to my family, whom I intend to protect. Third, to Italian-Americans, whose reputation I mean to cleanse.''

They were tight-eyed. ''Gentlemen?'' He drank, and watched over the rim as slowly his partners each managed a sip of their drinks, no more.

Joe set his glass down. He kept his voice very low, so they wouldn't think he was leading up to a scene. ''And I would very much appreciate it if you three would work with me to see that all three parts of my toast come true. I think it's time to start looking at our legal options.''

''The only legal option that I can think of is prior restraint, and we've already discussed the impossibility of that.'' Tom was using his lawyer-to-client tone.

''Tom's right,'' Judd said. ''There's nothing we can do but wait and then sue for libel.''

Joe could feel his blood pressure start to climb. He was on the cusp of losing control of his temper. The others were watching him warily, so he took a few slow, deep breaths to regain his composure.

''I didn't call this meeting for a lesson on the law against prior restraint. I know it as well as any of you,'' he began very quietly. ''But a court may not see a band of itinerant journalists, trying to stick their collective nose up a community's ass, as necessarily what the First Amendment intended. Correct me if I'm wrong, but I believe the right of freedom of the press was expressly meant to ensure free and open debate. A collective effort in a town that has only one paper could be construed as outside First Amendment protections. Why not try it?''

''I have to admit, it's a sexy argument,'' Spencer responded. ''I'd be willing to give it some thought.''

''Look, let's give it a shot,'' Joe pressed them. ''The worst that can happen is the situation remains unchanged. Hell, if we succeed, look at the impact we will have had on constitutional law in this country.''

His partners were nodding their assent. Were they just massaging him again? Or had he rung a bell this time? He couldn't be sure. And suddenly he knew: he wasn't going to wait around to find out.

CHAPTER 10

JOE HAD set up a date to meet with his cousin Tony at Tony's office in the Goldcor packinghouse. The Glendale packinghouse had been Tony's brainchild. A graduate of the University of Arizona's agriculture college, he had spent years at loggerheads with Uncle Joe over every new idea Tony tried to implement in their farming operation. As the eldest of the next generation of males, Tony was the family's "crown prince." He knew it, and his uncle knew it. Tony's ideas were vetoed not on the basis of their merit, but because Uncle Joe saw him as a young pup trying to grab authority before his time. Joe knew from experience how exhausting a relationship with his Uncle Joe could be.

Standing before a glass wall facing the packing lines, waiting for Tony, Joe watched tangerines being sorted, graded and packed. This shed had become the largest Sunkist packinghouse in Arizona.

"Sorry to keep ya waiting," Tony announced as he burst into the office.

"Union trouble?"

"Nah. Immigration. It's settled. If these goddam Mexicans would learn to speak English, it'd help ya figure out who's legal and who isn't. Okay, what's up?"

Tony kept one eye on the fruit dancing along the conveyor belt and the other on his cousin while Joe filled him in on what he had learned about the IRG during the last five months —keeping his facts close together and any embellishments far apart. Conversations with Tony lasted only as long as he wanted them to. When he was finished, even if you were in the middle of a sentence, he'd say, ''Okay, goodbye,'' and either walk out or hang up.

In Tony's eyes, and he sincerely hoped in everyone else's, he was the ultimate tough guy. This image was carefully nurtured, not nearly so much for the sake of his masculinity as to provide him with a cover. Tony was a man exerting half his energy on self-control—so much energy that it was visible, and he knew it. If he could strut, bark and bellow convincingly, perhaps he could hide his fear of what family members, only in private, referred to jokingly as the ''family curse,'' an inability of Corelli men to control their moods. On five occasions, he'd seen his Uncle Joe collapse and wind up in the hospital after several days of being wildly out of control. Tony's father had followed the same pattern. His Uncle Vince had been debilitated by these moodswings during the last decade of his life. As for Tony, when the rage would well up inside him, he'd rip a telephone out of the wall or shove a fist through a door all the way up to his elbow just for release. He lived in constant fear of going over the brink. With each new explosion, he tightened his grip on himself and his terror mounted proportionately. Though Joe's problems with control were less severe, he saw his future in every outburst of Tony's. Now—before Tony might decide to terminate the meeting—Joe forced his own attention back to what had brought him here.

''So what I need you to do, Cousin Anthony, is bring to the law firm the pressure of a substantial client. You pay us a healthy fee. You want your name protected! I never thought I'd say this about Judd and Spencer, and I can't even begin to tell you what it means to me to say it about Tom, but I'm beginning to wonder whether the only way to get them to respond is to send in the cash. It almost seems to me they're getting their jollies off playing with my head. Y' know, we put the whole ballgame together from scratch. Just the four of us! I really love those guys, but sometimes it's as though we're on different planets.''

''I'll think about it and get back to ya,'' Tony said, and picked up his phone.

Time was up. Joe grabbed his briefcase, held up his hand in a parting gesture and left.

As he drove back to his office, it came to him. A street fight, that's what this was! Joe had gone to his partners—the wrong guys! What the fuck did they know about street fighting? Tony understood. So would others. Johnny Riccio'd pick up on it real fast. He was a fellow refugee from Avenue U who was now an executive in the stock market. A no-bullshit guy with a heart of gold and balls of steel. Joe jotted down his name. Who else?

CHAPTER

11

"OKAY, GUYS, it's your turn. Irv, you start," Joe ordered. The boys had begun to arrive at Joe's house at six-thirty on a Tuesday evening. Steve Ankewitz, Rocky Parlati and Joe's cousin, Tony, were the first to show up. After the others had gotten there and everyone had had a drink at the bar in the family room, Joe filled them in.

Irv, the honorary Italian, had wanted in from the beginning. "Well, I been kinda involved for a while now, ever since I set Joey up with Benny Soleri. I wanna stay involved. I wanna help. Seems to me, from growin' up in Chicago, Italians get a bum rap. Almost as bad as Jews. That's it."

Sitting next to Irv was Pete Grandella, six-four and handsome—minus a hundred pounds. Pete's mother was Uncle Joe's sister and, on his own, he was one of Joe's favorite relatives. "I'm here because I'm getting tired of every time I walk into a coffee shop, everyone gets up and fuckin' leaves. After those Barnes articles came out, my foreman'd say, 'Hey, Pete, ya gonna get me killed if I don't do a good job?' I got real tired of that crap. Irv, remember the night Joe and I came into the Polo Club and I belted the guy who was taking pot shots at us for being Corellis? You threw him out! Our family was getting it in the paper day in and day out because of labor problems. Between illegal aliens and Mafia, it really hurt."

"Was it worse after Barnes got killed?" Jeff Amobile asked.

"Ya know, Jeff, it didn't bother me. So the son of a bitch was dead."

"No. I meant the harassment."

"We didn't get any harassment. The guys they arrested had no connection with us. That fuckin' guy Simpson was nuthin more than a two-bit punk! We were raised to be proud that our grandfather had the courage to testify against the Mafia. One of Joe's father's porters had his tongue cut out because he wouldn't tell where grandpa was."

Pete paused and looked to Joe for confirmation. Joe nodded his head. "Okay, Jeff, baby, you're on," he said.

Jeff Amobile looked like a Mediterranean version of Benjamin Franklin. He had meandered through his share of Eastern prep schools, started college at Yale and finished up some place in England after a tour of duty in Vietnam as a Marine. In spite of himself, he wound up with a degree in architecture at about the same time his parents retired to Scottsdale. That seeming as good a place as any to start up his firm, he soon followed.

"I grew up in New Haven, where the Yale community never even heard of Italians! My father ran the A. C. Berkeley Company for Archer Berkeley. How much bigger a WASP could ya be than Archer Berkeley? A. C. Berkeley was a brilliant man, but he couldn't implement his ideas. My *father* ran the show, but we didn't have the honor of socializing with the Berkeleys."

"All right, last but not least, Johnny Riccio, Wall Streeter extraordinaire." Joe smiled as he pointed to his old friend who had so far sat quietly listening to this group, some of whom he was meeting tonight for the first time.

"I'm easy, guys. Joey called me and said, 'Hey Johnny, I'm gettin' into a street fight. I need ya.' So here I am."

"All right, guys, any ideas?"

"Joe, I think we need to fight these assholes with their own weapons and play by their rules," Pete offered.

Irv Wolfe leaped forward in his seat. "I totally disagree with you! If the Constitution is fair for one group, then it should be fair for every group. So we say, 'Look, you cocksuckers, if you publish articles that aren't true. . . .'"

"You're gonna pay," Pete finished.

"Yeah, you're gonna pay."

"But not the way Barnes paid," Joe said. "Whoever blew him up should have discredited him by showing him up for the fuckin' banana that he really was. Instead, now the guy's larger than life. Look, guys, these reporters've been here for a few months. Now they say they have to stay another couple of months because they found more than they expected. Jerk me off easy! This is already becoming one of the coldest winters on record back East, and it's not even Thanksgiving yet. You think they're in a hurry to go home? Let me tell you, when your boss has paid for you to vacation in the sun, you'd damn well better have something to show for it. So I think we have to conclude that they will print, no matter what.

"Now, my partners think I'm off the wall. I can't, on my own, possibly do all the research necessary to present a federal court with the kind of argument and documentation that it'd take to get a foot in the door. They aren't willing to commit enough of the firm's resources to help me, so that's out. Right now I'm inclined to deal with the reporters directly. We should be able to come up with a strategy for minimizing the negative impact of their series."

"Do you think that minimizing is the most we can hope for?" Rocky asked.

"I'd like to think we could win, but we can't. However, if we deal with these guys one-on-one, maybe we can keep them from printing in, say, L.A. or Denver or Chicago, whatever."

"What about the direct approach?" Johnny suggested. "Go to their headquarters. Introduce ourselves. Tell them we're interested in their project and ask them what they've uncovered."

"Hey, look, Johnny," Irv objected. "We don't need you for talking. With your looks you could romance the broads and get 'em t' tell ya everything."

"That's very interesting, Irv. Do you always lead with your prick, or is tonight special?"

"Okay, guys, time out!" Joe laughed. "Irv, get yourself another drink and relax. Look, maybe we can carry Johnny's idea one step further—offer to help them. Who knows, maybe we could alter their outlook?"

"I say we set 'em up," Jeff offered.

"How are we gonna do that, Jeff?" Joe asked.

"They're probably gonna show us, each of them, how to do it. We won't have to devise anything."

"That's right." Irv was rubbing his hands together, as if he could hardly wait.

"Each of them will have his own bad habit," Jeff said. "All we have to do is identify it and then capitalize on it."

Pete spoke up. "I say we use women. They're gonna be here for months—they gotta get horny."

"Let's dig up some information on their individual backgrounds," Rocky offered. "If we found skeletons in any of their closets, maybe they'd think twice about what they write."

"If we hung out at the bars they frequent, we might pick up all sorts of stuff," Joe suggested.

"The best idea I've heard so far is to meet them," Pete said. "Once we know who they are, we use their own tactics on them: innuendo and lies!"

"You can't do that!" Johnny jumped in. "You don't have the power of the press. *They* have the power of the press! We're dealin' with hit men with typewriters! Whatsa matter with you fuckin' guys?"

"Let's fix 'em up with some broads and get pictures. Mail 'em to their wives."

"Hey, Pete, you're gettin' dirty," Jeff teased.

"Yeah, I'm gettin' dirty! You're damned right!"

Pete's suggestion provoked comment from practically everyone simultaneously.

"Hey, great, Pete, great!" Irv started yelling. "Can I be the photographer?" He broke up laughing.

"Maybe we should wire some hookers," Pete, on a roll, suggested.

"I second that," Irv said.

"Okay," Rocky asked. "When we get something, whatta we do with it?

"Ah, all ya can do is use it personally, 'cause they're gonna write what they want, anyway," Irv responded sadly, sticking steadfastly to his theme.

"What do we know about these fellas so far?" Jeff asked, resting a cold washcloth on his face. "You say Benny Soleri's been reporting back. What does he say?"

"Benny came into the Polo Club the other night, said these guys are eatin' like they're goin t' the electric chair."

"Eating like pigs isn't exactly the kind of thing I was lookin' for, Irv," Joe said sardonically. "We only got three months till they're ready to publish. At this rate we'll still be here trying to decide what to do when the articles hit." Joe stood and clapped his hands for attention. "Let's get focused, make some decisions, and draw up a plan."

"You aren't gonna get them to like you, so forget that one."

"No one suggested that, Irv. Let's sort out the ideas that have been presented," Joe ordered, trying to bring sanity to the proceedings.

"Okay. Let's get anything we can on them to persuade them that they have something to lose if they write a story we don't like," Tony said decisively.

"I don't think we should throw out the possibility that we might get a couple of them to question what they're doing here," Joe added.

''I think the idea of wiring some hookers is great!'' Irv put in. ''We know the bars. We have access to the guys through Benny. Maybe he could let them know he could fix them up.''

''Hey, how about we bug their rooms?'' Jeff suggested.

''Why should we play that kind of dirty game, Jeff?''

''We shouldn't, Joe. If we get caught, we've given them ammunition,'' Pete said, shaking his head vehemently.

''I thought this was a street fight. Where did all these ethics come from?''

''It's a street fight with rules, Jeff,'' Rocky said.

''I say we find some black pimps who control the hookers and buy their time to make contact with these guys and then report back to us anything they can find out,'' Pete suggested.

''You guys are all nuts!'' Tony said. ''How do you think you can find a real hooker you can trust?''

''There's something in this,'' Johnny said. ''Guys with a few drinks unda their belts will brag like crazy to a broad. We tell the girls what we wanna know, put a recording device on 'em an' let 'em make friends with the reporters. But we can't use hookers. We need girls we can trust—and who won't get carried away with love for the work.''

''I'll see if my girlfriend will help out,'' Pete volunteered.

''I got two I can ask who I know would work out,'' Steve said.

''I know one I think will go along, so I think we've got enough girls. Now, let's plan a sting.''

''What do you mean by a sting, Jeff?'' Irv asked.

''We get pictures of these guys with the girls. Not in bed—a public place is good enough. Then we get reefers for the girls, and they plant 'em on these guys, then—''

''Hold it!'' Joe shouted.

''Joe, you buy this and I'm out!'' Pete warned.

''Why are you out if we do a little marijuana?'' Jeff asked. As I see it, this is no holds barred—whatever works! I question your commitment.''

"I'm here. My commitment's been made. Does that mean I have to like every suggestion I hear?"

"Okay, guys!" Joe yelled. "Time out! I want you all to understand somethin'. Now, listen hard. I'm a long way from the neighborhood. I'm willing to listen to any and all suggestions, but in the last analysis, this is my party, and nobody's gonna step out of line. Now, any other suggestions? The floor's still open."

"I'd like to say something."

"Okay, John. Go!" Joe said.

"I have yet to hear anyone suggest the truth."

"Like what, Johnny?" Joe asked.

"Like Barnes was all wet. Off target. There was no investigation following his series, because there was nothing to investigate. That the entire series was ancient history about a lot of dead torpedoes, plus innuendo and guilt by association about the living."

"Ya know, maybe they need to see some of the editorials that appeared in other papers around the Valley after 'The Hidden Cancer.' If we do a mailing, maybe that's the one to do."

"Do you still have any of those, Joe?" Pete asked, sounding tired.

"Do I still have them? My good man, I've got the whole series and everything that followed. Don't forget, I had Uncle Joe yelling 'Sue!' at me every day. I kept meticulous files, just in case."

Just in case had come to pass.

CHAPTER 12

A WHOLE day at home was never easy and, lately, was becoming nearly unbearable for Joe. But he was determined to make an effort. Despite everything, he had a lot more to be thankful for than most people.

He'd awakened early, as usual, but tried to go back to sleep—as if a few more hours' sleep would even dent the tiredness he felt inside him. He couldn't fall back to sleep anyway, but he postponed going downstairs, and lay there thinking about how Thanksgiving had been his father's favorite holiday. That man, who never forgot he was Italian for more than three minutes at a time, always put out a flag on Thanksgiving, although nobody on their street did it even on the Fourth of July. How many times had he heard his father say, ''God bless America!''

Joe wanted to hear it now. He reached for the phone. Angela was on the extension, talking to one of her girlfriends. ''I'm on, Joe. Joseph and I had breakfast hours ago. You ever coming down for yours? I'd like to get started on dinner.''

He wanted to slam the phone on her head. Saying that whole speech at him while some other broad was listening in! But he wasn't going to let her get to him. ''I'll be down, but first I want to call my father.''

''I'll get off,'' Angela said.

He put down the phone, waited a full minute by the clock on his bedside radio, and picked it up again. The only reason she'd gotten off so fast was to hurry him up. He called his parents' house, and had a leisurely talk with his mother before his father got on. Joe talked to him briefly about what was happening, leaving out the worst stuff.

"Listen, Pa. Lemme tell ya why I'm callin'."

"Pepino, you meana you needa better reason dena to talk to you mama and me?"

Joe laughed. "You're right, Pop," he said. "But I gotta special reason. Don't laugh at me."

He waited.

"Wella?" his father said.

"Promise you won't laugh."

"Shoo I promise. Whatta you do somethin' stupida?"

"Probably, but that's not it. Pa, say 'God bless America.'"

"Ma whatta you *pazzo*?"

"Please say it. Like you always do. God bless America. Just like that. Please?"

"Ma shoo. Gah blace Ahmeriga. Gah blace Ahmeriga. I say it okay?"

"You said it beautiful, Pa. Thanks. Talk to ya later."

■ ■ ■

HE HAD thought Angela would be pleased at his taking Joseph out on his bike. They'd be out of her way, and besides, she was always complaining he didn't spend enough time with the boy. But by then she was angry with him, and so they left with her glaring after him.

He barely cared any more, but why wouldn't she too make an effort today, if only for the boy's sake? Exerting a little of his notorious will, he put their argument and her out of his mind, and concentrated on Joseph. Angela was right about one thing. He didn't spend enough time with his son.

They ended up in the park, sharing a big tree trunk with their bikes. Joe described to Joseph the bike he had in mind for him for his tenth birthday. A Jaguar of bikes! He loved it when Joseph's eyes lighted up like that.

"Papa?"

"Mmn." Joe felt relaxed for the first time in weeks, and had begun drifting off.

"When Mama asked if you wanted to go with us to church before, why'd you laugh?"

"Did I laugh?"

"She didn't think it was funny."

"No, I guess she didn't. I guess I laughed from surprise."

"Because she should have known, right? Because you never come to church with us."

Joe looked at his son. How much a kid his age took in! "I'll tell you this, Joseph. If I went to church, I'd definitely go with you." He roughed up his son's hair.

"When you were my age, did you go?"

"You bet I did. Your grandmother would have slit my throat if I didn't go with her."

"When'd you stop? She lose her knife?"

Joe laughed. "No, she's still got her knife." The boy was intent on him, wanting more.

"I was years older than you when I stopped. Years and years older."

"Ten?"

"A lot older than ten."

"Why'd you stop?"

"Oh, Joseph, you ask a whole lot of questions."

"If I don't ask questions, how'm I going to learn anything about you?"

Joe looked at the boy's upturned face. Was he really that interested in him? How ironic. Angela had lost interest in anything he might have to say so long ago he couldn't say when, but here was her son, the desire to know about Joe flushing his cheeks.

"You're absolutely right. Okay. Why don't I go to church? Well, first off, you should know that I think of myself as a Catholic. We're all of us Catholics. Like all the popes are Italian, all the Italians are Catholics. Nearly a hundred per cent. And in the old country, it was like family, the Church. You didn't belong to it, it belonged to you. Every small town had its own saint—San Gennaro, San Rocco, San Giuseppe, San Antonio, Santa Rosalia. . . ."

"Was I named for San Giuseppe?"

"You know you're named for your grandfather!"

Instantly, the boy retreated. And as quickly, Joe was sorry he'd raised his voice. "I guess if you go back far enough," he said, "a Giuseppe in our family was named for San Giuseppe."

He searched the boy's face. It was all right. He'd been forgiven for his outburst. Joe felt an urge to grab his son to him, and cradle him in his arms, as if he could protect him not only from *his* temper but from the family temper, which he'd probably inherited right along with Joe's eyebrows. Instead, he smiled at Joseph, who took the smile as an invitation to proceed. "Tell me more about those saints," he said.

Joe settled his back more comfortably, and said, "Well, according to my father, each town's patron saint was held personally responsible for that town's well-being. Every year, the saint's feast day was cause for a big celebration. His statue was paraded through the streets while everyone cheered and threw flowers." Joe was surprised how readily it all came back to him. "Gran'pa told me that when the year was bad, the people blamed their saint, so instead of flowers they'd throw rotten vegetables at the statue as it went by."

"Sounds like a lot more fun than church."

Joe chuckled. "Does, doesn't it?"

"Can I stop going with Mama to church?"

"No."

''When can I?''

''When you're grown. For Chrissake, you just made your first communion!''

''Don't get mad.''

''I'm not mad. I just don't see why you're in such a hurry to grow up. I'd give anything to be your age, without a worry in the world. Except pleasing my papa, of course,'' he added, holding the boy's eyes until he nodded.

■ ■ ■

''I WAS getting ready to call the police,'' Angela greeted them.

''Sorry. We got to talking and forgot the time. Is dinner ready?''

''Dinner was ready an hour ago! Just because we finally have a peaceful Thanksgiving without your family, you think you can show up when you feel like it?''

''Turkey needs to cool, anyway. I'll carve it and we can eat,'' he said calmly.

Even if Angela set things on the table so they bounced, everything was delicious. Maybe if the phone hadn't rung, they'd have gotten through dinner without any more trouble. But who knew?

The first call was from Herb Steinberg. When Joe came back to the table, he said, ''Herb's sources at the paper tell him that Grogan—the guy from *Newsworld*—views the IRG's mission as establishing future protection for all reporters by punishing Phoenix for having allowed one of their kind to be killed.''

''He had to call you this minute to tell you that? Don't Jews celebrate Thanksgiving?''

Joe stared at her. Then he decided to turn her implied insult into a joke. ''I bet today he is. With that kind of vendetta mentality dominating the project, once the series hits, Herb's clients will be lining up to sue. What's your opinion? Think he's counting his clients—I mean his blessings?''

''How would I know?''

He leaned forward, his fists clenched under the table. "You should know because he's my friend. He doesn't want me hurt, or others like me."

"Tell me, Joe, are there really any others like you?"

The phone rang. Count *your* blessings, lady, he thought as he went into the den to take it.

It was Don Perrino. "There's so much noise in my house, I had to escape to the bedroom, so I thought I'd take a chance you could talk a minute."

"Sure, I can talk. What's up?"

"First, tell me, you heard anything from Northridge since we talked?"

"Yes. He's pretty much established himself as a liaison with Grogan. Grogan thinks Parker's a reformer who would like the chance to help them clean up the state."

"Has he learned anything?"

"Some. The IRG's focusing heavily on the 'Hidden Cancer' article on Detroit. Right now they're questioning everybody about the Mother Goose debacle."

"Great," Don said. "That ought to go a ways toward helping me digest the four portions of sweet potatoes I just ate. Listen, I think you better be ready for a call from Mark Windman. My sources are convinced he believes there's a direct and ongoing connection between Detroit gangsters and Goldcor."

"That evens us up, pal. I'm not through my dinner yet, and you feed me this?"

When Joe returned to the table this time, Angela didn't say a word. She and Joseph were eating dessert.

Joe took his place at the table. "How's the pie, son?"

"Super. Mama warmed it up."

"Only way to eat apple pie," Joe said.

And waited, watching Angela take small bites of her slice, and chew them daintily. She didn't so much as glance in his direction.

He got up and went into the kitchen. The remainder of the pie was in the oven, the door ajar. He took it out and touched it. Still warm. He hesitated. Eat some, or push as much of the pie as was left into her face? Think about Joseph, he told himself.

So he cut a slice and ate it standing at the sink, looking out the window. Could Thanksgiving be this grim in any of those other homes? He shuddered. He put his plate in the sink and rinsed it. Then he went to the bar, took a bottle of cognac and a glass, and went into his den. This was the one door even Angela didn't knock on.

He drank cognac for a long time. It was dark out when his vision began to blur. He turned on the lamp next to his chair, but nothing cleared up. Then he tasted the salt at the side of his mouth. His son was asking questions. He wanted his son to be someone who asked questions. But when Joseph got around to asking him—and he knew it'd be soon—why his mother and Joe couldn't ever stay in the same room without fighting, what would his answer be?

CHAPTER

13

THE WORLD was turning its attention to Christmas. Joe's clients were frantic to close deals before the calendar year ran out. He was logging a hundred calls a day. The endless round of Christmas parties took what was left of his time. At one of those parties, around mid-December, he ran into Parker Northridge.

"Good to see you," Parker said, clearing his throat. "How are things at CBP&W these days?"

Parker, careful to shake every available hand at a gathering, would approach an acquaintance with an air of eager tension. His head, led by his jutting chin, rotated on his stiff neck as he greeted each member of a group personally. Propelled by a finely tuned internal alarm, he moved from person to person with military precision.

"Hectic! There's nothing like the practice of corporate law to take all the fun out of the holidays."

"Tell me about it."

"Have you heard anything recently about the IRG?" Joe asked, his voice walking an even line.

"Not much. So far as I've heard, they haven't uncovered anything new."

"How do you account for that?"

Well, I don't know, but I suspect that Bruce Babbitt has something to do with it. He keeps claiming that Barnes's death was the work of organized crime, as though he's on to something. Put yourself in their place. The Attorney General, in a state you know nothing about and are trying to investigate, talks about organized crime as though this were Palermo. Where would you look?"

"Point well taken," Joe said. "But every indication is that the best they've come up with is some five-year-old articles that local people laughed at."

"Because five years ago Barnes's news was already thirty years old!"

Northridge knew it. Joe certainly knew it. But, when push came to selling papers, would it matter?

■ ■ ■

RIGHT AFTER the New Year, Joe decided to take one more shot at his partners.

Judd was off skiing, so he and Spencer met in Tom's office late the following Saturday afternoon. At the outset, Spencer and Tom admitted that they had put on the back burner Joe's request to research the possibilities of a prior restraint. He'd been right. They weren't in his corner.

"Look, fellas, since we last spoke, clients of ours have been contacted by the IRG. Tony gave one of them a tour of the Goldcor packinghouse. Vito Garbi has had several requests for an interview. It's not just me overreacting anymore. We have worried clients to consider. Sean Kelly from the *Herald* is on this team. So are some other locals. We have to expect the series to appear in Arizona and not just out of state."

"Joe, you know as well as I do that it is absolutely impossible to get a prior restraint order," Tom said, obviously irritated that the subject kept coming back like a bad penny.

"I don't know it's impossible! I know it's never been done. And I know it's not easy. If it were, I'd stop batting my head against the wall trying to get help from you guys and do it alone. But I believe that in this firm with all these former law clerks, three Watergate prosecutors and two law professors, we could give it the old college try! You can't tell me that with all these fuckin' geniuses, we gotta roll over and play dead!''

Joe's voice and blood pressure mounted quickly as he spoke. By the time he was finished, he was shouting and pounding the desk with his fist. The last time he'd felt this helpless, frustrated and angry, he'd nearly strangled a priest.

As an alternative to strangling his old buddy Tom, Joe slammed out of his office.

The wood held. Too bad offices as expensive as theirs came with such strong doors, Joe thought.

CHAPTER 14

LATE-JANUARY flowers bloomed outside, but for Joe this winter was cold and bleak. He was proofreading a trust he had just completed drafting when a call came through from Judge Paul Lorano.

''Have you seen cheek?''

''What?''

''Maybe it's chick.''

''What's chick?''

''It's some magazine.''

''Never heard of it.''

''There's an article in it that I'm gonna send over to you. It's got all these naked ladies with snakes and animals. It's disgusting! There's even some broad with an elephant!''

''What the fuck are you sending me this piece of shit for, Lorano?''

''Because these great reporters from the IRG gave this magazine a scoop!''

''Christ! Let me send my runner right over to pick it up! What's the name of it, again?''

''Chick.''

''Like in chicken?''

''Na! C-H-I-C.''

''You asshole! That's 'sheek.' It's French. It means fashionable.''

''Maybe fucking elephants is in fashion? Whattaya think?''

An hour later, the CBP&W messenger returned from the courthouse with a sealed manila envelope marked ''Personal and Confidential.'' The Larry Flynt classic cover picture was a naked girl sitting on a couch with her legs spread farther apart than Mother Nature would have thought possible. The banner story was ''How the Mob Rules Phoenix.'' Incredible! Strung together under the main headline were topics the issue explored. ''Blood, Death, Clap, Cruising, Manson, Vodka, Girls, Girls!'' In order of importance, no doubt. To the right, in bold print: ''Blockbuster Holiday Issue.''

He turned to page seventeen and began to read. In the middle of the sixth paragraph from the end, he slowed down.

> When somebody kills a reporter, a good reporter doing his job, every newspaper should show solidarity and make it apparent to other people who might have the same idea that it's more trouble than it's worth. Create an object lesson by saying, ''We'll bust your balls, we'll bust a whole community's balls if people in that community think they can take out reporters.'' Whoever killed Dan Barnes is less important than that every illegal-thinking member of Phoenix remembers it with great distaste for the rest of their lives because of what happened afterward. In the course of that you hope to throw light on everybody involved, higher-ups, but the deeper thrust is to buy life insurance for every reporter in the U.S.

Unbelievable! This wasn't investigative journalism, it was a bona fide street fight.

The *Chic* article was genuinely scary. Joe had copies mailed to Arla Perkins, the Governor, the Attorney General, the County Attorney, newspapers around the Valley and the IRG reporters. Jan, his secretary, called Joe's allies who lived out of town and suggested they find a copy of the magazine. The locals got hand deliveries.

■ ■ ■

THE MINUTE Parker Northridge finished reading his copy, he was on the phone to Joe.

"Do you believe a Pulitzer Prize-winning journalist being willing to give an interview to a magazine that is beneath trash?"

"Yeah, well a friend of mine in Denver just gave me a history lesson. I didn't know anything about Joseph Pulitzer—I just figured the guy was a distinguished journalist. Forget it. Pulitzer helped invent yellow journalism! Selling papers was his only goal, and he didn't give a flying fuck how he did it! It's perfectly appropriate for a hard-on like Grogan to have won a Pulitzer!"

"I know you're upset, Joe, but do you realize that you're shouting?"

"Yeah, I know I'm shouting, and I'm getting fuckin' sick of being asked that question! I've got a call coming in on another line. Talk to you later."

Joe hung up the phone, leaned back in his chair and took a deep breath. A lot of people were telling him to calm down these days. How the hell could he? Calls came in all day long from everywhere and everyone. Every time these reporters belched, Joe got an update.

Jumping out of his chair, he went for his liquor cabinet. He poured himself a drink, and drained the glass in one swallow. He had to calm himself down! He was racing, and he didn't want anyone to see it. He was about to pour a second drink when his phone rang.

It was Rocky Parlati. So much for settling down.

"I went right out and got the magazine."

"Yeah."

"I was embarrassed to buy it. I took one look at the cover and browsed around the store until there was no one at the cash register to see me holding the goddam thing. I haven't felt like that since I was sixteen, buying my first pack of rubbers."

As Joe laughed, he could feel the tantrum in him ease a little.

"Remember I told you I was working on a little project of my own? Well, I've been out to *Newsworld* a few times, trying to make contact with someone who could give me leads on where Grogan and his boys might be coming from in this fancy investigation. I started up a conversation with a real cute executive secretary who works there, and we've gone out a few times."

"Anything from her?"

"Hey, that's a personal question. Even friendship has its limits."

"Ah, yes. Funny. You know what I mean."

"Not yet, but I'm in there humping."

When Joe hung up, he felt considerably better. Smut, he thought, was like anything else: good and bad. Their kidding about the girl from *Newsworld* was good smut—wouldn't hurt anybody. Larry Flynt's rag was bad smut. Chances were, it would hurt a lot of people.

CHAPTER

15

JOE WAS staring at a picture of Angela on his desk. In her sterling Tiffany frame, she looked exactly the way a wife was supposed to look in a picture on her husband's desk. Placid, content, smiling at him. Nothing like the face she'd shown him when he'd gotten home sometime after two this morning.

■ ■ ■

SHE'D BEEN sitting in the living room, leafing through a magazine. Soft music was playing on the stereo, and in the equally soft light and a loose midnight-blue negligee sheer enough to reveal that that was all she had on, Angela looked not bad for a very pregnant woman.

Tired as he was, he'd read her signals and made a move on her. But she'd pushed him away, said he smelled of liquor and cheap perfume. He knew he should just walk away, but he'd pinioned her arms and, close up, told her the perfume couldn't be cheap because the woman who'd been wearing it was anything but cheap.

When he'd let go of her arms, he moved away fast. But she hadn't made a move toward him. Instead, she'd smiled. "You earn it, you're entitled to spend it any way you like," she said.

Then she'd gotten up and walked out of the room, leaving him to his rage. Her not getting mad was worse than when she threw things. Did she really not care at all? Had they reached that point?

He'd poured himself a nightcap, and as he drank, it came to him that she'd set him up. Sitting there waiting for him all decked out in that negligee that hid absolutely nothing—it was her way of spitting at him. Telling him that she was beyond his grasp.

Well, things he needed more than Angela were beyond his grasp. Peace, for example. When was the last time he'd felt at peace? He couldn't remember.

Damn her for not caring what was happening to him! He felt fury well up in him. He thought of going after her, showing her she wasn't beyond his grasp. . . .

But he didn't care enough. Instead, he'd had a second night-cap. And a third. He didn't remember pouring a fourth, but that must have been the one that put him to sleep on the couch—where he'd awakened with a crick in his neck and an ache in his soul.

■ ■ ■

THE HOURS since had done nothing to alleviate either one.

The buzzer. ''Irv Wolfe,'' Jan said.

Joe sighed. No, there was no peace. He pressed the button and said hello.

''I just had some visitors here at the dress shop who weren't interested in clothes.''

''Oh, what did they want?''

''Information about Harry Rosenzweig.''

''Harry? That's interesting, Irv, because I've been talking to Phil Evans and Mark Jennings, and they're pretty upset about the IRG's interest in him. I hope you weren't shooting off your mouth.''

''Whattaya mean, Joey? I told 'em he never did one thing wrong in his life.''

''Okay, but I've been getting a lot of feedback from people that you're talking too much, so I'm just warning you. Which ones came to see you?''

''Windman and Oskowski, Ostriski, or however the fuck ya say 'is name.''

''What else did they want to know?''

''Well, they seem to think I'm one of d' contact guys in Arizona for the Chicago mob.''

Joe got hysterical. ''Gee, Irv, they must have found out we made you an honorary Italian.''

''It ain't so funny. They was askin' me questions about Jimmy Fratianno. They say I was seen with him. They said the police tole 'em I help Allen Dorfman launder Teamster money. And they think Harry and me are in business.''

''What'd you tell them, Irv?''

''What did I tell 'em? I tole 'em the truth. I grew up in a rough neighborhood in Chicago. A lot of people I hung out with got into the rackets. Others are lawyers and judges. Period. But Harry, I tole 'em, Harry's straight. Anyway, I gave 'em passes to the Polo Club. How much ya wanna bet they come t'night? Joey, you should come over.''

■ ■ ■

FRANK LA BATE was in town from Denver on a real-estate deal he was doing with Steve Ankewitz and a group of outside investors. After the meeting, Joe asked Frank to have a drink with him at the Polo Club.

''Great! Listen, an interesting coincidence. My daughter's doing this research paper for history on Ben Franklin. She's telling me that he wrote a series of essays on the abuse of freedom of the press. I had them copied for you and the guys. When you've got some time, look them over. I thought it was kind of unique that someone so involved in the struggle for independence would then worry about the press having too much freedom.''

''Thanks, I'd like to read that.''

■ ■ ■

AS THEY drove into the parking lot of the Polo Club, they noticed two men sitting in a white Ford.

"That's odd, don't you think, Frank? Why would two guys be sitting in the dark in a car in Irv's parking lot, unless maybe they're casing the joint?"

"We should tell Irv."

They opened the beveled glass doors into the vestibule. Seated at a highly polished oak podium in front of a stained-glass wall was a played-out broad who wore her thirty-odd years more like fifty. Her blonde, kinky hair was stringy, and her make-up looked as if it was left over from yesterday.

"Hi, Joe," she said, tilting her head to her shoulder.

She jumped down off her stool to open the stained-glass doors that led into the club. She wore a tight, red skirt that conformed so completely to her thighs that, from the rear, she looked like a squat fire engine.

"Who's your friend?" she asked as she eyed Frank.

"Oh, uh, Charlene, this is Frank," Joe mumbled as he opened the door and shoved Frank through.

Inside the bar, Frank, a schizophrenic mixture of one of the boys and priest, rolled his eyes into his head and said, "Where did Irv find that *putana*?"

Joe pointed to the left where Frank saw a hand-carved mahogany staircase that led down to the sunken dance floor. "He paid $14,000 for that fuckin' thing because he wanted the joint to have class, and then he puts that dilapidated broad out there. Go figure it."

Joe and Frank walked to the head of the stairs and looked around the bar below for Irv. Just as they spotted him sitting on his usual stool, talking to a man who had his back to them, Irv, with his left hand hidden under the bar, signaled them not to join him. So Joe and Frank turned left at the bottom of the stairs and went to a table in the corner.

"What was that all about?" Frank asked.

"My guess is he's talking to one of the reporters and either doesn't want me to hear what he's saying or has some scenario in mind that he wants us to go along with."

Frank nodded. "I bet you're right. There's one of the reporters now, dancing with Kay. I remember that guy from a time I went to the Adams with Steve."

Joe looked for Kay. You couldn't miss her. She was about five-ten, with black hair that looked like she arranged it each day by sticking her finger into an electric socket. With her was a plump, blond man who was just tall enough, given the fact that Kay was wearing six-inch spikes, to be nose to nipple with her emaciated chest.

"You know who the guys in the parking lot are, Frank? Reporters. If these guys are here, that's who *they* are. I hear that for every one you see, there's another posted as a lookout. These jokers think they're in a James Bond movie. It's a fuckin' farce!"

"Hi, Joe. Frank. In town again, huh?"

They smiled at the pretty, young cocktail waitress who had just walked up to the table to take their order.

"Hi, honey," Joe said. "Bring us two Chivas and sodas and one Irv Wolfe."

She smiled. "I'll tell him," she said as she walked away.

They were watching the reporter climb all over Kay when Irv joined them.

"Who's that dancing with Kay?" Joe asked.

"Mark Windman."

"Did you arrange that?"

"Nah. She was sitting with me at the bar when they came in. All of a sudden this chump's over her like wallpaper. I never saw nobody so wired. He should get his glands checked."

"Who were you talking to at the bar?"

"That's Stan Ostrowski. He seems to be an okay guy."

"What have you been talking about?"

"Harry. But don't worry, Joe. I remembered what you said, and I seen to it that Harry gets a clean bill of health."

"Now, what the fuck does that mean, Irv?" Joe asked with some alarm. Irv's idea of a clean bill of health might very well be reported as an epidemic of bubonic plague.

"Well, I tole 'em I talked to Harry after I spoke to them this afternoon, and he's real upset about the questions they been askin'. This Ostrowski says they're real sorry about asking all those questions, and he's tired of poking his nose into other people's business, and he thinks Harry and I are real nice guys. See?" he said with obvious pride.

Joe leaned across the table until he was practically eyeball-to-eyeball with Irv. "And while he was telling you this, Irv, did you feel his hand on your cock?"

"Whattaya mean?" Irv asked, looking wounded.

"You believe that shit? Snooping is his profession. His vocation! And he's sorry he asked you questions? Irving, jerk me off real slow."

Joe sat back in his chair. With vast effort, he grabbed hold of his temper and reined it in.

"What else happened, Irv?"

"Nuthin."

"Irv, don't pout."

"I offered to buy 'em dinner. They didn't want none. I brought Vicky ova to meet dis Ostrowski. He wasn't interested, but meanwhile Windman was. Ostrowski tells me not to tell anyone they're here, 'cause his boss don't like them goin t' places like this."

"Sure. That's why two more are out in the parking lot, covering the rear."

"I don't know nuthin about that, Joey. All I saw was two of them. But lemme go check outside."

"Is that it?" Frank asked.

"No. I tole 'em they should meet Harry themselves and see what a great guy he is. I tole 'em I'd set it up. I tole 'em I'd pay 'em to tell me who's spreadin' all dose lies about me and Harry.''

''Good, Irv. Good. Now they can say you tried to bribe them.''

Shaking his head in disgust, Joe got up and turned to Frank. ''Get your drink and let's go talk to Ostrowski.''

Irv jumped up ahead of them and offered to go along to make the introductions.

The three men walked up to the reporter seated at the bar.

''Stan, I'd like you to meet a good friend of mine, Joe Corelli,'' Irv said. ''Joe, this is Stan Ostrowski. He's from Chicago.''

Ostrowski wore a brown moustache and a tan corduroy jacket. Joe shook his hand and introduced Frank as his partner.

''Irv tells me you're part of the IRG team.''

''That's right. I'm with the *Chicago Tribune*.''

''Maybe you can answer a question for me?''

''I don't like to talk shop when I'm out unwinding,'' Ostrowski responded.

''This isn't shop. Just a quickie. I saw the interview your leader, Grogan, gave *Chic* magazine. What would motivate you guys to give an interview to that kind of rag, especially before your series is even published?''

Joe could see from the look on Ostrowski's face that the question had come from left field. He watched him intently as the reporter fiddled with the stump of a cheap stogie. Joe reached inside his jacket pocket, pulled out a Partagas and offered it to Stan. Ostrowski studied Joe for a very long moment before finally taking it.

As Joe sat down at the bar, Frank walked away and joined Windman and Kay.

''Are you married, Stan?'' Joe asked, shifting the conversation to less confrontational ground.

''Yeah. I have a six-year-old daughter.''

''I have a six-year-old son. How long you been in Phoenix?''

''Too long,'' he responded with a wry smile. ''I really miss my daughter. Before I came here, I had been in California covering a story. I'm getting real tired of living in hotels, long distance being my only contact with my family.''

Joe showed the reporter a snapshot of his son, and the two of them spent the next twenty minutes comparing notes on their kids. Ostrowski was less wary by the time Joe asked, ''So, Stan, why *are* you here?''

''Well, I knew Barnes and I'm president of the Investigative Reporters Group. Barnes's murder was a tragedy that really requires some kind of response from his colleagues.''

As Ostrowski talked about vindicating the dead reporter and completing his work, Joe wondered how well he could have known Barnes because it became clear that Stan was sincere. Joe felt his hostility begin to ebb, at least as far as this man was concerned. Ostrowski really believed Grogan and Windman about the criminal infestation of Arizona. He talked about his investigation of Mother Goose's and all the people he had interviewed. Carl McBane, Paul Rogers, Tom Perry—all he heard from them were tales of corruption.

''Stan, all the men you've just mentioned were thrown out of the company, either because they were incompetent or because they lost out in a proxy fight. All you could possibly get from them is one side of the story.''

''Well, who else can I interview? Your father is dead.''

''My father is dead?''

''According to our records he died just recently, weeks before Barnes.''

Joe laughed. ''You got the wrong guy.''

''I've done the research. I know your father is dead.''

''Would you like to meet my father? We'll take a drive up Central Avenue, and you can meet him right now. He's probably working on his memoirs. Pop's a scholar. A historian. He likes to write late at night.''

''It can't be.''

''Look, fella, who should know better than me if my father is alive or dead?''

"We have this extensive family tree on the Corellis."

"Did you do it?"

"No, it was already up on the wall when I got here. But it's got the whole family and that's how I know your father is dead."

The thought of his family tree hanging on the wall at the IRG headquarters gave Joe an eerie feeling that he couldn't put a name to but hoped would pass before he came up with one.

"I don't know what you've got on your wall, but whoever is doing your research doesn't know what he's doing. Any time you decide you'd like to meet my father, just let me know."

"Well, who is Joseph T. Corelli?"

"My cousin."

"That's not the way they've got it on the chart. He's the one from Mother Goose's, right?"

"Right."

"Then he's the one I can't interview because he *is* dead, right?"

"Right. But you can interview Bob Goldwater. You can certainly interview Jack Klein, the president of the company. You can probably even interview Max White, the former president of Sunrise Valley Land Company, who might give you a different perspective on Carl McBane. Carl McBane is a guy who flimflammed a few deals into a company and then made a bad deal when he bought Mother Goose Coffee Shops. That deal probably cost him his company—although he did buy a few other pigs. Now, how do you expect him to feel about Mother Goose's or Joseph T. Corelli? Do you really expect him to give you honest answers?"

"Well, we do plan to interview Mr. Goldwater."

"Really? Have you set it up yet?"

"No. We're having trouble reaching him."

"He's out of town, but let me arrange it for you when he gets back."

"Thanks, I'd appreciate that." There was a new warmth in Ostrowski's smile.

Feeling drained, Joe was almost ready to call it a good night's work and go home. ''Just one last question, Stan. Have you ever subjected Chicago to this kind of screening?''

''No.''

''Well, think about that,'' he said, hopping off the barstool. ''I'll be in touch.''

CHAPTER 16

It was a gorgeous afternoon, low seventies, not a cloud in the sky. Joe had been sitting out by the pool for a long time, thinking about the IRG. Forget what the sky said; inside Joe bad weather was brewing, as unstoppable as any twist of nature. There was no denying it anymore. A lot of the people around him were telling Joe he was drinking too much. What they didn't know was that alcohol, which usually relaxed him, wasn't working. Even liquor was turning on him.

The situation at home was a disaster. Angela's attitude towards him alternated between irritation and fury. His partners looked at him quizzically. When he was at his most serious, people would say, "Joe, that's not funny anymore."

One thing that did help relax him was a good massage. He had a cute, little masseuse named Susie, who played Marvin Gaye records while she worked. Lately, Joe had started paying attention to the lyrics. He and Susie spent a lot of time talking about the message in Gaye's music. It became the only diversion that worked—even when he was with Ashley, his ghost seemed near. But he couldn't worry about the reporters while he was talking about Marvin Gaye. One day Susie handed him a book she'd just finished.

"I can't think of anyone I know who'd enjoy this as much as you," she said as she held out the paperback.

Joe looked down at the cover. In bold, black letters across the center of the book was "Joey." Above the title was the artist's conception of the gaunt face and fevered eyes of Joey Gallo. Suddenly frightened, he looked at her. What could he have told her? He was having difficulty turning the most ordinary thoughts into sentences these days. His mind was always racing to stay one step ahead of his fears. His partners were telling him he wasn't making sense. He had been interpreting their comments as a new ploy to get him to ignore the IRG. But could they be right? No! He shook them and his demons loose from his head and tried to smile casually.

"Why is that?"

"Because you're two smart Italians from Brooklyn. How many of those do you think I know?" she laughed.

On his way back to the office, he stopped at a record shop and bought a selection of Marvin Gaye tapes. He spent the rest of the day behind his desk reading the book and listening to Gaye's music. By the time he finished the book, it was no longer clear to him where Joey Gallo left off and he began. If the reporters kept investigating him, what would they find out? How much of what he read was really about him or just could have been?

■ ■ ■

HIS NEED to talk about the First Amendment, and the right of the press to ruin lives, was bordering on frenzy. He began to insist that everyone around him read *Joey,* listen to Marvin Gaye and hear him out on the First Amendment—then they'd understand!

But no one heeded him. Not even Angela, who, in the past, had always dropped everything when he needed to talk. She wouldn't listen to him—or to Marvin Gaye. Most puzzling of all to Joe, she wouldn't read *Joey*.

"I'm not interested in reading about these petty hoods from your past, and I don't know why you are," she told him.

"You know he wasn't a petty hood. Besides, I've never asked you to read a book for me before. You always wanted me to read books and talk to you about them, remember? Well, read this and we'll talk about it."

He thought she had understood that when you read all day to earn a living, you don't want to read for relaxation. Apparently she hadn't. Now she was getting her revenge. Or maybe it was just because she was pregnant. That was it! Women were never themselves when they were pregnant. They became fragile. Of course! She was too fragile to deal with this now. He'd be better off if he just left her alone.

He stopped coming home unless he was sure she was asleep. He left in the morning before she woke up. Oddly enough, the less he slept, the less sleep he needed.

His thoughts turned to Ashley. Ashley was passionate, Ashley was terrific looking, Ashley was intelligent, but what clinched the relationship for him was that she *cared*.

CHAPTER

17

ONLY HIS allies, whom he'd christened the Hardheads, would listen to anything he had to say.

When he arrived at his office, he found a message from Mark Jennings.

''Ah, Joe. Glad you could get back to me,'' Mark said in his slow, western drawl. ''Harry asked me to call and fill you in on his interview with the IRG. He thought you'd like to hear the details.''

''Sure would, Mark. Bob and I have agreed to be interviewed and our turn is coming up in a couple of days. It'd help to know what to expect,'' he said, drawing a deep breath and forcing himself to concentrate.

''Well, we met at my office. And I started out by saying that before Mr. Rosenzweig answered any questions, I expected them to tell us what they were doing in our city. My intention was to make it perfectly clear that because what they were doing was so unique, there were no established ground rules beyond whatever we would agree on then and there. An astonishingly obese man was their spokesman.''

''Grogan from *Newsworld,*'' Joe said. ''I've been hearing about him.''

''That's the one. He stated that they were here to investigate the connection between organized crime and politics in Arizona.

"I had decided, once we agreed to the interview, that we were going to limit the discussion to the most recent past. From everything we had heard about the scope of the investigation, all they had to go on was the ancient history Barnes dug up five years ago. Grogan's answer to that was the shibboleth that history is the father of today."

"I take it, then, that they tried to go back thirty years?"

"'Fraid so, Joe. The only reason we agreed to see them was to set the record straight on some unfavorable information they had on Harry. They are free to print whatever they've heard and then say that Mr. Rosenzweig, on advice of counsel, declined to be interviewed, so we had almost no choice but to see them. Interestingly enough, Grogan claimed that he only solicited the interview after Irv Wolfe had assured two other team members that Harry was anxious to talk to them."

"Boy, Mark, I don't understand Irv. I have told him repeatedly to keep his mouth shut. I have heard more stories that eventually get traced back to him. Sometimes he's an absolute menace."

"Well, be that as it may, I denied that Mr. Rosenzweig solicited an interview and made it clear that he did not waive his right to privacy. Look, Harry is not a public official, not a candidate for public office, and not, in my judgment, a public figure. He was there, I told them, because of the implication, as I read it, that if he didn't talk to them, the report might not be as favorable as it otherwise might be. I told Grogan that if in fact he did have unfavorable information, then we were there by consent. If he did not, we would consider that we were there by ruse and deception and proceed accordingly. Further, I told him I'd determined that he might legitimately go back to 1965 when Harry became Chairman of the Republican Party. Since he refused to discuss the scope of his inquiry in advance, we had decided that anything preceding that date was irrelevant.

"He then gave me a lecture on Supreme Court decisions concerning the First Amendment. He said that the Court does not require the press to submit written interrogatories before an interview, and any time limitation would render the interview worthless. I never thought I'd need someone of his ilk to lecture me on the First Amendment.''

''It sounds like you got off to a lousy start.''

''Yes. Because they came with an agenda headed by Harry's connection to Willie Bioff, and that goes back to the forties. Why did Harry ask the paper to kill the story that Nelson was really Bioff? The answer should have been obvious. The man did nothing illegal here in Phoenix. He wasn't wanted by the law. Why expose him and force him to go somewhere else? What would that accomplish?

''And it went downhill from there for almost two hours. I'm just waiting to see what they write. If they go back to the Nelson/Bioff story, we will think long and hard about an invasion-of-privacy suit.''

''Mark, what about the other reporters? Is there anything I should know about them?''

''This is Grogan's show. Good luck.''

''This has been very helpful, Mark. Thanks.''

Joe hung up the phone and went out to Jan's desk.

''I'm going out. If Stan Ostrowski calls, tell him I'll meet him for lunch at the Phoenix Country Club tomorrow at noon. I want to give him some reading material before his pals come out to my house.''

■ ■ ■

DRIVING UP to the club the next day, Joe found Stan Ostrowski walking back and forth on the sidewalk.

''Glad you could make it,'' Joe said with enthusiasm.

''I wasn't sure I was coming until I got here. This is a violation of all Grogan's rules.''

''What do you mean?''

''Going out alone without another team member.''

''What made you do it?''

"I didn't think we'd be able to talk freely with someone else around. The truth is, you're the first person I've met since I came to Arizona who's had the guts to call a spade a spade and not worry about the impression he's creating. Not only that, but I've been thinking about your question."

"What question?"

"Not to change the subject, but this view is magnificent!" Ostrowski said as he sat down near the window in the main dining room. "What a great place to get away from it all!"

Joe looked out the window at the golf course. The flowers were at their most brilliant this time of year. But he couldn't remember the last time he felt he had gotten away from it all anywhere.

"Stan, that view is part of what people leave gray, grimy cities like Detroit and Chicago for. They get here and the sun shines every day. The scenery is clean and beautiful. The quality of their environment and the ease of life, day to day, are so superior to almost anywhere they came from, that people believe everything is rosy. It's hard to get all fired up about the things that worry people elsewhere. What's more, people tend not to pry. The likelihood is that I'll accept whatever you tell me about you without question. Phoenix isn't unique. That's the Sunbelt mentality."

Joe watched the reporter closely as he spoke. Stan had read him. "Now, what was my question?"

"Oh, yes. You asked me what would happen if I were to subject Chicago to the same kind of scrutiny that we're putting Phoenix through. Last night at dinner I asked Windman that question about Detroit, and Grogan about New York."

"What did they say?"

"Nothing. What could they say? We all know the answer," he said with a shrug. "So, where's this reading material you have for me?"

Joe opened his briefcase and took out three sheets of paper. "These are editorials that appeared around the state after Barnes's famous 'Hidden Cancer' series was published, disassociating the papers from Barnes's findings. Before I give them to you, I want you to know something. No matter what a person does, no one has the right to blow him away, but Barnes was no hero."

Stan set the pieces down on the table next to his plate.

■ ■ ■

WHEN JOE got back to the office, Jan told him that Tom had been looking for him and wanted to see him just as soon as he returned. As he walked down the hall to Tom's office, he was thinking that the more he talked to Ostrowski, the more he liked him. He wasn't a glory boy. He wasn't an egomaniac. He was just an honest guy trying to get at the truth. Well, Joe'd find out if his judgment was sound soon enough. Ostrowski had confirmed that his interview would be on the twenty-ninth, and Bob Goldwater's the following day.

"Joe!" He was passing Spencer's open door.

He stopped and went in. "Yeah, Spencer?"

"On your way to Tom's office?"

"Yeah."

"I'll be down in a minute. I want to see you, too."

"Okay."

When he got to Tom's office, Judd was there. Finally, bells went off.

"Well, well, well. What have we here? A spontaneous gathering of the big four?"

Spencer followed him into the office and closed the door.

"I understand you have some firm interview dates set up with the IRG," Tom began.

"My, my! Good news travels fast. Or is it bad news?"

"Well, Joe," Spencer responded in his deep bass voice, "that depends on how we handle it."

"We?"

"Well, yes. You'll need the advice of counsel, and Judd and I decided we were the logical choices."

"Oh, yeah? What do I need lawyers for? Am I on trial?"

"No. Of course not," Judd answered. "It's just that the firm has a vested interest in what these reporters say, and we feel that you've been too close to this project for too long to be objective."

"Do my ears deceive me?" he said in mock surprise. "The firm has a stake in this?"

"Look, Joe," Tom said with rising irritation, "there have been times lately when you've let your temper and your penchant for profanity get out of hand. We feel we owe it to you *and* us to see to it that you don't say anything that we may all regret."

"Let me see if I understand this. It's not Joe Corelli who needs representing—it's the firm. Is that how this whole patronizing pitch translates out?"

"There's no need to get testy," Spencer said. "You've been under great strain, and we'll just be there to help. I'll assist with questions about business transactions, and Judd will be keeping his eye peeled for a potential lawsuit."

Joe studied each of them in turn. "Okay. You wanna come to my party? Come. Jus' remember, it's goddamned fuckin' generous of me. You guys haven't done a fuckin' thing for me so far. But ya wanna come, come. But make sure ya understand, if the firm has suddenly decided it has an interest in this, then it's not just a selective interest. You're in this with me from here on in, or no deal. Got it?"

CHAPTER

18

THE HOUSE was U-shaped, lined with glass on the inside, cradling a pool between the two ells. Behind the pool loomed Camelback Mountain. Joe had spent the last hour pacing from one end of the house to the other. The kitchen faced the street, and each time he came to the front, he'd look out the window. Angela had posted a cloth banner on the refrigerator: "When life gives you lemons, make lemonade!" Joe chuckled to himself. The last few times he'd looked out, he was sure the same white Ford station wagon had driven by. Despite his partners' warnings about being calm and rational, he had downed half a bottle of Rémy Martin and had broken into a sweat. It was working. Joe was loose, and he was ready.

Angela was washing the breakfast dishes.

"Would you watch the cars passing by while you're standing here?"

"Sure. What am I looking for?"

"Three men in a car. I think they've driven by a few times already, casing the joint," he laughed nervously.

She shrugged and went on with what she was doing. After about ten minutes, she called him.

"Joe. A station wagon with three men in it just drove very slowly past the house, made a U-turn at the corner and is headed back this way."

He ran to the front door and opened it just as the car pulled into the drive. The man in the back seat jumped out first. Wearing a flannel shirt, polyester pants, a pair of saddle shoes, and a smug look, he sauntered up to Joe, held out his hand and introduced himself as Fred Penwick. Right behind him was an overweight younger man wearing a pullover sweater across the top of which a flock of geese flew from right to left. Below them, pulled over his pot belly, was a marsh whose reeds swayed as he walked. Jake Smith. The tallest of the three, David Holloway, greeted Joe and followed the others into the house. Joe thought to himself: Moe, Larry and Curley.

Angela had set up an urn of coffee on one of the tables by the pool.

"The day is too beautiful to stay inside," Joe announced as he ushered the reporters outside.

While they were helping themselves to some coffee, Judd and Spencer arrived.

"Gentlemen, let me introduce you to my partners. Judd Peters and Spencer Winthrop. David Holloway, Fred Penwick and Jake Smith."

While the men shook hands and exchanged greetings, Joe turned away to look up at the top of a tree near the back wall. When he was sure he had his guests' attention, he waved his arm and yelled, "Okay, Angelo, you can take your Uzi and go home. These guys are all right."

The reporters looked confused, Judd and Spencer alarmed. Joe laughed himself silly.

"Let's get underway, men!" he shouted, clapping his hands.

They all took seats around the table. Joe had set up a tape recorder that was loaded and ready to go. Fred Penwick had brought one, too, and plugged his in next to Joe's.

"Before we go on tape, fellas, let's establish some ground rules. If you get to ask me questions, I get to ask you questions. I'm not gonna answer your questions unless you answer my questions. Just so you understand, even though you're interviewing me, I have the right to ask questions, too. Now, whether or not you answer is, I suppose, your prerogative. I'm not so foolish as to think you're gonna tell me your sources, but I may ask you questions related to your sources. For example, you may talk about 'authorities.' I won't ask you which authorities, but I may ask you if they were police officers, state troopers, politicians. You might say the FBI. Then I might say, the FBI in Phoenix, Arizona? The FBI in Washington, D.C.? The FBI in Milwaukee, Mr. Holloway?

"Next, how are you gonna use the tapes? Are they solely for information purposes to assist you in evaluating these discussions and determining whether to write something about them? That's fine. That's the same way we'll use the tapes, just to have a record of what went on. They are not for your publication. They are absolutely my property. They are not for your dissemination. Is that agreed?"

"Agreed," Holloway said.

"Mr. Peters and Mr. Winthrop reserve the same right to ask questions. Just so you understand. Did you bring any data with you? Any writings, any pictures, any materials that I will be asked to look at? If you did, anything I'll be asked to look at, I'll want a copy of. The tape will, in a sense, be referring to an exhibit, so I'll need a copy. Do you agree?"

"Yes," Holloway said again.

Joe turned to Fred Penwick. "I understand you have my family tree on the wall of suite 1939 at the Adams Hotel. Is that true?"

"Well, it's not a tree. It's kind of a chart."

"I want a copy of that chart if I'm going to go forward with this meeting. Is that agreed to?"

"Yes, it's agreed to."

"All right, then, let's go on tape."

They turned on their recorders—except that the reporters' didn't work. They fussed, fiddled, shook, plugged and unplugged, but they couldn't get it started.

Joe folded his arms across his chest, leaned back in his chair, and enjoyed the show. Finally he said, "Hey, Spencer! Is this their lucky day or what? What do you say we let them have a copy of our tapes?"

For the next four hours, most of the interview centered on real-estate transactions. Holloway and Smith told Joe that they were the IRG's experts. Fifteen minutes into the session, it was apparent to Joe that they knew as much about real estate as he knew about astrophysics. Holloway didn't know the difference between a deed and a mortgage, or a deal structured for tax purposes as opposed to a straight, all-cash investment in raw land. He didn't understand the distinctions between a limited partnership and a general partnership. Joe's six-year-old son could have asked more intelligent questions than these crackers. Joe leaned back and gave them relaxed answers.

Then: "Just to get on a little different subject," Fred Penwick said, "What is your relationship to Mike Franco?"

Joe didn't move a muscle, but his antennae were immediately erect. Just how far into his past had these guys gone? Were his worst fears about to stand up and salute? He took a deep breath. Another. The important thing was to keep himself under control. About an hour earlier, he had switched from coffee back to cognac. Everyone else had joined him; yet, while they were becoming more relaxed and less formal, he was feeling more agitated.

"Mike Franco went to law school with me at Notre Dame. Class of . . . Honey!" he called to Angela, who was on her way out with a bucket of ice. "What year did I graduate?"

"From what?"

"Law school."

"Nineteen sixty-seven."

"His wife, Ann, was one of my wife's closest friends."

"Please refer to Ann in the present tense," Angela corrected him as she turned to go back into the house.

"Excuse me. She *is* one of my wife's closest friends. She and Mike are divorced. Mike, my wife doesn't like. First time they came to my house, he brought a bottle of J&B scotch, and we watched the Notre Dame-Air Force game. The Irish won it 34-7. We got plastered. The same night, I watched Potter Stewart judge the Moot Court finals. . . ."

"Uh, did you ever handle any investments for Mr. Franco?" Penwick wasn't going to let Joe change the subject.

"No."

"You did not handle any investments for Mike Franco?"

"I handled one deal for Mr. Franco as a trustee in Arizona. Mr. Franco came to me in about nineteen—I'm gonna speculate now—about 1972 and said he was a trustee for a trust and wanted to invest in some limited partnerships. Did Goldcor have any deals for him? I said yes, we had an apartment deal for him. 'If you'd like to invest, here's the deal.' And I told him the deal. The deal was the Roman Village apartments on Thirteenth Street and Osborn, and the Northview apartments on Central Avenue, all in Phoenix. He bought two apartment houses."

"As trustee?" Judd asked.

"As a limited partnership interest held in trust."

"A what?" Penwick asked.

"A limited partnership," Joe responded with irritation. He had already explained what that was to these clowns. Weren't they listening?

"Oh, right. Excuse me. Were you aware of who the limited partners were and who the general partners were?"

"The daughter of a judge. That's all I was aware of."

"Joe will answer as best he can," Spencer interrupted. "But we won't get into the attorney-client province."

"Agreed, we won't. We'll ask the questions. If you can respond, you'll respond."

"Go on!" Joe cut in. He wasn't in any mood to watch two amateurs parry.

''Did Mr. Franco suggest why he was coming to Arizona? I mean of all places. He's from Boston, isn't he?''

''Yeah. Lemme tell ya about it. Joe Corelli got him through law school, baby. He used to come to Joe Corelli to teach him what it was all about in agency, torts, criminal law, contracts, constitutional law, tax law. Yeah, he came t' Arizona cause I got him through law school! Because he loves me—that's why he came to Arizona.''

''To the extent that you can comment on that, do you know who the other members of the apartment partnership were?''

''I don't know what you mean by 'other members.' But let me try again. He established a trust. He asked me to draw up a trust agreement for some six-year-old girl—I'd have to look in my files in my office to tell you her name.''

''Would Bell be right?'' Penwick looked like a kid with a Popsicle.

''Bell! Right on, baby!''

''To your knowledge, would that be the daughter of a judge?''

''I already said that. Movin' on!''

''So he came to you and said, 'Hey, I've got some money here for a trust for the six-year-old daughter of a judge. I'd like to invest in something that you might think is worthwhile out there.' Is that more or less accurate?''

''Yeah, you're close.''

''Who else was in this partnership?''

''Only Goldcor Incorporated.'' Joe's voice started to lower and take on a gravelly quality that even his partners hadn't heard before.

At that point, the tape recorder clicked off. Joe got up, turned the tape over and began testing to see if it was working.

''*Uno, due, tre, quattro.* Testing! *Uno, due, tre, quattro.* Okay! We're going, baby. Sony! The Japanese contingents! We're on the air, baby! Shoot!''

Spencer laughed, pretending this was a normal aspect of Joe's sense of humor.

''How much did Mr. Franco contribute to this partnership?'' Penwick asked.

''Two hundred thousand dollars,'' Joe answered as he lit a cigar.

''Did Goldcor have any other business dealings with Mr. Franco?''

''No. Now, may I ask you a question?''

''Go ahead.''

''Why Mr. Franco?''

''Well, there's a strange sequence of events, a suspicious set of circumstances. I'd like to get to the bottom of it.''

''Shoot your best shot.''

''I'd like to know why records relating to business transactions between Goldcor and Franco were found in the bottom of a trunk of a car registered in Mr. Franco's name that was stopped by Customs. The two individuals in the car were busted for narcotics coming across the border.''

''Who was driving the car?''

''Where was that?'' Spencer interjected.

''Somewhere on the Canadian border.''

''I asked you who they were!'' Joe whipped at Penwick.

''We don't have the names of the people who were arrested—we're checking it now. What we're asking is—''

''Let me tell you something!''

''Joe, let him finish,'' Spencer advised.

''Have you heard anything about it?'' Penwick said.

''Have I heard anything about it? Yeah, I've heard something about it! Butch called me. Lemme tell ya the story. Franco called me and he says, 'What's this? Somebody's got my name on the Canadian border linking me to Goldcor!' And I said, 'Butch! Are you nuts? What are you talkin' about? What the hell are you talkin' about?' An' he says again, 'Somebody got my name in the back of a trunk on the Canadian border.' 'Hey, Butch, cool it. This is bullshit. This is absolute bullshit. Unless you keep all your legal files in the trunk of your car. Fuck, our deal's almost five years old.' Who was in the car?''

''We don't have the answer. So what's your response?''

''Believe me—let me tell you straight out—you're jerkin' off!''

''No!'' Judd looked frantic.

''Relax, Peters. Lemme tell 'em.''

''But, Joe, the answer—''

''Judd baby, it's bullshit!''

''The answer is you don't know anything about it,'' he insisted. ''Franco told you about it.''

''But he heard the same bullshit from them.''

''Joe. Joe,'' Spencer tried to break in. ''But, I mean, presumably—''

''That's so fuckin' ridiculous! That's preposterous! That is so fuckin' preposterous!''

''Joe! Just a second,'' Judd persisted. ''Whether it's bullshit or not, the question is whether you know anything about it.''

''I know absolutely nothing about it!''

''All right,'' Penwick continued. ''When did Mr. Franco call you and inform you?''

''About three weeks ago.''

''What did he say with regard to—''

''He said what I tole ya, an' I tole him, 'Don't worry about it.' So Butch says, 'Tell those reporters whatever they wanna know. We got nuthin to hide. An' please, tell 'em for me that they're wastin' their fuckin' time!' ''

''Just what do you find ridiculous about this?'' Holloway asked.

''That anyone would find records with Franco's name on the Canadian border! You're talkin' about a deal that went down five years ago. You expect me to believe that Franco's carryin' around files of a deal, where there's been no activity for at least four years—in the trunk of his car. Whattaya think, he's a fuckin' hobo? He's a prominent lawyer in Boston. This is so much poppycock! You guys're in the twilight zone.''

''Are you suggesting it didn't happen?'' Holloway asked again, taking over the questioning.

''I'm suggesting it didn't happen! For all I know, you fuckin' guys manufactured this story! You can bust me!''

''Hey, hey, Joe! Just calm down!'' Spencer said. ''Look, there's no way in the world we can dispute the records you found. You guys have ascertained the records were found, fine. But the statement is very clear that there's no basis that anyone here knows for linking Goldcor and the Canadian border. There's no basis for linking Franco and the Canadian border, as far as anyone here knows. We can all speculate about it, but some of the adjectives used, like ridiculous and preposterous, are because no one knows anything about it.''

''Absolutely no connection! That's so much bullshit!''

''Did Mr. Franco, in his telephone conversation with you, offer any explanation, based on what he knew about it, as to what had happened?'' Penwick asked as he resumed the questioning.

''He laughed! He said, 'What do you know about it?' I said, 'It's bullshit! That's so much shit, I can't believe it!' So much shit!''

''So you have no idea. . . .''

''You guys are gettin' your information from a buncha ignorant scumbags! It's so much horseshit!''

''Let me tell you our position now. We came across this information, and we just want to know if you know anything about it.''

''All I'm tellin' you is from my heart. I'm tellin' you from my heart! It's pure, unadulterated bullshit!''

''Listen,'' Judd interrupted. ''You offered that as an explanation to a question we asked and that is, 'Why all of this about Franco and North Village Partnership, and a trustee under a trust?' And your explanation is that some documents were found in the back of a car at a Customs station in Canada. I may be naive, but I don't see what connection that has to the prior questions.''

''The point is, sir, that if these papers were found in the trunk of a car, allegedly bearing some form of narcotics, this is a suspicious occurrence, and we'd like to find out about it.''

''No doubt about it,'' Spencer acknowledged. ''Sure.''

''So that led to these other questions about Franco?'' Judd asked, still dissatisfied with the explanation.

''All we are doing is attempting to ascertain, from Mr. Corelli, a factual background on a number of transactions—''

''That may or may not have any relationship whatsoever,'' Judd added.

''Absolutely right. We have other things to bring up. We are not saying that this is all a chain of events, and, based on his answers, we'll finally make a determination—''

''Lemme tell you something. Unlike my distinguished colleagues here, I'm from the streets. And my street sense tells me that you jokers are playin' with yourselves. It's bullshit, but go ahead,'' Joe said.

''Were there other records?'' Spencer asked.

''I have very limited information.''

''What were the records?'' Joe asked, suddenly realizing that in all this time no one had established just what they were talking about.

''Look,'' Spencer said, dismissing the question, ''no one here has any information, so let's just go on.''

''Well,'' Penwick resumed, ''I think we're off the subject. Let's get back to the subject.''

Joe stood up and turned off the tape recorder. ''There will be no other subject, gentlemen. This interview is over.''

He walked across the lawn to the door, where he waited as the reporters gathered their belongings. Fred Penwick walked into the house last, and as Joe closed the door behind him, he put his arm around Fred's shoulder.

"So, what do you think of my house, Mr. Penwick? I noticed you looking around when you arrived."

"It's very nice."

"Can you afford a house like this on a reporter's salary?"

"Not even close." Penwick chuckled at the far-fetched idea.

"Do you think I can afford to buy a house like this on a lawyer's salary?"

"I wouldn't know."

"Just for the record, I can." Joe tightened his hold on the reporter's shoulder and spoke in a whisper. "I bet you think I'm some spoiled-rotten trust baby, and somebody gave me the money, right? Or maybe you figure because I'm Italian, I'm a hood. You see my wife over there? Pregnant as God knows what? She looks harmless, doesn't she?" He put his mouth up close to the reporter's ear. "She's a killer! Not one—four hits to her credit. Don't for a minute think we'd bother her in her present condition. She needs to take it easy, keep her feet up, give her trigger finger a rest. Besides, all that hormonal turmoil they go through might make her queasy. But as soon as she has the kid, she'll be back on call."

Joe let go of Penwick and solemnly shook the reporter's hand. "Now don't forget," he said. "Background only. I don't want to go reading about my wife's peccadilloes in the paper."

CHAPTER

19

SUNDAY MORNING was cold and gray. Low-lying clouds nestled like cotton balls in the curve of Camelback Mountain. A fine mist permeated the air. They'd have to meet inside today.

Angela had set up the coffee in the living room, but Joe decided to bypass coffee and go directly to cognac. Judd and Spencer had lectured him yesterday about his language and general decorum, which he attributed to too much coffee. He had to be calm today, not only because he had to assist Judd as Bob's attorney, but because he wanted to go up against Grogan with all his faculties sharp.

At ten a.m. they started to arrive. First Bob Goldwater, looking as cool as if he were about to play golf. Judd Peters was next, and Joe saw the alarm in his eyes when he noticed Joe's snifter. Saved by the bell—the reporters arrived. Penwick and Stan Ostrowski greeted their host and walked in, leaving him with a clear view of Grogan.

Despite all he'd heard, Joe was unprepared for the sight before him. Grogan's gray hair wasn't simply disheveled from the wind; it looked as if he'd just lifted his head from the pillow after a sleepless night. The smooth, puffy parts of his face were clean-shaven, but black stubble protruded from between his jowls. He maneuvered his bulk into the living room and onto the couch.

When he sat, his fat belly oozed out between the buttons of his shirt.

As everyone introduced himself, set up tape recorders and got the preliminaries out of the way, Joe kept wondering what kind of person would choose to look like that? Was it his way of saying "up yours" to one and all? Did he need a body that reflected the enormity of his ego? Or was he so profoundly insecure that he had to insure the kind of negative response in others that made him feel comfortable? Whatever the answer, Joe decided, anyone who looked like that had to be dangerous, for no other reason than that his head was in trouble.

The day went smoothly. Grogan did most of the questioning. Based on Mark's description of the Rosenzweig interview, Grogan was much more civil to Bob than he'd been to Harry. For seven hours, Bob answered questions with his usual unflappable candor. A good deal of the time was devoted to Mother Goose's, Uncle Joe and Mel Adelbaum. Joe could see that Bob was doing a good job of making his points with Ostrowski.

Joe was pleased with himself. He kept his cool almost effortlessly. He represented Bob with appropriate professional detachment. Throughout, he kept his eyes on Grogan.

Buried in the flesh of the reporter's right hand was a pen with which he took microscopic notes. A fuckin' anal retentive, Joe thought. A Pall Mall was tucked into the corner of his mouth at all times, the ash ending up on his shirt. Grogan's breathing was so labored that it caused a rhythmic wheeze, like that of a faint whistle. How long could someone in his condition go on living? The boys on Avenue U would take book on it.

When the session came to an end, Joe picked up a file he had earlier placed near at hand and turned to Grogan.

"I wonder if I could have a private word with you, Mr. Grogan?"

"Sure. Where?"

"Just outside by the pool. It's stopped raining."

As they turned to the door, Judd interjected, ''Excuse me. I've got to be running, and I need a minute with Joe before I head out.''

Joe nodded, and he and Judd walked into the kitchen.

''What's up, Peters?''

''It went very well today. Why do you want to chance talking to Grogan?''

''C'mon, Judd, I'm not gonna blow it. Ya know, freedom of expression? What I'd really like to do is take the son of a bitch to my kid's playroom, lock the door and see which one of us comes out alive. But we learn, don't we, to curb such instincts in this civilized society of ours? So don't you worry, Peters. Thanks for comin', I love ya.''

Joe walked back towards Grogan, who was again seated, and pointed toward the pool. With great difficulty, Grogan hauled his body off the couch and followed.

''I want to show you something,'' Joe said, as he pointed to the left. ''That's Barry Goldwater's house.''

''I know.''

''Oh. I didn't know you knew. You're from New York. Ya know, I'm from New York, too.''

''Yeah. I knew that.''

''Where'd you know that from, the chart you have on your wall?''

''What chart?''

''Come on. Does it say where I was born? When?''

Grogan regarded him with mute eyes.

Joe got to the point. ''Ya know, Mr. Grogan, I don't even understand why you're here. You've been in Arizona for the better part of the last four months. I know you know there's nuthin here. There're some interesting, spicy stories you could write, but not one of national or even local consequence.

''So I don't know why you're here, Mr. Grogan. I could speculate. Nice weather? Ya gettin' enough to eat? I'm not gonna break your balls. I'll make you an offer. And that offer's because

Newsworld's in Westchester County. I'll fly back to New York, and I'll take you in a chauffeur-driven limousine—that I'll pay for—I'll take you for a ride and I'll personally point out to you more active Mafia figures within a five-mile radius of your paper's offices than are alive in the entire State of Arizona.

"Why aren't ya there, Mr. Grogan? What are ya doin' here?"

"All that has nothing to do with anything."

"Wrong. I read in the *New York Times* that they think you guys should investigate your own cities. I read that other reporters weren't particularly happy with this project, thinking that maybe you were taking the First Amendment too far. Mr. Grogan, there's a bar in your neighborhood called Club Sahara. It's owned by Carmine "Big Barracuda" Lombardi. Now, you know who he is, don't you? He probably lives within two miles of where you live. Do you write stories about him and all the guys who own all the bars out there? What are you doin' in Phoenix, Mr. Grogan? What do ya have against the Italians in Phoenix, Mr. Grogan?"

"I don't know what you're talking about."

"Truly, Mr. Grogan? Then you listen closely to the tapes of the last two days and tell me what percentage of the people you and your playmates inquired about had Italian surnames."

"Look, our editor at *Newsworld* is Peter Petrillo, so don't hand me that shit."

"You don't have to get defensive, Mr. Grogan. I was just inquiring."

With Grogan looking uncomfortable, Joe moved in on him. "But you know, Mr. Grogan, I'm glad *you're* here, 'cause yesterday you sent the rookies. Where you got those guys from is beyond me. They reminded me of the Three Stooges. Penwick seemed to have the most experience, only he's not smart enough to accomplish anything. But now I have you, the boss. You ask intelligent questions. You can follow a line of reasoning. You remember what we're talking about. I'm impressed. Smith isn't even a reporter, and Holloway, your real-estate expert, doesn't know shit from third base about real estate. All Penwick wants to do is look at my house and ask smart-ass questions. Only Ostrowski's a different animal. Ostrowski's a prince!

"Let me tell you something, Mr. Grogan. I've got a little First Amendment background myself. I thought it was a tremendous stronghold of freedom that you guys should be able to express your opinions freely on any subject—with virtual impunity. I did.

"I stopped thinking that about five years ago, in 1971, when Mr. Barnes wrote a series of articles that you undoubtedly have read. Just so you understand, in my opinion that was the biggest pile of garbage and the most abusive misuse of the First Amendment that I personally had ever encountered. Just so you understand.

"It was, Mr. Grogan, until two weeks ago. 'Cause two weeks ago I got this magazine."

Joe pulled *Chic* out of the folder he had tucked under his arm. He watched closely for a reaction. He had to give the fat bastard credit. Grogan didn't even wince. The guy must be a hell of a poker player.

"I don't even know how to pronounce it. Chick, Cheek? A judge here in Phoenix gave it to me, Mr. Grogan. Now, I read all about your project in the *New York Times*. How you're a Pulitzer Prize-winner, a veteran journalist, and this was a project to vindicate Dan Barnes and the work he did. Mr. Grogan, you haven't published one word of this series yet, you and all the other Pulitzer Prize-winners who are here. Yet you gave a scoop to Larry Flynt? You got animals here with women, dogs—the worst piece of shit. How much did ya get paid for this? Was your project running out of money? This is who a Pulitzer Prize-winner gives his scoop article to? The first time your group's findings were gonna be discussed at any length? You expect me to take you seriously, Mr. Grogan? I ain't gonna take you seriously no more!

"Let me read you something, Mr. Grogan, that may end up being your undoing. Listen to what you said."

The reporter looked at the page that Joe turned to and immediately asked, very defensively, "How do you know I said that?"

"Mr. Grogan, it's in this magazine!" Joe said, his intensity rolling like thunder in his chest. "It's in quotes and this magazine only quotes you, Mr. Grogan. This was an interview with you, Mr. Grogan, the Pulitzer Prize-winner."

"But I—"

"You say," Joe began reading, pronouncing every word slowly and distinctly so the reporter was forced to focus on each one, 'Cops have a great idea in their solidarity. When you kill a cop, everybody's after you. I think newspapers should adopt that attitude. When somebody kills a reporter, a good reporter'—

"I'll give you the benefit of the doubt on that one, Mr. Grogan.

"'When somebody kills a reporter, a "good" reporter doing his job, every newspaper should show solidarity and make it apparent to other people who might have the same idea that it's more trouble than it's worth. Create an object lesson by saying, *"We'll bust your balls, we'll bust the whole community's balls,* if people in that community think they can take out reporters." Whoever killed Dan Barnes is less important than that every illegal thinking member of Phoenix. . . .'

"Mr. Grogan! You're gonna decide who all the 'illegal thinking members of Phoenix' are? And how are you gonna do that, tell me? And all these clowns, those monkeys you sent over here yesterday, are they gonna decide who the illegal thinking members of Phoenix are? Are you kidding me, Mr. Grogan? One of those guys got indicted for bribing a police officer. Another of your reporters is AWOL. Don't look so surprised, Mr. Grogan. You think we haven't been doing our homework, Mr. Grogan? We have our sources, too, Mr. Grogan. Now, is Mr. Penwick an illegal thinking member of Indianapolis? Is Mr. Woolf an illegal thinking member of Tucson? You guys don't even understand what a washout Dan Barnes was until somebody decided to blow 'im away. And you're gonna decide who the illegal thinking members of Phoenix are?''

''You know you—''

''I haven't finished. 'That every illegal thinking member of Phoenix remembers it with great distaste for the rest of their lives because of what happened afterward.'

''I got a lot of distaste to date, and I'm sure I'm gonna have a lot more distaste by the time you get outa town. You got a lot of innocent people having terrible distaste, Mr. Grogan. Just so you understand it. Let me go on. 'In the course of that you hope to throw light on everybody involved, higher ups, but the deeper thrust is to buy life insurance for every reporter in the United States.' To buy life insurance for reporters?

''Mr. Grogan, now I ask you, do you think the founding fathers intended the First Amendment to be used to buy life insurance for reporters? Is that what the First Amendment is all about, Mr. Grogan? That any time a collective group sets out to do something, they can abuse the privilege they've been given? The freedom that protects their right to act—use it for any purpose? You think you're gonna buy fuckin' life insurance, Mr. Grogan, with the First Amendment? That's not how I understand it, Mr. Grogan. That's not how I understand the First Amendment, just so ya know.

''Now I wanna tell ya one last thing,'' Joe continued, in an increasingly raspy voice. ''I lived through Dan Barnes in 1971. I saw the aftermath of Dan Barnes, with grown-ups, with kids. The adults suffered. But the kids really got hurt! Kids with Italian surnames were embarrassed to go to school. Kids didn't know how to explain it to their friends. Kids cried! I had a son who was one year old then, Mr. Grogan. Thank God, he was only one. Today, Mr. Grogan, my son Joseph is six years old, going on fourteen. He's very smart! He hears everything! You hurt Joseph, Mr. Grogan, an' I'll kill you!''

CHAPTER 20

HIS ARM hurting was what awakened him. He yanked it out from under his body, and opened one eye. There was no sunlight coming into the bedroom. He reached out his hand toward Angela, but remembering, pulled it back. With the baby coming so soon, she was hardly sleeping at all. She would open the sofa bed in the den, but after an hour or two of tossing, she'd move to the big chair in the living room, where she was relatively comfortable, and she could at least doze there the rest of the night. It seemed reasonable enough. But he wondered what her excuse would be for staying out of his bed once the baby came. He didn't care much. Hell, he didn't care, period. He was glad it was still dark, not time to get up. He'd sleep a little more. He needed more. Where had he read that waking up before morning was from worry? He couldn't remember, but it fit. He had worries; that was for sure. But what about? He reached to remember, but couldn't. Couldn't be that bad if he couldn't remember. He turned on his side, nestled his head on his arms, and let go, drifting slowly off . . . content that when it was time to get up, his alarm would tell him.

■ ■ ■

THERE WAS such powerful blackness it reached down to his toes and immobilized them. His whole body was held in place by the unrelenting blue-blackness, a darkness impenetrable as the jungle he could only hear and smell. The blackness had edges, sharp enough to cut through centuries of jungle growth. He was at the center, and the edges were all around him, closing in slowly but inexorably. When they reached him, he knew, it would all be over. And then the terrible waiting would seem easy compared to what would happen to him, the blades coming at him from every angle, aimed at every limb and organ. And his blood would run unnoticed in the blackness until all the life had run out of him, drop by excruciating drop. He howled into the blackness, but the sound was drowned out by the roar of animals laughing at this pitiful prey. He howled louder, his lungs emptying themselves of every sound within him. Again, and—

■ ■ ■

A HAND was shaking his shoulder. Not the executioner holding him down between the blades. Not the hand of a rescuer, either, lifting him out to safety. The hand belonged to a woman, whose powers were of a different order. He felt the hand. Not loving. Not Ashley. Impersonal. Angela. Of course. He wasn't in the jungle; only in the jungle that was his life. He shook his head clear of the dream. Blinked his eyes open. The room was very light. He must have turned off his alarm and fallen back to sleep. He could do it again, sleep. Especially if waking meant looking into Angela's face. He clenched his eyes shut. Maybe she'd go away. But the hand touched him again, pushing his shoulder back and forth. She always was a persistent bitch. "What time is it?" he asked Angela.

"It's half past two, Mr. Corelli."

Joe turned slowly on his back and located the face that went with the voice. Definitely not Angela. Whatever else she was, even in her ninth month Angela was still pretty. This face had never seen a pretty reflection. It was attached to a body that was much too thin. No woman should be so thin. There was nothing to grab onto. And with that pasty complexion she shouldn't wear white. Blue might help. Or a warm rose. Why didn't women know what looked good on them? That . . . uniform didn't . . .

Joe's eyes flicked rapidly around the room. "What the fuck!" he said, sitting bolt upright.

"Now, Joe, we want to stay calm," the uniform said.

Her voice was reedy, like her body. He hated it instantly. And why was she talking down to him? Nobody talked down to him! And where the hell did she come off calling him by his first name?"

"You have ten seconds to tell me where 'we' are, and who you are," he said in a voice that could cut a diamond.

The uniform's mouth thinned out even more; she was trying to smile. "Of course. You're in St. Paul's and I'm Mrs. Pearlstein."

Mrs., huh? Well, there never was any accounting for tastes, was there? "Now, Mrs. Pearlstein, tell me what I'm doing in St. Paul's."

"Well, you've been sleeping, mostly. You came in because you were very tired and needed a lot of rest." Her lipless mouth spread in a tight smile again. "And you've been getting it."

Her voice was like a metal dipping-stick going in and out of a vat of maple syrup. He wanted her out of his room. But he hadn't gotten enough from her yet. He'd rather have asked someone else, but he wasn't about to put off knowing even a minute longer. "And just how long have I been catching up on my sleep?"

"Since day before yesterday. I'm sure you're feeling a bit rested by now, aren't you?"

"I feel fine," he said. The truth was, if it weren't for the two-dozen questions pounding in his head, he wouldn't mind going back to sleep for a couple more hours.

"Ready?" Mrs. Pearlstein was asking.

"Ready for what?"

''I told you,'' she said with transparent patience, ''that it's good you're feeling rested, because Dr. Hammer is waiting for you in his office.''

Quickly he ran down the list. Rappaport was his dentist, Miles his orthopedist, Cranston his head doctor, and Erskine his doctor when he got a cold every four years. ''Who's Dr. Hammer?'' he said.

''Your doctor.''

''I haven't got a Doctor Hammer.'' Firmly. ''There's been some mistake.''

''You can discuss that with Doctor Hammer,'' she said.

■ ■ ■

DOCTOR HAMMER was about thirty, with one of those faces that show what he looked like as a baby and what he'll look like as an old man, but there's never one moment when you can say, here's a man in his prime.

Joe took charge of the situation and asked Doctor Hammer some basic questions. He got answers that would bounce in any bank. Under any other circumstances, Joe would have told this man off swiftly and been on his way. But his instinct told him not to blow up for any reason. So, very calmly, he said, ''Couldn't you at least take me off some of these medications? It sounds like a chemical avalanche.''

''Mr. Corelli, you're not getting any medication you don't require. And you really must take it as prescribed. It's for your own good, I assure you.''

''Doctor, I don't know you. Why should your assurances mean anything to me?''

Doctor Hammer made a church steeple of his hands and looked at him. Joe wished he could smash the man's pale face in for him, but he knew that was a wish his fairy godmother wasn't going to deliver. At least not now. He retreated. ''Look, Doctor, I'm not into taking a bunch of drugs. But the nurse says I'm supposed to take them all.''

''That's her job,'' the doctor said blandly.

''But *you* can cut back this stuff.'' He took a deep breath. ''Please.''

''I'm sorry, Mr. Corelli, but right now you need what I've prescribed in order to stay calm. You must realize how important it is for you to remain calm, not to get upset.''

''You're upsetting me! For Chrissake, can't you see that?'' The doctor sat up straighter in his chair. His hand moved almost imperceptibly toward a buzzer on his desk. He was about to send for reinforcements. He thought Joe was crazy.

Well, why not? He was a doctor for crazies, wasn't he? The whole horrendous thing had its own internal logic.

Joe forced himself to sit back in his chair. ''Look,'' he said. ''I realize that when I came in here I was exhausted beyond reason. But these past couple of days, I've gotten lots of sleep. I'm better. At least take me off the Thorazine. I've heard too many horror stories about that shit. And it gives me terrible dreams.''

''Oh?'' Doctor Hammer looked as interested as if Joe had left off a dirty joke in the middle.

He was damned if he was going to tell this guy that in all his dreams he was either dying or dead already. Fuck him. ''I don't remember them specifically, but I wake up upset—and you said it was bad for me to get upset.''

The doctor smiled. Joe wished he had a fast print-out on his IQ.

''We'll think about taking you off the Thorazine, but in return I want you to think about joining our therapy sessions starting today.''

''Sure,'' Joe said. The guy wanted to deal, he'd deal. On the outside, Joe would never give his word and then renege. But this wasn't the real world, so he wasn't giving his real word.

Only saying what the doctor wanted to hear. He *had* to get off the Thorazine.

It wasn't that Joe didn't think he needed help. He knew he needed help. But not what this guy was offering. He didn't need help from an enemy like Hammer, but from his family and his friends.

Where the hell was everybody?

CHAPTER 21

SOME PRAYERS are answered more slowly than others. It wasn't the next day, but the day after that, that Miss Dwyer, another gem in white, told Joe he had a visitor.

Joe rushed to the visitor's lounge. Who had come? He practically ran into the room and—head on—into Tony. He was right about blood: when push came to shove, blood was all that counted. Angela and he were not related by blood—except for the time he'd hit her—the one fuckin' time out of thousands he'd wanted to—and her lip split. As for his partners coming to see him, they didn't have any blood at all, let alone his. But Tony—Tony was real family.

He laughed with the joy of recognition, and hit Tony on the back. "You got no idea how glad I am to see you," he said. The thought came from nowhere: You were always five steps ahead of me in losing control. How come I'm in here instead of you? He shoved it aside. The fact was, he was here, and the point was, Tony was here to straighten things out for him.

Tony had moved away toward the window. Backed off? That thought, too, Joe pushed away. He walked over to a couple of chairs near the window. "C'mon," he said to his cousin. "Let's sidown."

Joe moved his chair a couple of feet back, putting extra space between them. He didn't want Tony to feel he was pressuring him in any way. He didn't want Tony to leave before he could explain things to him, and with Tony, there was always the danger the spirit would move him to walk.

"We gotta talk, Tony," he said, making sure to keep his voice steady. "I can't stay in this place. This Doctor Hammer I pulled is wet behind the ears out of med school. And fer Chrissake, he's from someplace in Utah. Shit, I didn't even know where Utah was until I came to Phoenix. I mean, what's in Utah except that fancy temple? Do they even have a decent medical school? This guy keeps asking me questions, but he ain't about to tell me anything. I've seen him three times already, but he refuses to give me a rational explanation of what's goin' down here. He just keeps tellin' me to take my medication, like I was a kid or a senile old man. And the nurses—Tony, the nurses are off the wall! They won't leave me alone. They keep sayin' t' me that I'm making too many phone calls. They say—so fuckin' sweetly—I oughta be restin' and forget the outside world. Christ, I've had more rest the last few days than I've had altogether since Christmas! I'm so rested I'm near ready to be laid out. And it's not only all the rest that's doin' me in. They keep giving me this Thorazine shit that makes me feel worse than when I checked into this rotten hotel. Tony, take my word for it, this ain't La Costa."

Tony hadn't said a word. He let Joe let it all out, and Joe was grateful. Tony, who was always in a hurry, was sitting there like he had no place to go all day. And Joe could see in his eyes that his cousin was feeling for him. So he was surprised that when Tony finally said something he said, "Joe, what you probably ought to do is get yerself moved to the third floor." He took a deep breath.

Tony nervous? That was a new one. "What's so special about the third floor?" Joe asked, keeping it light.

"It's a . . . the . . . ward, you know. . . ."

''Tony, I'm very calm. I'm not gonna let you have it, no matter what you say. So let *me* have it. What's on the third floor that ain't here? I mean, we got all kindsa amenities.''

''The psychiatric ward,'' Tony said. You could see it hurt him to say it.

''I see,'' Joe responded, knowing suddenly how Caesar must have felt.

''No, you don't, Joe. Look, just agree to go through all their tests—they got a whole battery of these tests—and they'll prove there's nuthin wrong with you.''

''Tony, I'm not crazy.'' Softly, oh so softly. He'd never known a scream could come out so softly.

''A course not. That's the whole idea. To show 'em that. Then you can check outa this joint with a clean bill a health, and you can either take off to La Costa or go wherever y' want. Everybody'll be satisfied. You won't be bugged by these nurses, and there'll be a lotta people you can talk to. Whattaya say?''

Joe wasn't sure. Not even close. But in a situation where everyone was keeping things from him so he knew almost nothing, he did know two things: Tony understood how scary the moodswings were, that was one. The second was, he loved Joe. Joe didn't have a better bet going than that.

''Okay,'' he said. ''On two conditions.''

Tony grinned. ''My cousin the wheeler-dealer rides again.''

''Maybe yes, maybe no. These are the conditions. You get them to discontinue the Thorazine, and you bring me some books to read.''

''I'll get ya the books for sure, and I'll try on the Thorazine.

''Not good enough. No more Thorazine or no third floor.''

Tony nodded. ''No more Thorazine. What books ya want?''

''Let's see. *Trinity*. And *Roots*. And *Joey,* of course.''

''Anything else?'' Tony looked at him, waiting patiently. It was amazing that Tony hadn't ended this meeting with the abruptness with which he bolted from almost any conversation.

Joe felt very grateful, but knew it'd embarrass Tony if he told him. So he said only, ''That's the lot.'' Joe got up. He would have liked Tony to stay longer, to talk more. But it felt so good being the one who ended the visit, he didn't want to take a chance on pushing his luck.

''Hey,'' he said as they walked to the elevator together. ''I did wanna tell ya, they tested my heart, and it was okay.'' He punched Tony playfully in the chest. ''Cousin Anthony, babe, you and me, our hearts are all right. Ya know?''

Tony looked him straight in the eye, and nodded solemnly. He could've kissed his cousin for that. But then Tony put out his hand, and again was solemn as they shook each other's hand. Tony wasn't big on speeches, but that serious handshake was better than a speech, better than a hug or a kiss. Because now Joe knew for sure: no more Thorazine. Even if Tony had to organize a caper to steal their whole supply.

Family.

Still, he'd been in here four days. Ashley was right not to risk coming there and bumping into anyone, but where the fuck was Angela?

CHAPTER

22

NOTHING IN his past had prepared Joe for the third floor. If one word had to sum up his whole life till now, colorful might be as good a choice as any; if one word would have to describe the third floor, it'd be colorless. As if drabness were a wonder drug for mental illness.

As soon as you got off the elevator, there were these steel doors. Like something out of a forties movie about the pen. If Joe had been thinking halfway clearly, he'd have turned back then and there. Once you were on the inside of the steel doors, it was harder to turn back, Joe thought. Hah! Who said his sense of humor had lost its subtlety. Maybe his joke was a little sick, but what do you expect?

Joe stayed in his room. He'd worked hard to afford the kind of house he lived in, and he didn't like living in this putrid-green room in which the bed and desk and chair and single picture were all hospital-issue ascetic. Fortunately, Joe thought, the powers that be had not yet thought of a way to keep out the sunlight. Joe watched the sun play on the walls, admiring the noble, if hopeless, effort. If the sun could not cheer up the room, it could and did cheer him up a little. He'd sit at the desk, pulled close to the window, and look out, sucking in the warmth on his face. If he closed his eyes, the sun felt as caressing as Susie's hands. He missed Susie, but he missed the Marvin Gaye tapes she played even more. Boy, what he wouldn't give to hear some of those lyrics now. Well, they couldn't take everything away from him. He could play the songs in his head. He'd heard them enough times so his mind knew them as well as his gut. He listened now, and the honesty of that voice was as if Gaye were singing inside Joe's own heart. Sometimes he thought that this man, whom he'd never met, knew his every thought and disappointment and hope. Like God.

"Joe."

A soothing voice and a hand on his shoulder. He'd known He would come. Joe reached up and patted God's hand.

The hand wrenched away.

Joe turned. "Tony! Wow! I musta been daydreamin'. I thought you wuz Marilyn Monroe."

"Ain't she dead?"

"I tole ya I wuz dreamin'." He laughed, hoping.

Tony continued to look very, very uncomfortable.

It'd pass. "Got all my stuff?" Joe asked him.

"Yeah, I got it."

Did Tony realize he kept taking one step back after the other? If he didn't stop, he'd be out the door any second. Joe shouldn't have said what he did about Marilyn Monroe. But he had to think fast, and Tony knew he liked blondes, and Monroe was the blonde of blondes. He couldn't very well have told him he thought God had come in and touched him. He had to be careful. God was out there. Not in here. Goddammit, not in here for sure!

But out there, yes. Out there everything was in His sight, in His hands. Oh, yes. "Look, Tony. Look outa the window. Whattaya see?"

But Tony's eyes were glued on him.

"Hey! I said out the window!"

Tony moved slowly, as if he were walking toward him in Joe's pool. When he came close, he glanced once, real sharp, at Joe. Then he bent and looked out the window.

''Well, what do you see?'' Joe insisted.

''It's nice out.''

''Go on.''

''It's a sunny day. Beautiful.''

''That's God, Tony! Recognize God. When ya see God, ya reconcile eternity in a second. Listen to Him and understand.''

''I do,'' Tony mumbled.

''Good. I love ya, Tony. God loves ya.''

Joe turned to the books on the bed. ''Where's *Joey*?''

''Well, why don't you read that after you read these?''

''Look, Tony, we made a deal upstairs. Now, don't fuck the deal over! You want me to go back to the seventh floor? I'll check out, just like I checked in. You go get *Joey,* or I check out. Get it?'' Tony looked confused and upset. He had to make him understand. ''The book gives me a lot of comfort. This isn't Joe of a week ago talking. This is Joe of today. I feel a lot better. I wanna read these other books, but there's some great stuff in *Joey* that I really like reading. So go get it.''

''All right,'' Tony agreed reluctantly.

Joe got up and put his arm around Tony's shoulder as he walked him to the door.

''Come here, Tony,'' he said when they were out in the hall. ''I want you to see something.''

Joe steered him to the room opposite his and stopped in the open doorway. The acrid odor of burned hair drifted toward them, causing Tony to step back involuntarily. The room was very dark. Joe flipped on the light, revealing a white-sheeted examining table, with foot and arm restraints and a thick leather strap draped limply across the middle. On a shelf behind the head of the table was a piece of equipment that looked like a large radio with headphones.

''What is this?'' Tony asked with irritation.

''This is the house torture chamber,'' Joe said. ''The electroshock room. I don't know exactly what they do t' ya in here, but I know they ain't gonna do it t' me. I ain't even goin' t' stay close by—in case they get any funny ideas about tryin' anythin' just cause I'm in the immediate neighborhood—so I'm gettin' my room changed.''

Tony, still staring at the equipment, shuddered.

Joe put his arm around his cousin's shoulder. ''Don't be scared, Tony. I won't let 'em get me.''

Why did Tony pull away like that? He tried to hide it, but he didn't want Joe's arm on him. Joe didn't like that.

''Hey, cousin, it's not catching.''

''I know.'' But he was standing a good two feet from Joe.

''It's in the blood,'' Joe said. Fuck 'im. Remind him it could be him in here instead of me.

Tony's fists clenched, but he kept his arms at his sides. Well, Joe could exercise a little control, too. After all, Tony had brought the books. And he'd come to see him—twice in one day. Which was twice more than anyone else.

''Hey, cuz, where is everybody? You been my only visitor, ya know.''

Tony shrugged.

''I asked ya, how is everybody?''

Tony studied the squares on the floor.

''How's my fuckin' wife? Why ain't she got her ass here to see me?''

''I guess she's upset, Joe.''

''Shit, she's been upset since the day she got pregnant this time.''

''Yeah, that's it,'' Tony said.

Tony wasn't looking at him. Joe hated to be lied to.

He grabbed Tony's lapel and pulled his face down to his. ''No, that isn't it, not all of it. I wanna know why my wife hasn't come to see me. Tell me!'' Slowly, he released Tony.

His cousin was staring at him. And he hadn't lifted a finger against Joe. Finally, he shrugged. Then he said, ''Joe, she's scareda ya.''

''She oughta be scared. When I'm outa here, I'm gonna—after she has the kid, a course—I'm gonna throw her the fuck out—lettin' me rot in here without coming to see me.'' He took a shallow breath. ''What's she scareda me for, anyway?''

Tony examined his nails. He bit off a hangnail.

''Ya done givin' yerself a manicure? Why would Angela be scareda me, enough to stay away from here?''

Tony's eyes looked like those of an animal that's felt the bullet.

''Christ Almighty, that's it!'' Joe hollered. ''She put me in here! That bitch on wheels put me in this place!''

''Joe, you gotta stay calm.''

''Why da fuck should I stay calm? What're they gonna do, throw me in the looney bin?''

He began to laugh at his cleverness, and couldn't stop, it was so funny. He was laughing so hard his eyes shut, and when he opened them Tony was headed for the steel door. In the second it took Joe to start after him, he was on the other side. Joe ran to the door. He wasn't finished! But Tony had his back turned and was pretending he couldn't hear him. Joe banged on the door, but Tony didn't turn. And then the elevator came, and his cousin vanished.

And Joe knew he'd never be back.

He began to howl then, because no one but Tony had come, and Joe had driven him away with his dumb jokes and his questions and his pushing Tony too far, and now he was never coming back and Joe would die in this place. Feelings of terror assaulted him from every direction, engulfing him like flames. He saw two orderlies coming at him, but he was faster than they were, faster than the flames. He ran toward his room and slammed the door and leaned back hard on the closed door, holding them out—the flames and the terror—and the men who wanted to capture him so he wouldn't be able to fight off the terror. It took every iota of his strength to keep them out.

But they were winning anyway. Their voices were sliding under the door. Grabbing at his feet. He danced a desperate dance so the voices couldn't get hold of his feet. And as he danced, the things in his head fell off their shelves and bumped into each other and started breaking. The whole inside of his head was under siege. It was terrifying having his thoughts break apart. Nothing was holding. Nothing!

He was out of control. Suddenly, he knew it, and knew, too, that if he was out of control, they had him where they wanted him. He'd lost control before, and landed here. He couldn't let them win again. He refused to lose it again!

With the shards of strength he had left in him, he willed himself to inhale deeply. Slowly, he took in all the air his lungs could hold. Then, lungs filled, fists clenched, eyes squeezed shut, he held his breath until every muscle in his body cried out for release. A little at a time, a slow leak whistled through his parted lips, a finger relaxed, multi-colored spots grouped and re-grouped forming kaleidoscopic patterns, knees folded and he slid gently to the floor.

CHAPTER

23

CALM. It was over. He had won! He had no idea how long he had been sitting there, when he gradually became aware of knocking on the door. The energy with which he got to his feet surprised him, but when he opened the door and saw Dr. Hammer, he was glad he had it.

"Before you say anything, I just want you to know that Thorazine is out," Joe announced, *in charge*. "I'm not taking it anymore. I can't sleep. If you got any problems with that, check with my cousin Tony. I told him that's the deal. No more!"

Joe kept his eyes glued on Hammer to see how he was taking this news. The pallid man did not back off. He didn't look scared. He had his head tilted to one side, nodding calmly.

"That's fine," he said then. "Certainly. But I do strongly recommend that you continue the lithium. It's critical to stabilizing your moodswings."

"Okay. That doesn't seem to do anything to me. The Thorazine's worse than I've read about. I'll gladly take the lithium to get off the other stuff."

"All right, then you'll continue the blood tests, so we can determine how your body metabolizes the medication?"

"Yeah. Now, I'd like to leave in the not-too-distant future. I'm feeling great. I have a lot of things going on. I really have to get back to work. I can't be fooling around here, reading books.''

''Well, yes, I'm certainly aware of that. However, the morning and afternoon blood tests are critical to your recovery, so you must stay here for the time being.''

''Look, Dr. Hammer, my office is in walking distance of this hospital. I could stop here on my way to work for the first test, and come back in the afternoon for the second. Why do I have to stay here?''

''Well, we have to be certain that we've allowed enough time for all the possible negative reactions to the drug to occur here where you can get immediate attention, not to mention the importance of getting the blood before you've eaten anything. It's not that I don't trust you to come in. It's just that we must be very careful in striking an extremely delicate balance.''

As the man spoke, Joe became so absorbed with his own perspiration that it was all he could focus on. Large drops broke out on his forehead; rivulets ran down his neck, soaking his shirt; he couldn't keep his hair dry. ''Is this terrible sweating connected to the medication?'' he asked Hammer.

And realized that the doctor had vanished.

■ ■ ■

JOE WAS having second and third thoughts about his decision to transfer to the third floor. The place was noisy: bells and whistles all day long. And the night sounds were scarier. He had come here of his own volition, but he couldn't leave freely. No one could. People coming in had to ring buzzers to get clearance. Phone calls were limited to two a day, except in cases of emergency, and then someone from the staff had to go along to verify the call. His first priority was to figure out how to get more contact with the outside world. In the morning, he'd call Skip Waxman with a list of phone calls he wanted made. At the end of the day, based on whether he had any visitors and what he had accomplished, he'd decide how to use his last call. It was unwise to talk too much or ask too many questions. He adopted the principle of *omertà*.

At six o'clock, Joe was stretched out on his bed thinking about how his partners had double-crossed him again, when a Brunhilde in white poked her head in the door. He wanted to ask her where her horned helmet was, but decided against it. No one ever laughed at his jokes anymore. His mood plunged like a diver off a high board. He tried to keep afloat in the deep, chill water of his despair while the nurse told him it was time for dinner. When she left, he buried his face in his pillow to muffle his sobs. Would anyone ever laugh with him again? Could he ever indulge the bizarre streak that existed in everyone without frightening the people around him? What would happen if he lost his temper? Everyone loses his temper sometimes. And what about enthusiasm? Just how enthusiastic would his friends allow him to be before running for the butterfly net? The precariousness of his life washed over him in huge, frightening waves. His panic was rising like a dangerous tide, but he couldn't afford to let it submerge him. He pulled himself out by an act of will: he had to go to dinner before he became conspicuous by his absence. He washed up and put on a fresh, white dress shirt and his favorite plaid pants. He combed his hair carefully. Some of the people around here were astonishingly disheveled, and Joe made up his mind that he would not be one of them.

The tables in the dining hall could accommodate six to eight people. Joe looked around, trying to decide where to sit. To the far left, sitting all alone, was a brawny Mexican kid whom Joe had noticed earlier. The second they made eye contact, the boy looked away. Two tables over, and closer to the door, an old man struggled to get the food to his mouth with violently trembling hands. Across the table from him, a young woman of about thirty watched impassively. Her sandy-colored hair was pulled back severely and tied with a scarf, accentuating her angular Nordic features. Her high-necked white blouse gripped her throat, and a gray suit jacket added a superfluous shield.

Immediately across from the doorway, a distinguished-looking elderly man with snow-white hair and an ascot sat at a table humming *Tales of the Vienna Woods* as he ate. Next to him, a woman about the same age wearing a loosely fitting, flowered housedress was clutching her cane as though some invisible hand were trying to wrench it from her. Across from them, an Indian woman, face like a pancake, jet-black hair cut Buster Brown style, was coaxing them to take the jar she was offering.

"Oh, God," thought Joe. "How did I get here?"

He felt desolate. What little appeal the food on his tray had had, vanished.

"Mr. Corelli," the nurse called out as he passed her table on the way out. "Mr. Corelli! You have to stay here!"

They'd see about that.

CHAPTER

24

HE READ page after page of *Joey,* especially about his confinement in Attica. Joe focused on how Gallo protected himself. Joey was very quiet, very reserved. Never shot off his mouth! Never lost his temper; bit his tongue. He couldn't afford to have the nurses write bad reports about him. No, that was him. For Joey, it was the guards. Maybe Joe had better start thinking about self-preservation.

■ ■ ■

AS HE stepped out into the hall next morning, most of the patients he had run across yesterday, and some he had not, were lined up in front of the nurses' station.

"Mr. Corelli, will you please get in line for your medication?" The redhead from the day before was signaling with her finger where she wanted him to stand. One after another, the inmates took paper cups from the nurses, dumped the contents into their mouths and washed the pills down with water. It was eerie—like something out of a science-fiction movie: tranquilized slaves blindly submitting to their captivity. Then it was his turn.

"What are these?" he asked, putting as much authority in his voice as he could.

"The yellow-and-gray capsules are lithium. The others are Navane."

"That's not Thorazine, is it?"

"No. Now, please take your pills. You're keeping the others waiting."

"Then they'll just have to wait. What am I taking this for? Dr. Hammer discussed lithium with me, nothing else."

"The Navane just helps you stay with an idea until you're ready to give it up, rather than have it take off on its own. I'm sure the doctor will explain it more thoroughly when he comes by."

"Okay. I'll hold them till then."

"I'm sorry, but that's against hospital policy. Medication cannot leave this desk. I have to note on your chart that I saw you take it."

He was watching her face and was unable to detect any trace of hesitation in her explanation. Quickly, Joe decided that he had more to lose by continuing to challenge her than by going along, so he swallowed the pills and went in to breakfast.

As he sought out a table, he became aware that the Mexican, sitting where he had the night before, was glaring at him ominously. Throughout the meal, Joe sensed that the Mexican was not taking his eyes off him, and it was making him very uncomfortable. He finished eating quickly, and was starting out of the dining room when one of the nurses stopped him.

"Mr. Corelli, we'd like you to join a group-therapy session we're having this morning."

That it was couched as a request in no way modified the covert message. A refusal would be interpreted as misbehavior. So instead of making his first phone call, Joe followed her. Six patients had already arrived: two of the catatonic schizophrenics, the man who had shoved past him last night in the dining room, another comatose mealtime companion, a slinky blonde and a kid who looked like an extra in *On the Waterfront*.

The subject of today's discussion was how to respond. The nurse kicked off by telling a personal experience obviously intended to be an example of appropriate behavior.

''If some son of a bitch did that to me, I'd punch his fuckin' lights out!'' declared Grumpy.

''But Mr. McNamara, all he did was take my parking spot. It's simply excessive to respond to a discourteous act with violence,'' she pointed out reasonably.

About midway into the session, the therapist looked at Joe and asked, ''Now, Joe, let's imagine that your mother says to you, 'Joe, I hear from some of my friends that your partners are shysters. What kind of people are you associated with?' How would you answer her?''

Before he could respond the young hoodlum shouted, ''I'd tell her to get fucked!''

''Freddy, it's not your turn,'' the nurse said firmly. ''Mr. Corelli, please proceed.''

She was looking for a reading on his state of mind. He could see the score sheet: paranoia, lucidity, self-control. He had taken enough psychology to know the kind of answer that would get him high marks on his sanity report card, and went for it. About halfway through his response, one of the catatonics leaped from his seat, grabbed his head and ran shrieking from the room. Even more amazing than this outburst was the lack of reaction from anyone else. This therapy sucked! For the remaining forty minutes, Joe sat quietly, smiled politely and nodded attentively. When the session was over, he got his copy of *Roots* and decided to take it to the reading room.

''Reading room'' was something of a misnomer: a large television dominated the shabby room that was sprinkled with rickety card tables and green and yellow plastic chairs. The TV was on, though no one was watching it. Only a few listless patients were around. Once he'd turned off the TV, the prospects for reading seemed good.

Half a page into the book, Joe felt a fluttering on his arm. A tiny, shriveled, transparent hand was trying to get his attention. He looked up to find the old woman with the cane smiling down at him with a toothless grin.

''Are you my father?'' she asked expectantly.

''No,'' he said kindly, managing to hide his surprise.

''I've been waiting for him to come and get me. Do you think he'll be here soon?''

Covering her hand with his own, Joe was shocked by its frailty. He struggled successfully to hold back the tears that suddenly filled his eyes, and tried to reassure her.

''I'm sure he'll come very soon. I'm sure. Don't worry.''

She smiled gratefully and haltingly made her way to the next prospect in her quest for the soul presumably long departed.

Joe ordered himself not to let this place destroy him. He'd spent countless hours fighting depression and now, for the sake of his mental health, he was locked up with people who'd make anyone suicidal. He wanted to read. Okay, read!

Ten minutes had elapsed when the Mexican kid appeared. While he turned on the TV, he and Joe exchanged surreptitious glances. Pulling a chair close to the set, the boy settled in to watch the television with one eye and Joe with the other. When Joe failed to react, he raised the volume. Still no reaction. For all practical purposes, Joe was alone with a six-two, 215-pound, psycho eager for a fight. He decided to wait quietly while the boy played out his hand.

The confrontation was deflected when a nurse approached Joe and asked him to come to an arts-and-crafts class.

''I don't do those things.''

''Well, it would be very good for you. The work will calm you down. Get your mind off what you're reading. It would be better for you not to read and go work with your hands.''

''At what?''

''Oh, lots of things. We make belts and pottery and shape metals.''

''Look, miss, I told you, I don't do that kind of stuff! I don't know how to do it, and I don't want to learn. No way. If you want me to, I'll come watch for a while and socialize, but I'm not making any belts. The last time I made a belt, I was in summer school after the sixth grade. I remember, we wove four strands of colored plastic together. I got so sick of it, after weaving about two inches, I turned it into a key chain. And I already got a key chain, so don't go gettin' any ideas.''

CHAPTER 25

"HEY, STEVIE, what's goin' on?" Joe boomed, delighted to see his pal. Joe desperately needed someone he could relax and be himself with, and Steve was made to order.

"Hey, Joey baby!" Steve shouted with delight, slapping Joe on the back. "You're lookin' good. I call Skip every day to see how you are. He told me about the crazy phone system around here."

Joe grimaced. "Well, it won't be for long. I'm getting stronger all the time. I'm sure I'll be out in a few days. Ever since they stopped giving me that fuckin' Thorazine, I've felt a lot better."

"Yeah, I know what you mean. Sometimes the cure is worse than the disease."

"It's worse than that. I don't know how that stuff can cure anything. You know, Steve, nobody wants to talk to me."

"That's not true, Dolly. Everybody's rooting for you, but they don't like a lot of visitors in this place. It's easier to go to Moscow!"

"No, no. That's not what I mean. No one will talk to me about why I'm here or what happened. I'm not allowed any opinions on this place or the treatment because I'm nuts. It's like the medicine. They give me this lithium, because they say I get too excited. I admit I was really racing for a while, and I did do some bizarre things, but since I've been taking the medicine, I can tell that I'm bouncing less.''

''You'd have made some bouncer,'' Steve said, trying to make a joke out of it.

But none of this was funny to Joe. ''Bouncing! Up and down, from thought to thought!'' But, of course, Steve didn't know what it was like. He spoke softly now. ''Nobody listened to me about the reporters, because I lost track of what I was saying. I was so excited that my head raced ahead of my mouth. I can't explain it, but everybody treats me like a piece of blown glass.''

''Don't be too hard on them, Joey. People are afraid you're embarrassed. They just don't want to upset you.''

''I know—and they're right, I am embarrassed. But I've been embarrassed before, I'll get over it. The question is, will they?''

''Absolutely! Give them time. No one will even remember this. And there's one thing *you* should always remember. *You* checked yourself into this place—on your own. You knew when you needed rest. And you got it. All by yourself! You shouldn't be embarrassed.''

Joe shot an irritated glance at his friend. ''Now you're doing it, Stevie.''

Steve blushed. ''I'm sorry. Why does your hand shake?''

Grateful for the concern in Steve's voice, Joe admitted, ''I don't know. I don't know why I sweat so much, either. I wanted to ask Dr. Hammer the other day, but I couldn't hold the thought. By the time I drifted back, he was gone.''

''I don't understand,'' Steve commented, confused. ''What do you mean, drifted?''

''It's hard to explain. Sometimes I feel like my head is filled with cobwebs. They're giving me a drug called Navane to help me make my way through them.''

''You should feel lucky that they know so much. Who would have thought you could take a pill to help you think?''

''I don't feel all that lucky. It's terrifying. The next time *you* look in the mirror, see a mass of chemicals looking back at you.

We're just collections of atoms. As long as they behave, life goes on without a hitch, but Christ, one of 'em takes off on its own and all hell breaks loose. Think about it, Steve. It's dehumanizing. Love, pride, fear, hate—human emotions are nothing more than chemistry in action. I take lithium, and I'm more and more in control. I take Navane, and I'm concentrating better. I still have terrible moments, but they're fewer and shorter, and each time I wrestle for control, it's easier to win. Do you see what I'm saying? It's all chemistry!''

''God, Joe, what an idea! Think of it. You could mix emotions in a test tube! And then what would happen to the spirit, the soul?''

Joe smiled wanly and shrugged. ''Buddy, I've gotta get out of here. I've got too much to do to sit around reading books and watching psychos make pottery. The people in this hospital are morons. The other day a nurse told me that reading was bad for me.''

''Listen, bubbala, be patient. You're a lot better. I'm sure you'll be out soon.''

They walked together to the steel door, both of them run out of steam.

''Some door,'' Steve said, punching the metal lightly.

And Joe remembered.

''You broke into my house the morning I checked into this joint!'' he yelled.

''Those partners of yours had their heads up their fuckin' asses.''

CHAPTER

26

WHEN STEVE was gone, and it was too late, Joe saw that his temper had crossed him again. Instead of lashing out at Steve, he could have asked him why he'd broken the door down at Joe's house. And who had put him up to it. Steve'd never do anything like that on his own. Steve *was* his friend. He had to keep straight who was and who wasn't.

■ ■ ■

AFTER DINNER there was a town-hall meeting. The patients were expected to gather around and talk, make contact, relate. The Mexican sat opposite Joe and glared at him throughout the session. For some reason, his hostility and resentment were increasing.

After the town hall, Joe watched the staff set up a record player and bring in Coke and popcorn for the patients. He was trying to calculate whether his attendance at the town hall was enough socializing for one evening when the blonde caught his attention. Her bright green dress, laminated to her otherwise naked body, undulated toward him. In one continuous movement, she coiled herself onto the couch next to him. At that very moment, music filled the now-converted dining room. Not feeling very imaginative, Joe was about to ask his new companion to dance when the Mexican loomed up in his line of vision.

Alarm broke the spell that suggested this might really be a place where you'd ask a woman to dance, as Joe realized that the boy was either unable or unwilling to mask his rising animosity.

■ ■ ■

BY THE time Joe got to bed, his nerves were so jangled he knew that unless he took some measures to protect himself he'd never sleep. As he looked around his room trying to formulate a plan, it occurred to him that he could use its six chairs to create a maze that would trip anyone entering the room in the dark. After the trap was set, he took the last chair and put it next to his bed—only tonight he changed beds. If this kid had observed which bed he slept in and decided to attack him while he was sleeping, he'd lunge at the wrong bed. Joe made up the bed at the window as though somebody were in it, but he'd be in the bed near the wall that would allow his right hand to rest next to a chair and his left against the wall. This way, if he had to protect himself, he could grab the chair with his right hand and clobber an assailant. After all his precautions were in place, he took his copy of *Joey* and turned to the chapter on Attica.

> Survival was the one, all-encompassing problem Joey faced in prison . . . he spent most of the first three years of his sentence in isolation. . . . Incessant psychological pressure had to be endured before Joey's case was ready for court. . . . He is locked in 22 hours a day. He was locked in for five months without being afforded a walk.

Joe closed the book. Nine years, he thought. Nine years of hard time. Joey Gallo had made it. No, he hadn't. Not really. He was only out a short time when they got him. It happened on his forty-third birthday. Joe even recalled the date: April 17, 1972. He even remembered the hour: five a.m. Joey had been eating *scungilli* at Umberto's Clam House on Mulberry Street in New York's "Little Italy." His family had been with him, and his bodyguard. But that time even Pete the Greek couldn't help Joey. Five bullets had shredded Joey's body. He'd lunged uncontrollably through the restaurant, and then collapsed at the center of the intersection of Hester and Mulberry. It seemed to fit, Joe thought: Joey's life ending in the streets, where it had begun. Joe felt a huge sadness. For Joey, being dead. For himself, being in here. Was dead worse or better than being in here? Joe wondered. And decided: it was worse. Because dead was forever, and in a few days he'd be out of here. This wasn't forever; it wasn't nine years in Attica, either. He could do it.

■ ■ ■

JOE AWAKENED to discordant notes being pounded on the piano in the arts-and-crafts room next door. Even though he had never seen the Mexican go anywhere near it, he knew instantly that it was the kid playing now.

CHAPTER

27

JOE LAY very still, breathing shallowly, and stared at the ceiling. Abruptly, the playing stopped. He shifted his gaze from the ceiling to the door, and waited for it to open. In the shadows, Joe made out a hulking figure holding an enormous kitchen knife above his head. The figure took a few steps into the dark room, tripped over the first chair and fell into the second. The minute he tripped, Joe grabbed the chair by the side of his bed, sprang to his feet, and as his attacker collapsed into the second chair, Joe brought the one in his hand down on the Mexican's head. Recovering quickly, his assailant fled from the room.

The noise had attracted the attention of the guards, who began chasing the Mexican. By the time Joe got to the other end of the hall, the guards were tightening his straitjacket.

Joe glared at them. "Keep him the fuck off this floor! Enough is enough!"

■ ■ ■

NEXT MORNING, instead of his usual call to Skip, Joe phoned Tony. He was nervous because their last meeting had ended badly, but Tony acted as though nothing had happened.

So Joe described the events of the night before and said, "Tony, get me the fuck out of this place!" When he'd hung up, Joe placed the same call to Tom Brady.

"We'll take care of it immediately, Joe. Maybe you should go back to the seventh floor."

"Tom, don't you believe the story?" he asked. "It's the God's honest truth! I'm as calm and level-headed as I've ever been, so don't think this is some figment of my imagination. You check for yourselves what went on here last night."

Not fifteen minutes later, a hunchbacked man with a beard approached Joe.

"I'm Dr. Zimmerman. From the things I've been hearing, I'd say you must be harboring a great deal of hostility."

Instantly, Joe knew Tom *had* checked—and snitched. Still, he laughed. "What? Are you kidding me? A guy tries to kill me, and I'm harboring hostility. You bet I'm harboring hostility," he continued, starting to shout. "You tell me to make belts, but who's watching the loonies around here?"

"What I suggest for you, and many of my patients, is to hit the punching bag in the corner of the rec room. It's the best way to let off steam."

"Hit the punching bag, huh? Maybe I'll do that. I used to hit a speed bag, but I've never hit the heavy one."

Before Joe could take Dr. Zimmerman's advice, Dr. Hammer arrived for his daily thirty-minute meeting.

"Look, I've gotta get outa this place. First of all, I can't go through another night like I had last night. You tell me I'm supposed to rest. How can you sleep when a guy comes in your room with a butcher knife? So if I'm supposed to rest, this is the wrong place to be. Furthermore, I'm perfectly fine. All I needed was a nice rest. These pills you're giving me are great. I'll continue taking them. But I'm gonna check out."

"Oh, no, no. Give us a few more days. Your blood tests are coming along very well. You're reacting positively to your medication. What happened last night will never happen again, I can assure you."

"How can you assure me? You've got all these crazy people running around here. What's next?" he shouted.

"Tomorrow you can have a pass," Hammer countered, trying to pacify him. "You can take a walk outside, then come back. But you're not quite ready to leave yet."

Joe didn't argue. He'd make his own decision.

■ ■ ■

THAT AFTERNOON, Judd Peters and Larry Axelrod came to visit. They said they'd come to get his input on the letters they were writing to the IRG participants. But he would have given odds that Dr. Hammer had called them to say he was having increasing difficulty keeping Joe in the hospital, and it might help if they could relieve his anxiety about work. He didn't ask. No point, when he didn't trust their answers.

Judd began the meeting by repeating his doubt that the IRG would publish anything detrimental to Joe, the firm, or their clients.

"Look, Judd, the *New York Times* said on February 7th that these fuckheads are going to publish on March 15th, and here it is March 2nd and we haven't done anything yet! I don't understand it. What the hell is going on?"

"We still don't know who's going to publish the series or what it's going to say," Judd answered.

"I don't want to wait until I see what they say. I want them to know the kind of exposure they'll have if they aren't goddam careful about what they say. Now go do it!"

The meeting had given Joe neither comfort nor reassurance. Not a single question about what it was like for him there—or even how he'd landed in the hospital.

They knew! In the moment he realized that, he saw, too, that they had been the ones behind locking him up. He had been thinking it had to be Angela. How else explain that she still hadn't shown up? But Angela wouldn't have done anything like that on her own. She wouldn't have dared. His partners dared. They must have figured their little world was safer with him inside here. Joe felt betrayed—from all directions. Well, maybe it was better to know where he stood.

And maybe it would be better if *they* knew where they stood. Where they all stood—like it or not—together. Perhaps the time had come for a little shock treatment. He had plenty of time on his hands. Why not write the article that could appear if those reporter clowns really did their homework? Yup! That was just what he would do. Conjuring up images of Barnes writing "The Hidden Cancer," Joe spent the better part of the afternoon writing in the same serrated style.

THE PHOENIX PROJECT

Tilting the Scales of Justice

Prominent Phoenix attorney Joseph P. Corelli, of 4230 East Lincoln, Paradise Valley, Arizona, was identified by local sources as having as many Mafia connections as anyone in the State of Arizona. Yet he sits perched at the top of The Valley Center, the state's tallest building, directing the fortunes of one of the Valley's most prestigious law firms, Corelli, Brady, Peters & Winthrop.

Mr. Corelli's family has long been in partnership with Senator Barry Goldwater's brother, Robert W. Goldwater, in a corporation called Goldcor, Inc. Informed sources state that the Arizona branch of the Corelli family brought Joseph P. Corelli, 36, to Phoenix from New York in order to enlist his financial and legal expertise in various family enterprises. Mr. Corelli's first task upon arrival was to form the predecessor corporation of Goldcor, Inc., Goldcor Investment Corporation, in 1970, to acquire the sprawling Marblehead Ranch, north of Glendale, Arizona. That same ranch was previously owned in part by Joseph Zerilli (FBI No. 79517C), a reputed Mafia kingpin from Detroit. Zerilli and Peter "Horseface" Licavoli of Tucson are under constant local law enforcement surveillance. Since that time Corelli has served as the president of Goldcor and a member of its board of directors. Former Republican State Chairman and chief advisor to Senator Goldwater, Harry Rosenzweig, has also served on Goldcor's board. Additionally, Mr. Corelli has represented Bob Goldwater, another member of the Goldcor board, in a variety of matters, both business and personal.

Mr. Corelli came to Arizona in 1968, after long association with reputed Mafia figures in New York. While living in Brooklyn, Joseph P. Corelli was in the employ of well known Cosa Nostra chieftain, Carlo Gambino (FBI No. 2525631). Gambino was identified by Joseph Valachi as head of one of New York's five organized crime families. He died in Brooklyn early this year, and authorities reported a procession of crime figures in attendance at his funeral.

In addition, Corelli worked for mobster Mauro ''Ace'' Fiore, reputed to be a Gambino ''soldier,'' and was an advisor to labor racketeer Raymond D'Allesandro. Through Corelli's association with D'Allesandro, he began his involvement with the Teamsters and its international vice president, Anthony ''Tony Pro'' Provenzano (FBI No. 374286).

A local informant, shielded by the Federal witness protection program, has also linked Corelli to Thomas Cutrone, Dominic ''Lilo'' Ferrara, Salvatore D'Allesandro and the notorious mob executioner, Joseph ''Joe Bonehead'' Bonfiglio, all members of New York crime families. He is also reported to have had close ties with the infamous Joey Gallo, who was gunned down in a New York restaurant five years ago.

A series of mysterious meetings have been taking place this past year between Corelli, Rocky Parlati, 35, of New York and Philadelphia, Frank La Bate, 38, of Denver and John D. ''Johnny Boy'' Riccio, of Redondo Beach, California. Meetings have occurred at The Polo Club, owned by Irv ''Big Red'' Wolfe of Chicago, an establishment frequented by numerous Mafia chieftains and underlings.

During an interview at Corelli's palatial Paradise Valley residence, he said the meetings at The Polo Club were being held to ''promote Italian-American unity.''

It is indeed curious that the Corelli law firm was retained by the Attorney General of the State of Arizona to assist in the investigations relating to the Embassy corporation and criminal infiltration of the state's racetracks. Have the scales of justice been tilted?

TOMORROW: The Political Thugs:
Barry, Harry & Bob

Joe read over his article. He smiled. Every word was true; every implication, false. Could they write something like this?

Yes, if they did their job. Could he sue? Sure, with little probability of success. Could this ruin him? Absolutely!

Joe was wired! He decided to take Dr. Zimmerman's suggestion and hit the punching bag. He had just begun to hit the bag when the Mexican kid walked in. As soon as he saw Joe, he froze. Enraged that the kid was on the loose again, Joe began to hit the bag harder and harder, never taking his eyes off him. While the two of them stood, locked in eye contact, the bag started hitting the wall. Little by little, the wall crumbled, until by the time Joe stopped, drenched and drained, he had punched his way through it. He walked to the door, turned, glared at the Mexican, who was still watching him, and grabbed his throat. "If you bother me one more time, you cocksucker, I'm gonna rip your fuckin' heart out. You understand what I'm sayin', you scumbag?" He turned and stalked out of the room.

■ ■ ■

ONCE AGAIN, Joe went to bed with *Joey*.

> With every cruel blow that sends me tumbling, I return with chin thrust forward and defiance emanating from the entire me. FATE, I challenge you! I fight—we fight or quit and be crushed by the sick, crying, howling hordes of humanity searching for a way out of the TRAP! We bounce back ALWAYS! Joey Gallo #18140. *A letter to Jeffy, his wife.*
>
> So what Joey had been doing, whether in solitary or not, was to lie down on his stomach on his cot, bury his head in his pillow or blanket and scream silently. He would scream in every way short of letting any sound come out. He would do this quite deliberately and in an organized way, thinking about the Nazi and everybody else he saw as an adversary, trying to work out his rage so that he wouldn't be provoked into losing his temper. *Dr. Bruce.*

That night, Joe screamed soundlessly into his pillow, thinking about the Mexican. It worked. He felt enough relief to patrol the halls himself before going to sleep.

CHAPTER

28

JOE AWAKENED refreshed and excited. He had a pass and decided to walk to his office and check his mail.

As he was leaving, feeling great, Dr. Zimmerman accosted him. "Joe, did you do what I said?"

"Yeah, I murdered that bag."

"Let me see your hands."

Joe held out his hands so the doctor could see them—and for the first time saw it himself.

"Your hands are black and blue! Why did you hit the bag so hard?"

"Dr. Zimmerman, you told me to hit the bag until I felt better. That's exactly what I did. And I feel better."

"But your hands are black and blue."

"Dr. Zimmerman, I really don't give a fuck about my hands! I feel better."

Joe walked out into the free world.

The brisk breeze and the exercise aired out his mind, so that by the time he got back to the third floor he was much less annoyed.

That lasted ten minutes.

He was confronted by a frantic Dr. Hammer. "You violated hospital policy by leaving the grounds!" he yelled. "Now what am I going to do with you?"

"Hey, what the hell are you talking about, I violated hospital policy? You told me I could take a walk. You didn't tell me where I had to walk. I took a walk to my office. My first thought when I went outside was to go across the street to the Italian restaurant, but I decided I needed exercise more than some food with taste to it. All I did was pick up my mail and come back."

"Well, I got a very angry call from your partner, Tom Brady, wanting to know what you were doing in the office disrupting things."

"People may have been surprised to see me, but nobody seemed bothered. I certainly wasn't disrupting anything. So just calm down. I'm not one of your standard yo-yos, so don't try to intimidate me. You told me I could take a walk. I took a walk. Period."

As Joe finished, he realized how extreme this man's reaction was to such an innocuous event. Hammer's hair was so soaked with perspiration it looked as though he'd just gotten out of the shower. Even on this cool day, he had loosened his tie because he was clearly overheated. He was acting like one of Joe's young associates who had made a mistake and was distraught about what to do next.

"You psychiatrists are one worse than the next," Joe said. "One tells me to hit the punching bag. Then he says I hit it too hard. You tell me I can take a walk. Now you complain that I walked too far. You guys could drive someone bananas. Look at you! You're soaked with perspiration. The other day I was going to ask you why I suddenly sweat like that. I was gonna ask you if it's the lithium. Does lithium make *you* sweat, Dr. Hammer?"

Joe paused only long enough for Hammer to recover from his jab. Then he told him the news. "I'm getting out of here, and that's a fact."

Hammer stormed off.

Joe hadn't used either of his daily phone calls yet, so he called Herb Steinberg.

''The great man speaking!''

''Herb, you got an hour?''

''Sure, Joey. What's up?''

''Look, I'm in St. Paul's, locked up on the third floor with bars, locks, buzzers and whistles. When I first got here they were giving me a drug that was killing me. Then one night some fuckin' psychotic tries to kill me. When I call my cousin and Tom to tell them I'm leaving, they tell me I can't—maybe because my wife's out there with papers ready to commit me if I don't stay. You know what I've been doing since I got here? Arguing with nurses who tell me it's bad for me to read—I should make belts instead. You should see this guy Hammer. He's supposed to be my shrink. I think this guy's way sicker than I am. Herb, you gotta get me outa here!''

''Joey, you know what this sounds like? It sounds like *Dial M for Murder.* I'll be there inside of an hour.''

''Don't let them give you any static. Sometimes they don't like all the guests I'm having. Just get in the door!''

■ ■ ■

WHEN HERB arrived, Joe sat him down and told him the whole story in sequence. This time Joe was cool, calm, rational —mostly. Occasionally, the old ferocity appeared and he'd call someone a fuckin' asshole.

Herb looked hard at his friend, and hard inside himself, and decided. ''Joe, long as we've known each other, I've been straight with you.''

''Goes both ways, Herb. You know that.''

''Yeah. That's why I don't wanna start it being different now. I've got a confession to make.''

''I'm no priest, Herb.'' He said it as much to make Herb less tense as to stall his friend a minute and call up his reserves.

Herb grinned tightly. ''That's all right. I'm no Catholic.'' He wiped his upper lip. ''This confession's to you, Joe.''

''Then there's nothing to worry about. It's me sitting here, the same Joe as always, listening to my old and very good friend, you, Herb.'' Joe meant every word, he discovered, and that made him able to sit back and relax his shoulders.

Body language was Herb's legal specialty. He stopped sweating. ''Yeah, that's what I think. That's why I'm gonna tell you what I did.'' A visible breath. ''When we got off the phone, I called Tom Brady.''

This time it took effort, but Joe kept his shoulders down. If he tightened up, if he leaned forward, Herb might remember that even the same old Joe sometimes turned on a dime.

''I was a little apprehensive. You did sound very agitated. You know?''

Joe nodded. ''I know. Go on.''

''Well, I told Tom we'd talked, and I was comin' over here, but I was . . . well, concerned about your condition, and did he have any information?''

''Did he?'' Joe wasn't knocking himself out to sound calm, he really felt that way. A good sign, he noted. He was able not to lose sight of the fact that Herb was on his short Friends list, not his long Enemies list.

''. . . you'd come in here, voluntarily,'' Herb was saying. ''And although they had some papers drawn up so you could be kept here. . . .''

Joe locked his shoulders in place.

''. . . if you changed your mind, the papers had a time limit on them that had run out. He was worried you'd take it into your head to leave before it was good for you.''

Joe permitted himself to smile uncensored the smile that came from his gut. A smile that acknowledged a betrayal he'd been telling himself was beyond Tom. A smile that knew whose good Tom was worried about.

Herb read at least the second part clearly—enough reason on its own for the sideways smile on Joe's face. ''That's what I thought too,'' he said. ''Tom said he was afraid if you came out, you'd stop the medication, or drink while you're on this Navane stuff.''

''I won't stop the medication, Herb. It's helping me.''

Herb nodded, as if he were checking off a want list. ''That's good, Joe. I'm sure glad it's helpin'.''

''Tom have any more information for you?''

Herb frowned.

''C'mon now. This isn't getting to me. You can tell, can't you?''

''That isn't it. It got to me!''

''Well, relax and tell it real slow.''

Herb tried to sit back, but his body bounced forward like a ball on a string. ''He told me you'd gotten out on a pass, and come over there, and scared the bejeebees out of everyone.''

''Herb, I didn't do anything to scare anyone.''

''I figured he must be exaggerating, because you wouldn't fuck yourself that way. He said somethin' else, Joe—I wanna get this all out and over with, okay?''

''Okay.'' Joe was amazed at how easy it was not to get up and throw a chair through the visitor's room window. That would frighten Herb away, and he couldn't afford to do that. And knowing that *was enough* to keep him calm.

''He said the reporters are still around, and he doesn't want you calling them. I got the definite feeling he likes you being here inside because your contact with everyone on the outside is limited. Joe?''

''I'm listening with both ears, Herb. But I'm not upset. You're telling me things I already knew, if only in my dreams. Herb, you're helping me by telling me all this.''

''I hope so. Joe, they want you in here until the reporters leave town.''

''And what did you tell Tom?''

Now Herb sat up straight. ''I told him you're not only my very good buddy, but you're my client, and you just hired me to get you outa here, and I was on my way over to do just that.''

Joe leaned forward and touched his friend's hand. ''Thanks, buddy.'' He hoped two words were strong enough to telegraph all the gratitude he felt.

''You know one thing? I don't think Tom's all bad. I mean, he seems to feel guilty about you.''

''Yeah? That's interesting. In what way guilty?''

''Says they shoulda seen it comin'.''

All the times he'd tried to get Tom and the others to take the IRG threat seriously, to give him some real help, they'd fed him legal placebos. They were so busy placating him, they hadn't seen how deep his turmoil went. Tough shit! ''Right,'' he said. ''Well, I hope he doesn't feel too guilty about that. He could've had me put away months or even years ago. He could've built the firm all by himself.'' He latched onto Herb's eyes. ''The truth, old friend. So help you God. Do you think I belong in here?''

''Bullshit! I'll tell you what I told Tom. I said I'm not gonna keep you in the hospital because he and your other partners don't want you talking to some reporters.'' Herb grinned. ''I told him kinda loud, Joe.''

''Didja?'' Joe smiled. This one was pure pleasure.

Herb stood to go. ''Time to get down to it. I want you to know I'm sorry I called him, Joe. I should've taken your word for everything.''

''Forget it. I already have.''

Herb beamed gratefully, and put out his hand. ''I'll have you outa here tomorrow,'' he promised.

■ ■ ■

THAT EVENING, Judd and Larry were back.

''Well, Joe,'' Larry began. ''We're completing a draft.''

They should have had the sense to put it another way. ''What good is a draft? These guys are gonna publish in a week. We can't send them a letter warning them not to publish after they've published! It only does some good if they get the letter *before* they publish! This letter has to go to thirty-two papers! If the presses are ready to roll, they won't pay any attention. You've gotta get off the dime!''

Larry was hopping from one foot to the other, like there was a real dime he was trying not to land on. Joe turned away in disgust.

''You know,'' he said to Judd, ''all this time we've been talking, you always said you were going to help, you were going to help. Back at our first meeting you were there to help. But you never understood what my concern was. I told you I had some personal concerns and some concerns about the firm. Here, Peters,'' he said as he held out several sheets of paper. ''This is the article, parts of which Dan Barnes could have written in 1971, but he had no research capability and didn't look much beyond his own work. Now we've had thirty reporters here for the better part of six months. Maybe they've done some research. Read this article, guys. This is what I'm concerned about.''

He threw the pages at Judd, who missed them. As Larry bent to pick them up, Joe said, ''You always were slow to catch things, Judd, old pal.''

CHAPTER

29

JOE AWAKENED early. One more day and he'd be a free man. Notre Dame had beaten San Francisco, 93-82! It was an omen. Nothing could go wrong now—he was sure of it! He decided to start packing and was gathering his papers when Larry arrived, bearing copies of the long-awaited letters.

''All I can say is I hope we're not too late,'' Joe observed dryly after reviewing them. I have good reason to suspect the *Chicago Tribune* won't publish. Do you think we can get jurisdiction over out-of-state papers?''

Larry looked troubled. ''What for? What are you talking about?''

''Well, I want to get a restraining order against them.''

Larry's face was in bold print: here Joe was, getting out and as crazy as ever. ''That's impossible!'' he said with mounting alarm. ''The high nine laid that issue to rest a long time ago in *Near v. Minnesota*.''

''Yeah, yeah. I know all about that. But if you've got ten minutes more to hang around this fuckin' place, let me paint you a picture.''

Larry didn't look as if he wanted to stay, but he sat down.

''Okay,'' Joe said. ''We do a Brandeis brief in about three days—because that's all we've got. Then on Thursday or Friday we present it to Judge Muecke or Judge Craig and ask for an injunction. We start with Blackstone and all that stuff, and we trace freedom of the press back to the Constitutional Convention and all the debates that surrounded the Bill of Rights. We latch onto Thomas Jefferson's star and lay out what expression was intended to be protected and what was not. There was a whole lot of disagreement on what was sacred and what was out of bounds.

''You know, Skip Waxman's been helping me and some of the others on this, and I asked him to bring me my files. Here, read some of what Jefferson had to say about an unbridled press. When you get a chance, read some of the cases in the early 1800s to give you the flavor of the debate.

''Then we succinctly trace the history of the First Amendment for the court, through *Near* and *New York Times v. Sullivan* to date. The fact of the matter is that none of the reported cases has dealt with anything like what we're facing today. The IRG itself acknowledges that nothing like this has ever occurred in American journalism. It's precisely for this reason that a number of our bastions of a free press, the *New York Times,* the *Washington Post* and the *Los Angeles Times,* refused to participate in the IRG. We subpoena some guys like A. M. Rosenthal and Ben Bradlee. And somebody from Los Angeles. We also subpoena the *Chicago Tribune* and Stan Ostrowski.''

''No way, Joe! The *Chicago Tribune*? They're part of the IRG team.''

''Larry, you're not listening. My sixth sense tells me they've had it and they're ready to walk away from the whole mess. Their man Stan Ostrowski's disillusioned. We can get him and some of the other disgruntled IRG guys.

''Larry, I know it's more than a calculated risk. It's a real fuckin' long shot. But that's where a maverick judge comes in. We urge him to do what's right—and carve out a place in history for himself!

"We introduce the *Chic* magazine article to show what a bunch of jokers these IRG guys are. Here, look at this article from the *Wall Street Journal*."

Larry glanced at the paper. "Joe, this is all very nice, but it's not enough to make for a Brandeis brief in the true sense of the word."

"Larry, Louie Brandeis I'm not, but are you ready for my coup de grace?"

"Sure," Larry said, but it sounded like a shrug.

"We get two or three experts on the Third Reich and have them testify how Hitler used the press—specifically, collective journalism—as an instrument of suppression throughout his regime. Maybe we get that guy Shirer, the one who wrote that best-seller on the Third Reich. Perhaps we get an expert on Goebbels, and paint for the court just how devious a group of journalists can get when cloaked with an impenetrable shield.

"Look, I can't tell you exactly how we do it. But I know it can be done! If nothing else, the case gets national attention and the subject gets some sort of preliminary airing."

"I have to admit I'm fascinated," Larry said. "But the attention may be bad for our clients, because when we lose—I mean, if we lose—then more people will pay attention to the IRG series than otherwise would have. Plus, Joe, I doubt that we have enough time."

"You know, Larry, you remind me of the shrink in this joint who told me the other day to take out my hostility on a punching bag. When my hands got black and blue, he chided me for hitting the bag too hard.

"I've been talking to Tom, Judd and Spencer for five months on the subject of a prior restraint. Perhaps my thoughts were not as well formulated as they are today, but nobody was willing even to listen to an approach. All I keep hearing is *Near v. Minnesota*. I say fuck *Near v. Minnesota*! This is a very different case with infinitely more far-reaching consequences. Consequences for us, our friends, our clients and, as I see it, in the long run, for the future of the First Amendment. What we'll be doing will shore up the First Amendment. Even if that weren't an offshoot, I'd still say go for it!

"I've been doing a lot of reading in this place. Let me read you something I found the other day. It's from Camus.

> If anyone, knowing it, still thinks heroically that one's brothers must die rather than one's principles, I shall go no further than to admire him from a distance. I am not of his stamp.

"Please don't tell me we don't have enough time! We once had more than enough time to produce our most scholarly work product. Now, we have to go to the mattresses. Axelrod, you know anything about street fights? Shit, if the guys from my neighborhood knew anything about the law, they'd get this job done overnight!"

CHAPTER

30

''JOE! Good to have you back! You look wonderful. How are you feeling?'' Jan greeted him with enthusiasm.

''Fine. What's going on?'' He hoped the pleasure he felt at her reception showed.

''Larry said to let him know when you got in.''

''Okay. Tell him I'm here, and please get me some Sanka. We're starting fresh. Day One!''

Joe walked into his office, feeling a bit tentative. But everything was exactly as he had left it. Still, in a way, he felt as if he were seeing it for the first time. He took a sip of Sanka and cringed, inhaled deeply and forced himself to focus on the day ahead. Joe had just settled himself behind his desk when Larry came in.

''Welcome back.''

''Thanks, Larry. I assume you have the firm's letter?''

''Yes, in what I believe is its final form. Why don't I wait while you read it?''

''Okay,'' Joe said, as he took the document.

A careful review of the letter revealed meticulous attention to detail. Finally satisfied, Joe returned it, with only a few corrections, to Larry.

''Good changes. I'll get it out right away,'' Larry promised as he got up to leave. ''I'll catch you later. Judd's waiting for me to go over to Goldcor to review our letter with Bob Goldwater.''

''What do you mean you and Judd are going over? The guy who knows more about this whole thing than anybody is me. I'll be coming along.''

''I don't think that's a good idea. It's your first day back. You should take it easy.''

''Look, Larry, give me a break. I'm ready, willing and able to go over there. Get me a copy of the Goldcor letter so I can review it, and then we can all go together.''

Larry studied him for a very long moment. Apparently concluding there was no point in arguing, he went back to his office to get the letter. While Joe waited, the phone rang.

''Where the hell have you been?''

''You first. Who the hell is this?''

''Stan Ostrowski, from Chicago.''

''Stan! Nice to hear from you. I've been in a fancy nut house. That's because I'm a big-shot lawyer. Now, if I were an underpaid journalist, I'd have gone to stay with my mother.''

''Well, I can see your vacation has improved your sense of humor. Your office said you were on a cruise. You sound rested.''

''Would you believe me if I told you my office was lying? I really went to Cabo San Lucas and did some fishing.''

''Fishing? How would a New Yorker get into fishing?''

''Don't they teach you guys geography in Chicago? New York's on the ocean. Trust me, I wouldn't lie to you. I used to live in walking distance of Sheepshead Bay—one of the biggest fishing ports in New York.''

''I guess I have the typical midwesterner's view of New York: concrete and steel. Well, before you tell me about the ones that got away, I have a few things to tell you.''

''Shoot!''

''I think I've got some good news for you, Joe. I resigned from the IRG.''

"That *is* good news. I knew you weren't one of them, so I can't say I'm completely surprised. What happened?"

"Well, they had a board meeting last Friday in Indianapolis. The subject was a deal that had been made by the Indianapolis crowd and a literary agent they hired. The plan was to get everyone to agree not to do anything on their own and collaborate on an IRG-censored version of the Arizona project. Can you imagine a journalist agreeing to censorship? They've turned into a power-hungry machine."

"No, Stan. They always were."

"I don't believe that." Stan sounded sad. "We started out as a fraternity and turned into a pack of jackals. The minute I objected to the concept of an 'official' version of the project, I was bombarded with hostile questions about my intentions. Anyway, today they issued a statement saying that I was expelled."

"Well, I seem to remember having said to someone once—or was it twice—'Don't believe everything you read!'"

"No one will be reading anything about the Arizona project in the *Tribune*. We aren't going to publish. I have another piece of news. There'll be nothing in the articles about your law firm."

"Dynamite. That's real nice. You're okay, Ostrowski. *Grazie*!"

As soon as he put down the phone, Joe's head was in gear. If the IRG was going to steer clear of CBP&W, then their attack was going to be focused on Goldcor, the Goldwaters and Rosenzweig. Without those three, the IRG didn't have much of a story to go with. Good thing he was going over to Bob's. Judd and Larry were the wrong guys to prep anyone for a street fight.

■ ■ ■

IN LIGHT of his apparent lack of interest in the matter, Joe was surprised to find Tony waiting for them with Bob at Goldcor's offices.

"To what do we owe the pleasure of your company, Cousin Anthony?" he began with friendly sarcasm.

"What are you talking about? I've been involved for weeks, particularly in the drafting of this letter."

"How come you suddenly found religion?"

"Well, you have to admit, you went to extraordinary lengths to get my attention."

The first joke. All eyes were on Joe. He laughed. They laughed. Their focus shifted to the business at hand.

It was over.

CHAPTER 31

JOE AND everyone around him spent the few remaining days that week in a countdown to the second Sunday in March. Joe had set his alarm for four a.m.—the time the *Herald* was delivered to its distributors. When the alarm went off, he threw on a pair of shorts and drove to the nearest Circle K.

On the front page of the paper, in a box to the right, headlined in large black letters was ''Our Creed'':

THE VALLEY HERALD
Phoenix, Arizona, Sunday March 16, 1976

For some time now, several journalists, mostly from other states, have delved into organized crime in Arizona.

Today, the first of a series of stories about crime in Arizona has been released for publication. Although these articles have been made available to this paper, The Valley Herald did not participate in the project. After meticulous screening, we have decided not to publish this series.

We have heretofore published some of the material in the series—only after painstaking verification of the data. Some of the other material made available to The Herald contains charges without sufficient documentation or proof to justify publication.

Our creed is predicated upon honesty and decency. Always, The Herald strives to be truthful and accurate. To report that which we have not determined to be truthful and accurate would be a violation of Our Creed.

Joe couldn't believe his eyes. "I'll be a son of a bitch!" he shouted to the deserted store. Jumping into his car, he drove home. He had to tell someone. Forget Angela. And he couldn't very well call Ashley at home at this hour. But how could he bear just standing around and waiting for the world to wake up? It was 6:30 in New York. Did he dare awaken his friends? Absolutely. He began with Rocky Parlati.

"Who the fuck is this?"

"It's Joe!"

"For Chrissake, do you know what time it is?"

"Yeah, I know, but I couldn't wait to tell you. The *Herald* has decided not to publish!"

"Did we do that?"

"Who knows? It'd be nice to think so, wouldn't it? The point is that, based on their assertion that there isn't enough proof to justify publication, the *Indianapolis Beacon* can't publish, either."

"Why not?"

"Because Arla Perkins, the Publisher of the *Herald,* is also the President of the *Beacon*. If there isn't enough documentation to publish in one paper, how could there be justification for publishing in another?"

"Well, well, well. Maybe Jeff got two birds with one stone."

"Yes, sir! And listen to this: The *Herald* denies having participated in the project."

"You can't be serious!"

"You bet your sweet ass, I am."

"Keep your eye out, Joe, to see if anyone in the local media, or the papers in surrounding communities, calls them on that. Maybe some of the participants will say they're liars. I just wanna see if their colleagues let them get away with that bullshit."

"My only regret is that I wasn't around to see Penwick's face when he found out that Perkins is taking a pass."

Rocky laughed. "Serves the little prick right. So, what does our scorecard look like so far? Last week it was the *Chicago*

Tribune, the Oklahoma and Washington papers are probably out, and now we have Phoenix and Indianapolis. Is that right?''

''Yeah. Not bad for a bunch of rookies. Let's start calling the rest of the boys and see if we bagged any more. I'll call Franco. Who do you want to take?''

Monday, Joe rammed into an unexpected wall!

CHAPTER 32

IT TOOK several readings for the words to penetrate. Then he turned to the second article from Indianapolis. And then, from the same paper, two more equally inane exposés. On the same day!

One Perkins paper couldn't find enough proof to publish anything, and the other could publish nothing else. Four articles in the same day on the same subject.

On the nineteenth, *Good Morning, America* interviewed Senator Goldwater. In his characteristic, straight-from-the-hip fashion, fueled by anger at the IRG's attack on his home, he challenged the IRG to name one nationally known gangster in Arizona today, to which Bob Grogan immediately responded: Joe Bonanno. As soon as the show was over, Amy Mayer of ABC News called Goldcor looking for Bob. When she was told that he was not available, she called Stan Ostrowski, who suggested she call Joe.

■ ■ ■

"MS. MAYER wants you to call her. She got your name from Stan Ostrowski," Jan reported. "She'd like you to appear on *Good Morning, America* for an interview."

"How about that?" He made no attempt to disguise his pleasure. "Looks like my relationship with Ostrowski is still paying off.'' He picked up the phone and called Stan. He was out on assignment, so Joe left a message saying, 'Thank you for the forum. JPC.'

Then he went to see Tom.

''I don't see how you can accept the invitation unless you know the questions in advance. We have lawyer-client privileges to consider.'' Tom, ever cautious, went on. ''We just can't afford to have you go on national television and refuse to answer on the grounds of confidentiality. You know the press. There's no such thing as a good reason not to answer a question. Considering their typical stand on submitting questions in advance, I can't see how we can work it out.''

Back in his office, Joe called Amy Mayer.

''I got your message and would love to come on the show, but I've got to have the questions in advance.''

''We can't do that. It costs us spontaneity and our viewers will think the show's rehearsed. Senator Goldwater didn't get the questions.''

''Well, I'll spare you the benefit of my insights on that subject. Let's just say you've made my case.''

''I'm sorry, but it's not our policy. If you change your mind, please call.''

The following morning Joe found a message from Amy Mayer saying that he would have the questions the next day.

''Well, isn't this interesting?''

Jan smiled at Joe, acknowledging his triumph.

The promised questions didn't come in the morning. A call from Amy Mayer did.

''I have invited Bob Grogan to come on the show Monday to speak for about ten minutes. I'd like you to watch the show and then at 9:00 a.m., a writer will call you to discuss the questions we'll ask you on Tuesday. You should fly in late Monday, after we've spoken to you. Can you work that out?''

''Sure.''

''Okay. The last flight to New York from Phoenix leaves at 2:50 p.m. We'll have a prepaid ticket waiting for you at the airport. You get to New York at 9:13. Take a taxi and get a receipt—we'll reimburse you for everything. We've made a reservation for you at the Warwick Hotel. A limo will pick you up at 7:00 a.m. and bring you to the studio. You'll be on the air from 7:40 to 7:50. David Hartmann will be your interviewer. A limo will take you to Kennedy in time to catch the 9:00 flight back to Phoenix.''

''You don't mess around, do you? I'll look forward to our meeting.''

''Same here.''

Joe hung up, prepared a memo on his *Good Morning, America* plans and sent it down to Tom's secretary.

Joe didn't intend to wait for the questions. The first order of business was to decide exactly what he wanted to get into his conversation with Hartmann. When he knew the questions, he'd fit his answers to them. He had to be absolutely clear. Use terms any reasonably intelligent viewer would understand. Present his views in such a way that they could be grasped quickly. He told Jan no calls and, pulling over a yellow legal pad, began excitedly to make notes.

He had no idea how long he'd been at it, but he was reading over what he had, feeling pleased, when Jan buzzed him. ''Your wife's on the line.''

Jan was aware that Angela knew not to call him at the office except in an emergency. He pushed the button quickly. ''What's the matter with the baby?''

''Nothing's the matter with her.''

''It's Joseph!''

''Joe, nothing's wrong, period.''

He sat back. ''What's up, then?''

''I was just wondering if by some wild chance you were planning to be home for dinner.''

"Why?" He hadn't had dinner at home in weeks.

"Your mother's coming over, and I wanted to have the right story ready."

"You didn't tell me she was coming."

"I'm telling you, right? I just talked to her."

"What's the occasion?"

"No occasion. She just sounded like she really wanted to see the baby, and this afternoon she has her sewing club. How about you, Joe? Would you like to see the baby?"

"Angela, I played with her before I left this morning. And I don't need to account to you about my time with her. Plus, I don't intend having an argument with you to spoil what, until this call, has been a first-class morning."

"Sorry. I didn't mean to upset you." Angela didn't usually retreat this quickly. "Tell me, what's so special about this morning?"

She sounded really interested. That was Joe's first solid clue. Angela didn't give a damn about his mornings. Or how he spent his nights, either.

He decided to go along for the ride. "I got an invitation to go on *Good Morning, America* Tuesday morning, with the questions in advance so I won't get caught off-guard the way Barry was."

"That's terrific, Joe! Your new blue shirt with that maroon Valentino tie would look great on TV."

She should have taken acting lessons. Her voice was too bright. It gave her away.

But he had to admit she was arousing his curiosity. "What do you think?" he asked. "Should I say yes?"

"What kind of question's that? After all you've gone through to get this far, you'd have to be crazy to pass up a chance like this."

"Does that mean you don't think I'm crazy?"

"C'mon, Joe. It's just an expression." For a moment, she sounded small—scared. Then she perked up. "You are going, aren't you?"

This was getting to be fun. "So you think it's a great idea?"

"Absolutely."

"Thanks for telling me. I appreciate it."

"You don't seem to notice, but I am still in your corner, Joe. What about this evening?"

With you in my corner, sweetie, the corner might as well have spikes. "Tell my mother I've got to get ready for the show."

"I'll tell her," Angela said, trying without success to hide her dread of an evening alone with Joe's mother.

"Have fun," Joe said, twisting the knife just a little.

Immediately, he dialed his mother's number. "Hi, Ma. How are you?"

"Fine, my dear. And you?"

"I'm on top of the world, Ma. Angela tells me you're coming over tonight. I was just wondering, what made you pick tonight?"

"Who picked it? I had a date to go to the pictures with Mina Blumberg. But your wife made such a point of it, I figured I'd better cancel Mina. It's not exactly often she invites me over. I should say yes, no? I did wrong, Joe?"

"No, Ma, of course not. I'm just sorry I have to work tonight. Angela'll explain it all to you."

"You're not going to be there?"

"I wish I could be."

"*You* wish?" She sighed. "Sorry, son, I shouldn't have said that."

"It's okay, Ma. Look, you'll play with the baby, you'll have a good time."

"Sure. That baby's one beautiful little girl."

"Takes after you, Ma. Gotta go. Love you."

He replaced the phone slowly. He was so close that the answer was breathing in his chest. Another minute—two at most—he'd have it figured.

A knock. He looked up at Tom standing in his doorway. Hell, who needed a minute? The last piece of the puzzle was standing right in front of him. Angela's call for a reason she'd gone to some trouble to concoct. Her enthusiasm. Christ, it was as plain as the expectant look in Tom's eyes. Joe wished Sally D was around so he could get some odds on it that Tom had put Angela up to sounding hot about his going on the program just to put him off doing it.

"Tom," he said, smiling. "Come on in. I was just talking to Angela. Telling her about *Good Morning, America*. She thinks it's a great opportunity and I'll knock 'em dead. I have to tell you, it's loyalty like that that turns a good day into a great one."

He watched with hidden glee as Tom worked to get hold of himself, enough to proceed with whatever next dumb move he had in mind.

"Joe, we feel that it's not in your best interests to accept this invitation at this time."

"Why not? There is no other time."

"We don't think you're strong enough yet to handle a subject that's so emotionally stressful."

"You mean you still think I'm nuts?"

"No. I just think that in light of all you've been through, the risks outweigh the rewards."

It wasn't working. Joe was determined. Tom started to lose his temper, and before long they were engaged in a shouting match that had Tom on his feet, flailing his arms. For the second time in a short while, Joe wanted to level him. In the midst of Tom's tirade, Jan buzzed Joe. "Ms. Mayer is on the phone."

"Put her through."

''I just wanted you to know that our producers have decided to give Jack Anderson the opportunity to interview you, but he won't agree to submitting his questions in advance.''

When Joe hung up, he turned to his partner and said, ''Well, Thomas, you lucked out again.''

CHAPTER

33

THE MEDIA ran true to form. Every single IRG article was read over the air in its entirety, with no invitation to any of the victims to respond.

Spin-off articles started to appear. *West Coast* magazine featured "Da Goombah From Arizona" sprawled across its cover, with a picture of Barry, in a cowboy hat and a bolo tie, surrounded by gangsters and looking out at the world through a lurid sneer. The IRG was believable! Barry threatened the world's largest lawsuit, but that didn't stop anyone.

While Corelli, Brady, Peters & Winthrop waited for their retraction requests to be turned down before preparing libel suits, others did not.

Danny DiGiorgio, sports information director of the Phoenix Suns basketball team, was the first person in the nation to sue the IRG. In April, he filed suit for defamation, negligence, gross negligence and invasion of privacy for the publication of the following paragraph.

> Action in the football season is heavy on the University of Arizona Wildcats and Arizona State's Sun Devils and in the basketball season, the main betting goes down on the Phoenix Suns. Much of the gambling fraternity can be found at the Brighton Beach Bagel

> Emporium, a popular Sunday morning gathering spot on North Central Avenue where gamblers talk odds and munch on some of the best Nova Scotia salmon and cream cheese with chives west of New York. Danny DiGiorgio, sports information director of the Suns, has a chair reserved for him at the Emporium and is close friends with Harold Pincus, the shop owner. . . . DiGiorgio said that when he found out Pincus was into gambling he told Pincus he wouldn't be able to come to the store anymore. DiGiorgio said Pincus promised to stop gambling.

The implication was clear. The man's career was professional sports, where gambling is strictly prohibited. Yet these clowns published an article linking him to gamblers and bookies because they all ate bagels in the same restaurant.

And then there was Andrew May, the subject of IRG sleuth Sid Wyman's "Alaska Connection." May hired Herb Steinberg to "Sue the bastards!" In vintage Steinberg prose, the complaint renamed the team of reporters "the defamation squad" and went on to charge that they "conspired and joined in an unlawful scheme and an agreement of joint venture to form a vigilante task force . . . to investigate, expose and defame the political and business institutions of the State of Arizona, its prominent citizens and others, such as May, who were not public officials or public figures, for the express purpose of avenging the death of a fellow reporter, Dan Barnes." The suit went on to charge that the publisher defendants authorized their employees to "investigate, expose and defame Arizona people fortuitously targeted by the conspirator joint venturers"; that pursuant to their conspiracy, "the defamation squad descended upon Phoenix in furtherance of their vengeful and irresponsible scheme." That they "prepared and published, both in Arizona and throughout the United States, false and malicious polemics impugning the character and reputation of numerous people, including May."

Herb's rhetoric was just the relief Joe needed as he waded through complaint after complaint in an effort to synthesize the arguments. Little doubt remained that he'd be drafting complaints of his own before long. At the end of April not one of the firm's requests for a retraction had even been acknowledged.

In the large conference room at CBP&W, victims and attorneys gathered to decide what action to take.

CHAPTER

34

"HELL, when I sued *Fact* magazine, every week there was a new story somewhere—rehashing the article, my complaint, and regurgitating the entire mess. What do we stand to gain by keeping our names in the mud?" Barry asked.

"The people who know us, know it's bull. I'm too old to go through a libel suit," Bob added.

"But isn't that the point, Bob? We've gone all our lives with impeccable reputations. Why should we go down the chutes without a fight? I'm too old not to! What do you think, Joe? Should we do it?"

"Harry, I can't make that decision for you, but if we do it, it'll mean taking depositions all over the country. It'll demand a lot of your time. I don't know if the Senator has it. It'll cost a fortune. This will be a big commitment, across the board."

"Well, why don't you take it on a contingent-fee basis?" Bob asked.

"Look, Bob. If you decide to sue, we'll do it any way you want, even though it doesn't make any economic sense for us. Very few people can justify the cost of bringing a libel suit. Hell, the deck is stacked! And Harry, some court might decide you're a public figure. Republican State Chairman, former member of the City Council."

''Well, Joe,'' Barry said, ''give us your best legal judgment. What should we do?''

''Much as I'd like to do it, Senator, my advice is not to go forward. The other people suing have much more isolated issues. It's easier to bring a suit on one or two allegations. They've got a hundred different theories about you guys. We would have to test all or most of those issues.''

When the meeting broke for coffee, Judd drew Joe off to a corner. ''After everything we have been through on this subject for the last nine months, I can't believe I'm hearing you right!''

''What do you mean?''

''I just never thought I'd hear you advise these people not to sue.''

''You know, Judd, I wondered all along if you were paying attention. I asked you to help me address a unique event in the history of American constitutional law. The upshot of our case for a prior restraint, under the circumstances, was not at all a foregone conclusion. True, it was a real long shot, but one with little pain for our clients. Had we prevailed, we wouldn't be sitting here today. But you and those other partners of mine jerked me around till I wound up at the funny farm. I sure hope you ain't gonna jerk me around no more!

''Now I'm advising our clients based on libel, an area of the law where only us lawyers get rich. The IRG has published. We no longer have a sexy constitutional question. Just the well established law of libel to be brought in a very traditional context.

''Insteada wastin' my time on fuckin' lawsuits, I'm gonna do all the meticulous research it takes and write me a book about street fights in Phoenix!''

BOOK
VI

PEACE BE WITH YOU

PHOENIX 1986

CHAPTER 1

LARGE, CRYSTAL teardrops swung from the ceiling, glancing darts of light off the mirrored walls and chrome furnishings. Harsh but for abundant plants, Avanti was the first restaurant in Phoenix with panache. As Joe looked over the menu, he wished the owners were as restrained about their food as they had been about the decor. He didn't have the energy to make a decision. Giving up, he leaned back and sipped his drink, trying to unwind.

As he sat wondering about his partners' likely reactions, Benito, one of the owners, noticed Joe sitting alone at his favorite corner table, and aimed in his direction.

"Good to see you, *Signor* Corelli," he greeted Joe as he extended his hand. Joe gazed up at Benito's broad, affable face and smiled. The restaurateur was a tall, powerful-looking man who wore his silk shirt unbuttoned to reveal a large, gold medallion and enough hair to compensate for the dearth on his head.

"Are you expecting someone, Giuseppe?"

"No, Benito. I came alone to enjoy your wonderful food and relax. Have a seat. Let me buy you a drink."

"*Grazie*. So how come I no see you for so long?"

"I've been busier than usual."

"Ah, *sì*. We beena busy, too. Dee new place in La Jolla hasa got us a crazy. Times like dis you happy you in business wit' you friends. No?"

No. What friends? "Tell me, Benito, how do you like being in the United States?"

"I like. Dis is a good place to make money, anda women, ah. . . ." He looked at Joe knowingly while he twisted his cheek between his fingers. "American womena lovea men wit' accents, 'specially d' Eetalian ones."

"What about being Italian in this country? You know, coming from Italy, do you feel any prejudice?"

"Prejudice? No. Whatta you mean?"

"Like your character? Do people question your honesty?"

"No more den in Eetaly. Why you aska dis question?"

"I was just thinking, you know, while we were talking, about the difference between being an Italian-Italian and an Italian-American. Successful Italian-Americans are looked at with suspicion. You know, Mafia, Cosa Nostra, Black Hand. Like that stuff that's going on in New York these days. The Commission investigations! I just wondered if being from Italy you felt the same thing?"

"You know what I notice 'bouta you American Eetalians? You gotta lousy image. For example, I see deesa television commercials with Eetalians. You ever notice dey all are fat? How come? In Eetaly nobody's fat. Deesa fat Eetalians is an American invention. No? How come you getta such bad press?"

"I don't know, Benito, but, believe me, I've been asking myself that very question for a helluva long time."

"Well, I notice for all d' Eetalians in this country, Americans don't know nothing about you. Where you all been? Americans invented disa public relations! Well, maybe no. I don't know, but where's d' Eetalians' public-relations man?"

"Whatsa matter with you, Benito? We got Mario Puzo!"

"Ah!" he exclaimed, tossing his hand into the air. "You see, dere's another problem. In Eetaly, the government hasa regular purges of Sicilians, because dey no trusta dem. At leasta, you can tell who'sa who. Here you alla treated the same. You Americans no can tell dee difference, so all Eetalians gotta voices likea san'paper, ana dey fat, ana dey sloppy, ana dey carry guns o' knives. How come nobody educates deesa people?''

The idea that Italians discriminated against Sicilians in the same way that Americans were prejudiced against Italians was a new concept for Joe. After Benito left, another thought stayed in his mind. Where *were* the public-relations men? Why had the American public swallowed *The Godfather* whole? Why were Italians always portrayed as sinister or dangerous or, for that matter, fat?

The evening provoked quite a few questions, no answers and one decision. Avanti would be the perfect place to throw a party for all of his off-the-wall friends, to celebrate the completion of his manuscript. Ten years was a long wait for a gig.

■ ■ ■

''JOE, got a minute?''

Joe put down his pen and signaled Tom to come in. Tom had changed a lot over the years. He had become a compulsive runner and it showed, in both his appearance and his personality.

Joe's old friend who used to struggle with his weight was now the quintessential jogger: stringy, leathery, weather-beaten, a grim countenance, the whole nine yards! Joe's hospitalization and the IRG invasion had dealt their relationship a series of blows from which there were still leftover marks. The firm had grown. They had their own building now. Corelli, Brady, Peters and Winthrop ranked with the state's top firms in both size and prestige. But these two old classmates barely knew each other anymore. Tom's running worried Joe. It seemed he ran more to save his soul than his life. His wife had moved—Joe didn't know why; they were no longer close enough for him to offer Tom an ear.

''I just saw Frank La Bate in the parking lot,'' Tom was saying. ''He asked me how I liked your book. He was as surprised to learn I hadn't read it as I was to learn that it was finished.''

As Tom paused, searching Joe's face for a response, Joe stared coolly back at him, waiting for him to get to the point. After all these years, Joe had learned how to make ice.

''Evidently all your friends have read it and discussed it over dinner.'' Again, Tom paused.

Joe remained impassive. He had no inclination to make it easy. For one solid year he'd worked to write this book, not to mention the eight years he'd researched and thought about it, with everyone humoring him. Now it was his turn.

''I wonder if you'd have any objections to my reading it?'' Tom asked, finally.

''Not a one.'' Joe swiveled around in his chair and took a copy of the manuscript off his credenza.

He handed the box to Tom and said, ''Let's keep this between you and me. I don't have to tell you that this is a sensitive subject. We don't want a bunch of scared rabbits runnin' around this firm, do we?''

CHAPTER 2

THREE DAYS LATER, Joe found himself discussing the book over lunch with Judd Peters. So much for confidentiality. But as he listened to Judd, his irritation with Tom subsided. For a couple of guys who had been patronizing Joe for a long while, they were certainly paying attention to him now.

"I enjoyed reading your book, Joe. I was kind of surprised that you got the color of my eyes wrong."

Joe shook his head in disbelief and started to laugh. "Here, Judd. Open wide. I'll have it corrected immediately!"

Judd smiled. Time had marked him physically only with some gray hairs. "It flows well. I don't necessarily like everything you say, but far be it from me to tell you not to say it."

■ ■ ■

BACK AT the office, Joe found a message from Tom. As he walked into Tom's office, Joe caught sight of his manuscript on the bookshelf. Hundreds of paper clips marked the pages that Tom wanted to discuss. As Tom spoke, he removed the shiny metal clips from each page. There were enough of them to form a chain to shackle him. Had Joe been willing to deal with all of Tom's problems, he'd have had to write a new book.

"Spencer is getting very frenetic, Joe," Tom was saying, coming to the last of his complaints.

"Why would Spencer be getting frenetic? I thought this was just between you and me."

"Well, I just felt I had to disclose it to him."

"Well, when you disclosed it to him did you also disclose enough of your own objections to create anxiety before he had an opportunity to read it?"

"Well, I did share some of my problems with him, but you know Spencer. He looks at things differently, and he's very, very concerned. He can't understand why you didn't give him a copy."

"Tom, after you and I square it away, I don't have any problem giving Spencer or anybody else in this firm a copy. I've got nothing to be ashamed of, nothing to hide, nothing to be embarrassed about. This is the story I'm going to tell."

"But it's your perceptions."

"Obviously, it's my perceptions. I'm not going to write a book about your perceptions. If you have some perceptions and would like to share them with me, share them with me. And then, to the extent they impact on my perceptions, I may change things."

"Well, but Spencer is concerned about other matters. What will some of the New York firms think about this? Why would you bring up things from your past?"

"Because they're essential to the book!" he snapped, cutting Tom off. "They are critical to understanding what went on. Why I reacted. When I reacted. How I reacted. You can't change certain things—because they're *true*."

Increasingly irritated with the way the conversation was going, Tom shifted his weight in the chair. "I don't think I have to remind you, Joe, that Spencer's father used to be with Cravath and that we frequently get referrals from them. What would they think about this book?"

"What would they think about this book?" Joe responded, leaning across the desk to confront Tom. "Are you completely out of touch with reality? You've got Tom Barr representing

Time magazine in the Sharon case. Freedom of expression? You've got David Boies representing CBS in the Westmoreland case. Now, you're not really telling me that these people are gonna opt for censorship when they're the bellwether of free speech in this country! So if Winthrop believes this book will have a negative impact on them, he's dead wrong. If he raises that issue with me, I'll tell him just that.''

Getting nowhere, Tom decided to shift the focus of the conversation. ''Well, all right, Joe. You handle it, but I feel this book could have serious ramifications for the firm.''

''Sure—but they could be good as well as bad. If they're good, they could be very good. If they're bad, how can they really hurt us?''

''How can they hurt us, Joe? Manic depression?''

CHAPTER

3

BINGO! So, now he had it! That's what this encounter is really about. He's ashamed of me! After all his efforts to see to it that not one word about mania leaked out into the community, here I am, blowing it all. His partner's a nut, and Tom can't live with it.

"I don't have anything to hide," Joe said evenly, looking Tom in the eye. "We're talking about ten days in my life. Do they undo all the rest? It's critical to my story. I'm not troubled about the truth. Years ago when Barnes wrote 'The Hidden Cancer,' you were worried about the article that called Uncle Joe a Detroit mobster. I told you then, if we lost clients because of it, fuck 'em. Anyone who could have believed that story was a chimpanzee, and I didn't want to represent chimpanzees anyway. Remember? Well, I feel the same way now. If we lose clients because of the book, then good riddance!"

"The mention of Barnes leads me to another problem," Tom said, letting Joe's outburst pass without comment. "Some of us are friends with Buck Kirby. He was just honored by B'nai B'rith with their Torch of Liberty Award for his staunch defense of the First Amendment. You know how many other tributes he's received lately for the same thing? Given the mood in the community about its publisher, how can you possibly attack the *Herald* like this?"

"Brady, are you whacked out? Give me a fuckin' break! Buck Kirby's just like some of these other Perkins imports. Here a few years from the East, an outsider from South Carolina—suddenly we country folk are gonna learn about the First Amendment from the city slicker? The great war hero devotes space in the paper to run the First Amendment up his flagpole. The *Herald* reeks with self-serving pronouncements about its loyalty to principles of free expression. Kirby's an egomaniac! I wouldn't give you a plugged nickel for 'im."

"Fine. But you know, he's dated one of our clients. It could be embarrassing."

"Look, Tom." Joe was beginning to feel weary. "I don't want to embarrass anybody. I disagree with you about Kirby. Whom he dates is irrelevant. If it were my sister, it wouldn't change my thinking. I'm going to tell my story. If you're worried because he's vindictive, I agree. I'll run the risk that the power he wields will come right down on my head when the book gets published. But the story is too important to me for me to be intimidated by that kind of fallout. Don't you think that a bunch of people at the *Herald* are going to agree with me? Kirby's not exactly loved around there. I'm willing to take the risk."

"Maybe the firm isn't." Quietly.

"I don't think it's the firm's risk. It's Joe Corelli's risk." Even inside, he wasn't shouting.

"Well, Spencer feels otherwise."

"Does he, now? Has Spencer asked you to speak for him? Let him tell me that himself—after he's read the book. How can he criticize a book he hasn't read? Unless, of course, you read it to him?"

The two men stared at each other. When it became clear that Tom was not going to react to his last jab, Joe said, "So, if he's uptight, it's his problem, not mine. If he wants to read it, fine. Why didn't all these concerns arise when we were getting paid to represent Bill Clemens? We were the voice crying in the wilderness! We were representing a guy who was being pilloried by the paper day in and day out. Now we have a new issue. We have to worry about what the paper thinks of us? You want me to limit my freedom of expression because the paper may not like it? What kind of fuckin' irony is that?''

CHAPTER

4

A WEEK LATER, Spencer in person: "I think the Notre Dame story should be reworked to show that you really didn't take the pages after all," he began.

Wonderful. "Why is that?"

"I think it will stand us in very bad stead."

"What the hell do you mean by that? Spencer, I was seventeen years old! I made a mistake. I intended to reverse it but got caught in a trap first."

"But why tell it that way?" Spencer persisted. "Why not make it look like the university really screwed you?"

"They *did* really screw me! But I really took the pages, Spencer, and I would rather tell a true story. You think if I change the story, I'll look like I'm a better lawyer or a nicer person? I happen to love Notre Dame. I don't know if you love Harvard, but I love Notre Dame. That happened to me. I was real pissed at Notre Dame at the time. But they've been awfully good to me since then. It's over!"

"All right, Joe, fair enough. Let's look at this from another angle. You may want to be a judge someday, or maybe you'll want to run for public office. This will hurt you."

Joe gave him only unrelenting eyes for a response.

"I see that doesn't concern you. Well, what about other people in the firm? Judd's President of the County Bar Association.

Hasn't he told you he's thinking of running for State Bar president?''

''Yes, he has. But he's also told me it wasn't his place to tell me what to say in my book. He seems to have more respect for my freedom of expression than you and Tom put together. Maybe that's why he's president of the bar.''

Sidestepping Joe's shot, Spencer continued. ''What about Kirby?''

''What about him?''

''It's my considered opinion that this book in its current form will hurt the firm's reputation. I think you should tell your story because it's a fascinating one. I'm not trying to censor you, but I believe you should make some inconsequential changes for everyone's sake, yours included. The book should be fictionalized. Take it out of Phoenix and move it to Albuquerque or Salt Lake.''

''Spencer! Spencer, before you go any further.'' Joe held up his hand. ''These were real events. Real people were hurt, and the paper's still at it. Did you see what they just did to the guys in Lake Havasu City? They've just finished regurgitating Barnes's articles and the IRG's articles. Stories that are ten years old! How many more times are they going to rewrite this bullshit about people with Italian names? Spencer, I *have* to keep my story in Phoenix. I've got something to say about ending this crap, and I've got to stop it in Phoenix. It's very important to me. I owe it to my old man and my Uncle Joe.''

''But what about Buck Kirby?''

''Spencer, spare me! I've already heard all this Kirby bullshit from Tom Brady, and I don't need to hear it again.''

''He'll punish you for the rest of your life. Heaven knows how it will impact on the firm. Can you imagine the field day the muckrakers at the *Herald* will have with your book?''

''Listen to me, Spencer. And listen real close. You've read the book? Then you know that I've dodged real bullets more than once and Thorazine bullets a bunch more times. How many times can I die? So what in the fuck are Buck Kirby and those other broken-down valises going to do to me? A couple of those guys have picked up where Barnes left off. Under Kirby's nose, they continue to tear at a bunch of decent institutions and people in this Valley. You really think I give a fuck what those derelicts have in store for me? Let them shoot their best fuckin' shots. And you know what? They better not miss! Spencer, *read the book*."

CHAPTER

5

DURING the next several weeks, the younger members of the firm found opportunities to swoop down on Joe, take a pot shot, then vanish.

Joe waited.

When Spencer Winthrop believed he had Joe sufficiently primed, he came by for a second visit. Short. Not sweet. "This book is so troublesome to everyone in the firm, Joe, that you are just going to have to speak to the entire membership about it, even some of the associates."

Running his fingers through his hair, Winthrop paused briefly and began again, hardly able to disguise his frustration. "Where do you shine off messing with Buck Kirby? Don't you realize he'll have you for breakfast?" Spencer had broken into a sweat; Joe coolly watched each new globule form.

Finally, he said, "You're banking on my blowing up. But I'm not going to blow up. You want it? You've got it. I will talk to every partner, every associate, every secretary, the file clerks, the messengers, you name it! One-on-one, three a day, for breakfast, lunch, drinks, dinner. If people are truly concerned about the book, I'll talk to everyone individually. But they have to read it first. I won't speak to anyone who's worried just because they've accepted your view or Tom's."

Joe sat back in his chair and waited for Spencer's next move.

Winthrop chose to retreat.

It was too good to last, of course. Right after lunch, Spencer came calling again.

"Well, Joe, I've thought about our conversation this morning, and I've spoken to several members of the Executive Committee. We've decided it's not a good idea for you to speak to the young partners or the associates. You intimidate too many of them. You should talk to the Executive Committee because there are several other matters we'd like to discuss with you, as well."

"Like what?"

"Well, we feel this book has been an all-consuming passion and that you haven't been attending to other concerns of the firm."

"Hold it right there, Spencer," Joe said, cutting him off. "That's history. Last year, I took part of my sabbatical and finished the book. You and I both know that. It's not an all-consuming passion, but I intend to complete the project. It would have been done already except for everyone here telling me to rewrite it, fictionalize it, or whatever. I already told you that I owe this story to my father and my Uncle Joe. Maybe, in that sense, it has been a passion. You know, Winthrop, my old man didn't go to Harvard. He didn't even graduate from high school in Italy. But he cared about this country. As much as your father, I guarantee you! Someday I'm going to let you read his memoirs. With the Statue of Liberty and Ellis Island celebrations coming up, who knows, you might learn something in advance."

"I understand all that, Joe," Spencer said. "But you'll still need to see the Executive Committee."

CHAPTER

6

NO SOONER had Spencer left his office, than Joe picked up the phone and called Johnny Riccio. The following night, he was on a plane to Los Angeles to have dinner with Steve Ankewitz and Johnny.

Despite its Santa Monica location, Carmine's could just as easily have been in Coney Island, not only because of the decor but also because of the proprietor's accent.

''Okay, Joey,'' Steve began, diving right in. ''Who's on this bloody Executive Committee?''

''Tom, Spencer, Peter Rigby, Burt Rosen, Fox, and Lex Barclay.''

''The last two guys are nonentities. And Barclay's a three-dollar bill. Scratch 'em!'' Steve ordered with a wave of his hand. ''Unless, of course, Ashley can do you some good.''

''How come you aren't on it?'' Johnny asked.

''Because I founded it to bring the newer guys into the leadership of the firm. For a while, it looked as if the big four were united against everyone. We had a bunch of complaints that no one else had any meaningful input into major decisions. So we split up. Spencer and Tom went on the committee. Judd and I were off. If he and I were also members, there wouldn't have been any sense in having it.''

''Who can you count on in this group?'' Johnny asked.

"I sent all these guys a copy of the book before I left town, telling them I wanted it read before the meeting. Rigby sent his copy back saying he'd read it in its third printing. It's nice that Pete's in my camp, but not useful—he's not known for speaking up at meetings or making waves of any kind. Then there's Tom. What's he gonna say? We've been together for twenty years. He doesn't agree with everything I do, but. . . ." Joe shrugged and then abruptly changed the subject.

"Let me tell you what really bugs me. I've asked these guys for an agenda four different times. I haven't seen a piece of paper yet. It would take a *stupido* not to realize they don't want to put anything in writing."

"What do you think, Joey?" Johnny said wryly. "You think they're gonna tell you on paper not to publish your book?"

"I'll tell ya, Joey," Steve interjected. "Every time I see that Winthrop, I break out in hives. He looks at me like I smell bad. You'd think I hadn't paid that law firm of yours a half a million dollars over the years. Ah, who gives a fuck? That's his problem, not mine." Steve settled back in his chair to contemplate injustice.

"How much do you trust Spencer, Joey?" Johnny asked.

"Are you shittin' me? About as far as I can throw him. The guy's been talking out of both sides of his mouth for too fuckin' long. If he hasn't told me, 'I couldn't agree with you more,' a hundred times and then proceeded to piss all over my ideas, I'll cop your joint!"

"Well, I guess that covers Spencer," Johnny said, chuckling. "What about Stevie's *lantzman*?"

"Lemme tell ya about Burt," Steve broke in. "I kinda like 'im, but he's gonna seize on any opportunity he can get. This is a chance to break up the big four. At long last, here's a subject about which you guys strongly disagree. He's gonna find a way to look like Sir Galahad to those other fuckin' troublemakers you have in that firm. He's too much of an opportunist to pass on this one. Ya know what makes me laugh?" Steve continued,

''Rosen's got this big First Amendment poster on his office wall. I wonder if he'll take it down after he 'advises' you not to publish.''

''Not a fuckin' chance!'' Johnny exclaimed. ''Let's get back to the lineup. So, Joey, you're pretty sure Tom's in your corner?''

''I'm not sure of anything anymore, Johnny, but look at it this way. We've been together since law school. I'm his only kid's godfather. He baptized my daughter. I convinced my Uncle Joe to stake him on his first house in Phoenix and to guarantee a $75,000 loan for us to start the firm. What else can I say?''

''Hey, Joey! He ain't one of us,'' Johnny said, shaking his head. ''I've seen enough of this *cedrulo* over the last ten years to know he ain't got no compassion. No heart. Plus, he ain't got no balls. He's not gonna stand up if he sees a risk in it to him.''

''Not only that, Joey,'' Steve added. ''Lately, he's been a different guy from the one I met years ago. He must have a lot on his mind. Trust me, buddy, it's not you. Anybody who does all that running has got to have serious problems. Can't you see that? Look at *his* life, for Chrissake, and don't let him play shrink to you!''

''Joey, baby,'' Johnny chimed in. ''Don't you see that this is finally his chance to be *numero uno*! Listen to Johnny Boy. Don't bank on 'im. Not that he ain't gonna be torn. But he'll smell the green! Whatsa matta, you gotta short memory? Think about Sally D and Joe Bonfiglio. Boyhood friends. They were best men at one another's wedding. They each baptized and confirmed the other's first son. I betcha they teamed up to waste a few guys. When Sally went away, Bonehead split fifty-fifty with the D'Allesandros to take carea Sally's wife and five kids. Then, wouldn't you know it? Old man Gambino wants Bonfiglio tattooed, and who does he call on? Sally D! Right? In the great Sicilian tradition! Who else could get Bonehead out on a fishing boat? Sally fits Bonehead with a pair of cement shoes and dumps him in Sheepshead Bay. Joey, listen to Johnny Boy. Don't let Tom Brady take you fishing!''

CHAPTER 7

JOE LET HIMSELF into the room and dropped his briefcase on the table. As he crossed over to the window, he removed his jacket and tossed it over the arm of a chair. He had no trouble locating her among the women around the pool. Even lying down she held herself differently from most women. She was wearing a white suit that italicized her tan and her blond hair. And her body. Even from this distance, anyone who wasn't legally blind could see she had one helluva build. Of course, he didn't need to look out the window. He could see her in his mind. Without the bathing suit.

It had been three years and eight months since they'd been to bed together. It was two years and one month since she'd agreed to see him again. But only as friends. Her eyes had been as sure as her voice. He didn't blame her. Their lovemaking had always been a promise between them. He hadn't been able to fulfill his end of the promise, and she had, after a year and a half, forgiven him. Maybe between them sex without a promise wasn't possible. In any case, he'd agreed to her terms. By then he'd have agreed to any terms she set, so much did he want to be in the same room with her again. Smell her fragrance, half perfume, half her. Look into the clarity of her eyes. Hear her voice that always soothed the demons.

How often he wished he could have kept the promise. Married her. It wasn't that he couldn't stand living with her kids, it was that he couldn't stand living with them while not living with his own. Truth and consequences. He watched her shift on the chaise and glance up at the window. Both had understood without saying it that he'd reserve the room at the Biltmore they used to have every Wednesday afternoon. Made it seem, back then, more like their place. Now she smiled, a very small smile. Maybe he should have asked for a different room. Without hurrying, she gathered her things and walked toward the door. He moved away from the window, his face closing in on itself. In the old days, she could hardly keep from running once he'd arrived. This isn't the old days, he reminded himself sharply.

God knew! He opened the top button of his shirt, loosened his tie, and worked his neck muscles. The time with her meant too much to fuck it up with his tension. Right now, he'd give a thousand bucks for three minutes with Susie. His own hands were accomplishing nothing.

He didn't hear Ashley's footsteps in the carpeted hall, and she had the door open before he could reach it. He stepped back. No touching allowed. Her rules.

"Hi," she said.

"Hi." His voice cracked. A puberty-stricken man of forty-four.

She pretended she hadn't noticed. "Got time for me to take a real quick shower before we talk? I'm kinda sticky." She held up a container of the hotel's suntan lotion.

"Sure," he said, not pressing his luck with a longer sentence.

She kept her word. He'd never met a woman who could shower and dress and put on a face faster than Ashley. He was still soaping her breasts in his mind when she turned off the water. Not three minutes later, she emerged from the steamy bathroom dressed in lavender slacks and a matching silk shirt. Nice. The lady knew what looked good on her. The lady knew a lot. About him, most everything.

He'd ordered a bottle of Roederer Cristal because it was her favorite. He handed her a glass, and raised his toward her silently.

She smiled and sipped the champagne. "We're not celebrating yet, are we?"

"Far from it."

"Don't frown like that. Lying by the pool, I figured out a way to make sure there will be something to celebrate."

"You're here with me. That's something."

"Thanks. But I meant about tomorrow."

"Tomorrow is going to be a stinking experience," he said. He tried to slow down the anger. Took a sip of the Roederer. Another. "Lex drop any hints?" he asked in a calmer voice.

She shook her head. "He didn't say anything. He wouldn't, of course. But he was humming while he shaved this morning."

"Fucking fag!"

"He's my husband," she said quietly.

Joe nodded. Guilty as charged. It *was* his fault she was still married to Lex.

Ashley changed her tone to change the subject. "Listen, Joe. I meant it when I said I had an idea."

"When did I ever not listen to you?"

"You never didn't listen to me." It was one of the things she most loved about him.

"Joe, you know I can blow the lid off CBP&W."

Joe smiled. Kind of. He knew what she meant. "Baby, I've never had any use for stool pigeons. So just forget it."

"But I . . . I don't think Lex would have told me if all that shit weren't true," she said. Lex wasn't a subject she liked dwelling upon. The truth was, she'd never discussed him with anyone except Joe—not even Brenda, her best friend.

Joe, seeing pain in her eyes, said, "True or not, forget it. And forget Lex—at least for now."

"I'm not talking about Lex and me. I'm talking about you—Joe Corelli, Italian street fighter—your whole future. I could send them an anonymous note. . . ."

"They'd laugh it off as a crank letter from a dissatisfied client. CBP&W lawyers don't do those things."

"Right. Well, I could threaten Lex."

"No." Firmly. "That would hurt you as much as him."

"If it'll help you. . . ."

"Even if I were agreeable, I still wouldn't do it. Not at your expense. No way. Hey, don't go looking so sad. I got something of my own to use on them."

He went to his briefcase and took out a few pages, stapled together. "This isn't the original. I want to save that. I had it typed up. When my mother was going through my father's things after the funeral, she found these journals. She figured that since I was his namesake, I should have them. My old man kept them for years and years. He used to write nights. Nobody knew what. Stuck in one were these separate sheets."

"Is it a story?"

"It's a letter. To his grandchildren. Ash, he wrote it thirty years ago." Joe swallowed, but the lump in his throat seemed permanent. "To *my* kids. I'm gonna shove this in Winthrop's face."

He handed her the pages, reached for a Camel, and tried to think about something that wouldn't tighten the screws in his back.

She read slowly.

America

I write this for you, the sons and daughters of my sons and daughter. I am Giuseppe Corelli, your grandpa. I write this for you even though you are not born yet, because I love you already, and I want be sure you know about my America.

I think a lot about America. I been thinking about her a long time. Before I come here, when I a boy in Calabria, America is land of promise to me.

Life for the Calabrese was not so good in those days. Not so good before or after, neither. Not everybody free to leave, but I one of the lucky ones. When I get my exit visa, I was skinny boy with fuzz on my lip like a peach. My mama pack all my things in one cardboard valise belong to my Aunt Marianna. I visit all my aunts and uncles and cousins, and I promise to send each one picture of me in America. Kissing my papa and mama goodbye is hardest thing I ever do. How I know I see them again? I decide no to leave. But my papa, he brush away tears from his eyes and push me out door. He believe—we all believe—in America is better future.

Still I not sure I leave if I know before what trip going to be like. Thatsa big ocean. And bumpy. It take too long to get across. Parts of the ship are like a palazzo—from our deck we can see above bright lights twinkling like stars all night, and we can hear the music, like a love song from a far planet. Where we are, in steerage, is no palazzo. It is dark, even in daytime, and always damp. Sometimes too hot, sometimes very cold. Always, always, too crowded. On this ship, Calabrese like me, and Napoletani, Barese, Siciliani—nobody remain stranger. Could be you meet somebody's elbow or his knee before you meet his face. *So* crowded. People packed in like grapes in a box they get nervous, edgy—many many fights for a few inches of space. I keep away from the nervous ones. My papa warn me a black eye make it harder to find job quickly.

The worst thing was the noise. Crying . . . screaming . . . babies . . . women. A girl give birth to a dead baby—she scream a whole day and two nights. There was laughter, too. Some good laughter, some ugly. But all the trip, not one moment of silence.

Was a lot of sickness on the ship. Some bad sickness. Some only seasick. People all around throwing up. But not your grandpa. I do not get seasick. I make up my mind, and I do not. The mind is wonderful thing, children. If you master of your mind, nothing—nobody—become your master.

Finally, early one morning, in the mist we see her. Like an appearance by the Virgin! To myself I call her Our Lady of Promises. And I bow my head—there is no room to kneel—and I pray. I think I already know that in America I too busy to stop and pray a whole lot, so I say very good, very long prayers this morning—to last me and God a long time.

Ellis Island make me want to get right back on that terrible ship and go home to Reggio. They push us into lines, they push us toward benches, they push us upstairs, push downstairs. Worst, they know nothing about us. I stand behind a Siciliano, back of me is family from Torre del Greco, but to man in charge we all the same. Eyetalians, he calls us. Eyetalians! I swallow my tongue, and I shake my head. Yes, sure, I Eyetalian. But to me I say, they wrong they think they make us all into this mishmash Eyetalian.

After Ellis Island, everything better. They was right in Calabria. Our Lady of Promises no fake. You willing to work hard, seventeen, eighteen hours a day, six days a week, and you strong and you no cheat the boss, you make good money. I here only one month, my boss call me reliable. He not look angry so I say, thank you, Boss. At home, I search for this word—dictionary, my first American book. Beautiful word, reliable. I think to myself, you betcha life I reliable. I going to be bigga success in America.

Down at the market where I work, I meet all kinds people. Irish. Jew. Colored. All kinds. Some nice, some not so nice. The same to me. I say, Hello, how you today, so long. Some nosey body ask me personal question, I pretend I no understand. When my work finished, I say, Goodbye. I go home.

One time, a few years go by, this Jew, nice man, he invite me and your grandmama to big dinner his house. Jew Holy Day, about how God help them leave Egypt—like he help me leave Calabria. They like us, these Jews, they remember, good and bad. My Maria Teresa, your grandmama, she say I never forget nothing. What kind of man forget? Somebody do me good, I remember always. Somebody cheat me—worse, insult me—I remember till one of us dead. Anyway, we go early to Jew's house. Lotsa talk, reading, prayers in their language. Wine is too sweet. No food. I think I eat a horse. Finally, the wife bring out food. No macaroni, but fine meal anyway. Couple weeks later, your grandmama say we have to invite back. Reciprocate, she say. She know words like this. I look up. Right away, I like this word. Mean you even. I say, Good, invite. Maria Teresa cook two days. Feast she give them. Everybody have real nice time. Me too. A month go by and Jew invite us again. This time I say, No thank you. Basta. They very nice people, but better to stay with you own.

Here where we live, with our three sons and daughter—be you parents someday—almost everybody like us. Maybe the man on Ellis Island no stupido. Here, soni Italiani. We together in one neighborhood. Strong this way. Nobody bother us.

Don't think nobody try. Outsider always trying to make trouble becausa we stick together. I think this make them nervosi. Some it make good and scared. Okay by me. They scared, they leave us alone.

I wish I not have to tell you about the others, our own who make trouble. The small time peanut crooks to the bigshot gangsters with their Cadillac cars the colors of my little girl's room. *Stay away from them all*. Makes me sick how they turn this land of opportunity inside out—into opportunity to do bad. I ashamed they ours.

I angry, too. Because at work some people move away from me, like they not sure about me. Me who never in my life take one nickel I not earn. Then I say to myself, they see us living together so close. We rubbing up against each other every day in the neighborhood. Maybe natural they wonder if this sickness, this crookedness, rub off.

But then I hear another voice in my head, and this one angry again. Because the few rotten ones give the real Americans excuse to keep us all down. They say we all a *little* crooked, have criminal mentality. So they keep us out of their big businesses and their government—they afraid we contaminate them. A very ugly word, contaminate. I know we start it, we stick together. But itsa they who quarantine us!

Still I think Lady of Promises genuine dream. Life here in America is better. How can life be good if there is shame and anger? I tell you. You listen good. I live each day with honor, so I know and God know I am honest man. And I live each day with hope. In my heart ana my soul, I have this hope—so beautiful my hope—that your parents going to be honest like your grandpa and grandmama, and they bring you up to be that way, too, so *in your lifetime* the "real Americans" will finally understand that we honest Calabrese and Bolognese and Siciliani are not special. The bad ones are special.

That day come, so help me Gesù Cristo. That day we really belong here.

God bless you. God bless America.

Your grandpa,
Giuseppe Corelli
July 4, 1954.

When, finally, she looked up, her eyes were wet. He handed her his handkerchief.

"Don't waste this on them," she said softly, laying the pages on the table.

"I want to make them ashamed of themselves."

"Oh, Joe, don't you see? You need a certain amount of class, like your father had, to feel ashamed. They'll only feel embarrassed."

He stared at her. How had she seen it and not he? He reached for the letter, straightened it with the flat of his hand, and put it back into his briefcase. Then he looked at her. "So what do I do?" he asked.

She met his eyes without blinking. Then she moved. Without a word, she stood and came over to his chair. She took his hand and raised him up. Then she led him over to the bed and began to take his clothes off. Usually, he was the aggressor, and it was important to him. But he let her. *Was* the aggressor? Had been. Should he remind her that they didn't do this anymore? God couldn't demand of anyone that he be that fair. Besides, he'd rather die than stop her.

When he was naked, she took off her own clothes, and lay down beside him. He wanted her more than he ever had, but his body didn't seem to be getting the message. Again, she moved; again, without a word. She made love to him until his blood throbbed and he took over.

■ ■ ■

AFTER A long time, he whispered, "Why?"

She kissed his chest. "I couldn't find the words right off to tell you that I know tomorrow'll be hard, but you're more man than that whole fucking Executive Committee put together, and they only think they have what it takes to silence you. No matter who says what inside that room, you're going to walk out of there with your book and your *soul* intact."

She sounded so sure, but he could feel the arrhythmia in his chest. What if she was wrong? What if he didn't have it?

''Joe?'' Her head was burrowed into his shoulder. ''Make sure everyone knows that even if we couldn't go all the way together, what we had was. . . .'' Her whisper faded altogether.

He pressed a fist against his eyes. ''No other woman came close,'' he said.

''Say it in the book?'' Her voice was trembling. Was it possible that she who was so sure *about* him wasn't sure *of* him now?

''Hell, if you want, I'll hire the Goodyear blimp and write it across the whole Phoenix sky.''

She laughed. ''The book will do nicely,'' she said.

No one is ever sure on his own, he thought. He had to be certain. ''You really think it'll happen, then?'' He turned her chin so she was looking at him.

She nodded. ''Your way,'' she said. ''The truth.''

He moved so they were as close as two bodies can get. And he held on to her. He'd known he needed to see her before he could face that meeting tomorrow. But he'd had no idea how much.

''Ashley,'' he whispered.

''I love you, too,'' she said.

CHAPTER

8

JULY 23, 1986. The Executive Committee of Corelli, Brady, Peters and Winthrop met, with Spencer Winthrop presiding.

"Is there an agenda for this meeting?" Joe asked when the tribunal had assembled.

Lex looked at Spencer. Spencer turned to Tom. "We can just breeze through most of the matters, Joe," Tom said quickly.

As Spencer began to pontificate, Joe surveyed his partners. He had hired all save Tom. It was no small irony that they should be gathered here, under the roof he had built, to judge and to censor him. These six attorneys, four of them former big-league law clerks, were bent on proscribing his freedom of speech. Had he gone through the looking glass? Whatever, this was his third time around on trial and, by God, it would be his last!

"Of course, we wouldn't tell you not to publish," Spencer was saying. "But if you decide to, it should be a fully fictionalized version. We firmly believe that to be in your best interests and, concomitantly, in the interests of the firm. It goes without saying that we wouldn't want to pressure you, especially after your herculean effort. But, in all candor, Joe, I haven't the faintest idea what some people around here will do if you go ahead with your book as is. You know, we've lost control of the troops and it just isn't like it used to be. Some of our newer partners simply don't see things the same way."

All eyes were glued to the immaculate tabletop. Joe stared at Tom until the silence forced him to look up at his colleague of two decades. Barely audibly, Tom whispered, "I agree."

Tempted to retort, "Gimme a fuckin' break," Joe bit his tongue and stood. The insult of a pair of loaded dice!

As he walked toward the door of the massive conference room of the firm that had borne his name for almost fifteen years, Joe stopped at Tom's chair and whispered to him to step outside.

In the hall, he waited until Tom gave him his eyes. Then it took only a minute.

"Brady, it's time to say *arrivedérci*. I'm history. But you got a bad memory. I told ya more than once, *life's a street fight*. Just so ya know—on my father's grave! When the *war* is over, this Italian's gonna come out on top! *Ciao*!"